Y0-DBN-736

From "Sis" 2019
" " /
Happy 70!
Hope You Get a
chuckle
or 2!!

MEDICINE FOR A MERRY HEART

AS PRESENTED BY DR. OF LAUGHTER: LARRY ELLIS

Bob, I hope you enjoy the book.
Larry Ellis

BookVenture Publishing LLC
1000 Country Lane Ste 300
Ishpeming MI 49849
www.bookventure.com
Hotline: 1(877) 276-9751
Fax: 1(877) 864-1686

Ordering Information:
Quantity sales. Special discounts are available on quantity purchases by corporations, associations, and others. For details, contact the publisher at the address above.

Printed in the United States of America.

Library of Congress Control Number 2017950417

ISBN-13:	Softcover	978-1-64069-650-1
	Pdf	978-1-64069-651-8
	ePub	978-1-64069-652-5
	Kindle	978-1-64069-653-2

Rev. date: 07/22/2017

CONTENTS

FOREWORD

This book is a result of entertaining various audiences over 60 some years by Mr. Ellis. “My hope is that much laughter is generated in these pages. The patience of my wife, who’s heard most of these jokes numerous times is much appreciated. My thanks go out to the folks who laughed at the audacity of me telling some of these stories & lines. Your laughs were a tonic for my soul.” If I may quote the late Bud Reese, entertainer from Kirksville, Mo. “Don’t try to hold in the laughter, it might go down & spread your hips!”

ANIMAL JOKES

I stopped by to see ________ & I was amazed to find him playing chess with his dog. I watched them for a while & I said, "I can hardly believe my eyes, that's the smartest dog I've ever seen!" _______ says, "Nah, he's not so smart, I've beaten him 3 outta 5 games."

Rush Limbaugh & his chauffer were out in the country & accidentally hit & killed a pig that ran out in the road. Limbaugh told his chauffer to drive up to the farm & apologize to the farmer. So they drive up to the farmhouse, the chauffer gets out & knocks on the door. They let him in & he was there for what seemed like hours. When the chauffer came out, Rush asked him, "What took you so long?" The driver said, "Well, the farmer shook my hand, then he offered me a Pepsi, then his wife brought me some cookies, & his daughter showered me with kisses." Limbaugh says, "Well, what in the world did you tell them?" Chauffer says, "I told them 'I'm Rush Limbaugh's driver & I'd just killed the pig!"

Remember that cat that I don't get along with? Well, it's been 3 years now & I decided to do something about it, so I took that cat from my house in Lee's Summit out to Swope Park & left him. When I pulled in the driveway, there was that cat. So, the next day I drove over North of the river to Richmond & again, that cat beat me home! So, the next day I took that cat plumb down deep in the Ozarks, I mean I went way back in the boonies. Six hours later I called Shirley & asked her, "Is that cat there?" She says, "Yes, why?" I said, "Put him on the phone, I'm lost & need directions home!"

Which reminds me. Life is like a dog sled team. If you ain't the lead dog, the scenery never changes.

I was out walking my dog & it got away from me & attacked a woman out in her front yard. She ran into the house & sent out her husband. Of course I was beside myself & I said, "Sir, how about a settlement, will 50$ do?" He said, "Sure, & if you come around next week, I'll give you more.

Spring must be almost here cause I saw an 'Ah bird' in my back yard today, An 'Ah bird' lays a square egg & when its finished it says, "ahhhhhhh".

______ had a $10,000 coon hound. All you had to do to get a raccoon the size you wanted was to show the hound a stretching board the size you need & you didn't even have to back your pickup truck out of the shed, that dog would go to the woods & bring it back. He had that hound for about 3 years & one day his wife left the ironing board out on the porch. They haven't seen that hound since.

Hear about the man who crossed a dog & a hen? He got pooched eggs.

Do you know how to make an elephant fly? First, you get a great big zipper.

Three dogs were in a bar. A bulldog, a Doberman & the Taco Bell Chihuahua. In walks a beautiful collie & says, "The one of you that can use the words 'liver' & 'cheese' with originality can take me home!" The bulldog says, "I hates liver & cheese." She says, "No, that won't do." The Doberman says, "I love liver & cheese". She says, "That's not original." & the Chihuahua sidles up to her & says, "Liver alone, cheese mine!!"

That reminds me--Outside of a dog, a book is man's best friend. Inside a dog, it's too dark to read.

Two elephants came out to the beach but the lifeguard ran them off. They couldn't keep their trunks up.

Too much junk mail. The Dairy Farmers Association sent me a booklet on non-fat milk---I just skimmed through it.

I had an uncle who was a great magician, or he would have been if it wasn't for his pet parrot. He'd bring that parrot on stage & every time--that parrot would give away his tricks. For instance if he was doing a card trick the parrot would say; "Aauk card up his sleeve, card up his sleeve" & the people would boo him. If he was doing a rabbit in the hat trick, the parrot would chime in & say, "rabbit in his coat, rabbit in his coat". It got to where he had a hard time getting a job. His last job was on an ocean liner & the ship got caught in a terrible storm & sunk. The only 2 survivors were my uncle & that parrot. There they were floating on a large piece of debris about 10 feet long, the parrot on one end & my uncle on the other. Three days went by & neither had spoken a word. Finally, the parrot spoke up & said, "Okay, what'd you do with the ship?"

A bear walks into a bar & says, "I'd like a beer----------------& some of those peanuts." The bartender says, "Sure, but why the big paws?"

A pair of cows were talking in the pasture. One says, "Have you heard about the 'Mad Cow Disease' that's going around?" The other one says, "Yeah, makes me glad I'm a penguin."

Went ice fishing down at the lake. There was a boy there fishing about 12 years old & he'd already caught 3 nice bass. So, I decided to cut a hole about 10 feet from him so maybe I could have some luck too. An hour & a half went by, he'd caught 4 more & I hadn't caught a one. So, I went over to him & asked him; "How are you catching those fish so easily?" He says, "Mmmmmmm!" I said, "What?" He spits into his hand & says, "Keep your worms warm!"

Research has found that Kitty Litter takes the odor out of your shoes. Unless you have a cat.

I was fixin' to make a batch of moonshine & my cow got into my mash & drank it. Yep, it ended up killin' my cow.
() Why would that killer?
Well, it turned her milk into eggnog & I milked her to death!

To cut expenses when Kansas reduces the 'personal property tax, Animal Control in Overland Park will be taken over by Asian restaurants.

A vulture boards an airplane carrying 2 dead raccoons. The flight attendant looks at him & says, "I'm sorry sir, only one carrion allowed per passenger."

What's ground beef? A cow with no legs.

It's been raining cats & dogs down home. I know, cause I just stepped in a poodle.

They're trying to reduce taxes in Overland Park, Ks. . Now Animal Control will be taken over by Asian restaurants.

I used to have a pet parrot but it had a foul mouth. One day I got so frustrated with him I said, "One more word of profanity & you go into the freezer." So he says, "Darn" . I grabbed him & put him in the freezer & pretty soon his eyes get accustomed to the darkness & he sees this dressed 'butterball' turkey in there & he says to this turkey, "All I said was 'Darn', what in the world did you say?"

I followed _____ up those gravel roads to here. He didn't know I was back there, but I saw him run over a jack-rabbit. He stopped his car & I stopped & watched. He went back to his trunk, got out a spray can & he sprayed that rabbit. The rabbit's ears started wiggling & he sprayed him again & the rabbit got up & ran off about a hundred feet, turned around & waved at _____, then he ran off another 100 feet etc. until that rabbit was plumb out of sight. _____ threw that can in the ditch & drove on. I pulled up to where he was, got out & got down in the ditch, picked up that can. You know what it was? Permanent wave & hare restorer.

Once upon a time there were 3 baby snakes. Let's see there was Wiggles, Squiggles & Junior. They were all very good little snakes, of course snakes live in a snake pit. Now Junior like to talk a lot & as you know when snakes talk they hiss. It was a Tuesday & Junior's Mom was doing the ironing & Junior was laying around the pit hissing & hissing & it got on his Mom's nerves. So she said, "Junior I'm tired of you lying around the pit hissing, why don't you go over to Mrs. Potts pit & hiss a while." So Junior went over to Mrs. Potts pit & pretty soon he started hissing again. Mrs. Potts says, "Junior, you're driving me crazy, if you have to hiss all the time, why don't you go back to your own pit & hiss. So, Junior went back home to his own pit & it wasn't long 'til, you guessed it, he started hissing again. Junior's Mom says, "What're you doing back here, I thought I told you to go over to Mrs. Potts Pit & hiss awhile." Junior says, "I did, but she got tired of my hissing too & sent me back home." Junior's Mom says, "Oh that Mrs. Potts, I can remember when she didn't have a pit to hiss in!

Why don't elephants like martinis? Have you ever tried to get an olive out of your nose?

What is that pink stuff between an elephant's toes? Slow clowns.

An elephant & a giraffe were down by the river & the elephant picked up a snapping turtle with its trunk & threw it across the river & a hundred feet beyond. The giraffe asks, "Why did you do that?" The elephant says, "That's the snapping turtle that bit my trunk 30 years ago!" TURTLE RECALL.

Did you hear that NASA is planning to send a group of Holsteins into orbit? Apparently they're calling it the 'Herd Shot Around The World'.

Holstein. That's the only Jewish cow I know of.

Did you ever notice that the duck is the only animal who walks as if he's ridden a horse all day?

An elephant escaped from the zoo & got into a very nearsighted old lady's vegetable garden. She looked out her window & called the police. She said, "There's a huge beast in my garden!" The policeman asks, "Well, what's it doing Ma'am?" She says, "It looks like it's pulling my lettuce with its tail!" "What's it doing with it Ma'am?" "Well sir, you're not going to believe this!"

So this penguin walks into the license bureau & says, "Has my father been in here?" & the clerk says, "I don't know, what does he look like?"

______I followed ______ up from Saniflush, mostly on gravel roads. He didn't know I was following him & I saw him run over a jack-rabbit. He stopped, got out, opened his trunk & got out a spray can. He sprayed that rabbit once & it wiggled its ears. He sprayed it again & it got up & ran about 100 yards, turned around & waved at him. It ran another 100 yards, turned around & waved at him. That rabbit kept doing that until it was out of sight. _____ threw that spray can into the ditch, got back in his car & drove on. I pulled up from where I'd been watching him, got down in the ditch to see what was in that can. It was permanent wave & hare restorer.

Why are turkeys wiser than chickens?
Ever heard of Kentucky Fried Turkey?

Birds of a feather flock together & mess up your car.

I took the wife out to eat at one of them fancy restaurants last night & I asked the waiter; "Do you have any wild duck?" He said, "No Sir, but we can take a tame one & irritate it for ya."

Went out to _____'s farm this week to buy us a hog for butchering. We went down to the hog lot & I picked out one that suited & as we headed back to the house I saw this nice fat pig in the front yard with a wooden leg. I said, "What's the deal on that pig with the wooden leg _____. He said, "Well, Larry, that's not just a pig, that's a hero." I said, "What do you mean?" He said, "My 10 year-old grandson almost drowned in the pond last summer, but that pig floated him right out of there." I said, "That's amazing, but what about the leg?" _____ says, & that ain't all. About 6 months ago the house caught on fire & that pig rooted the back door open, woke us up, we put out the fire. I tell you that hog's a life saver!" I said, "That's a miracle, but how come he's got a wooden leg?" He says, "Well, with a pig like that, you don't eat him all at once!"

Let's play horse. I'll be the front & you be yourself.

Do you know research has found that Kitty Litter takes the odor out of your shoes---unless you have a cat.

A man walks into a restaurant with a fully grown ostrich behind him. The waitress asked them what they wanted. The man says, "A hamburger, French fries & a coke. The ostrich says, "I'll have the same." When the bill came, it was $9.41. The man pulled the exact change out of his pocket. The same thing happened every day Monday through Thursday----same food----ostrich says, "same thing---exact change. Friday came along & the waitress asked, "Same thing?" The man says, "No, this is Friday, so I'll have a steak, baked potato & a salad." The ostrich says, "I'll have the same." The waitress brings the bill, it's $32.63. The man pulls the exact change out of his pocket & the waitress says, "Now, wait a minute, how do you always manage to have the exact change to pay your bill?" He says, "Several years ago I was cleaning the attic & found an old lamp. When I rubbed it, a genie appeared & offered me 2 wishes. My 1st wish was that if I ever had to pay for anything, I would just put my hand in my pocket & the right amount of money would always be there." The waitress says, "That's brilliant! Whether it's a gallon of milk or a Rolls-Royce, the exact money is always there, but, what's with the ostrich?" The man sighs, "My 2nd wish was for a tall chick with big eyes & long legs who agrees with everything I say."

I'll never take _____ hunting with me again. Went to an old friend's farm down in Pettis County, pulled up to the house. I said, "Wait here & I'll make sure it's alright to hunt today." My friend said, "Sure, you can hunt today, but would you do me a favor?' He said, "I've got a mule that's old & sick & he needs to be put down, but I don't have the heart." I said, "Sure, I'll take care of it for you, where is the mule?" He said, "Down in the barn." I went back to the car acting mad. I said, "That rascal won't let us hunt, I think I'll just go down to his barn & shoot one of his mules!" So,

I go to the barn & shoot the mule & then I hear 2 more shots. I holler at ______, "What are you doing?" He says, "Hey, I shot 2 of his cows too!"

Why some men have dogs & not wives:
The later you are, the more excited your dogs are to see you.
Dogs like it if you leave a lot of things on the floor.
A dog's parents never visit.
Dogs find you amusing when you're drunk.
Dogs like to ride in the back of a pickup truck.
And last, but not least:
If a dog leaves, it won't take half your stuff.

Did I ever tell you how ______ made his fortune? He'd go out to California & buy Angus bulls for a cheap price, then bring them back here & sell them for a big profit. Why he became the biggest Bull Shipper in this part of the country.

Two partners ran a men's clothing store in Pleasant Hill years ago. You talk about shrewd salesmen. One time they had this purple suit for several months & they were so used to being able to sell that it really frustrated them. In fact, one of them got so mad after trying to sell that suit one day that he told his partner, "I'm going home & I'm not coming back until you sell or burn that purple suit!" So, he went home & about 2 hours later his partner called him & said, "Come on back to the store, I sold that purple suit." So he came back to the store, but when he got there his partner was bruised, scratched & bitten. I mean he was a mess. So, the one that came back says, "What'd you have to do, fight the guy to get him to buy that suit?" His partner said, "No, but I had quite a tussle with his seeing-eye-dog."

Two dogs were out for a walk. One dog says to the other, "Wait here a minute, I'll be right back." He walks across the street & sniffs a fire hydrant for about a minute, then rejoins his friend. The other dog says, "What was that all about?" The 1st dog says, "Oh just checking my messages."

() HOW'S YOUR CALF DOING?
Calf? What calf?
() THE SICK ONE I TOLD YOU TO GIVE 2 TABLESPOONS OF CASTOR OIL.
I didn't say calf, I said cat, c-a-t cat!
() OH NO! YOU GAVE A CAT THAT MUCH CASTOR OIL?
Well, yeah.
() WHAT HAPPENED?
The last time I saw him, he was headin' up over the hill with 3 other cats. One was digging, one was covering up & the 3rd was looking for new ground.

It's been so cold that the Fire Department here in Pleasant Hill's been spending a couple days a week breaking dogs loose from fire hydrants.

My neighbor was bitten by a rabid dog. The Dr. called him to his office & told him the bad news, that he was infected. My neighbor immediately pulled out a notebook & began writing furiously. The Dr. said, "Now, take it easy, there's no need to start writing your will, you'll pull through." & my neighbor says, "Will? What are you talking about, this is a list of the people I'm gonna bite!"

Do you know what a polled Hereford is? It's a cow with an opinion.

I went to the racetrack & bet on the horses. I bet on the politest horse ever. He let all the other horses go in front of him.

Why did the horses get a divorce? They didn't have a stable relationship.

After a talking sheep dog gets all the sheep in the pen, he reports back to the farmer: "All 40 accounted for." The farmer says, "But I only have 36 sheep!" The sheepdog says, "I know, but I rounded them up."

I drove by a house the other day & I saw a sign that said: 'Talking Dog For Sale'. I went up to that dog laying on the front porch & said, "What have you done with your life?" The dog said, "I've led a very full life, I lived in the Alps rescuing avalanche victims. Then I served my country in Iraq. And now I spend my days reading to the residents of a retirement home." I was flabbergasted & I asked the dog's owner, "Why on Earth would you want to get rid of an incredible dog like that?" The owner says, "Cause, he's a liar, he's never done any of that!"

What do you call an alligator in a vest? An investigator.

A guy walks into a bar with a frog on his head. The bartender says, "Where in the world did you get that?" & the frog says, "Would you believe it started out as a wart on my rear?"

Two old sows in the barnyard. One says to the other; "Heard from your boar friend lately?" The other one says, "Yup, had a litter from him last week."

I love cats, they taste just like chicken.+

_______ & I went fishin' one night last July & he sat down on a stump & a rattlesnake bit him right on the rump. He said, "Do something Larry!" So, I drove to town & the Dr. told me to cut an 'X' on the site of the bite

& suck the poison out. When I got back out there _____ says, "What did the Dr. say?" I said, "He said, You're gonna die!"

I ran over a cat on the way through town, so I stopped & went up the nearest house & knocked on the door. A lady came to the door & I told her, "Ma'am, I'm sorry, but I ran over a cat & I thought it might be yours." She said, "It might be mine, what did it look like?"
I went (look dead). She says, "No, I mean before you hit it!" (I looked terrified.)

Shirley & I went out to a fancy Chinese restaurant on our anniversary & we ordered a special dinner. When the meal arrived it was in a cast-iron pot. The 1st thing I noticed the top of that pot lifted & I could see two little beady eyes. I jumped up & hollered at the waiter. I said, "There's something strange in that pot!" He says, "What did you order?" I said, "The chicken surprise." He says, "Oh, I apologize sir, this is Peeking Duck."

_______ was late for school & the teacher asked him what was the problem? He said, "It ain't my fault, you can blame it on my Daddy. The reason I'm 3 hours late is Daddy sleeps in the nude!" The teacher says, "Now ______ you'll have to explain what your Daddy's sleep attire has to do with you being late." He says, "You see, teacher, at the ranch we got this here lowdown coyote. The last few nights he done et 6 hens & killed Mom's best milkin' goat. & last night, when Daddy heard a noise out in the chicken pen, grabbed his shotgun & said to Ma, "That coyote's back again & I'm gonna git him!" He hollered at us kids, "You younguns stay back!" He was naked as a jaybird, no boots, no pants, no shirt. To the henhouse he crawled, just like an Indian on the snoop. Then he stuck that double barrel through the window of the coup. He forgot about our old hound dog Zeke & he had woke up & came sneakin' up behind Daddy with his cold doggy nose. "Teacher, we been cleanin' chickens since 3 o'clock this morning."

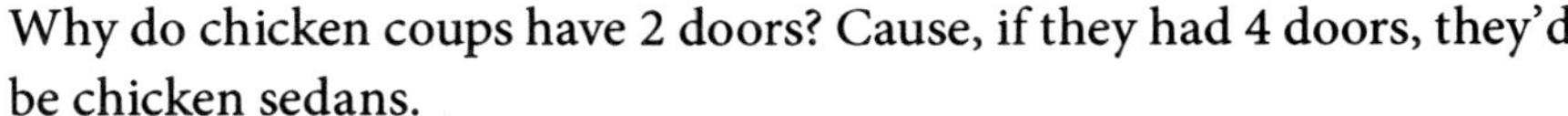

Why do chicken coups have 2 doors? Cause, if they had 4 doors, they'd be chicken sedans.

Two philosophical hens were sitting next to each other talking about life as chickens when one said, "Did it ever occur to you that with all the eggs we lay, there ought to be more of us?"

In my hometown there was a tavern that owned a monkey that would often sit on a pickle barrel & play the harmonica. A customer saw that the monkey's tail was hanging in the barrel & told the bartender. The barkeep said, "Don't bother me with it, go tell the monkey!" So, the customer approached the monkey & said, "Do you know your tail is hanging in the pickle barrel?" The monkey says, "I don't know, hum a couple of bars & I'll see if I can pick up the melody."

A lion sprang upon a bull & devoured him. After he had feasted, he felt so good that he roared. The noise attracted hunters & they killed him. The moral of the story is: When you're full of bull, you should keep your mouth shut.

() HEY LARRY, HOW ABOUT IT, CAN I SELL YOU THAT INSURANCE POLICY?

Well, yes, go ahead & see if I'm eligible.

() HAVE YOU EVER HAD A SERIOUS ACCIDENT?

No.

() YOU MEAN YOU'VE NEVER HAD AN ACCIDENT IN YOUR LIFE?

Never, except when the bull tossed me over the fence.

() AND YOU DON'T CALL THAT AN ACCIDENT?

No sir! He did it on purpose!

If a pig loses its voice, is it disgruntled?

What happened to the little frog who sat on a telephone? He grew up to be a bellhop.

I have a white hen that lays brown eggs.
() WHAT'S SO WONDERFUL ABOUT THAT?
Well, can you do it?

I was stopped by a game warden leaving a lake with 2 buckets of fish. The game warden says, "Do you have a license to catch those fish? I said, "No sir, these are my pet fish. Every night I take these fish here down to the lake & let them swim around for a while. Then I whistle & they jump back into the buckets & I take them home." The warden says, "That's a bunch of hooey, fish can't do that!" I said, "Well, I'll just show you!" So, I poured the fish back into the lake & we stood there waiting. After several minutes the game warden says, "Well?" I said, "Well what?" He says, "When are you gonna call them back?" I said, "Call what back?" He says, "The fish!" I said, "What fish?"

How do you make a hot-dog stand? Take away his chair.

A farmer called the Sheriff & said, "Speeders are killing my chickens!" So the next day some county workers put up a sign that said: "SLOW-SCHOOL CROSSING. Three days later the farmer called back & said, "That sign's not helping, the people ignore!" So, the sheriff sent some workers out again & they changed the sign to read; "SLOW-CHILDREN AT PLAY". Three more days went by without results & the farmer called the sheriff again & asked, "Could I make my own sign, that one's not working?" The sheriff says, "Sure, go ahead." Three weeks later the sheriff called the farmer to check on the situation. He asked, "How's your sign working out for you?" The farmer says, "Great, not one chicken has been killed since I put it up!" Well, that got the sheriff's curiosity up & he drove out to see what that sign said. It said, "NUDIST COLONY---GO SLOW & WATCH FOR CHICKS."

A dog walks into a bar & says, "Hi, my name's Bob & I'm a talking dog. Isn't that something? Ever heard of a talking dog before? Not one as smart as me I'll bet. How about a drink for a talking dog?" The bartender says, "Sure, the toilet is right down the hall."

What do you call a dog with no legs? Scooter.

I have an American Legion dog. He stops at every post.

When I was a kid, I had a dog with no legs.
() WHAT DID YOU CALL HIM?
I didn't call him anything. What's the use in calling him, he didn't have no legs so he couldn't come if you did call him. But I had an uncle who could whittle real good, so he whittled that dog 3 wooden legs & after that we called him 'tripod'. One night we had a terrific storm & the lightning struck his dog-house & burnt that dog plumb to the ground. After that, anytime the dog wanted to go anywhere we pushed him around in a wheelbarrow. One day grandma was pushing that dog around & that dog got to chasing a rabbit & like to have run grandma to death.

I went fishing this morning, but after a short time I ran out of worms. Then I saw a cottonmouth snake with a frog in its mouth. You know frogs are good bass bait. Knowing the snake couldn't bite me with the frog in its mouth, I grabbed him right behind the head, took the frog & put it in my bait bucket. Now, the dilemma was how to release the snake without getting bit. So, I grabbed my bottle of Jack Daniels that I use for medicinal purposes only & poured a little whiskey in its mouth. His eyes rolled back & he went limp. I released him into the lake with no problem & carried on fishing, using the frog. A little later, I felt a nudge on my foot. It was that snake, with 2 more frogs!

I think we're gonna start raisin' hogs under our house.
() WOW! WHAT ABOUT THE SMELL?
Oh, they'll get used to that.

The Fire Department's been busy this week. It's been so cold, they had to spend 2 days breaking dogs loose from fire plugs.

The early bird may get the worm, but the 2nd mouse gets the cheese in the trap.

Two race horses are in a stable. One says, "You know, before that last race that I won. I felt a pinch in my hindquarters." The other horse says, "Funny, I felt a pinch in my hindquarters before the race I won too!" A dog walking by says, "You idiots, you're being doped. They're injecting you with a drug to make you faster!" The 1st horse t urns to the other & says, "Hey, a talking dog!"

() SAY, I WENT BY YOUR HOUSE TODAY & ALL YOUR CHICKENS WERE OUT IN THE FRONT YARD.
Yeah, they heard some men were going to lay a sidewalk & they wanted to see how it was done.

() SAY LARRY, HOW DID YOU EVER MAKE YOUR NEIGHBOR KEEP HIS HENS IN HIS OWN YARD?
Oh, that was easy. One night I hid half a dozen eggs under a bush in my yard & the next day I let him see me gather 'em. I wasn't bothered after that.

What do puppies think when they see you looking through a newspaper? They probably think; "Why in the world is that guy reading a toilet?

When I got home today my wife was just bawling & I said, "What's wrong Honey?" She said, "The dog ate the pie I made for you!" I said, "Don't worry, I'll buy you another dog!"

There's a knock on the front door. The man of the house opens it & looks down to find a snail sitting on the stoop. He picks up the little critter & throws it as far as he can. Three years later, there's a knock. The man opens the door, looks down, & there sit's the same snail. The snail looks up & says, "What on Earth was that about?"

A woman has a parrot that she enjoys, except all it says is "Let's Make Love". She talked to her pastor about the embarrassing problem & he said, "You should bring your parrot over to our house because we have a nice parrot that's always saying, "Let Us Pray, Let Us Pray." So the lady brings her parrot over to the pastors home. She walks in with her parrot saying, "Let's Make Love, Let's Make Love" & his parrot says, "My prayers have been answered."

Well, ______, I'm glad to see you. That crate of chickens you sent me busted open just as I was going to take them out & they ran all over the place. I chased them through my neighbor's yards & I only got back 11! () You did okay, I only sent you 6.

Went ice fishing down at the lake. There was about a 11 year old boy already there with a hole cut in the ice & he had 3 nice bass. So I cut a hole about 10 feet from him & got to fishin'. An hour went by & he'd caught 3 more & I hadn't caught a thing, so I went over to him & said,

"How come I can't catch fish like you can?" He says, "MMMMM". I said, "What?" He says, (spit) "Keep your worms warm.

What happened to the little frog who sat on a telephone? He grew up to be a bellhop.

Research has found that 'Kitty Litter' takes the odor out of your shoes. Unless of course you have a cat.

Help keep your city clean---eat a pigeon!

A guy went on a 2 week business trip to Europe & he left his cat with his brother. Three days before he heads home, he calls his brother & asks him, "How's my cat doing?" His brother says, "She's dead." "Dead ? What do you mean she's dead? I loved that cat. Couldn't you have found a nicer way to tell me? You could have told me she got out of the house last week. Then you could have called & said you found her up on the roof & we're having trouble getting her down. Then when I called you from the airport you could have told me that the Fire Department was there & scared her off the roof & the cat died when it hit the ground." His brother says, "I'm sorry, you're right, that was insensitive, I won't let it happen again." & the brother who's cat died says, "Alright, alright, forget about it, how's Mom doing?" The insensitive brother says, "She's up on the roof & we're having trouble getting her down!"

How do you tell the difference between a fiddler & a dog? The dog knows when to stop scratching.

A pair of chickens walk up to the circulation desk at a public library & say, "buk-buk-buk." The librarian decides that the chickens want 3 books & give them to them. About noon the chickens return; "buk-buk-buk."

Another 3 books. The librarian decides to follow the chickens. They leave the library, go out of town into a park. The librarian hid behind a tree & watched. She saw the chickens throwing the books a frog in a pond, to which the frog was saying; "Rrredit-rrredit-rrredit."

Two dogs walk over to a parking meter. One says to the other, "How do you like that? Pay toilets."

A butcher watching over his shop & he sees a dog come in, so he shoos him off. Later that dog comes back, so he goes over to the dog & the dog has a note in his mouth. The note reads, "Can I have 12 sausages & a leg of lamb, please." The dog has a $10 bill in his mouth too. So, the butcher takes the money & puts the sausages & lamb in a bag & places it in the dog's mouth. The butcher is so impressed & because it's closing time, he locks up & follows the dog. The dog goes to a crossing, puts down the bag, jumps up & presses the button with his paw, waits patiently for the 'walk' light to come on & crosses the street with the bag in his mouth. The dog comes to a bus stop, looks at the timetable & sits down on the bench. Along comes a bus, the dog walks around in front, looks at the number, & goes back to his seat. Another bus comes, again the dog looks at the number, notices it's the right bus & gets on. The butcher by now is dumb-founded & follows the dog on the bus. The bus goes through town & into the suburbs & the dog's looking at the scenery. Eventually he gets up, moves to the front of the bus, stands up on his rear paws, pushes the button to stop the bus & gets off with the groceries in his mouth. The dog & the butcher are walking along the road & the dog turns into a house, he walks up the path & drops the groceries on the step. Then he walks back down the path, takes a big run & throws himself against the door. He does this again. There's no answer at the house. Finally the door opens & a big guy comes out & starts scolding the dog. The butcher runs up & stops the guy, "What in Heaven's name are you doing? The dog is a genius. He could be on TV!" The guy says, "You call this clever? This is the 2nd time this week that this silly dog's forgotten his key!"

What do you get when you have 10 rabbits in a row & they all take one step backward? A receding hare line.

I went horseback riding today.
() WELL, SIT DOWN & TELL ME ALL ABOUT IT.
I can't.
() YOU MEAN YOU CAN'T TELL ME ABOUT THE RIDE?
No, I can't sit down.

() THEY TELL ME WHEN I'M IN THE SADDLE I'M A PART OF THE HORSE.
Yeah, but they didn't tell you what part.

______'s been having trouble with his prize bull. He called his Veterinarian & the doc gave him some pills to give that bull & they worked great. So, I asked him, "Do you have any idea what's in them pills?" He says, "No, but they taste kinda salty."

Did you hear about the 2 elephants who came down to the beach, but the lifeguard ran them off? They couldn't keep their trunks up.

It's been so hot that the cows are giving evaporated milk.
It's been so hot that farmers are feeding their chickens crushed ice to keep 'em from laying hard boiled eggs.

Did you know you can teach your dog to play fetch by tying your cat to a boomerang?

() I HEARD A MULE KICKED YOU YESTERDAY.
Yes he did.

() WHERE DID HE KICK YOU?
Well, if my head was in New York & my feet in California, he'd have kicked me in Omaha.

What do you get when you take a bovine & divide its circumference by its diameter? A cow pi.

Did you hear about the rabbit who wouldn't let his dentist give him Novocain---cause he was an Etherbunny.

Two goldfish are in a tank & one says to the other, "Do you know how to drive this thing?"

So, I walk into a restaurant & ask, "How do you prepare your chickens?" The cook says, "Oh, nothing special. We just tell 'em they're gonna die."

Went to see my uncle down home. He's on his deathbed & a lot of friends & family were gathered in to help make him feel more comfortable. They gave him warm milk to taste but he refused to drink it. Then a neighbor remembered a bottle of Irish Whiskey in his pickup truck & generously poured an amount into the warm milk. Now folks, my uncle is a teetotaler & a rather pious gentleman old farmer, but he tasted that milk & then drink a little more & before long the entire glass was empty. In a whispery voice his last words were, "Don't sell that cow."

So, here's the situation: There I was---out in the wilderness---a bull coming at me in one direction & a bear in the other, & I only had one shell.

() WHICH ONE DID YOU SHOOT?"
I shot the bear, cause I could shoot the bull anytime.

Where do you find a dog with no legs? Exactly where you left it.

What do elephants & tomatoes have in common? Neither one can ride a bike.

Did I tell you how Ty made all his money? Years ago he bought pure bred Angus bulls out in California & he'd bring 'em back here & sell 'em at a big profit. Why, he became the biggest 'bullshipper' in this part of the country.

A man walks into a restaurant with a full-grown ostrich behind him. The waitress asks them for their orders. The man says, "A hamburger, fries & a coke." & the ostrich says, "I'll have the same." The waitress brings the order & says, "That'll be $9.41 please." The man reaches into his pocket & pulls out the exact change. This went on all week. Every day he paid with the exact change. So, the man & the ostrich came in on Friday night & the waitress says, "The usual?" The guy says, "No, this is Friday night, so I'll have a steak, baked potato & a salad." "The same," says the ostrich. Pretty soon the waitress brings the order & says, "That'll be $32.63." Once again the man pulls the exact change out of his pocket & places it on the table. The waitress couldn't hold back her curiosity any longer. She says, "Excuse me sir, how do you always manage to always come up with the exact change in your pocket every time?" He says, "Well, several years ago I was cleaning the attic & found an old lamp. When I rubbed it a genie appeared & offered me 2 wishes. My 1st wish was that if I ever had to pay for anything, I would just put my hand in my pocket & the right amount of money would always be there." The waitress says, "Wow, that's brilliant, most people would ask for a million dollars & have it spent in no time---but you'll always be as rich as you want for as long as you live.!" He says, "That's right, whether it's a gallon of milk or a Rolls-Royce, the exact money is always there." So the waitress asks him, "What's with the ostrich?" He sighs, pauses & says, "My 2nd wish was for a tall chick with big eyes & long legs who agrees with everything I say."

Why don't oysters give to charity? Because they're shellfish.

I grew up in a small, flat Midwestern town where you could watch your dog run away for 3 days.

Roses are red, violets are blue, horses that lose are made into glue.
_____'s been on a diet where he goes horseback riding every morning. It's been partially successful. So far, his horse has lost 25 #.

I was wondering, can a vegetarian eat animal crackers?
I've been making a lot of money off the dachshunds I've been raising.
() OW?
I rent them out as stove pipe cleaners.

If there's one thing I've learned in this life, it's be decisive. Right or wrong, make a decision. The road of life is paved with flat squirrels who couldn't make a decision.

What do you call a cow with a twitch? Beef jerky.

It finally got cold enough to go ice fishing, so me & Elijah went out & we started to cut a hole in the ice when this voice spoke to us & said, "Don't cut a hole in the ice!" I said, "Elijah, was that God speaking to us?" And the voice came back & said, "No, this is the owner of this ice-skating rink!"

I remember the 1st time I went ice fishing. I went down to this lake & there was this lad about 12 years old settin' there fishin' through a hole in the ice & he'd already caught about 3 nice bass, so I cut me a hole in the ice about 10 feet from him & I guess I fished about 2 hours & I hadn't caught a thing & he'd caught 6 more. So, I went over to him & asked him, "How come I can't catch any fish this close to you & you've caught all these fish?" He says, "Hmmm---hmmm." I said, "What did you say?" He said, "(spit) Keep your worms warm!"

My brother accidently swallowed a frog when we were little.
() SWALLOWED A FROG! DID IT HURT HIM?
He's liable to croak any minute!

How do you identify a bald eagle? All of his feathers are combed to one side.

A lady went to the airport with a dog kennel. She said, "I want my dog on the plane first, & off the plane first in New York." When the plane arrived & they took the kennel off the plane, they discovered the dog was dead. One of the baggage handlers said, "What're we gonna do?" They thought & then another handler says, "I saw a cute little dog that looks just like that dog, let's get it & she'll never know the difference." So, they brought the dog to the woman & she said, "That's not my dog, my dog is dead!"

I crossed a horse with a black widow spider.
() WHAT DID YOU GET?
I don't know, but if it ever bites you, you can ride him to the doctor.

Did I tell you about my New York buddy Ralph? He's always dreamed of owning a cattle ranch & he finally saved enough money to buy the spread of his dreams in Wyoming. I went out to visit hi wile back. I said, "So, what'd you name the ranch?" He said, "We had a hard time naming it, but we finally settled on 'The Double R Lazy L Triple Horseshoe Bar 7 Lucky Diamond Ranch'." I said, Wow! So, where are your cattle?" He said, "None of 'em survived the branding."

A circus owner walked into a bar to see everyone crowded about a table watching a little show. On the table was an upside-down pot & a duck tap dancing on it. The circus owner was so impressed that he offered to buy the duck from its owner. After some wheeling & dealing, they settled for $10,000 for the duck & pot. 3 days later the circus owner runs back into the bar in anger. He says, "Your duck is a rip off!" I put him on the pot before a whole audience, & he didn't dance a single step!" The duck's former owner says, "What, did you remember to light the candle under the pot?

My great granddaughter was in the back yard digging a hole to bury her dead goldfish. Our next-door neighbor was watching her & she asked, "Izzy, what are you doing?" Izzy says, "I'm digging a hole to bury my dead goldfish." My neighbor says, "Well, don't you think that hole is a little too big for a goldfish?" Izzy says, "No, it's inside your darn cat!"

Did you hear about the pregnant bed bug? She had her baby in the spring.

A lonely guy bought a centipede & brought it home in a little white box. Later that day, the fellow decided he & his pet should spend some quality time together. So, he knocked on the box & said, "Hey, Buddy, wanta take a walk?" No answer. He waited a few minutes, then tapped again, "How about a stroll?" Again no answer from his supposed new friend. So, he decided to ask the centipede once more. This time he pressed his face against the box & shouted, "Hey, would you like to go for a walk?" At last a little voice came from the inside. "I heard you the 1st time! I'm putting on my shoes!"

What's black & white & black & white & black & white? A penguin rolling down the hill

---

What's black & white & laughing? The penguin that pushed him.

An elephant escaped from the zoo & got into the vegetable garden of a nearsighted ole lady. She looked out the window & saw that & called the police. She says, "There's a huge beast out in my garden & it's pulling up my lettuce with its tail!" The officer says, "Really? What's it doing with it?" She looked in the garden again & said, "Officer, even if I told you, you'd never believe it."

An old fellow passed away that lived 2 doors down the street. He passed away Tuesday & for several years now he thought he was a rooster. It was sad. The day after he died, the whole block overslept.

Speaking of roosters, did you hear about the farmer who bought a new rooster, put him out in the barnyard & the od rooster sidles up to him & says; "You know, we've got to decide who's the head rooster around here." The young rooster says, "Okay, how do we do that?" The old rooster says; "I'll tell you what, we'll run 10 laps around the barn & whoever finishes 1st is the head rooster!" The young rooster says, "That's fine with me, in fact, I'll give you a one lap head start, cause you're older." So, off they go & the old hens start cacklin' & makin' all kinds of noise & the farmer thinks there must be a fox killin' chickens, so he steps out on the back porch with his shotgun. Well, them roosters had gone about 5 laps & the young one was about to catch up with the old one. All of a sudden the farmer hauls off & shoots that young rooster & then he goes in & tells his wife, "That's the 3rd gay rooster I've bought in a year!"

Howard Rash (banjo picker extraordinary) is also an avid coon hunter. He invested in a special coon hound that cost $10,000. This coon hound was so special that you didn't even have to back your pickup truck out of the garage. All you had to do was show that hound a hide-stretching board of the size coon you wanted & that dog would go get & bring it back home. So, I went out to visit Howard & I noticed that the hound wasn't in the pen. I said, "Howard, where's your hound?" He said, "Oh, Wilma left the ironing board on the back porch the other day & we ain't seen him since."

What do you get when you cross a pit bull with a collie? A dog that rips your leg off, then goes for help.

Once upon a time there was a mole family. There was Papa mole, Mama mole & baby mole. They were traveling along under ground when all of a sudden Papa mole stuck his head up out of the ground & said, "I smell pancakes!" Then Mama mole stuck her head out of the ground & said, "I smell syrup!" Then baby mole stuck his head up out of the ground & said, "I smell molasses!"

A man walks into a bar carrying an ape in his arms. "I just bought this fella as a poet. We have no children, so he's going to live with us, just like one of the family. He'll eat at our table, even sleep in the bed with me & the wife." The bartender says, "But what about the smell?" The guy says, "Oh, he'll just have to get used to it, the same way I did."

A lady buys a parrot at the pet store. The salesman tells her, "That bird is so well behaved, you can take it anywhere." She was delighted & the next Sunday, she took her parrot to church with her. Things were great until, halfway through the sermon, the bird blurted out, "It's dang cold in here!" She was so embarrassed, she ran out & went toe pet store & jumped on the salesman: She said, "This 'good bird' swore in church today." The guy says, "I'm sorry, it sometimes does that in new environments. Next time, grab its feet & swing it over your head a few times, that should stop it." The next week the woman & her parrot were in church again & the parrot yelled, "It's dang cold in here!" She grabbed that bird & swung it above her head 6 times, put the bird back on her shoulder & sat down. The bird said, "Dang, it's windy too!"

I got a hold of some rejected Hallmark Greeting Cards. Here's one: My tire was thumping, I thought it was flat, when I looked at the tire---I found your cat----sorry.

A pig walks into a bar, orders 15 beers, & knocks 'em back. The bartender says, "You've had a lot to drink. Would you like to know where the bathroom is?" The hog says, "No, I'm the little pig that goes wee-wee-wee all the way home."

Two monkeys were playing in the jungle & they got bored & they were looking around for some mischief to get into, when they saw a lion sleeping. One of the monkeys said, "I'm gonna go down there & kick that lion in the rear & run & see what he does." So the monkey climbs down the tree, sneaks over to the lion, kicks him in the rear as hard as he can & then takes off running. So, the lion gets up & chases after him & he's catching up. The monkey runs right through the middle of a village, so he grabs a straw hat, a pair of sunglasses, a lawn chair & sets down reading a newspaper. The lion comes running up & asks, "Did you see a monkey run through here?" & the monkey says, "You mean the one that kicked the lion in the rear?" & the lion says, "That's in the paper already!"

Did you know I've got the biggest sheep farm in the state?
() OH YEAH? HOW MANY SHEEP DO YOU HAVE?
I don't know. Every time I try to count them, I fall asleep.

A guy walks into a bar with a bird. The bartender asks, "What kind of a bird is that?" The guy say, "A gulp." Bartender says, "A gulp? I've never heard of it!" The guy says, "It's like a swallow, only it's bigger."

Yesterday I was at Costco, buying a large bag of Purina Dog Chow for my loyal pet, Owen, The Wonder Dog, & was in the check-out line when a woman behind me asked if I had a dog. So, because I'm retired & have little to do, on impulse, I told her that "No, I didn't have a dog & I was starting the Purina Diet again. I said, "I probably shouldn't, cause I ended up in the hospital last time, but that I'd lost 50 pounds before I woke up in an intensive care ward with tubes coming out of most of my orifices & IV's in both arms. I told her that it was essentially a perfect diet & that the way that it works is to load your pants pockets with Purina Nuggets & simply eat one or two every time you feel hungry. The food is nutritionally complete, so it works well & I was going to try it again." She was horrified & she asked me if I ended up in intensive care, because the dog food poisoned me." I told her, "No, I had stopped to wee-wee on a fire hydrant & a car hit me."

A tourist rented a camel to cross the desert. The camel died in the heat & the man wandered, looking for an oasis. The tourist saw a man in the distance standing on a sand dune. He came up to the man & said, "I'm dying of thirst, do you have any water?" The man says, "No, all I have are these ties for sale, I'll sell you one cheap." The tourist says, "What am I going to do with a tie?" The vendor says, "What do you want from me? I sell ties, that's all!" The tourist drags on, then he saw an oasis with a restaurant! Is it a mirage or is it real? It was real & he started into the restaurant but the doorman stopped him & said, "You can't come in without a tie."

Two old hens were pecking away in the barnyard. Suddenly one of them looked over her shoulder & says to the other, "We'd better separate, here comes that cross-eyed rooster again & we don't want him to miss both of us!"

What can a pigeon do that 7 out of 10 farmers can't to? Make a deposit on a pickup truck.

Did I tell you my dachshund died?
() THAT'S TOO BAD, WHAT HAPPENED?
Aw, he met his end going around a tree.

A dead mule lay in front of our church for 2 days, so, finally our pastor called the Department of Health. Some smart-aleck answered the phone & the pastor told him about the dead mule & the guy said, "Well, don't you take care of the dead?" And our pastor said, "Of course, but 1st we get in touch with their relatives."

I dressed my dog up as a cat for Halloween. Now he won't come when I call him.

Phil's sure got that soft touch on the piano. He learned it when he was on the night shift in a dairy. He had to milk the cows without waking them up.

My dog died last week. I called him 'Handyman' cause he did a lot of odd jobs around the house.

I guess the funniest pet I ever had when I was a kid was a rooster. This rooster was quite a cassanova. I woke up one morning & found him lying flat on his back in the chicken yard, legs up in the air, lookin' deader than a door nail. As I was walkin' up to him I was talking out loud to him. I said, "I told you this would happen, you can't run around after every chick day & night!" He said, "Shhhh, when your romancing a buzzard, you gottta play it right."

Impression of a lovelorn worm: "I can't live without you, marry me."
"Oh shut up! I'm your other end!"

Then, finally we found a good way to make some money, we started raisin' hogs under our house.
() Gee whiz Larry, what about the smell?'
Oh, they got used to that!

BLONDE JOKES

______ took his blonde girlfriend to her 1st football game. They had seats right behind their team's bench. After the game, he asked her how she liked it. She said, "Oh, I really liked it, especially the tight pants & all the big muscles, but I just couldn't understand why they were killing each other over 25 cents!" _____ says, "What do you mean?" She says, "Well, they flipped a coin, one team got it & then for the rest of the game, all they kept screaming was: 'Get the quarterback! Get the quarterback'? I'm like---Hello? It's only 25 cents!"

How can you tell when a blonde's been using a computer? There's 'white-out' all over the screen.

Did you hear about the blonde that tripped over a cordless phone?

Did you hear about the blonde that thought a 'quarterback' was a refund?

So this blonde suspects her boyfriend's cheating on her. She takes off work early, comes home & finds him with another woman. She gets a gun out & points it to her own head. Her boyfriend says, "Oh, no, don't do that!" She says, "Don't worry, you're next!"

This blonde decides one day she's sick & tired of all these 'blonde' jokes & how all blondes are perceived as stupid, so she decides to show her husband that blondes are really smart. While her husband is at work, she decides she's gonna paint a couple of rooms in the house. Her husband got home from work at 5:30 & he smells the distinctive odor of paint. He walks into the living room & here's his wife lying on the floor in a pool of sweat. He notices she's wearing a ski jacket & a fur coat at the same time. So he asks her, "Are you okay?" She says, "Yes." & he says, "What are you doing?" She says, "I wanted to prove to you that not all blonde women are stupid & I wanted to do it by painting the house." So he asks her, "Why do you have a ski jacket & a fur coat on?" She says, "Well, I was reading the directions on the paint can & it said, 'for best results, put on 2 coats'."

Two blondes walk into a building. You'd think one of them would have seen it.

Three blondes were applying for the last available position on the Texas Highway Patrol. The detective conducting the interview looked at the 3 of them & said, "So, y'all wanta be cops huh?" They nodded yes, so he pulled a folder out with a picture on it & said, "To be a detective, you have to be able to detect. Notice things, such as distinguishing features & oddities such as scars etc. He stuck the photo in the face of the 1st blonde for about 2 seconds. "Notice any distinguishing features about this man?" She says, "He has only one eye!" "Of course he has only one eye in this picture, it's a profile of his face!" He says, "You're dismissed." He shows the picture to the 2nd blonde, she says, "He only has one ear." He says, You're dismissed." The 3rd blonde says, "This man wears contact lenses!" He says, "You're absolutely right! His bio says he wears contact lenses, but how could you tell that by looking at his picture?" She says, "Well, hellooo! With only one eye & one ear, he certainly can't wear glasses!"

Blonde pulls into the Wal-Mart parking lot & rolled down her car windows to make sure her Labrador Retriever had fresh air. The dog was stretched out on the back seat & she wanted to impress on him that he must remain there. So she walked backwards pointing her finger at her car, giving the order; "Stay, stay!" A man was walking by & told her, "Why don't you just put it in 'PARK'."

What goes vroom--screech--vroom--screech--vroom--screech? A blonde at a flashing red light.

A blonde & her father were walking down the street when he says; "Look a dead bird!" The blonde looks up & says, "Where?"

A brunette was doing her laundry & asked her blonde friend to help her find a match for her sock. The blonde says, "What for? Are you gonna set it on fire?"

A blonde goes into the Emergency Room at the hospital. The Dr. asks, "What's the problem?" She says, "I've shot myself in the hand!" He says, "I'll have to report this to the police, we're required by law to report all gunshot wounds. She says, "Oh please don't, you see, I was trying to commit suicide!" He says, "Well, if you were trying to commit suicide, how did you shoot yourself in the hand?" She says, "Well, I had my gun stuck in my ear & I thought, 'wow' this is gonna be loud!"

A blind man walks into a bar & says, "Wanta hear a blonde joke?" The bartender says, "I'm a blonde,& I don't appreciate it. The man sitting next to you weighs 265#, & is also blonde. The man behind you is 285# & he's blonde too. Now, do you still want to tell that joke?" The blind man says, "No way, not if I have to explain it 3 times!"

A blonde went to see a ventriloquist in one of the clubs here in town. With his dummy on his knee, he starts going through his usual dumb blonde jokes when the blonde stands up on a chair & starts shouting:

"I've heard enough of your stupid blonde jokes. What does the color of a person's hair have to do with her worth as a human being? It's guys like you who keep women like me from reaching our full potential as a person. Because you & your kind continue to perpetuate discrimination against not only blondes, but women in general, & all in the name of humor!" The ventriloquist was embarrassed & he started to apologize but the blonde yells at him, "You stay out of this Mister! I'm talking to that little runt on your knee!"

The TV News was interviewing a blonde this week. It went kinda like this:
"How old are you?" (she counts on her fingers, toes & breasts) "Twenty-two."
"How tall are you?" (she gets out a tape measure & measures) "5', 2"."
"I'll give you an easier question. What's your name?" (she bobs her head from side-to-side for about 15 seconds & says) "Jenny."
"Okay, but why were you bobbing your head like that?" She said, "Oh, that. I was going, 'Happy Birthday to you, happy birthday to you, happy birthday dear Jenny."

Two Mexicans were on a bicycle about 15 miles out of Phoenix. One of the bike's tires goes flat & they start hitching a lift into town. An 18 wheeler stops to see if he can help, they ask for a ride, they can't ride in the cab, not much room in the trailer "I'm carrying 10,000 bowling balls, but if you can manage to get in there, you're welcome to ride." So they squeeze themselves & their bike into the trailer & the driver shuts the doors. By this time, he's really running late, so he puts the hammer down & sure enough, a blonde cop pulls him over for speeding. The officer asks the driver what he's hauling. He says, "10,000 Mexican eggs." She says, "I don't believe you, open up that trailer!" She looks in the trailer, closes the door & locks it. She gets on the radio & calls for immediate backup & the SWAT team. The dispatcher wants to know why so many officers? She says, "I've got a tractor-trailer stopped with 10,000 Mexican eggs in it, two of them have already hatched & they've already managed to steal a bicycle!"

A blonde went to Florida on vacation. She was staying in the tallest hotel around, so she went up on the roof to sunbathe. She noticed that it was by far the tallest building anywhere around, so she decided to sunbathe in the nude. So she took off her bathing suit & while she was lying there in that warm sun, she heard footsteps coming. Right quick, she wrapped a towel around her, looked up & it was the hotel manager. He said, "Young lady, we don't allow nude sunbathing!" She said, "But there are no tall buildings close enough to see me!" He said, "I know, but you're lying on the skylight over the dining room!"

A blonde calls Delta Airlines & asks; "Can you tell me how long it'll take to fly from San Francisco to New York City?" The agent says, "Just a minute." The blonde says, "Thank you" & hangs up.

---

2 blondes were waiting at a bus shelter. When the bus came, one leaned in & asked the driver, "Will this bus take me to 5th Avenue?" The driver said, "No ma'am, I'm sorry." Then the other blonde leaned in & asked him, "Will it take me there?"

A blonde had a twitter exchange between herself & an apologetic Domino's Pizza. She tweets: "Yooo I ordered a pizza & it came with no toppings on it or anything, it's just bread." Domino's tweeted back, "We're sorry to hear this!" A few minutes later the blonde tweeted back, "Never mind, I opened the pizza upside down."

A blonde got pulled over for a traffic violation. She said, "Honestly officer, I wouldn't have pulled over had I known you were just going to criticize me."

What do you call it when a blonde dyes her hair brunette? Artificial intelligence.

I saw this blonde in the supermarket the other day, reading the back of a shampoo bottle out loud---"Wet hair--lather--rinse--repeat--wet hair--lather--rinse--repeat, wet hair------.

Stayed in a motel last night. I had a blonde knocking on my door 'til 3 in the morning. Finally I got up & let her out.

A blonde touring a farm asked the farmer about his cows, "Why do some cows have no horns?" The farmer says, "There are 3 cases. Some are born without horns, some are dehorned, & some knock their horns off fighting." The blonde says, "What about that one in the corner?" The farmer says, "Ah, that's the 4th case, that's a horse!"

A blonde goes into the post office to buy some stamps for her Christmas cards. She says to the clerk; "May I have 50 Christmas stamps?" The clerk says, "What denomination?" The blonde says, "God help us. Has it come to this? Give me 22 Catholic, 12 Presbyterian, 10 Lutheran, & 6 Baptists."

Did you hear about the blonde that sold her car so she would have gas money?

Three women escape from prison. A blonde & 2 brunettes. They find an old abandoned farmhouse to hide in. They find 3 burlap bags to hide in in case the law decides to search the old house. Sure enough, 2 cops show up. One searches outside & the other goes inside. The one that's inside sees the burlap bags & says, "Hey, there's 3 burlap sacks in here!" The other cop says, "Kick those bags to make sure it's not them hiding." So, he kicks one with a brunette in it & she yells, "MEOW" & the officer says, "Oh it's just a cat in there." Then he kicks another sack with the other brunette in it & she yells, "WOOF, WOOF" & the office says, "Well, that's just a dog." Then he kicks the sack with the blonde in it & she yells, "POTATOES-POTATOES!"

Three women go down to Mexico one night to celebrate college graduation. They get drunk & wake up in jail, only to discover that they are to be executed in the morning, though none of them can remember what they did the night before.

The 1st one, a redhead was strapped into an electric chair. They asked her, "Any last words?" She says, "I just graduated from Trinity Bible College & I believe in the almighty power of God to intervene on behalf of the innocent. They throw the switch & nothing happens. They all immediately fall to the floor on their knees, bet forgiveness & release her.

The 2nd, a brunette was strapped in & she gives her last words. She says, "I just graduated from the University Of Illinois School Of Law, & I believe in the power of justice to intervene on the behalf of the innocent." They throw the switch & nothing happens. Again, they all immediately fall on their knees, beg for forgiveness & release her.

The last one, a blonde (you knew it) is strapped in & says, "Well, I'm from Ohio & I just graduated from Ohio State University with a degree in Electrical Engineering & I'll tell you right now, y'all ain't gonna electrocute nobody if you don't plug this thing in!"

When blondes have more fun, do they know it?

___ & ____ were out shopping the other day & he locked his keys in the car. It took him an hour & a half to get his wife out.

Hear about the blonde mortician? A man was brought in to be prepared for the funeral. He had a real nice black, pinstriped suit on, but his wife insisted on a blue suit for him. Then another man was brought in who happened to have a real nice blue suit on. The blonde mortician called the 1st lady in to see if everything was to her satisfaction & she was elated with the blue suit. She said, "That's beautiful, how much was it?" The blonde says, "Oh, nothing, I had another customer with a blue suit & his wife wanted him dressed in a black suit, so I just switched heads."

I was out to Debbie's (a blonde) place this week & she's got a couple of new dogs. I asked her, "What did you name them?" She said, "Rolex & Timex." I said, "Well, whoever heard of naming dogs like that?" She said, "Well, hellooooooo, they're watch dogs!"

Why did the blonde take all her clothes off in the laundromat? Because the sign on the washing machine said: "WHEN THE MACHINE STOPS, REMOVE YOUR CLOTHES".

Two sisters, one blonde, one brunette, inherit the family ranch. Unfortunately, after just a few years, they're in financial trouble. In order to keep the bank from repossessing the ranch, they need to purchase a bull so they can breed their own stock. When the brunette leaves, she tells her sister, "When I get there, if I decide to buy the bull, I'll contact you to drive out after me & haul it home." The brunette arrives at the man's ranch, inspects the bull, & decides she wants to buy it. The man tells her he'll sell it for $599, on less. She has $600, so she pays the man & drives to the nearest town to send her sister a telegram. She walks into the telegraph office & says; "I want to send a telegram to my sister telling her I've bought a bull for our ranch. I need her to hitch the trailer to our pickup truck & drive out here so we can haul it home." The telegraph operator says, "Sure, I can do that, but it'll cost you 99 cents a word." Okay, she's got one dollar left, so she can send only one word, so after thinking it over, she says, "Sir, I want you to send the word 'comfortable'." The operator shakes his head & says, "How is she ever going to know that you want her to haul that bull back to your ranch if you send her just the word 'comfortable'?" The brunette says, "MY sister's blonde, the word is big & she'll read it very slowly---com-fort-da-bul."

My neighbor's a blonde guy. He calls the doctor & says, "My wife is pregnant & her contractions are only 2 minutes apart!" The Dr. says, "Is this her 1st child?" He says, "No, this is her husband!"

He's a cilly. His wife told me about this: A while back he was in the bathroom & his wife shouts; "Did you find the shampoo?" He says, "Yes, but I'm not sure what to do---it's for dry hair, & I've just wet mine."

Blond news: Suicidal twin kills sister by mistake.

What do you do when a blonde throws a pin at you? Run like the dickens, she's got a hand grenade in her mouth.

What does the post card from a blonde's vacation say? Having a wonderful time. Where am I?

How do you make a blonde's eyes sparkle? You shine a flashlight in her ear.

Why does a blonde only change her baby's diaper every month? Because it says on the box: "Good for up to 20 pounds."

My neighbor, who is blonde, came running up to me in the driveway just jumping for joy! I didn't know why she was jumping for joy but I thought, what the heck, & I started jumping up & down with her. She said, "I have some really great news!" I said, "Great, tell me why you're so happy." Out of breath from jumping, she says, "I'm pregnant!" I said, "I couldn't be happier for you!" Then she said, "There's more!" I said, "What do you mean—More?" She said, "We're gonna have twins!" I wanted to know how she knew? She says, "That was the easy part. I went to Wal-Mart & they actually had a home pregnancy kit in a twin-pack. Both tests came out positive!"

A blonde spies a letter lying on the doormat. It says on the envelope: "Do Not Bend!" She spends the next 2 hours trying to figure out how to pick it up.

What do you call a blonde in a tree with a brief case? The branch manager.

Two blondes went deep into the woods searching for a Christmas tree. After hours of subzero temperatures & a few close calls with hungry wolves, one blonde turned to the other & said, "I'm chopping down the next tree I see, I don't care if it's decorated or not!"

They're gonna start putting dimmer switches back in the floorboards in cars because blondes keep getting their foot hung up in the steering wheel.

CAJUN JOKES

Thibideaux was driving his car past Beaudreaux's house & saw a sign that read: 'BOAT FOR SALE'. Thibideaux marches up to Beaudreaux's front porch & raps hard on the front door & Beaudreaux opens it. Thibideaux say, "Beaudreaux! How long we ban frens?" "Well, all our lives Thibideaux." "Why don you tole me you gotta boat?" "I ain't gotta boat!" Thibideaux says, "Dat sigh out there say 'BOAT FOR SALE!" Beaudreaux says, "Oh, no Thibideaux! See dat ole '72 Ford pick-em-up truck over der?" "Yeah, I see dat ole pick-em-up truck." "& see dat '76 Chevrolet Ce-dan?" "Yeah, I see dat Ce-dan." Beaudreaux says, "Well, dey boat for sale!"

CHILDREN JOKES

On the last day of school the children brought gifts for the teacher. The florists son brought the teacher a bouquet. The candy store owner's daughter handed the teacher a pretty box of candy. The liquor store owner's son brought up a big heavy box. The teacher lifted it up & noticed that it was leaking a little bit. She touched a drop of liquid with her finger & tasted it. "Is it wine?" The boy said, "No." She tasted another drop. "Is it champagne?" "No." "I give up, what is it?" He says, "It's a puppy!"

That reminds me. I once played hooky from school & my teacher sent my Mother a 'thank-you' note.

Grandson stayed all night last night & I sent him to bed about 9 O'clock. 5 minutes later he says, "Grandad!" I say, "What?" He says, "I'm thirsty, can you bring me a drink of water?" I said, "No, you had your chance. Lights out!" 5 minutes later---"Grandad!" I said, "What?" He says, "I'm thirsty, can I have a drink of water?" I said, "I told you no! If you ask again I'll have to spank you!" Five minutes later: "Grandad!" "What?" "When you come in to spank me, can you bring me a drink of water?"

If your parents never had children, chances are you won't either.

My Mother taught me about anticipation: "Just wait 'til your Father gets home!"

My great granddaughter brought home her science exam paper the other day & she let me look at it. I'll bet the teacher got a kick out of reading these answers. Here's one of the questions: What happens to your body as you age? She answered: When you get old, so do your bowels & you get intercontinental.

I don't know how _____ gonna do in school this year. He'll be in the 7th grade. Before school ended this spring he tapped his teacher on the shoulder & said, "I don't want to scare you, but my Daddy says, if I don't get better grades---somebody's gonna get a spanking!"

Last school year, Cozy, my 7 year old great-granddaughter was in the 1st grade & the teacher was reading the story of "The Three Little Pigs". The teacher came to the part where the 1st pig was trying to acquire building materials for his home. She read: "And so the pig went up to the man with a wheelbarrow full of straw & said, "Pardon me sir, but might I have some of that straw to build my house with?" Teacher asked the class: "And what do you think the man said, "Cozy says, "I know, I know! He said, 'Holy smokes, a talking pig!'" The teacher was unable to teach for the next 10 minutes.

Do you know the difference between broccoli & boogers? Kids won't eat broccoli.

My neighbor read in the paper that it takes ten dollars a year to support a child in India, so he sent his kids there.

Did I ever tell you that when I was a kid we had a quicksand box in our back yard. I was the only child--eventually.

My grandson's been fighting with one of the boys next door & gave him a black eye. So I asked him why he did it & he said, "Well, they're twins & I wanted to have some way to tell them apart."

Did you hear about the cross-eyed teacher who lost her job because she couldn't control her pupils?

I was trying to help my grandson with his arithmetic homework. I said to him, "Suppose you reached in your right pocket & you found a ten dollar bill & you reached in your left pocket & found another one, what would you have?" He said, "Somebody else's pants."

A few years ago, after a family meal one night, 3 generations are sitting around chatting. My grandson's sitting on my knee & says; "Granddad, can you make a noise like a frog?" I said, "Why, do you want me to make a noise like a frog?" He said, "Well, last night Daddy said that when you croak we can all go to Disneyland."

What did the 'Tin Man' say when he got run over by a steam roller? "Curses, foil again!"

A 5 year old little girl answered the door when the census taker came by. She told the census taker that her Daddy was a Doctor & wasn't home, because he was performing an appendectomy. The census taker says, "My, that sure is a big word for such a little girl. Do you know what it means?" She says, "Sure, it means $1500 bucks & that doesn't even include the anesthesiologist."

I don't think my Mother loved me. As a child she always wrapped my school lunch in a roadmap.

Yeah, my folks moved 7 times by the time I was 13. But I always found them cause they'd take their mailbox with them so they wouldn't have to change their address.

______went to his childhood home, knocked on the door & asked to come in & look around. They said, "No, & slammed the door. Sometimes parents can be so rude.

My 4 year-old granddaughter who lives with us hollered at me this morning. She said, "Grandad, my toothbrush fell into the toilet!" I said, "I'll get you another one, that one's full of bad germs now." Then I threw her old one in the trash. The next thing I knew she was handing me my toothbrush. She says; "Then we better throw this one out too, I dropped it in the toilet last week!"

Do you know that 90% of Americans have children because of hereditary reasons, and it's a well known fact that if your parents didn't have any children, you won't either.

() WHO'S PICTURE IS THAT?
Oh, that's a picture of me when I was a baby.
() GEE, BUT YOU WERE A NICE BALDHEADED BABY
Wait a minute---you're looking at that picture upside down!

My Grandson's sure got a big appetite for a 6 year-old. On his last birthday, his Grandma told him, "Devan, if you eat more cake, you'll burst!" He said, "Well pass the cake & get out of the way!"

Saw my cousin the other day. You know, the one that started school in the 3rd grade at the age of 6. Yeah, that's right. He was so smart his Mother marched him right into the 3rd grade. The teacher told my aunt,

"Oh no, he has to start school in the 1st grade like everybody else!" So, my aunt says, "Let's just take this up with the principal!" They went to the principal's office & told him what the problem was & he told the teacher to ask my cousin some questions to see how smart he was. So, the teacher asks him; "What does a cow have 4 of, that I only have 2?" He says, "Legs." She says, "That's right." Now, what does the principle have in his pants that I don't?" My cousin scratched his head & said, "Pockets!" The teacher said, "That's exactly right." & the principal said, "Let that boy start in the 3rd grade, I missed both them questions."

Went over to meet our new neighbors next door. About a 10 year old boy answered the door & I said, "Are your Father & Mother in?' He said, "They was in, but they is out." Then I said, "Young man, where's your grammar?" & he said, "Oh, she's upstairs!"

Summertime. You know, this is my favorite time of the year--good hot weather. I remember when I was a kid, I'd ask my Mom if I could go swimming & she's say; "Wait'll you eat something."

I don't think my Mother loved me, cause she'd always pack my school lunch in a roadmap.

A man brought his son into the emergency room at the hospital cause he'd swallowed a bullet. But the Dr. didn't seem too worried about it. He just wrote out a prescription, handed it to the man & said, "Just give him this strong laxative, but be sure that for the next few hours you don't point him at anybody!"

I never really liked hide-and-seek when I was a kid. Especially since the time I hid in the closet & my family moved.

Each day the son of a town baker brought his teacher a salted pretzel. She told the boy that she appreciated the gesture, but her Dr. told her to cut down on her salt. The boy says, "Don't worry, I'll take care of it." So, for the rest of the week, the boy brought his teacher pretzels without salt. The teacher told the boy, "Tell your father the pretzels are very good & I hope it's not a problem removing the salt." The boy says, "No problem at all, on the way to school, I just lick it off."

My 6 year old great grandson asked me how old I was. I told him, "I'm not sure." He says, "Granddad, look in your underwear, mine says 4 to 6."

My 9 year old great granddaughter came home from school the other day & said, "Guess what? We learned how to make babies today." I tried to keep my cool & I said, "Well, that's interesting, how do you make babies?" She said, "It's simple, you just change the 'y' to 'I' & add 'es'."

I'm looking forward to summertime. Summertime makes me think of my childhood, & boy what a childhood I had. My parents sent me to a child psychiatrist. That kid was no help at all!!!

My 5 year old great granddaughter asked me how old I was. I told her 78. She was quiet for a moment, & then she asked, "Did you start at one?"

A 3 year old boy accompanied his Mom when she was pregnant with his little brother. She heaved a sigh & clutched her stomach. The boy says, "Mommy, what is it?" She says, "The baby brother you're going to have is kicking." The 3 year old says, "He's probably getting restless, why don't you swallow a toy?"

A scoutmaster asks his troop to list 3 important things to bring in case they get lost. Food, matches & a bandana. My grandson suggests a compass, a canteen of water & a deck of cards. The leader says, "Well, I can understand the first two items, but what good are the cards?" Devan says, "Well as soon as you start playing solitaire, it's guaranteed someone will come up to you & say, "Put the red nine on top of the black ten."

When my grandson was about 10, he asked me, "How was I born?" I said, "The stork brought you." So he says, "Well, how was Dad born?" I said, "The stork brought him." Then he asked, "Grandad, how were you born?" I said, "The stork brought me." He says, "You mean to tell me we haven't had a natural birth in our family in three generations?"

Did you know that _____ finished school in half the time. He was expelled in the sixth grade.

_____ told me his teacher didn't like him much. Even during fire drills she would tell him to stay in his seat.

He walked 6 miles to school & 6 miles back. I thought, that's strange, because the school's right across the street from his house.

As far as school's concerned, I can't say that he was in the top half of his class, but he was in the group that made the top half possible.

Well, Isabella has just finished her 1st week of school. She says, "I'm just wasting my time, I can't read, I can't write & they won't let me talk."

While back she was over to our house & opened the big family Bible. She was fascinated as she fingered through the pages. Suddenly, something fell out of the Bible. She picked up the object & looked at it. What she saw was an old leaf that had been pressed in between the pages. She said,

"Grandad, look what I found!" I said, "What is it Sweetheart?" She says, "I think it's Adam's underwear!"

The wife & I were traveling again this week & we stopped at a motel that had a sign that said: 'CHILDREN FREE' & they tried to give us 2 kids!

When I was born, I was so surprised I couldn't talk for a year & a half.

We've got some new neighbors across the street, so I went over to meet them & about a 10-year-old boy answered the door. I said, "Are your Mother & Father in?" He says, "They was in, but they is out." So, I said, "Young man, where's your grammer?" He said, "Oh, she's upstairs."

I remember one day I went to school---I couldn't get a table at the pool room. So, I had this nice shiny apple & I gave it to the teacher & she kissed me right here on the cheek. So, the next day, I brought her a watermelon.

I feel uneasy about being in a school again. But I spent 7 of the happiest years of my life in high school.

I played hooky from school once & the teacher sent my Mother a thank-you note.

My grandson told me that the harmonica I gave him was the best present I ever gave him. I said, I'm glad you like it. He says, "Yeah, Mom gives me $5 a week not to play it.

CHRISTMAS JOKES

Knock-knock:
() WHO'S THERE?
Rapture.
() RAPTURE WHO?
Rapture Christmas presents yet?

Just before Christmas, an honest politician, a generous lawyer & Santa Claus were riding in the elevator of a very posh hotel. Just before the doors opened they all noticed a $100 bill on the floor. Which one picked it up? Santa, of course, cause the other two don't exist.

Right before Christmas a young fellow takes his girlfriend down to the Plaza to Alaskan Furs. He told her to pick out the one she wanted & she picked out the most expensive sable coat in the store. The price was $33,000 & the young fellow writes a check for the amount & the salesman says, "Okay, we'll hold on to the coat until Monday morning & if the check clears, the coat is yours." So the guy goes back into the store on Monday morning & the salesman jumps on him; "Sir, you've got a nerve, you don't even have $500 in your bank account!" He says, "Hey, take it easy, I just came back in to thank you for the greatest weekend I ever had!"

Pedro & Rosita were out in the moonlight & Pedro says, "Rosita, let's sing 'Wee, Wee, Jew'." She says, "No, not again Pedro." He says, "Oh please Rosita, just one more time?" She says, "Okay Pedro, just one more time." 'Wee, wee jew a merry Christmas, Wee, wee jew a Merry Christmas'."

Last Christmas I told my wife I wanted an antique as a gift. She had my birth certificate framed.

Toys are the big thing with kids. I knew I was an unwanted baby when I saw my bath toys were a toaster & a radio.

I always wait 'til the last minute to do my Christmas shopping. It saves time, because there's so little to choose from. Last year I got my Mother a rake.

When I was a kid my Dad planted a tree in our living room.
() THAT'S REDICULOUS!
I know, but it kept our dog off the streets.

All this Christmas shopping's got me as broke as a pickpocket in a nudist colony.

On the 4th day of Christmas, my true love gave to me: 4 calling birds, 3 French hens, 2 turtle doves, & a lawsuit from the 'Save The Birds Foundation."

Do the 4 calling birds use A.T.& T.?

It's not too pleasant around the house on the holidays. My wife won't let me have my pipe in the living room. The bubbles make stains on the carpet.

We've always been unlucky with those plastic trees. My neighbor thinks it's artificial & our dog thinks it's real.

I'd like to get something for my wife---but nobody will make me an offer.

To save money on phone bills, I bought my wife a cordless phone.
() WELL, HOW'S A CORDLESS PHONE GONNA SAVE YOU MONEY?
Oh, it's a regular phone, I just cut off the cord.

() DID YOU BUY ANY CHRISTMAS SEALS?
Naw, I wouldn't know how to feed them.

Remember folks, batteries are very important at Christmas time. They're what make things work. I'm giving a dozen to my Brother-in-law.

Frankly, I didn't realize how tight things were 'til I talked to Santa Claus on the phone. We chatted a bit, then I said, "By the way Santa, how's Rudolph?" He said, "Delicious!"

I was talking to a lady back there before the show & she asked me if I was Santa Claus. I said, "No." & she said, "Well then, leave my stocking alone!"

Song title: "Don't Kiss A Girl Under The Mistletoe---It's More Fun Under The Nose"

When I was 10 years old I wrote a letter to Santa Claus. I wrote: Dear Santa Claus, I want a plane, a bicycle & my violin busted!

Here's the latest one I've written: "Thirty days have September, April, June & November & my uncle.
() WAIT A MINUTE, HOW COULD YOUR UNCLE HAVE 30 DAYS?
The judge gave it to him.
() WHAT FOR AND WHEN?
Two weeks ago when he was doing his Christmas shopping early.
() HOW EARLY?
Before the store opened.

You see a lot of new kinds of dolls at Christmas time. We have mechanical dolls that walk, talk, sleep, wet, burp, stretch, roll over, & emulate countless other human traits. But, now manufacturers have come up with the ultimate, called the 'welfare doll'. Wind it up & it doesn't work.

The 3 wisemen were firemen. They came from afar.

() YOU KNOW THE CHINESE SETTLE ALL THEIR DEBTS ON NEW YEARS DAY.
Yeah, but they don't have a Christmas the week before.

Last minute shopping: The husband who waits 'til Christmas Eve to shop for his wife & has to gift wrap a Slurpee from 7-Eleven.

Some Christmas carolers came by our house the other night. So, we passed out some fruitcake. The next thing I knew, they were singing 'Rock Of Ages'.

Peace on Earth is a wonderful thing.
() YEAH, BUT I STILL DON'T MIND AN OCCASIONAL PRICE WAR.

One little boy wrote to Santa: " Dear Santa, please send me 2 mongooses." This didn't sound right, so he changed it to; "Sir, please send me 1 mongoose, & while you're at it, send me another one."

The 1st thing a child learns when he gets a drum for Christmas is, that he's never going to get another one.

I went shopping at Sears. It was so crowded that when I scratched my back, 3 girls slapped me.

One of my 1st Christmas presents was a bat. I went outside to play with it & it flew away.

I'm sure glad you don't get everything you want for Christmas. I remember when I was 10 years old, I wrote a letter to Santa Claus. I wrote, "I want a plane, a bicycle & my violin busted."

I don't know what to get my Mother-in-law for Christmas, she didn't use what I got her last Christmas.
() WHAT DID YOU GET HER?
A funeral plot.

I gave my Grandson a BB gun. He gave me a sweater with a bull's-eye on the back.

The Christmas season is upon us again. What other time of the year do you sit in front of a dead tree & eat candy out of your socks?

I wish my wife would finish her Christmas shopping, I'd like to know what I got her.

Year before last we got a waterbed. She called it the 'dead sea'

She told me she wanted something to protect her & something she could drive. So, I bought her a hammer & nails.

I'd like to get something for my wife, but nobody will make me an offer.

I bought my Mother-In-Law a beautiful chair for Christmas, but she won't let me plug it in!

Never stop believing in Santa Claus—when you do, you get underwear.

Two blondes went deep into the woods searching for a Christmas tree. After hours of subzero temperatures & a few close calls with hungry wolves, one blonde turned to the other & said, "I'm chopping down the next tree I see, I don't care if it's decorated or not!"

Three stages of man: He believes in Santa Claus. He doesn't believe in Santa Claus. He is Santa Claus.

Phil wrote Santa Claus again this year: "Dear Santa, for this year I'm requesting a fat bank account, & a small body. P.S, This year, please don't mix them up like you did last year!

CIRCUS JOKES

My uncle was a clown for the Ringling Bros. Circus, & when he died all of his friends went to the funeral in one car.

In school, I was never the class clown, but more the class trapeze artist, as I was always being suspended.

DOCTOR-MEDICAL JOKES

I saw a sign on a plastic surgeon's office today. It said, "Hello, can we pick your nose?"

How did Michael Jackson pick his nose? Out of a catalog.

______ takes his wife to the Dr. She's been looking kind of sickly as of late. The Dr. checks her thoroughly, stands back, scratches his head, leans over & kisses her on the cheek. Immediately she starts looking the picture of health. ______ says, "Dr. what's the deal?" The Dr. Says, "_______ your wife needs to be kissed at least twice a week." _____ says, "Well, I guess I could bring her in on Tuesdays & Thursdays."

Lady down the street is a hypochondriac & the last time she went to see the Dr. she told him she was getting hard of hearing. She said, "Dr., It's getting so bad, I can't hear myself cough!" So, the Dr. filled out a prescription & she asked him, "Will this improve my hearing?" He said, "No, but it'll make you cough louder!"

Man goes to the Dr. Dr. says, "What's your problem?" He says, "Dr., I can't hear out of my right ear." The Dr. looks in his ear with his scope & says, "Sir, you have a suppository in your ear!" The man says, "Oh, now I know what I did with my hearing aid."

The most pitiful case in psychiatric history concerns the 2-faced woman who talked herself & tried to have the last word.

Guy had been to the Dr. & the Dr. called him & said, "I've got bad news & worse news. The bad news is, you only have 24 hours to live." Guy says, "That is bad news, but what could be worse news than that?" The Dr. says, "I've been trying to reach you since yesterday.

Best friends graduated from medical school at the same time & decided that in spite of two different specialties, they would open a practice together to share office space & personnel. Dr. Smith was the psychiatrist & Dr. Jones was the proctologist; They put up a sign reading: Dr. Smith & Dr. Jones; Hysterias & Posteriors. The town council insisted they change it. The Drs. Changed it to : Schizoids & Hemorrhoids. Not acceptable---they changed again to Minds & Behinds. Thumbs down again. Then came Freaks & Cheeks, Loons & Moons---forget it. Almost at their wits end the doctors came up with: Drs. Smith & Jones---Specializing in Odds & Ends. Everybody loved it.

I've got a neighbor with a weird problem. Yeah, the lady that lives next door went to see her Dr. with a cucumber in her nose, a banana in one ear & a carrot in the other ear. The Dr. said she wasn't eating right.

My wife was talking to our Dr. the other day & he said; "Your husband must have absolute rest & quiet. Here's some sleeping pills." My wife asked him, "When should I give them to him?" The Dr. says, "Oh, they're not for him, they're for you!"

I stopped by a drugstore last night & asked the pharmacist if he had anything for the hiccups. He said, "Wait right here!" I just looked around the store for a minute & he snuck up behind me & hit me over the head with a wet mop. I said, "What in the world did you do that for?"

He says, "Well, you don't have the hiccups do you?" I said, "No! But my wife does out in the car!"

An elderly man visit's the Dr. for a checkup. Dr says, "Mr. Smith, you're in excellent shape, how do you do it?" Mr. Smith says, "Well, I don't smoke, I don't drink & the Good Lord looks out for me." For weeks now, every time I go to the bathroom in the middle of the night, he turns the light on for me." This kinda concerned the Dr., so he finds Mr. Smith's wife in the waiting room & tells her what her husband said. She tells the Dr., "I don't think that's anything to worry about, & on the brighter side, it does explain who's been wee-weeing in the fridge.

My great grandson swallowed a bullet the other day, so we took her over to the emergency room at the hospital. The Dr. said, "Give him this strong laxative, but be sure that for the next few hours you don't point him at anybody.

A country Dr. went way out to the boonies to deliver a baby. It was so far out, there was no electricity. When the Dr. arrived, no one was home except for the laboring Mother & her 5-year-old child. The Dr. instructed the child to hold a lantern high so he could see, while he helped the woman deliver the baby. The child did so, the Mother pushed & after a little while, the Dr. lifted the newborn baby by the feet & spanked him on the bottom to get him to take his first breath. The Dr. then asked the 5-year-old what he thought of the baby. The 5-year-old says, "Hit him again, he shouldn't have crawled up there in the first place!"

Lady that lives down the street goes to the Dr. all black & blue. Dr. asks, "What happened?" She says, "Dr. I don't know what to do. Every time my husband comes home drunk on Bud Light he beats me up. Dr. says, "I have some real good medicine for that. When your husband comes home drunk on Bud Light, just take a glass of sweet tea & start swishing it in your mouth, but don't swallow. Just keep swishing & swishing until he goes to bed in his stupor." Two weeks later the lady comes back to the Dr. looking fresh & reborn. She thanks the Dr., she says, "That was a brilliant idea. Every time my husband came home drunk on Bud Light, I swished with sweet tea. I swished & swished & he didn't touch me!" Dr. says, "You see how much keeping your mouth shut helps?"

Name a major disease associated with cigarette smoking? Answer: Premature death.

Got a neighbor who had a serious hearing problem for years. He went to the Dr. & the Dr. fitted him with a set of hearing aids that allowed the gentleman to hear 100%. He went back in a month to the Dr. & the Dr. said, "Your hearing is perfect. Your family must be really pleased that you can hear again!" He says, "Oh, I haven't told my family yet. I just sit around & listen to the conversations. I've changed my will 3 times!"

Did you know that _____ worked as a candy-striper years ago? Well, you know how hospital regulations require a wheelchair for patients being discharged. One time she found an elderly gentleman already dressed & sitting on the bed with a suitcase at his feet, who insisted he didn't need _______'s help to leave the hospital. So, she told him all about the rules & he reluctantly let her wheel him to the elevator. On the way down ______ asked him if his wife was meeting him. He says, "I don't know, she's still upstairs in the bathroom changing out of her hospital gown!"

My neighbor's wife had been after him for weeks to paint the seat on their toilet. Finally, he got around to doing it while the Mrs. Was out shopping. After he finished, he left to take care of another project before she returned. She came in & undressed to take a shower. Before getting into the shower, she sat on the toilet. As she tried to stand up, she realized that the not-quite-dry epoxy paint had glued her to the toilet seat. About that time, hubby got home & realized her predicament. They pushed & pulled to no avail & finally in desperation, he undid the toilet seat bolts. She wrapped a sheet around herself & he drove her to the hospital emergency room. The ER Dr. got her into a position where he could study how to free her (picture this) . She tried to lighten the embarrassment of it all by saying; "Well, Doctor, I'll bet you've never seen anything like this before." The Dr. says, "Actually, I've seen lots of them, I just never saw one mounted & framed!"

I loaned a guy $5000 for plastic surgery. Now I don't know what he looks like!"

That dentist you sent me to wasn't painless.
() Why, did he hurt you?
No, but he yelled when I bit his finger.

Three surgeons were bragging about their skills: 1st one said, "I had a man come in who had his hand cut off in an accident. I put him back together & he is now a concert violinist!" The 2nd one says, " I had a man come in after a terrible car wreck who'd had his legs severed. He is now a marathon runner!" The 3rd surgeon said, "I've got you both beat, I came upon a terrible accident where there was nothing left but the back end of a horse & a pair of eyeglasses. That man is now in the United States Senate!"

My neighbor went to the Dr. & the Dr. told him he had a bad illness & only had a year to live. So he decided he'd talk to me, cause he knew I'd done some counseling . He explained his situation & he asked me if there was anything he could do. So I told him; "What you should do is go out & buy an old Dodge pickup, then go get married to the ugliest woman you can find, & buy yourselves an old trailer house in the Panhandle of Oklahoma." He says, "Will that help me live longer?" I said, "No, but it'll make what time you do have seem like forever!"

I accidentally butt-dialed my proctologist, & they had a full conversation.

A Norwegian was terribly overweight, so his Dr. put him on a diet. The Dr. said, "I want you to eat regularly for 2 days, then skip a day, & repeat this procedure for 2 weeks. The next time I see you, you should have lost at least 5 pounds." When the Norwegian returned the Dr. was shocked because the guy had lost 25 pounds! The Dr. says, "Why this is amazing! Did you follow my instructions?" The Norwegian says," Ya, I'll tell you though, I taut I was gonna drop dead dat 3rd day." Dr. asked him, "From hunger, you mean?" "No, from all dat skippin'!"

Once upon a time there was this very short man. He was so short that when it rained, he was the last to know.

He was so short that elevators smelled different to him than to the average man.

So, he goes to a psychiatrist & says, "I'm so short, I want to kill myself." The Dr. says, "Size doesn't matter, giant oaks from little acorns grow. A little acorn, no bigger than the nail of your thumb can become a 100 foot oak." The patient was relieved & left, in fact, he felt so good about himself, he took a short-cut home through the park & a squirrel ate him.

Another guy goes to a psychiatrist & says, "I think I'm an umbrella." The Dr. says, "A cure is possible if you'll open up." The patient says, "Why?, Is it raining?"

Did you hear about the secretary who, by mistake, dropped one of her birth control pills in the copy machine & it wouldn't duplicate.

I waited so long at the doctor's office that by the time they called me it was time for my follow-up appointment.

Do you know the difference between a proctologist & a podiatrist? Just a couple of feet.

Did you hear about the guy who fell into the machine at the upholstery shop? He's completely recovered now.

A pharmacist arrives at work & sees this fellow leaning against the wall with a worried look on his face. The pharmacist asks the clerk, "What's with this guy?" She says, "Well, he wanted some cough medicine, but I couldn't find any, so I gave him a laxative." The pharmacist says, "But laxatives won't cure a cough!" The clerk says, "Sure they will, look at him, he's afraid to cough."

Two green beans are crossing the freeway when one of them is hit by an 18 wheeler. His friend scrapes him up & rushes him to the hospital. After hours of surgery, the Dr. says, "I have good news & bad news." The healthy bean says, "Okay, give me the good news 1st ." The Dr. says, "Well, he's going to live." "So, what's the bad news?" "The bad news is, he'll be a vegetable the rest of his life."

One day a Dr. a farmer & the President of an HMO arrive at the Pearly Gates. St. Peter hesitates, because Heaven is getting kind of full. Finally he tells the Dr., "You may come in, for you have taken care of the sick in their time of need." Then he turns to the farmer & says, "And you too man, enter for you have grown food to nourish your fellow man."

Then St. Peter turns to the HMO Executive & says, “Well, I guess you can come in too--but only for 3 days!------------

---

Went to my Dr. this week. He checked me out & told me; “You could go anytime!” I said, “Great, I haven’t gone for five days!”

It’s been quite a week. Yesterday I was walking down the street wearing my eyeglasses & all of a sudden my prescription ran out.

Went to my Dr. yesterday & asked him. “What should I take when I’m run down?” He says, “The license number!”

A man walked into the Doctor’s office with a duck on his head. The Dr. says, “What’s your problem?” & the duck says, “I want you to get this man off my rear-end.”

What does the word ‘benign’ mean? Be nine is what you will be after you be eight.

I was in a highly stressful situation years ago & a buddy of mine recommended a Chinese psychiatrist he knew of. So, I got an appointment with the Doctor. He asked me “What wrong you?” I said, “I don’t know whether I’m coming or going!” He said, “Take off all cose.” So I did. Then he said, “Cwaw to waw.” I did. Then he said, “Cwaw back.” & I did. Then he said, “Put on all cose.” I did. I said, “What’s wrong with me Doc ?” He said, “You have ’Ed Zachary Disease’.” I said, “What in the world is ‘Ed Zachary Disease’?” He says, “Your face looks ‘edzachary’ like your rear.”

Went to my Dr. this week & while I was talking to him in the examination room his nurse came in & said, "Dr. there's a man here who thinks he's invisible." The Dr. said, "Tell him I can't see him."

I think I'm gonna change doctors though. Like he treated one woman for yellow jaundice for 3 years before he realized she was Chinese.

Hear about the new tranquilizer called 'Dangitol'. It doesn't relax you, it just makes you enjoy being tense.

I went to the Dr. for a complete examination this week. He looked at me after he was done & he said, "I can't find the exact cause of your trouble Mr. ______, but it's probably due to drinking too much." I said, "Gee, I'm sorry to hear that Doc, I'll come back when you're sober."

If 4 out of 5 people suffer from diarrhea, does that mean that 1 out of 5 enjoy it?

But, my memory's not as sharp as it used to be. Also, my memory's not as sharp as it used to be.

I went to a psychiatrist while back. He asked me, "What's your problem?" I said, "Every time I get into bed, I think there's somebody under it, I get under the bed & I think there's somebody on top of it, so it's top-under-top-under, all night long. I'm going crazy!" He said, "Just put yourself in my care & for $100 a visit, once a week, I can probably cure you in 2 years." I said, "Well, I'll have to think about it." So, about 2 weeks ago I ran into that Dr. on the street & he says, "Hey, why didn't you come back & see me?" I said, "Cause, my barber cured me for $10!" The Dr. asked me, "How'd he do that?" I said, "He told me to cut the legs off my bed!"

My Doctor asked if any of my family members suffered from mental illnesses. I said, "No, they all seem to enjoy it."

Did you hear about the cannibal who went to a psychiatrist? He was fed up with people.

Last week I noticed my gums were shrinking. Then I found out I was brushing my teeth with Preparation H.

() HOW YA DOIN' LARRY?
Well, I ain't feelin' too good lately.
() DID YOU GO TO THE DOCTOR?
Yeah, I did.
() DID HE FIND OUT WHAT YOU HAD?
Yeah, very nearly.
() WHAT DO YOU MEAN, VERY NEARLY?
Well, I had $40 & he charged me $37.50.

Oh well, we all have to go sometime---usually during the commercials.

My wife went to the eye doctor the other day & she said, "Dr. I've broken my glasses, do I have to be examined all over again?" & the Optometrist says, "No, just your eyes."

My Dr. tried kidnapping for a while, but nobody could read the ransom notes.

A Chinese fellow calls a dentist on the telephone: "Doctah wha time you fixie tooth fo me?" The Dr. says, "Two-thirty alright?" & the Chinaman says, "Yes, tooth hurtee me alright, but wha time you fixee?"

We need to watch our sweets during the holiday seasons of the year. Of course I knew somebody who used only sugar substitutes. After a few years he died of artificial diabetes.

The difference between bird flu & swine flu? For bird flu, you need tweetment & for swine flu you need oinkment.

Did I tell you I had my teeth bonded. They don't look any nicer, but they are a lot closer friends.

Phil underwent an operation at the hospital. When he came out of the anesthesia, he asked the nurse. "How come all the shades on the windows are pulled down?" The nurse says, "The house across the street's on fire, & we didn't want you to wake up thinking that the operation was a failure.

Ran into my psychiatrist yesterday. She was pushing a sofa down the street. I said, "What are you doing Doc?" She said, "Making a house call!"

A doctor gave a woman a full medical examination. He wrote out a prescription & as he did it, he explained the instructions: "Take the green pill with a glass of water when you get up. Take the blue pill with a glass of water after lunch. Then, just before bed, take the red pill with another glass of water." So, she asks the Dr., "Exactly what is my problem?" He says, "You're not drinking enough water!"

Two medical students walking along off campus saw an old fellow walking along all spraddle legged. One says to the other, "I bet he has 'Paltro's Disease'." The other says, "No, I bet he has 'Savitski's Syndrome'." So, they couldn't agree & they decided to just ask the old fellow, "Sir, we're medical students here at the university & we've been arguing about what your problem might be, would you tell us what it is?" The old man says, "Well, you tell me what you think it is!" The 1st student says, "I think it's 'Paltro's Disease'. The old man says, "That's what you think, but you're wrong!" The 2nd student says, "I think it's 'Savitski's Syndrome'." The old man says, "That's what you think, but you're wrong!" They said, "Okay old fellow, what is it then?" He says, "I thought it was gas, but I was wrong!"

My Dad said I was the cutest baby he'd ever seen, except that I had no nose. Then he discovered he was holding me upside down & backwards.

Yeah, when I was born, I was so surprised I couldn't talk for a year and a half!

Well, here I am, right in the middle of the rat race---& my Dr. took cheese off my diet.

A Dr. is addressing a large audience in Tampa. He says, "The material we put into our stomachs is enough to have killed most of us sitting here years ago. Red meat--awful, soft drinks--corrode your stomach lining. Chinese food is loaded with MSG. High fat diets can be disastrous, & none of us realizes the long-term harm caused by the germs in our drinking water. However, there is one thing that is the most dangerous of all & we all have eaten, or will eat it. Can anyone here tell me what food it is that causes the most grief & suffering for years after eating it?" After several seconds of quiet, a 75 year old man in the front row raised his hand & said, softly: "WEDDING CAKE!"

I almost drowned this week. I was having an acupuncture treatment in my waterbed.

Boy, I'm tired tonight. You remember George, my golfing buddy? Well, he died today on the 4th green. It was terrible. For the next 14 holes it was hit the ball, drag George, putt, drag George.

Do you know the difference between a bad golfer & a bad skydiver? A bad golfer says, "Whack---Darn!" & a bad skydiver says, "Darn---Whack!"

When you have a bladder infection, urine trouble.

I saw my Doctor today about my loss of memory.
() WHAT DID HE DO?
Made me pay in advance.

Last week I noticed my gums were shrinking, but I figured that out. I was brushing my teeth with Preparation H.

Do you know how Michael Jackson picked his nose? Out of a catalog.

My sister Mary's memory is just as bad as mine. We're both convinced we're an only child.

So, an attorney tells his client, "I have some good news & some bad news." The client asks, "What's the bad news?" "The bad news is, your blood is all over the crime scene, & the DNA tests prove you did it." "What's the good news?" "The good news is; "Your cholesterol is 130."

You have to be good-looking to live in _______ . Everyone there's had facelifts. The only way to tell if people are ugly is to look at their children.

I went to a psychiatrist about my son. He asked me what was the problem? I said, "He's always eating mud pies. I get up in the morning & there he is in the back yard eating mud pies. I come home for lunch & he's eating mud pies. I come home at dinner & there he is in the back yard eating mud pies!!" The Dr. reassured me, "Give the kid a chance. It's all part of growing up, it'll pass!" I said, "Well, I don't like it----& neither does his wife!"

A doctor in Duluth wanted to get off work to go hunting, so he told his assistant, "Ole, I'm goin' huntin' tomorrow & I don't want to close the clinic. I want you to take care of all my patients." Ole say, "Yes Sir, I'll do it!" So the Dr. goes hunting & comes back in the next day & asks; "So, Ole, how was your day?" Ole says, "Well, I had 3 patients. The 1st one had a headache, so I gave him Tylenol." "Bravo" the doc says. The 2nd one's stomach was burning & I gave him some MaaaaaLOX." "Excellent my boy, what about the 3rd one?" Ole says, "Well Sir, I was sitting here in the examination room & suddenly the door opens & a beautiful woman enters. Like a flame, she undresses herself, lies down on the table & shouts, "Help me, I haven't seen a man in over 2 years!" The Dr. says, "Thunderin' Lard Jesus, Ole, what did you do?" Ole says, "What else could I do? I put drops in her eyes.

Did you hear about the guy whose whole left side was cut off? He's all right now.

Support bacteria. They're the only culture some people have.

Did I tell you I've been seeing a reverse psychologist? During sessions he makes me lie face down on his couch.

One day, the General noticed a soldier behaving oddly. He would pick up every piece of paper he saw, read it, frown & say, "That's not it!" &

drop it. After a month of this, the General finally arranged to have the soldier tested. The psychologist found that the soldier was coo-coo & wrote out his discharge from the Army. The soldier picked it up, smiled & said, "That's it!"

I went to the hospital last week to donate blood. On the couch directly across from me was an Apache Indian. I looked over & asked him, "Are you a full-blooded Apache?" He says, "I was, now I'm a pint short."

My neighbor's Dr. told him he had a very rare & extremely contagious disease. The Dr. said, "We're gonna put you in an isolation unit where you'll be on a diet of pancakes & pizza." My neighbor asked him, "Well, Doctor, will pancakes & pizza cure my condition?" The doc said, "No, they're the only things we can slip under the door."

You know, I've been seeing spots in front of my eyes.
() HAVE YOU SEEN A DOCTOR?
No, just spots.

I wonder about my Dr. anyway. I mean it's okay to take out my appendix & my tonsils---but through the same incision?

Ty wanted to be a doctor but his folks couldn't afford golf lessons.

You know you're gonna have a bad day when you come out of your memory-improvement class & forget where you parked your car.

Ty was figuring his tax & tried to deduct 30 cases of Dr. Pepper as a medical expense.

I was talking to the nurse that works at the clinic & she said the old lady down the street came in to the Dr. the other day. The Dr. asked her, "What's your problem?" She says, "Well, I'm embarrassed to say it, but it's silent gas." The Dr. says, "What do you mean by silent gas?" She says, "It's like this, when I go to the grocery store, I have silent gas. When I go to church, I have silent gas, why just while I've been talking to you I've had silent gas. Now, what can you do for me?" The Dr. says, "I'll tell you one thing, the 1st thing we're going to do is check your hearing!"

I went to Dr. Bloomfield who's known for miraculous cures for arthritis. He had a waiting room full of people when a little ole lady, completely bent over in half, shuffled in slowly leaning on her cane. When her turn came, she went into the doctor's office & in 5 minutes she came out walking completely erect with her head held high. So I went up to her & said, "It's a miracle! You walked in bent in half & now you're walking erect. What did the Dr. do?" She said, "He gave me a longer cane!"

A lady goes to a psychiatrist & says, "My husband thinks he's a horse." The Dr. says, "I can cure him, but it will take a lot of visits & a lot of money." The lady says, "Oh, money's no object, last year he won the Kentucky Derby."

My neighbor's been gravely ill lately & he & his wife went to the Dr. for examination. After the Dr. examined him he motioned for my neighbor's wife to come out into the hall. The Dr. told her, "Your husband is very sick, there are 3 things you can do to ensure his survival. First, fix him 3 healthy, delicious meals a day. Second, Give him a stress-free environment & don't complain about anything. Third & finally, Give him lots of hugs & kisses. So, on the way home the husband asked, "What did the Dr. say?" She says, "I'm sorry, you're not gonna make it."

Five surgeons from different big cities are discussing who makes the best patients to operate on:

1st A surgeon from New York says, "I like to operate on accountants, when you open them up, everything inside is numbered.

2nd A surgeon from Chicago says, "Try electricians, everything is colorcoded.

3rd A doctor from Dallas says, "Librarians are the best, everything inside of them is in alphabetical order.

4th A doc from Los Angeles says, "You know, I like construction workers, those guys always understand when you have a few parts left over.

5th A surgeon from Washington D.C. shut 'em all up when he said; "You're all wrong. Politicians are the easiest to operate on. There's no guts, no heart, no brains, & no spine. Plus, the head & rear are interchangeable!"

A Doctor at a mental institution decided to take his patients to a baseball game. For weeks in advance, he coached his patients to respond to his commands. When the day of the game arrived everything went quite well. When the National Anthem started, the Dr. yelled, "Up nuts!", & the patients complied by standing up. After the Anthem he yelled, "Down Nuts!" & they all sat back down in their seats. After a home run by their team, the Dr. yelled, "Cheer nuts!" They all broke out into applause & cheered. When the umpire made a bad call against the star of the home team, the Dr. yelled, "Boo, nuts!" & they all started booing & cat-calling. So the Dr. was comfortable with their response & decided to go get a beer & a hot dog & he left his assistant in charge. When he returned, there was a riot in progress. So the Dr. hot a hold of his assistant & asked him, "What in the world happened?" The assistant replied, "Well, everything was going just fine until this guy walked by & yelled "PEANUTS!"

I was just thinking, we should have a way of telling people they have bad breath without hurting their feelings, like: "I'm bored, let's go brush our teeth." Or, "I've got to make a phone call, hold this gum in your mouth.

The Mexican word for the day is HERPES. Me & my friend ordered pizza. I got mine piece, then she got herpes.

() HOW IS YOUR BROTHER-IN-LAW WHO WAS IN THE HOSPITAL?
Oh, he's alright, but I don't think he'll be home for a while.
() WHY, DID YOU SEE HIS DOCTOR?
No, but I saw his nurse.

_____'s Dr. told him to slow down, so he got a job with the Post Office.

I went to visit an old friend out in the country at a mental institution. It was a beautiful day & all the patients were assembled on the steps of this mansion. They each had an apple in their left hand & an ordinary lead pencil in their right hand & they were keeping time by tapping on their apple with their pencil. They were singing 'Ave Maria' in 4 part harmony & it was so beautiful it brought tears to my eyes. When they stopped singing I congratulated my friend on their singing. I said, "That was great, what do you call the group?" He says, "Isn't it obvious, we're the Moron Tapanapple Choir."

Listen, I may be a schizophrenic, but at least I have each other.

I went to see my psychiatrist the other day & while I was waiting, a guy walked in with a duck on his head. The Dr. said, "What's your problem?" & the duck said, "I want you to get this man off my rear end!"

() WELL LARRY, DOES YOUR WIFE KNOW THAT YOU'RE SEEING A PSYCHIATRIST?

Yes, I told her the truth about it. I told her I was seeing a psychiatrist. Then, she told me the truth, that she was seeing a psychiatrist, 2 plumbers & a bartender.

I'm going to him because of my split personality. I think it's getting worse cause yesterday I ate in a restaurant alone & asked for 2 checks.

I've got a neighbor with a really weird problem.
() WHAT IS IT/
She went to see her Doctor with a cucumber in her nose, a banana in one ear & a carrot in the other ear!
() WHAT WAS WRONG WITH HER?
The Doctor said she wasn't eating right.

I just came back from my Doctor.
() WHICH DOCTOR?
He's been called worse.

He told me, "I've got some bad news for you, you could go anytime." I said, "Good, I haven't gone for 5 days."

My wife went to see her Doctor & told him, "Dr., I want a little wart removed." He said, "Well, you're in the wrong office Ma'am, the divorce lawyer's next door."

I remember when our 1st child was born. The nurse brought a beautiful brown-skinned baby into the waiting room & asked me; "Is this yours?" I said, "It must be, my wife burns everything."

If you can't afford a doctor, just go to an airport. You'll get a free X-ray & a breast exam, & if you mention Al Qaeda, you'll get a free colonoscopy.

A nurse walks into a bank totally exhausted after an 18 hour shift. She grabs a deposit slip, pulls a rectal thermometer out of her purse, & tries to write with it. When she realizes her mistake, she looks at the flabbergasted teller & without missing a beat, says, "Well, that's great---some rear-ends got my pen!"

A nurse told her hospital patient, "Sir, we have some onion soup for you." He said, I hate onion soup, I'm not eating any onion soup!" About 30 minutes later, she came back & gave the guy an enema. Later that day when his wife came to visit, she asked, "How are things going today?" He said, "Pretty good, but I'll tell you one thing, when they want you to have onion soup they'll give it to you one way or the other!"

() WHERE WERE YOU BORN?
I was born in a hospital. Up until then I was never sick a day in my life.

So, this dyslexic man walks into a bra----

Mywifeputmeonabrandiet.It'smorning,noon&night---bran-bran-bran.
() HAS IT KEPT YOU REGULAR?
Regular! I'm 30 days ahead!

Last Sunday morning, I woke up with laryngitis. I mean I couldn't talk above a whisper. I knew the Dr. wouldn't be in his office on Sunday, so

I went to his house. I knocked on the doctor's door, & the doctor's wife answered. I said, "(whisper) "Is the Doctor in?' His wife whispers back & says, "No, come on in."

A midget lady went to the Dr. with a rash, high on her thighs. The doctor told her to lie on the table, & he would take a look. The Dr. lifted her little dress, took a pair of scissors & snipped around, then he said, "Hop down, & see if that's better." She did & said, "Doc, that's wonderful, what did you do?" The Dr. says, "I just cut a couple of inches off the top of your over shoes."

Once upon a time there was this very short man. He was so short that when it rained, he was the last to know.

He was so short that elevators smelled different to him than regular height people.

So, he goes to a psychiatrist & says, "I'm insecure about my height. I'm so short I want kill myself. The Dr. says, "Size doesn't matter. Giant oaks from little acorns grow! A little acorn, no bigger than your thumb nail can become a 100 foot oak. The patient was relieved & left. He decided to take a shortcut home through the park & a squirrel ate him!

Went to my Dr. for a yearly checkup. He said, "Everything's fine, you're doing okay for your age." I said, "My age, I'm only 75, do you think I'll make it to 80?" He said, "Do you drink or smoke?" I said, "No." "Do you eat fatty meats or sweets?" "No, I'm very careful about what I eat." The doc says, "What about your activities, do you engage in thrilling behaviors like speeding or skiing?" I said, "No, I would never engage in dangerous activities," Then the Dr. says, "Well then, why in the world would you want to live to be 80?"

I went to see my neighbor in the hospital this week. I went over to his bed & he began to gasp for air frantically. I said, "Now, don't you worry my friend, we're praying for you., The church will look after your wife & we'll try to take care of your business. Now, is there anything else I can do for you?" He says, "Yes, will you please move, you're standing on my air hose!"

() WHAT'S THE MATTER LARRY?
Aw, the Dr. says I have to take one of these little white pills every fay for the rest of my life.
() AND WHAT'S SO BAD ABOUT THAT?
Well, he only gave me seven!

Have you heard the new statistics on sanity? One out of 4 Americans is suffering from some form of mental illness. Think of your 3 best friends. If they're okay, then it's you.

My Grandson's got him an apartment now. He's only been there one week & he's complaining about his neighbors: He says, "One woman cries all day, another lies in bed moaning, & then there's the guy who keeps banging his head against the wall." So, I told him, "You better keep away from them!" He said, "I am. I stay inside all day playing my tuba."

My cousin's the director of a mental institution & I asked him how Doctors decide to put someone in a place like that. He said, "Well, we fill a bathtub with water, then we offer a teaspoon, a teacup & a bucket to the patient, & ask him to empty the tub."
() I GET IT, A NORMAL PERSON WOULD USE THE BUCKET BECAUSE IT'S THE BIGGEST!
No, a normal person would pull the plug.

This crazy guy ran up to me today & kept yelling; "Call me a doctor! Call me a doctor!" I said, "What's the matter, are you sick?" He says, "No, I just graduated from medical school!"

Colonoscopies are important medical procedures that have saved lives. Here are some comments purportedly made by patients to physicians during their procedures: 1. Now I know how a Muppet feels. 2. Could you write a note to my wife saying that my head is not up there? 3. Any sign of the trapped miners Chief?

They turned me down as an organ donor. I don't mind that so much, it was why they turned me down. They said it was like getting spare parts from an Edsel.

My neighbor was in a terrible car accident last week & he was in surgery for 12 hours. They messed up though. They sewed a woman's lips on him & now they can't get him to shut up.

Do you know the difference between amnesia & magnesia? The person with amnesia doesn't know where he's going.

Saw a sign on the door of a plastic surgeon's office: 'Hello, Can We Pick Your Nose?'

DRIVER JOKES

A policeman pulled my neighbor over for speeding. The officer said, "I'm giving you a ticket for speeding & not wearing a seatbelt. My neighbor says, "Oh no, I was wearing my seatbelt!" The officer says, "Sir, I saw you put your seatbelt on when you saw me!" "Oh, no, I had it on all along!" About that time my neighbor's wife spoke up & said, "Officer, I learned a long time ago, never argue with my husband when he's drunk!"

Ah-yes. Someday we'll all look back on this & plow into a parked car.

I'd like to share an experience with you all, to do with drinking & driving. As you know some people have brushes with the authorities on their way home. Well, I for one have done something about it. The other night I was out for a dinner & a few drinks, & having far too much Vino, & knowing full well I was over the limit, I did something I have never done before. I took a bus home. I arrived safely & without incident, which was a real surprise, as I have never driven a bus before.

I was driving when I saw the flash of a traffic camera. I figured my picture had been taken for speeding even though I knew I wasn't. Just to be sure, I went around the block & passed the same spot, driving even more slowly, but again the camera flashed. I tried a 4th & 5th time with the same results & I was now laughing as the camera flashed while I rolled by at a snail's pace. Two weeks later, I got 5 tickets in the mail for driving without a seatbelt. You can't fix stupid.

When I die, I want to go peaceably, like my Grandfather--in his sleep---not like the rest of the passengers in his car.

A guy hails a cab in New York City & they're going down the street when the guy taps the cabby on the shoulder. Well, the cab driver goes berserk, runs up on the sidewalk & almost crashes into a store window. The cabby says, "Don't ever do that again!" & the passenger says, "I'm sorry, I didn't think a little tap on the shoulder would scare you." The driver says, "I'm sorry too, but you see this is my 1st day driving a cab. For the last 25 years I've been driving a hearse.

Did I tell you? My wife got 8 out of 10 on her driver's license test---the other 2 guys managed to jump out of her way.

I broke down on the way here. My car's okay, I just pulled over & cried.

Did you know that General Motors is coming out with a new car? It's called the 'Filibuster', & it's supposed to run forever.

I'm looking for a car that gets good gas mileage. I used to drive an Eclipse. I think it was a nice car but I couldn't look directly at it.

A policeman pulled me over on the way here & he asked me, "Do you have any ID?" I said, "About what?"

Did you hear about the director of the Department of Motor Vehicles who resigned on Tuesday. He tried to resign on Monday, but he found he'd been standing in the wrong line.

My Mother-In-Law always says that she never gets any phone calls. So, for her birthday last month, I put one those 'How's My Driving?' bumper stickers on her car. The phone's pretty much ringing off the hook now.

I knew it was going to be a bad day when I rear-ended a car this morning. The driver got out of the other car & he was a dwarf. He looked up at me & said, "I am not happy!" So, I said, "Which one are you then?" That's how the fight started.

Be careful driving home tonight. Remember, almost 96% of all people are caused by accidents.

Siamese twins walk into a bar in Canada & park themselves on a bar stool. One says to the bartender, "Don't mind us, we're joined at the hip. I'm John, he's Jim. Two drinks please. " So the bartender tries to make small talk while he's pouring drinks & he says, "Been on holiday yet?" John says, "We're off to England next month. We go over there every year, rent a car & drive for miles, don't we Jim?" Jim nods yes & the bartender says, "England, wonderful country--the history--the culture!" John says, "Nah, we don't like that British garbage, we can't stand the English, they're so arrogant & rude." So the bartender asks, "So why keep going to England?" John says, "Well, it's the only chance Jim gets to drive."

BARTENDER-DRUNK JOKES

3 drunks hail a taxi. The driver---seeing that they're wasted, decides to pull a fast one. So he switches the engine on, then quickly switches it off & announces, 'WE'RE HERE!' The 1st guy hands him the fare. The 2nd guy says, "Thanks." But the 3rd guy smacks the driver up side of the head. The cabbie says, "What was that for?" The drunk says, "That was for driving so fast!"

---

3 vampires walk into a bar. "Bartender says, "What can I get ya?" "Blood, orders the 1st vampire. "Make it 2 says the 2nd." Bartender looks at the 3rd & says, "What about you Buddy?" "Plasma," says the vampire." The barkeep says, "Okay, let me make sure I've got this straight, '2 bloods & a blood light'."

I was bartending one day when a guy spent all afternoon drinking until he was totally inebriated. About 4 O'clock he says, "Bartender, give me another drink." I said, "No sir, you've already had too much!" He says, "You're right, I'll just throw one of these darts and go home." He picked up a dart, threw it & got a perfect bullseye. He says, "Bartender, I got a bullseye, what's my prize?" I looked around & it was a nice day with the back door of the bar open & there was a turtle walking by. I went out, picked up that turtle & handed it to the drunk, I said, "Here's your prize." The next day, same thing, he was in there all afternoon drinking. About 4 O'clock he says, "Bartender, how about another drink?" I said, "No, you've had too much already." He says, "You're right, I'll just throw one of these darts & go home." Folks, you wouldn't believe it, he picked up a dart, threw it at the dartboard--perfect bullseye! He says, "Bartender, I got another bullseye, what's my prize today?" I said, "I don't know, what'd I give you yesterday?" He said, "A roast-beef sandwich on a hard bun."

I saw a drunk last night in the middle of the road on his hands & knees.
() Now, _____ just because a man is in the middle of the road on his hands & knees at midnight is no sign that he's drunk.
Well, I guess that's true, but he was trying to roll up the white line.

A drunk gets on the bus & sets right down beside a priest. He reeked of alcohol & tobacco & had lipstick on his shirt. You could see he'd been out all night. The drunk picked up a newspaper someone had left behind & started reading. Pretty soon he asked the priest, "Father, do you know what causes arthritis?" The priest says, "I sure do! Alcohol abuse, illicit living, smoking & staying out all night with ladies of the evening & most of all keeping your fellow man in contempt!" The drunk goes back to reading the paper & the priest gets to thinking about what he's said to an obviously lost soul, so he apologizes & asks, "How long have you had arthritis?" The drunk says, "Oh, I don't have arthritis, it says here in the paper that the pope has arthritis real bad!"

I was thinking about my bartending days again. One day I had this drunk at the bar. He says, "Bartender, give me another drink." I said, "No, I'll not give you another drink, schucks, you can't even hold your head up off the bar now!" So, he says, "Okay, then give me a haircut."

One morning around 1:30 a drunk calls & asks, "What time do you open?" I just hung up on him. About 2:30 he calls back, same thing, "What time do you open?" I slam the receiver down. About quarter to four he calls back & asks, "What time do you open?" I said, "11:00am, but I wouldn't let you in anyhow!" He says, "But I'm not tryin' to get in, I wanta get out, I'm locked in here.!"

I was downtown Kansas City, walking along & here's this drunk hanging on to a lamp post for dear life. I said, "Why don't you take the bus home?" He said, "My wife would never let me keep it!"

My neighbor's been trying to get her husband to quit drinking. She's tried everything. She even tried to scare him into quitting. One night she dressed up like the devil & hid behind the front door. When her husband came home, she jumped out from behind that door & said, "Boo!" He says, "Who are you?" She says, "I'm the devil!" He says, "Shake hands, I married your sister!"

A drunk walked into a lounge. After staring at a beautiful woman who was sitting at the bar for 10 minutes, he sauntered over & kissed her. She jumped up & slapped him silly. He said, "I'm sorry, I thought you were my wife. You look just like her!" She says, "Yuck, get away from me, you worthless, insufferable, no good drunk!" He says, "Wow, you even sound like her!"

A grasshopper hops into a bar. The bartender says, "You're quite a celebrity around here. We've even got a drink named after you." The grasshopper says, "You've got a drink named 'Steve' ?"

A drunk's talking to his wife at Thanksgiving dinner; "Shweetheart, thish ish delicious stuffing. How did you ever get the turkey to eat it?"

A man comes home drunk again at 3 in the morning. His wife is waiting for him. She says, "Where have you been?" He says, "To the Golden Bar! They have golden doors, golden floors & they even have golden bathroom fixtures!" She says, "I don't believe you!" He says, "You just call down there, you'll find out!" Next day she calls The Golden Bar & gets the bartender on the phone. She asked him, "Do you have golden doors?" "Yes we do." "How about the floors?" "Yes, they're golden too!"

"Well, do you have golden bathroom fixtures?" Silence for a while, then she hears the bartender say, "Hey Joe, I think I might've found out something about who might have trashed your saxaphone!"

A man walks into a bar with a slab of asphalt under his arm & says, "A beer please, & one for the road."

A woman is walking along in front of the building here with a duck under her arm. A drunk met her & says, "Where'd you get that ugly thing?" The woman says, "Sir, that happens to be a duck!" He says, "I know, I was talking to the duck!"

A teetotaler is seated next to a rock star on a flight to Texas. After the plane takes off, the musician orders a whiskey & soda. So the flight attendant asks the teetotaler, "Would you like one too?" He says, "No, I'd rather be tied up & ravaged by crazed women than let liquor touch my lips!" The the rock star hands his drink back & says, "I didn't know we had a choice!"

A man walks into a rooftop bar & takes a seat next to another guy. He asks the other guy; "What are you drinking?" He says, "Magic Beer!" Guy says, "Oh yeah, what's so magic about it?" He proceeds to show him. He drinks some beer, jumps off the roof, flies around the building & returns to his seat. "Amazing! Let me try some of that. He grabs the beer, downs it, leaps off the roof, & falls 30 feet to the ground. The bartender shakes his head & says to the 1st guy, "You know, you're a real jerk when you're drunk Superman!

Thinking of my bartending days. Most of the time it was very boring. One day I had a drunk passed out on the floor & he had an elaborate handlebar mustache, so for fun I took some limburger cheese & rubbed in his mustache. Pretty soon he woke up with a terrible scowl on his face. He got up & staggered outside, came back in & said, "It's no use, the whole world stinks!"

Did you ever drink a 'card table cocktail' " One drink & your legs fold up.

THE POLECAT: Once upon a morning dreary as I staggered weak and weary
Making my way homeward bleary from the festive night before
I was feeling less than steady, for the punch had been quite heady,
And I hoped my bed was ready waiting just inside my door;
That's of course providing I could recognize my own front door
I wanted sleep and nothing more

I saw a furry little creature and I hurried up to reach her,
Though I beheld a double feature with my eyes so red and sore.
Just a lost and lonely kitty with her fur so soft and pretty
And my heart was filled with pity knowing not what lay in store.
If I could have guessed the evil fate that lay in store--
I'd have wished to live no more.

Much too late I saw my error and I cried out then in terror
For I found myself the bearer of an aromatic gore.
This was neither half nor whole cat, but a lousy stinking polecat,
And I wished there was a hole that I could hide in ever more.
I was deep in desperate trouble, up the creek without an oar---
And the skunk had declared war.

Suddenly my eyes were burning and my stomach started turning
And my nose hairs all were churning; I felt rotten to the core.
Oh, I tasted in and felt it for the skunk had not withheld it
And I bet you could have smelled it all the way to Ecuador;
Strong enough to make a buzzard lose his lunch upon the floor---
And the skunk poured out some more.

As the polecat sat there gloating, I was filled with fear and loathing.
I would have to burn my clothing and go bathing far offshore.
I was perfumed so completely, I was reeking indiscretely.
Would I ever smell as sweetly as I always had before?
Would my friends still come to see me or invite me to their door?
Said the polecat, "NEVERMORE!"

Two peanuts walk into a bar & one was a-salted.

One day when I was bartending, a fellow came in & asked me if I'd give him free drinks if he's show me something amazing. I said, "Okay, but it'll have to be pretty amazing!" So, he pulls a Crown Royal bag out of his coat, pulls out a miniature baby-grand piano, a tiny stool & a gerbil. He sets that gerbil on the piano stool & that gerbil plays the piano like Van Cliburn. He said, "Well, bartender, what do you think of that?" I said, "Sorry, but you'll have to show me more." So, he reaches into another coat pocket & pulls out a bullfrog, sets him beside the piano & that frog starts singing 'Old Man River'. There's a drunk setting about 2 stools down the bar & he says, "I'll give you a hundred bucks for that frog!" The guy says, "You got him." The drunk puts the frog in his pocket & leaves & I told the guy, I said, "Mr., didn't you sell that frog kinda cheap?" He said, "No, that guy doesn't know that gerbil's a ventriloquist."

I tried to write a song about drinking, but I couldn't get past the 1st two bars.

There are 4 bars in this town & I haven't set foot in one of them---the other 3 are much nicer.

You know, drinking makes you handsome.
() I DON'T DRINK!
Yeah, but I do!!

I came home last night---rammed into the garage doors & pulled one of them right off. It's a good thing I didn't have the car!"

A man comes to Mrs. Smith's door & says, "There's been an accident at the brewery. Your husband fell into a vat of beer & drowned. Mrs. Smith says, "Oh, the poor man! He never had a chance! " The man says, "I don't know about that, he got out 3 times to go to the bathroom."

A cop stopped a drunk & asked him, "Why are you walking down the street with one foot on the sidewalk & the other in the gutter? " The drunk says, "Thank God you stopped me officer, I thought I was crippled."

_____: YOU'VE BEEN DRINKING, I SMELL IT ON YOUR BREATH. I haven't had a drop. I've been eating frog legs & what you smell is the hops.

A drunk gets on the bus late at night, staggers up the aisle, sits down next to an elderly lady. She looks him up & down & says, "I've got news for you, you're going straight to hell!" The drunk jumps up out of his seat & shouts, "Man, I'm on the wrong bus!"

A cop stops a drunk late at night & asks where he's going. The drunk says, "I'm going to a lecture about alcohol abuse & the effects it has on the human body." The policeman says, "Really? Who's giving the lecture at one in the morning?" The driver says, "My wife."

A guy walks into a bar, orders 3 shots & downs 'em all. So the bartender asks him, "What's up with the 3 shots?" The guy says, "My two closest buddies & I have gone our separate ways, & I miss them terribly. See, this glass here is for Tom, this one's for Bob & this ones mine. I feel like we're all drinking together, just like old times." So, every day the guy comes in & the bartender sets up 3 glasses. Until one day, the guy asks for just 2 shots. The bartender says, "I hate to ask, but did something happen to one of your friends?" The guy says, "Nah, they're okay, I just decided to quit drinking."

Say, didn't I meet you in Toledo?
() NO, I NEVER WAS IN TOLEDO.
Neither was I. It must have been two other guys.

Thinkin' about my bartending days. One day Clancy came into the pub & ordered a beer. He drank half, then threw the rest at me. Clancy apologized, explaining it was a compulsion he'd had for years that embarrassed him terribly. So, I told him to see a psychiatrist & warned him not to come back until he had. A few months later, Clancy again entered the bar & ordered a brew. He drank half & threw the rest all over yours truly.. I said, "Clancy, I told you not to come back here until you'd seen a shrink about your compulsion!"
Clancy says, "I have been seeing one." I said, "Well, it hasn't done any good!" He said, "Yes it has, I'm not embarrassed about it any more."

A man walks into a bar, sits down & orders a drink. He hears, "Nice tie mister." He looks around--no one's there. "Hey, nice shirt!" Nobody there. "Hey, nice suit!" He calls the bartender over & asks, "Who's talking to me?" The bartender says, "It's not me, it's the peanuts, they're complimentary."

My neighbor shared a personal experience about drinking & driving. He was out for an evening with friends & had several whiskies followed by a couple of bottles of rather nice red wine & vodka shots. Although he was relaxed, he still had the common sense to know he was slightly over the limit. That's when he did something he'd never done before--he took a taxi home! Sure enough, on the way home there was a police roadblock, but since it was a taxi, they waved it past & he arrived home safely without incident. That was a surprise to him, cause he'd never driven a taxi before.

While I was registering at a hotel, a drunk came in to the desk clerk & says, 'M-friend, I wanna room on the second floor." & the clerk says, "But you're Mr. Brown aren't you? We have you registered as occupying room 620." The drunk says, "That's perfectly correct 'ol boy, but I just fell out of it."

A policeman pulled a guy over & said, "Sir, I need you to breathe into this breathalyzer for me." The driver says, "I can't do that, I'm an asthmatic. If I do that, I'll have a really big asthma attack." The officer says, "Okay, then I'll need you to come down to the station with me & we'll have to do some blood work." The guy says, "I can't do that either, I'm a hemophiliac. If you do that I could bleed to death." "Okay, then, I need a urine sample from you." "I can't do that either, I'm a diabetic. If I do that, my sugar will get really low!" The officer says, "Okay then, I need you to step out of the car & walk this white line." The driver says, "I can't do that either!" The officer says, "Why not?" He says, "Because, I'm drunk!"

A guy goes into a bar, orders 4 shots of the most expensive 30 year-old single malt scotch, & downs them one after the other. The barkeep says, "You look like you're in a hurry." The guy says, "You would be too if you had what I have!" The bartender says, "What've you got?" The guy says, "Fifty-cents."

A group of guys were touring the Anheiser-Busch Brewery last week & while they were marveling at the process, one of them slipped & fell into a huge vat of beer. Brewery workers tried to save him while his friends waited outside. A half hour later the supervisor came out to tell the guys the bad news--their friend had drowned. One of the friends asked, "Do you think he suffered much?" The supervisor said, "I don't think so, in fact, he got out 3 times to go to the bathroom."

A drunk walked into the Police Station & said, "Offsher, you'd better lock me up. Just hit my wife over the head with a club. The Officer asked, "Did you kill her?" The drunk says, "I don't think so, thash why I want to be locked up"

A preacher was driving down a 2-lane road, late for a meeting & he comes up behind a drunk weaving back & forth & moving slow. Finally, he tries to pass on the right shoulder while the drunk's veering to the left, but the drunk swerves back & the preacher slips into the ditch. The drunk sees this in his rear-view mirror & he stops, walks back & asks, "Ish something wrong?" The preacher says, "No, I've got God riding with me. & the drunk says, "Well, you'd better let him ride with me, you're gonna kill him!"

Did you ever drink a 'Mickey Rooney Cocktail'? One drink & you're standing under the table.

Calls to mind the words of W. C. Fields, who said, "It was a woman who drove me to drink, & I never got a chance to thank her."

A duck waddles into a bar. Bartender says, "What can I get you?" The duck says, "Got any grapes?" "No, we serve beer, whiskey, nuts etc." The duck says, "Okay" & leaves. Next day the duck comes back into that bar, hops up on the bar stool & says, "Got any grapes?" The bartender says, "No, I told you yesterday we don't have any grapes, if you come in here tomorrow & ask for grapes, I'll nail your beak to the bar!" So the duck leaves. The next day the duck comes back into the bar & says, "Got any nails?" The bartender says, "No, why:" & the duck says, "Okay, got any grapes?"

A guy sits at the bar & says, "Today's my birthday, I'll have a birthday drink!" A man setting beside him says, "Amazing, it's my birthday too, how old are you?" The 1st guy says "36." The 2nd guy says, "This is uncanny---I'm 36~! Where're you from?" The 1st guy says, "Pittsburgh." The 2nd guy says, "This is incredible, that's where I'm from! Where'd you go to school?" The 1st guy says, "Pittsburgh Catholic." The 2nd guy says, "I can't believe it, that's where I went to school." Well about that time the phone rang & it was my boss & he asks me, "Do you have any customers?" I said, "There's no one here except the drunken O'Brien twins."

Have you heard about the new alcoholic beverage on the market called Bourbon Renewal? After a few drinks your old neighborhood starts to look a lot better.

After a heavy night at the pub, a drunken man decides to sleep off his drunkenness at a local hotel. So he gets a room, but several minutes later he staggers back to the reception desk & demands his room to be changed. The clerk says, "But sir, you have the best room in the hotel!" The drunk says, "I insist on another room!" & the clerk says, "Very good sir, I'll change you from room 502 to 525, but would you mind telling me why you don't like 502?" The drunk says, "Well, for one thing, it's on fire!"

Did you hear about the lady visiting France on a wine-tasting trip? She drank too much, fell from her hotel window & ended up in a body cast. She swore never to get plastered in Paris again.

A blind man travels to Texas. When he gets to his hotel room, he feels the bed. “Wow, this bed is big!” The bellhop says, “Everything is big in Texas!” Later the man goes downstairs to the bar & orders a drink; a mug is placed between his hands. He says, “Wow, these drinks are big!” The bartender says, “Everything is big in Texas!” After a few drinks, the blind man asks the bartender the restroom is. The bartender says, “It’s the 2nd door on the right down the hall.” The blind man heads for the restroom but accidentally enters the 3rd door, which leads to the swimming pool, & he falls in. Scared to death, he shouts, “Don’t flush it, Don’t flush it!”

A nearsighted drunk at a cocktail party goes up to the host & says, “Excuse me, but do lemons have wings?” She says, “Of course not!” He says, “Oh, in that case I’ve just squeezed your canary into my drink.”

These 2 drunks are out for a stroll & they were staring up at the sky & one of them says, “Beautiful night ain’t it, look at the moon.” The other one says, “That’s not the moon, you moron, that’s the sun!” So, they’re still arguing when a 3rd drunk staggers over & they said, “Help us out here buddy, look up, is that the sun or the moon?” The 3rd guy says, “I don’t know, I don’t live around here.”

A man is sitting at the bar drinking away his sorrows. Suddenly he sees 2 squirrels burst through the front door & sit down next to him. He was amazed as he watched them order drinks & eat from a bowl of nuts. Finally, he can’t stand it any longer, his curiosity gets the best of him. So, he asks, “Where did you 2 learn to talk?” The squirrel closest to him says, “Wow, you’re drunk, there’s only one of me!”

A guy in a bar drinking all afternoon & evening & he finally decides it’s time to go home, so he tries to get off his bar stool & falls down. He pulls himself up & ends up rolling out the door, crawling over to a parking meter he pulls himself & he keeps going from parking meter to parking meter 'til finally he makes it home. The next morning his wife's standing over his bed & she says, "You were out drinking all yesterday afternoon & last night weren't you?" He says, "Yeah, how'd you know?" She says, "Cause, the bartender called & said you left your wheelchair at the bar."

Walked by a guy on the street. I guess he was drunk cause he was hanging on to a lamp post for dear life. I said, "Why don't you take the bus home?" He said, "My wife would never let me keep it!"

I saw a man lying in the gutter. I said, "Are you hurt?" He said, "I'm fine, I just found a parking place & sent my wife out to buy a car.

I came from a small town you know. It was so small that we didn't have a regular town drunk. Everybody had to take turns.

A drunk is standing on a street corner, & a cop passes by, & says, "What do you think you're doing?" The drunk says, "I heard the world goes around every 24 hours, & I'm waiting on my house. Won't be long now, there goes my neighbor!"

You might be a redneck if you think loading the dishwasher means getting your wife drunk.

A man walks into a bar with a giraffe & they proceed to get blitzed. The giraffe drinks so much it passes out on the floor. The man gets up & heads for the door to leave when the bartender yells, "Hey! You can't leave that lyin' there!" The drunk says, "That's not a lion, it's a giraffe!'

A guy walks into a bar & orders a drink. After a few more he needs to go to the can. He doesn't want anyone to steal his drink so he puts a sign on it saying, "I spit in this beer, do not drink!" After a few minutes, he comes back & there's another sign next to his beer saying: "So did I!"

I was out in the park barbequeing a chicken on a spit the other day when a drunk happened by & just stared at it. I said, "What's your problem?" He said, "I don't know if you know it sir, but the music's quit & your monkey's on fire."

DUMMY/ JOKES

_____ goes out to buy a new Cadillac. Finds one he likes. Salesman says it's $33,333.00. "How much would you take off if I paid cash?" Salesman says, "Twelve and a half percent." _____ says, "Okay, I'll think about it." He goes across the street to a café, has a cup of coffee & tries to figure this on a napkin. He can't get it done so he asks the waitress to refill his coffee. He said, "While you're here, tell me, how much would you take off for twelve and a half percent of $33,333.00?" She said, "Everything but my earrings!"

I just watched my dog chase his tail for 10 minutes, & I thought to myself, Wow, dogs are easily entertained. Then I realized: I just watched my dog chase his tail for 10 minutes.

I hate it when people forward bogus warnings on the internet, but this one is real! And it's important! So please send this warning to everyone on your e-mail list: If someone comes to your door saying they are conducting a survey on deer ticks & asks you to take your clothes off & dance around with your arms up, do not do it!! It's a scam, they only want to see you naked. I wish I'd gotten this warning yesterday. I feel so stupid now.

Two guys get laid-off at the underwear factory. They go to the unemployment office. Joe goes into see the agent.. She asks him, "What do you do?" He says, "I'm an underwear stitcher." She says, "Okay, that's unskilled labor, you'll get $300 a month ." Then Moe goes into see the agent & she asks, "What do you do Sir?" Moe says, "I'm a diesel-fitter."

She says, "That's skilled labor, you'll get $600 a month." Moe goes out & tells Joe, "Hey, I'm getting $600 a month!" Joe gets mad & goes back into the agent & says, "Why am I only getting $300 a month & Moe's getting $600?" She says, "Well, you're an underwear stitcher, that's unskilled labor, Moe's a diesel-fitter, that's skilled labor." Joe says, "What do you mean 'skilled', I stitch the elastic on the underwear, hand them to Moe, he holds them up & says, 'diesel fitter, diesel fitter'."

I don't get these people who, instead of buying a 4 or an 8-pack of toilet paper, buy the single individual roll. What? Are they trying to quit?

One of our ______ went hiking in the Irish countryside. He came upon a shepherd with a large flock. He tells the shepherd, "If I can guess how many in the flock, may I have one?" The shepherd says, "Okay, go ahead!" He says, "287." "You're exactly right, go ahead & pick you out one." So, ______ slung one over his shoulders to carry it home. The shepherd says, "If I can guess your occupation, may I have that animal back?" "It's a deal!" "You're a ________ ." "That's amazing! How did you know that?" The shepherd says, "Put that dog down & we'll discuss it."

I was in a restaurant yesterday when I suddenly realized I desperately needed to pass gas. The music was really loud, so I timed my gas with the beat of the music. After a couple of songs, I started to feel better. I finished my coffee, & noticed that everybody was staring at me--then I suddenly remembered that I was listening to my Ipod.

Poland's worst air disaster occurred today when a 2-seater Cessna plane crashed into a cemetery late this morning in Central Poland. Search & rescue workers have recovered 300 bodies so far.

My folks were really proud of me when I graduated from high school. So were my wife & kids.

Light travels faster than sound. This is why some people appear bright until you hear them speak.

13% of Americans are illiterate. & I know some of them can't even read.

Vacations: People drive thousands of miles to have their pictures taken in front of their cars.

Moe & Joe work in a warehouse. Moe wants some time off, so he climbs up onto the rafters & hangs upside down from his knees. The boss comes in & asks, "What do you think you're doing?" Moe swings back & forth yelling, "I'm a light bulb, I'm a light bulb! So the boss says, "I think you need some time off, go home. Now as Moe starts to leave, Joe follows him & the boss says, "Where do you think you're going?" & Joe says, "Well, you can't expect me to work in the dark!"

Four cowboys were talking around the campfire one night & one of them says, "What do you think is the fastest thing in the world?" The 1st guy says, "I think it's your brain, for instance if you hit your thumb with a hammer, you instantly know it hurts!" The 2nd guy says, "I think it's your eyes cause if you blink your eyes for an instant, nothing changes, it looks the same!" The 3rd guy says, "There's no doubt in my mind that it's lights cause, you turn on a switch & instantly the room lights up. The 4th cowboy says, "Well, I think it's chili-peppers!" They said, "That's ridiculous, what makes you say that?" He says, "Well, I went to Hosea's last night & had a real good Mexican meal with lots of chili-peppers & they woke me up in the middle of the night & before I had a chance to think, blink, or turn on the light, they hit me.!"

There was a tragedy at the Tightwad library. All the books were lost in a terrible fire. Both of them just blazed out of control! Worst part of it is, one of 'em hadn't even been colored in yet.

The school board in Tight Wad has decided to discontinue it's Driver Education program. The mule died.

Bubba & Leroy were in K-Mart & they decided to get in on the weekly raffle. They bought 5 tickets each at a dollar a pop. The following week, when the raffle was drawn, each had won a prize. Leroy won 1st place--a year's supply of gourmet spaghetti. Bubba won 6th prize--a toilet brush. So about a week or so had passed when they met again at K-Mart & Bubba asked Leroy how he liked his prize & Leroy said, "Great, I love spaghetti!" So Leroy asked Bubba, "How's about you, how's the toilet brush?" Bubba says, "Not so good, I'm thinking about switching back to paper."

Two Slobovians were building a deck on the back of their house down the street & they had lumber stacked on the roof & everywhere you could imagine. Well, this 2 X 6 slipped off the roof & cut one of em's ear off. So, they started looking for that ear & the other's said, "Hey, I found your ear!" & the 1st one said, "No, that's not my ear!" "Well, who elses ear could it be?" He said, "I don't know, but that couldn't be my ear, cause my ear had a pencil on it!"

Two guys go ice fishing. They start to cut a hole in the ice & a voice booms out; "Don't cut a hole in the ice!" One guy says to his buddy, "Was that God?" The voice came back, "No, the owner of this ice skating rink!"

There's a new scam that's being pulled mainly on older men. What happens is that when you stop for a red light, a nude young woman comes up & pretends to be washing your windshield. While she's doing this, another person opens your back door & steals anything in the car. They're very good at this! I guess I'm too easily distracted. They got me 7 times Wednesday & 5 times Thursday. I wasn't able to find 'em today.

I've been getting into astronomy, so I installed a skylight. The people who live above me are furious!

Yesterday I was walking down the street wearing my eyeglasses & all of a sudden my prescription ran out!

Today I bought some powered water, but I don't know what to add.

Well, I've got a flat tire out there on my car. I ran over a bottle about a mile back.
() MY GOODNESS, COULDN'T YOU SEE IT & DRIVE AROUND IT?"
Naw, the guy had it in his hip pocket.

A student asks the teacher; "Why am I the tallest one in the third grade? Is it because I'm Irish?" The teacher says, "No, it's because you're 18!"

The teacher says, "There are two words I don't allow in my class. One is 'gross' & the other is 'cool'." So _____ says, "Okay, what are the words?"

My wife & I've been having short-term memory problems, so we went to this Dr. we read about & the program he put us on really works good!
() I'D LIKE TO SEE THAT DR. TOO, WHAT'S HIS NAME?
Okay, help me with this. I need a name of a flower--it has a long green stem--& thorns.
() ROSE?
Yeah, that's it. Hey Rose! What's the name of that Doctor?

It's almost Christmas & _______'s just getting over Halloween.
() WHAT HAPPENED TO HIM OVER HALLOWEEN?
Aw, he burnt his face bobbing for French fries.

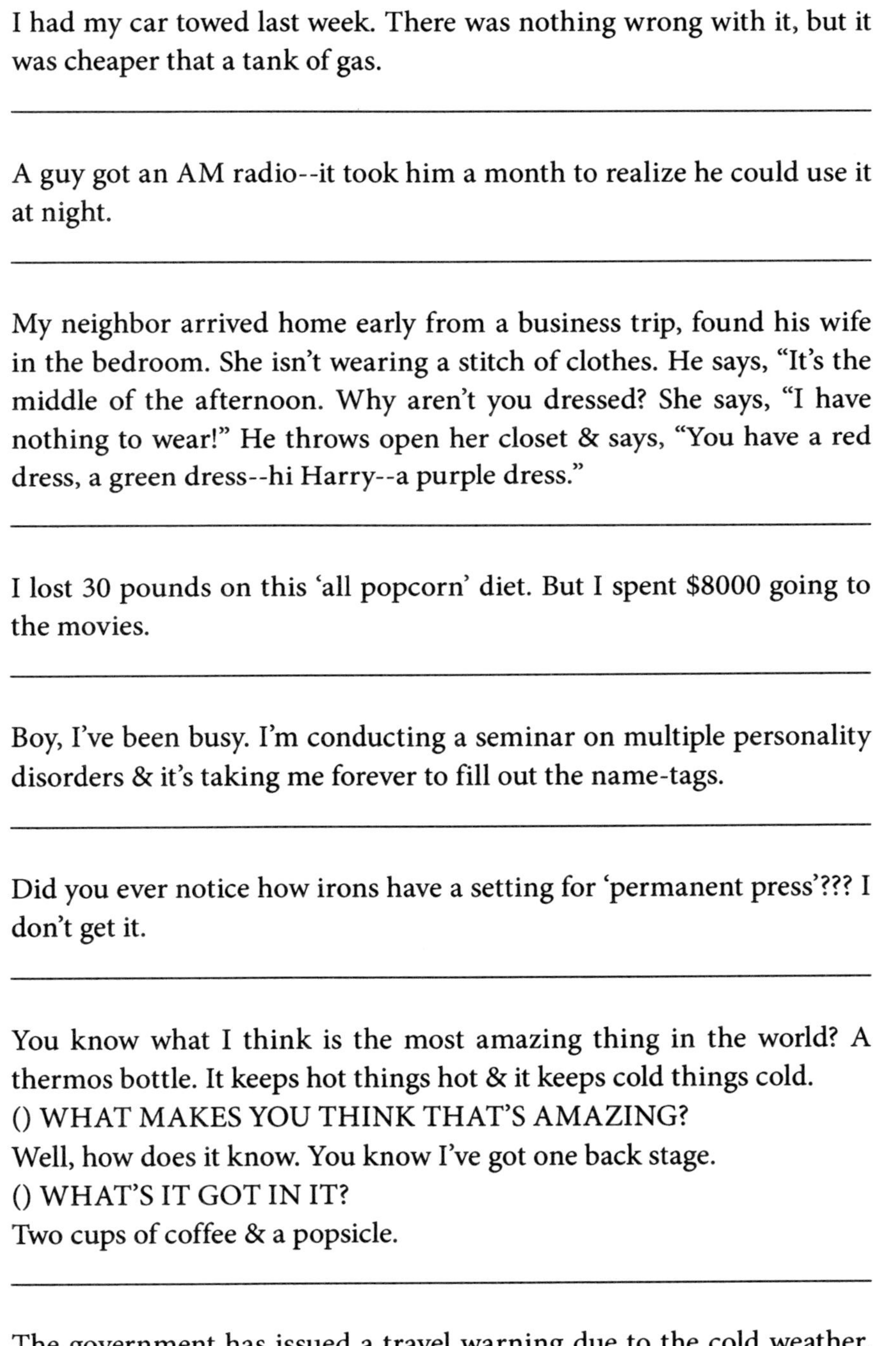

I had my car towed last week. There was nothing wrong with it, but it was cheaper that a tank of gas.

A guy got an AM radio--it took him a month to realize he could use it at night.

My neighbor arrived home early from a business trip, found his wife in the bedroom. She isn't wearing a stitch of clothes. He says, "It's the middle of the afternoon. Why aren't you dressed? She says, "I have nothing to wear!" He throws open her closet & says, "You have a red dress, a green dress--hi Harry--a purple dress."

I lost 30 pounds on this 'all popcorn' diet. But I spent $8000 going to the movies.

Boy, I've been busy. I'm conducting a seminar on multiple personality disorders & it's taking me forever to fill out the name-tags.

Did you ever notice how irons have a setting for 'permanent press'??? I don't get it.

You know what I think is the most amazing thing in the world? A thermos bottle. It keeps hot things hot & it keeps cold things cold.
() WHAT MAKES YOU THINK THAT'S AMAZING?
Well, how does it know. You know I've got one back stage.
() WHAT'S IT GOT IN IT?
Two cups of coffee & a popsicle.

The government has issued a travel warning due to the cold weather. They suggest that anyone traveling in the current icy conditions should make sure they have the following: shovel, blankets or sleeping bag, 24 hours worth of food, deicer, rock salt, flashlight with spare batteries, road flares, empty gas can, first aid kit, booster cables. I looked like an idiot one the bus this morning.

A hermit leaves the solitude of his rural home & ventures into town for the 1st time in his life to try to get a loan. Inside the bank, he tells the manager; "I want to borrow $10,000 to build a bathroom in my house." The banker says, "I don't believe I know you, where have you done your business before?" The hermit says, "Out back in the woods."

Did you hear about the 2 guys that froze to death in a drive-in movie theatre? They went to see 'Closed For The Winter'.

When _____ got out of high school he tried to get a job as an F.B.I. agent. They gave him a preliminary verbal test. They asked him: What's the capital of New York State? He answered, "New York City." What's the capital of Missouri? "Kansas City." Who shot President John F. Kennedy? "I don't know." They said, "Well, we want you to think about that & we'll call you later." So, he went home & his Mom asked him if he got a job with the F.B.I., & _______ said, "Yeah, they've already put me on a murder case."

Joe & Dave go hunting. Dave keels over. Frantic, Joe dials 911 on his cell phone & blurts out, "My friend just dropped dead! What should I do?" A soothing voice replies, "Don't worry, I can help. 1st let's make sure he's really dead." After a brief silence the operator hears a shot ring out. Then Joe comes back to the phone & says, "Okay operator, what do I do next?"

_______ was riding along with me from the auto repair shop & I told him, "_______, I'm turning now, see if the blinker is working." He said, "Sure!" & he rolled down the window & stuck his head out & said, "Yep, it's working, wait, no it isn't, yes it is, no it isn't, yes it is!"

() WHAT IS THAT YOU'RE CHEWING?
It's called 'Trick Gum'--the more you chew it, the smarter you get. I'm gonna chew this one second & have a lot of swell ideas.
() GOT ANY MORE?
I've only got one stick left. I'll sell it to you for ten dollars.
() HERE'S THE TEN DOLLARS.
Here's the gum.
() BOY, IT'S ALL RIGHT, IT TASTES GOOD. DO YOU THINK I'LL GET SMART FROM THAT? FUNNY, I DON'T FEEL ANY DIFFERENT. I THINK IT'S A JOKE.
Say, you're smarter already.

Everyone has a photographic memory. Some people are just out of film.

I remember when we got our 1st remote controlled TV set. The salesman installed the set in our house, then he took the remote control plum down to the barn & switched channels with no problem. About a week later, Dad called the salesman & complained about the remote control. The salesman asked Dad, "Doesn't it work?" Dad says, "Oh yes, it works just fine. But it's getting to be quite a nuisance going down to the barn every time I want to change channels!"

For a long time I had the feeling someone was following me.
() BUT YOU DON'T FEEL THAT WAY ANYMORE?
Oh, I still feel that way---but I found out what it was. It was just my underwear creeping up on me.

How many of you folks remember your ABCs? Well, they've added 23 more letters since then.

A guy goes into a library & says to the librarian, "I'd like a coke, some fries & a hamburger." The exasperated librarian says, "Sir, do you have any idea where you're at?" He looks around & says, "Oh, excuse me! (then he whispers) I'd like a coke, some fries & a hamburger."

You know, I had a brand new Mercury. I loaned it to my brother last week. I said, "Treat it as if it was your own." He sold it!

The reason I bought that new car's because I wrecked my old one. Another fellow & I collided on one of those winding backroads. So we got out & traded insurance information in a gentlemanly fashion. Then he said, "Man, you seem a bit shaken up, how about a drink to settle your nerves?" So, I took his flask & swallowed a good snort & handed it back to him & he just put it away. I said, "Aren't you gonna have any?" He said, "Not 'til after the police get here."

(stomp your foot)
() WHAT'S THE PROBLEM ________?
Aw, I hate it when my foot falls to sleep this early---cause then I know it'll be up all night.

Did you hear about the 2 guys that froze to death in a Drive-In-Movie Theatre last winter? They went to see 'Closed For The Winter'.

A government surveyor drops by a farm in Eastern Minnesota & announces that he has some bad news. "I discovered that your farm isn't in Minnesota, it's actually in Wisconsin!" The farmer lets out a sigh of relief. He says, That's the best news I've heard in a long time. I was just telling my wife this morning that I don't think I can take another winter in Minnesota!"

A firing squad was formed in Slobovia for the execution of 3 gentlemen. Henry was placed against the wall, & just before the order to shoot was given, he yelled out, 'EARTHQUAKE'! The firing squad panicked & in the confusion, Henry jumped over the wall, & escaped. Charlie was next & while the squad reassembled, he pondered what Henry had done. Before they could shoot, he shouted, 'TORNADO'!" Again the squad scattered & Charlie slipped away to safety. Last in line was a blonde by the name of Mike. He thought, I see the pattern here, just scream out a disaster & hop over the wall. As the firing squad raised their rifles & took aim, Mike grinned smugly & yelled, 'FIRE'.

() SAY LARRY, THAT'S A BAD GASH YOU HAVE ON YOUR FOREHEAD, HOW DID YOU GET IT?
I bit myself.
() OH, COME ON NOW, HOW COULD YOU BITE YOURSELF IN THE FOREHEAD?
I stood on a chair.

I suppose you think I'm a perfect idiot?
() OH, NO, NONE OF US IS PERFECT!

Did you hear about the guy who put on a clean pair of socks every day? By the end of the week, he couldn't get his shoes on.

Headlines: Suicidal twin kills sister by mistake.

I know a guy who's addicted to brake fluid. He says he can stop any time.

_______ & his wife are listening to the radio when they hear the weather report: "A snow emergency has been declared. You must park your cars on the odd-numbered side of the street." So, ______ gets up & moves his car. Two days later—the same thing. "A snow emergency has been declared. Park your cars on the even-numbered side of the street."

______ gets up & does what he's been told. Three days later: "There will be a foot of snow today. Park your cars on the----& the power goes out. So, ______ asks his wife, "What should I do?" She says, "Well, this time, why don't you just leave the car in the garage?"

You know what my greatest fear is? I fear that one day I'll meet God, he'll sneeze, & I won't know what to say.

I was visiting my Grandson & his wife last night when I asked if I could borrow a newspaper. He says, "This is the 21st Century, Granddad, we don't waste money on newspapers. Here, you can borrow my iPod." I can tell you, that bloody fly never knew what hit it.

Dennis, Jim & Kevin are all taking a memory test. The Dr. asks Kevin, "What's 3 times 3?" He answers, "274." Hmmmm. The Dr. turns to Jim & asks, "What's 3 times 3?" Jim says, "Tuesday." So the doc asks Dennis, "What's 3 times 3?" Dennis says, "Nine." The Dr. says, "Great, how did you get that?" Dennis says, "Simple, I subtracted 274 from Tuesday."

Say, have you got a box 50 feet long by 1 inch square?
() NO. WHAT DO YOU WANT THAT FOR?
It's my brother's birthday & I wanta send him a garden hose.

I was gonna wear my camouflage shirt tonight, but I couldn't find it.

I had an accident opening a can of alphabet soup this morning.
() WERE YOU INJURED?
No, but it could have spelled disaster!

How can you tell if a redneck is married? There's tobacco spit stains on both sides of his pickup truck.

I went to school to become a wit---only got half way through.

I just heard this in the news last night: In Europe they're gonna start driving on the right side of the road, like we do here. Polish officials are starting on a trial basis, so they're having just trucks drive on the right side for the first two weeks.

Is it me—or do buffalo wings taste just like chicken

I had the worst study habits in the history of high school, until I found out what I was doing wrong.
() WHAT WERE YOU DOING WRONG?
I was 'highlighting' with a black magic marker.

I never really liked 'hide-and-seek' when I was a kid. Especially since the time I hid in the closet & my family moved.

My sister has a lifesaving tool in her car designed to cut through a seat belt if she gets trapped. She keeps it in the trunk.

() ARE YOU GOING TO THE MOVIES AFTER THE PROGRAM TONIGHT?
No, I ain't going.
() WHAT GRAMMER! YOU SHOULD SAY; I'M NOT GOING, THEY'RE NOT GOING, HE IS NOT GOING, SHE IS NOT GOING. GET THE IDEA?
Sure---nobody ain't going.

() NO, NO! TRY THIS. CONSTRUCT A SENTENCE USING THE WORD 'ARCHAIC'.
Okay, I've got it: We can't have our cake and eat it too.

() CAN YOU TELL ME THE MEANING OF THE WORD 'UNAWARE'?
Sure. Unaware is what you put on first and take off last.

() HAVE YOU EVER ADDRESSED THE PUBLIC?
Oh, yeah, I've addressed thousands of people in Madison Square Garden.
() WHAT DID YOU SAY?
Popcorn, peanuts, soda pop.

One teacher I had was trying to make use of her psychology courses. She started our class by saying; "Everyone who thinks their stupid, stand up!" After a few seconds, I stood up & the teacher said, "Do you think you're stupid Larry?" I said, "No, Ma-am, but I hate to see you standing there all by yourself."

I was readin' the ads in the paper today. One of 'em said, "Chain saw for sale, only used one time. Call 555-2625 & ask for Lefty.

Back on the front page it said, "A lady stabbed her husband 152 times. She said she couldn't shut off the electric knife."

You might be a redneck if: You've ever been pumping gas & another customer asks you to check his oil.

Or, your wife owns a camouflage nightie.

Or, your wife & ex-wife are sisters.

Did you know that in China a woman has a baby about every 3 seconds! Somebody ought to find her & stop her!

Did you hear about the Slobovian who entered the Indianapolis 500? He made 90 pit stops---3 for gas & the other 87 to ask for directions.

They've raised the minimum drinking age for Rednecks to 32. They want to keep alcohol out of the high schools.

Did you hear about the 3 million dollar Red Neck lottery? The winner gets $3.00 a year for a million years.

Two rookie police officers find 3 hand grenades in the street & decide to take them to the station. The younger officer says, "What if one of them explodes?" & the other one says, "It doesn't matter, we'll say we only found 2."

FARM JOKES

Hear about the farmer that bought a new rooster, put him out in the barnyard & the old rooster says; "You know, we gotta decide who's the head rooster around here!" The new rooster asks, "Well, how do we do that?" The old rooster says, "The last several times we've ran 10 laps around the barn." The new rooster says, "Okay, that sounds fair, but I'll give you half a lap head start cause your older." Off they went with all the old hens cackling & making noise. After about 3 laps the new rooster was about to overtake the old rooster. Because of all the noise in the barnyard, the farmer thought a fox was in the henhouse, so he stepped out on the porch with his shotgun, took a bead & shot the new rooster deadern'a door nail. He came back in the house to put up his gun & his wife wants to know what all the commotion's all about. He says, "Aw, that's the 3rd gay rooster I've had in a year!"

You know if we don't get some rain we're gonna have a crop failure. I've seen a few crop failures in my day. In 1947 the corn crop was almost nothing. We cooked some for dinner & my Dad ate 14 acres of corn at one meal!

We fed an old hen sawdust out of desperation instead of oatmeal---she laid 12 eggs & sat on them & when they hatched, 11 of the chickens had wooden legs & the twelfth one was a woodpecker.

Did you hear about the farmer who put a tuxedo on his scarecrow? It didn't protect his corn, but it attracted a better class of blackbirds.

I overheard 2 farmers talking in the lobby. One of them says, "How's your banker treating you?" The other one says, "Oh, he's helping me get back on my feet. Just yesterday he repossessed my pickup truck."

The Missouri Department of Government Offices claimed a local farmer here was not paying proper wages to his help & sent an agent out to investigate. The agent tells the farmer, "I need a list of all your employees, & how much you pay them." The farmer says, "Well, there's my farm hand who's been with me for 3 years. I pay him $200 a week plus free room & board. Then there's the mentally challenged worker. He works about 18 hours every day & does about 90% of all the work around here. He makes about $10 per week, pays his room & board, & I buy him a bottle of bourbon every Saturday night so he can cope with life. He also sleeps with my wife occasionally. The agent says, "That's the guy I want to talk to---the mentally challenged one." The farmer says, "That would be me!"

He's just bought a new tractor. It doesn't have a seat or a steering wheel. It's for farmers who've lost their rears & don't know which way to turn.

FAT JOKES

Well, the media's always talking about how overweight we are in this country, but we had this problem when I was a kid too. Why, I went to High School with one guy that was so fat--his picture in the yearbook was on page 41, 42 & 43!

When he lived at home, he was so fat, they had to let the shower curtain out.

He ran away from home as a kid & had to take the truck route.

_____ told me he had the body of a Greek god. I had to explain to him that Budda is not Greek.

Did you see the headlines today? It said, "Floor Collapses at Weight Watchers Meeting!"

Well, I didn't make it to the gym today. That makes 1,508 days in a row.

Do you collect antiques? I saw an add in the paper that said; "For sale, Antique desk suitable for lady with thick legs & large drawers."

I helped move my nephew yesterday.
() OH, DID HE BUILD A NEW HOUSE?
No, he's just really fat.

Shirley noticed me standing on the bathroom scale sucking in my stomach. She says, "Ha! That's not gonna help." I said, "Sure it does, it's the only way I can see the numbers."

If you are always straightening things, you have OCD. If you are always eating things, you have OBCD.

I was at the grocery store yesterday & I overheard a little girl talking to her mother. They passed a very large lady in the aisle & the little girl blurted out, "Mama, that lady is fat!" The mother told the little girl, "She can't help it, it's in her genes." The little girl said, "Well Mama, some of it's in her sweater, too!"

I'm a little depressed today. I was looking at my birth certificate and it suddenly occurred to me---I've gained 194 pounds.

GOLFING JOKES

I went golfing with Dennis, Kevin & Cliff. We got behind a foursome slower than molasses. It took forever to play 18 holes. We finally got back in the locker room & here's these 4 slow guys on the other side, so we started making fun of them, like: 'Slowpokes', 'Old Fogies' etc. About that time the golf pro came over & said, "You gentlemen ought to be ashamed of yourselves, cause all four of those guys are blind." Boy, did we feel bad. Dennis said, "I'll pay their green fees." Kevin says, "I'll pay for their golf carts." & Cliff says, "I'm gonna buy them all dinner." The golf pro looked at me and said, "What are you gonna do for them mister?" I said, "I'm not gonna do anything for 'em, they coulda played last night!"

In my position as a homicide detective I've been investigating the murder of Juan Gonzalez. It looks like he was killed with a golf gun.
() A GOLF GUN? WHAT IN THE WORLD IS A GOLF GUN?
I don't know, but it sure made a hole in Juan.

Long ago when men cursed & beat the ground with sticks, it was called witchcraft. Today, it's called golf.

A golfer accidentally turned over his cart. Elizabeth, a young golfer who lived in a luxurious home next to the fairway, heard the noise & yelled over to him. "Hey, are you okay? What's your name?" He says, "Ken." She said, "Forget your troubles. Come to my home, rest up & I'll help you get the cart up later!" Ken says, "That's mighty nice of you, but I don't think my wife would like it." Elizabeth says, "Oh, come on!" She was very pretty & persuasive. He says, "Well, okay, but my wife won't like it!" After a delicious martini & some driving & putting lessons, Ken thanked the lady & said, "I feel a lot better now, but I know my wife is gonna be real upset." Elizabeth says, "Don't be foolish, she won't know anything. By the way, where is she?" He says, Under the cart."

() TELL ME SOMETHING, WHY DON'T YOU PLAY GOLF WITH _____ ANYMORE?
Well, would you play golf with a man who moves the ball & puts down the wrong score while you're not looking?
() I CERTAINLY WOULD NOT!
Well, neither will _______!

I was out golfing with my buddy, Fred today. A funeral procession came driving by & he took off his hat & watched it go by. I said, "Why Fred, that's very respectful of you." He said, "Aw, it's the least I could do after 37 years of marriage.

HALLOWEEN JOKES

Which ghost is the best dancer? The boogieman.

What do witches get a hotels? Broom service.

Why do witches ride brooms? Vacuum cleaners get stuck at the end of the cord.

Two monsters went to a Halloween party. Suddenly one said to the other, “A lady just rolled her eyes at me! What should I do” The other monster says, “Be a gentleman, & roll ‘em back to her.”

---

3 vampires walk into a bar. The bartender asks, “What’ll you have?” 1st one says, “I’ll have a blood.” 2nd one says, “I’ll have a blood.” The 3rd one says, “I’ll have a plasma.” The bartender says, “Now let me get this straight, that’s 2 bloods & a blood light?”

I hope the same thing doesn’t happen this year on Halloween. Last year I answered the door & saw a young boy dressed in a suit & tie standing there on the stoop. He says, “Trick-or-treat!” I said, “What are you supposed to be?” He says, “I’m an IRS Agent.” Then he takes 25% of my candy & doesn’t even say thank you.

Did you hear about the ghost that wore a rubber sheet? He was a bed wetter.

When I was a kid just about the meanest thing you could do on Halloween was push over an outhouse. About the 2nd time I helped do that we chose our outhouse for some terrible reason. The next day my Dad asked me, "Who pushed over the outhouse?" I said, "I cannot tell a lie, it was me Father." He said, "Well Son, I'm gonna have to whip you." I said, "But Dad, George Washington didn't get a whippin' for choppin' down the cherry tree cause he told the truth." & Dad said, "Yeah, but George's father wasn't up in the cherry tree at the time!"

Why do vampires drink blood? Because, coffee keeps them awake all day.

Why did the ghost wear a rubber sheet? He was a bed wetter.

A cab driver picks up a nun. She gets in the cab, & the cab driver won't stop staring at her. She says, "Why are you staring at me?" The cabby says, "I have an embarrassing question to ask you, but I don't want to offend you." She says, "My son you can't offend me. When you're as old as I am & have been a nun as long as I have, you get a chance to see & hear just about everything." He says, "Well, I've always had a fantasy to have a nun kiss me." She says, "Well, we'll just see what we can do about that, but 1st, you have to be single & you have to be Catholic!" He gets all excited & says, "Yes, I'm single & Catholic!" She says, "Okay, pull over & we'll see what we can do." She plants a whopper of a kiss on the cabbie, but when they get back on the road, the cab driver starts crying. She says, "My dear child, why are you crying?" He says, "Forgive me, but I've sinned. I lied, I must confess, I'm married & I'm Jewish." The nun says, "That's okay, my name is George, & I'm going to a Halloween party!"

A woman of the house 2 doors down got sick of her husband coming home drunk. So, she dressed up like the devil & hid behind the door. Here He comes staggering in & she jumps out & says, "BOO!" He says, "Who're you?" She says, "I'm the devil!" & he says, "Well, shake hands, I married your sister!"

I dressed my dog up as a cat for Halloween. Now he won't come when I call him.

A coffin maker was on his way to deliver one of his coffins one night when his car broke down. Not wanting to be late, he put the coffin on his head & began walking to his destination. A policeman saw him & asked, "Hey, what are you carrying & where are you going?" The man says, "I didn't like where I was buried, so I'm relocating."

IRISH JOKES

Why is it that when you ask an Irishman a question, he answers with another question?
Who told you that?

Paddy was in New York. He was patiently waiting & watching the traffic cop on a busy street crossing. The cop stopped the flow of traffic & shouted, "OKAY PEDESTRIANS!" Then he'd allow the traffic to pass. He'd done this several times, & Paddy still stood on the sidewalk. After the cop had shouted "PEDESTRIANS!" for the tenth time, Paddy went over to the cop & said, "Is it not about time ye let the Catholics cross?"

So ______ asks his teacher; "Why am I the tallest one in the third grade? Is it because I'm Irish?" The teacher says, "No, it's because you're 18!"

Why do people wear shamrocks on St. Patrick's Day? Cause regular rocks are too heavy.

Why can't you borrow money from a leprechaun? Cause they're always comin' up a little short.

How did the Irish Jig get started? Too much drink & not enough restrooms.

O'Connell was staggering down the street with a small bottle of whiskey in his back pocket when he slipped & fell heavily. Struggling to his feet, he felt something wet running down his leg. He says, "Please God, let it be blood!"

Pat & Ryan were getting ready to go on a camping trip. Pat said, "I'm taking along a gallon of whiskey just in case of rattlesnake bites! What are you taking Ryan?" Ryan replies; "Two rattlesnakes."

Gallagher opened the morning newspaper & was dumbfounded to read in the obituary column that he had died. He quickly phoned his friend Finney. He says, "Finney, did you see the paper? They say I died!" Finney says, "Yes, I saw it! Where are you callin' from?"

What's Irish & stays out all night? Paddy O'Furniture.

Two Irishmen were walking home after a night on the town when a severed head rolled along the street. Mick picked up to his face & said to Paddy, "Doesn't that look like Sean?" Mick says, "No, Sean was taller that that."

O'Connor always slept with his gun under his pillow. Hearing a noise at the foot of the bed, he shot off his big toe. He said, "Thank the Lord I wasn't sleeping at the other end of the bed, I would've blown my head off."

Patrick Murphy & Shawn O'Brien were lifelong friends. Patrick was on his deathbed & he said, "Shawn, would ya pour a good bottle of Irish Whiskey oer me grave so it might soak in me bones & I'll be able to enjoy it for all eternity." Shawn says, "Aye, 'tis a fine thing ye ask of me & I will pour the whiskey but, might I strain it through me kidneys first?"

Mick & Paddy were walking along in London. It was their first walk in the capitol.

Mick says, "Lord above Paddy, this is a great city!" Paddy says, "Why's that Mick?" Mick says, "Well to be sure, where else in the world would a complete stranger come up to you, make short idle chat, invite you to dinner & then offer you to spend the night at their house?" Paddy says, "Begorra, did that happen to you?" Mick says, "No, but it happens to my beautiful sister all the time!"

My buddy Mike O'Toole is rather fond of strong drink & he met his priest the other day & the priest asked him: "Mike, my son, how do you ever expect to get into Heaven the way ya act?" Mike says, "Sure, & that's aisy! When I get to the gates of Heaven I'll open the gate & shut the gate & open the gate & shut the gate & keep doin' that 'til St. Peter gets impatient & says, 'For goodness sake Mike, either come in or go out!'"

LAWYER JOKES

What's the difference between a dry cleaner & a lawyer? A cleaner pays if it loses your suit, but a lawyer can lose your suit & still take you to the cleaners.

Did you hear about the guy who's fed up with lawyers? He goes into a bar, starts drinking, pretty soon he hollers out, "All lawyers are jerks!" A guy next to him says, "I'm offended by that!" & the 1st guy says, "Why, are you a lawyer?" He says, "No, I'm a jerk!"

Hear about the lawyer that joined a nudist colony? He never had a suit again.

Overheard 2 burglars talking. One says, "You wouldn't believe my bad luck. I broke into a lawyer's house last night & he caught me. He let me go but told me "never to steal again"." His friend says, "He let you go? Why's that bad luck?" The 1st on says, "Cause, he charged me $500 for the advice!"

Word of wisdom: 99% of all lawyers give the rest a bad name.

The trouble with lawyer jokes is that lawyers don't think they're funny, & nobody else thinks they're jokes.

For example, today I was having a terrible day on the golf course. My tee shot disappeared into the trees. So, I was looking for my ball & when I found it--here's this guy lying on the ground beside it moaning & groaning & rubbing his head. He said, "I'm a lawyer & this will cost you $5000." I said, "I'm sorry, but I distinctly remember yelling 'fore'." He said, "Well, okay, you've got a deal."

Then there's that interesting new novel about 2 ex-convicts. One of them studies to become a lawyer. The other decides to go straight.

If a lawyer & an IRS agent were both drowning & you could only save one of them, would you go to lunch or read a newspaper?

Why do they bury lawyers 12 feet deep instead of 6? Because, deep down, they're really nice people.

Walking along the beach, a man finds a bottle. He rubs it & a genie appears. The genie says, "I'll grant you 3 wishes but there's one condition. I'm a lawyer's genie, so every wish you make, every lawyer in the world gets the same thing, only double!" So the guy thinks for a minute & says, "For my 1st wish, I'd like ten million dollars." The genie says, "Okay, lawyers get twenty million, what else do you want?" "I'd love to have a red Porsche." Zap! Instantly the car appears on the beach. "What's your last wish sir?" The guy says, "Well, I've always wanted to donate a kidney!"

What do you call a lawyer with an IQ of 50? Your honor.

() DID YOU EVER SPEAK BEFORE A LARGE AUDIENCE?
Yes.

() WHAT DID YOU SAY?
Not guilty.

A couple of attorneys walk into a diner, order drinks & pull lunches from their briefcases. The bartender says, “Sorry, but you can’t eat your own food here.” So, the lawyers looked at each other, shrugged their shoulders & swapped sandwiches.

Hey Dennis, what did your Dad do for a living?
() HE WAS AN ACCOUNTANT. WHAT DID YOUR DAD DO?
He was a lawyer.
() HONEST?
No, just the regular kind.

Our local United Way office realized they’d never received a donation from the town’s most successful lawyer. So, they called him to persuade him to contribute. They told him, “Our research shows that out of a yearly income of $500,000, you give not a penny to charity. Wouldn’t you like to give back to the community in some way?” The lawyer says, “First, did your research show that my mother is dying after a long illness & has medical bills that are astronomical.” “Well, No, No.” “Or that my brother, a disabled veteran, is blind & confined to a wheelchair? Or that my sister’s husband died in a traffic accident, leaving her penniless with 3 children? So, if I don’t give any money to them, why should I give any to you?”

How many lawyers does it take to roof a house? It depends on how thin you slice them.

A teacher, a thief & a lawyer all died & went to the Pearly Gates. St. Peter told them they had to pass a test before they got in to Heaven. So, he asked the teacher; “What was the name of the famous ship that hit an iceberg & sank?" She said, "The Titanic!" St. Peter said, "Go on in." The thief was next & St. Peter asked him, "How many people died on that ship?" The thief says, "That's tough, but lucky me, I just saw the movie, the answer is 1500." St. Peter says, "Go on in." Then St. Peter turned to the lawyer & said, "Name them."

Did you hear about the terrorists who took a courthouse full of lawyers hostage? They threatened to release one lawyer every hour unless their demands are met!

MARRIAGE, BOY-GIRL JOKES

There's a case of 'Mad Wife Disease' next door. Her husband was sitting quietly reading his paper when his wife walked up behind him & whacked him on the head with a magazine. He says, "What was that for?" She said, "That was for the piece of paper in your trouser pocket with name Laura Lou written on it!" He said, "Listen, 2 weeks ago when I went to the races, Laura Lou was the name of one of the horses I bet on. In fact, I bought you those flowers with the winnings!" She says, "Oh Darling, I'm sorry, I should have known there was a good explanation." 3 days later he was watching TV when she walked up & hit him in the head again, this time with a frying pan, which knocked him cold. When he came to he asked her, "What was that for?" She said, "Your horse phoned!"

But, love is blind, marriage is an institution. Does that mean that marriage is an institution for the blind?

Embarrassing moment: I was rummaging through the attic & came across my wife's love letters--they were dated last week.

Did you see that pretty girl on the 5th row?
() YEAH
She has nice even teeth. 1, 3, 5, 7 & 9 are missing.

Took my wife out to eat on Mother's Day to the Hyatt Regency Hotel in that Revolving Restaurant. Wouldn't you know it, that revolving mechanism quit working while we were up there & I thought we'd never get done eating, cause we had to get up & move to the next table about every 3 minutes.

There was a man & a very attractive woman sitting next to us & all of a sudden the man starts slowly sliding out of his chair & under the table. Funny thing was, the woman didn't seem to notice as her companion disappeared out of sight. About that time the head waiter came over & said, "Pardon me Madam, but I think your husband is under the table." She said, "No he isn't, my husband just walked through the door."

We finally got rid of our water-bed. I never did like that thing. My wife called it the 'Dead Sea'.

My neighbor came home & told his wife: "I've just been made a vice-president of our company!" She says, "So what, Vice-presidents are a dime-a-dozen, why the supermarket where I shop even has a vice-president in charge of prunes!" Well, he didn't believe her so he called up the supermarket & asked for the Vice-President of Prunes, & the guy asks him, "Packaged or Bulk?"

What do you call an Irishman who knows how to control a wife? A bachelor.

Definition of an Irish husband: He hasn't kissed his wife for 20 years, but he will kill any man who does.

Retirement is nice. This morning my wife said, "Whatcha doin' today?" I said, "Nothin'." She said, "You did that yesterday!" I said, "I wasn't finished."

() I'm gonna give you a driving test ______. If your wife were driving ahead of you & she put her hand out & gestured with her index finger toward the approaching corner, what would it mean?
It would mean the window's open.

It was our anniversary yesterday. We fell in love right before I went to the Navy. I remember writing home to my Mother: Dear Mom, I miss you. I miss Pa. But most of all, I miss the little potty under my bed." A couple weeks later she answered: "Don't worry son, you missed it when you were home too!

Well, I hope I can keep up with you tonight, I was out kinda late last night.
() Did your wife have much to say when you got home?
No, but that didn't keep her from talking for 2 hours!

She was already mad at me though. At supper last night she said, "This is rabbit stew we're having." I said, "I thought so, I just found a hair in mine."

She changes her tune though whenever she needs money. She calls me 'handsome' . She says, "Hand some over!"

You know, there are only 2 ways to handle a woman---& nobody knows either of them.

My neighbor had a terrible accident last week & he was in surgery for 12 hours. They messed up though. They sewed a woman's lips on him & now they can't get him to shut up.

He's the one that didn't have air conditioning until this summer. His wife told him she'd leave him if he didn't get an air conditioner. So he goes to the store & a salesman asked him, “Can I help you?” He said, “Yeah, I want to buy one of them window units.” The salesman says, “What size?” He says, “I need one with enough BTU to cool a BUT as big as a TUB.”

I just had another fight with the wife. Yeah, when it was over she came to me on her hands & knees. You know what she said? She said, “Come out from under the bed & fight like a man!”

My wife says she knows what Victoria’s Secret is. The secret is that nobody older than 30 can fit into their stuff.

I used to do some marriage counseling on the side. Sometimes my advice backfired on me though. For instance there was this young couple who came to me before they got married, only they didn’t come in together, they came in individually. The young lady was first, & she said, “I’m real worried about a personal problem I’ve got now that I’m about to get married.” I said, “What’s that?” She said, “Well, when I wake up in the morning, I have terribly bad breath.” I said, “That’s no problem, just keep your mouth closed until you get up & go brush your teeth & use some mouth wash.” Then her fiance’ came in to see me & he says, “I’ve got a real problem, my feet stink something terrible when I wake up in the morning.” I said, “That’s a problem we can overcome, all you have to do is wear socks to bed, get out of bed in the morning, wash your feet or shower & there you are.” So they got married & everything went real smooth for about 2 weeks. Then one morning about 4:30am he woke up & found one of his socks was missing. Now folks, he’d been alright if he hadn’t panicked, but commenced to thrashing around in the covers lookin’ for that sock & he woke her up & she forgot to keep her mouth shut & she says, “What in the world are you a doin’?” & he says, “You done went & swallowed one of my socks!”

My wife came home the other day & found me stalking around with a fly swatter. She asked me, "Killed any yet?" I said, "Yep, 2 males & a female." So she asked me, "How could you tell?" I said, "2 were on a beer can & one was on the telephone."

My wife went to bed before I did last night, so I took her a glass of water & an aspirin. She said, "Why are you bringing me that, I don't have a headache?" I said, "Gotcha!"

One couple in a small town got married to each other 3 times. The town is so small, they keep getting introduced.

() They tell me you married your wife cause her aunt left her a fortune. Well, that ain't so. I'd a married her no matter who'd left it to her.

My Mom & Dad got married to each other twice. Yeah, the 1st time it didn't work out.
() Why'd they get married again?
Oh, he got behind on his alimony payments so she repossessed him.

A feller that lives in Anchorage, Alaska's wife disappeared in a kayaking accident. The next day 2 grim-faced Alaska State Troopers showed up at his door. They said, "We're sorry Mr. Wilkins, but we have some information about your wife." "Tell me, did you find her?" The trooper says, "We have some bad news, some good news & some really great news. Which would you like to hear 1st ? Wilkins says, "Aw, give me the bad news." "I'm sorry to tell you sir, but this morning we found your wife's body in Kachemak Bay." Wilkins says, "Oh my Lord! Then what's the good news?" They said, "When we pulled her up, she had 12, 25 pound king crabs & 6 good sized Dungeness crabs clinging to her, & we feel you are entitled to a share in the catch." "Well, if that's the good

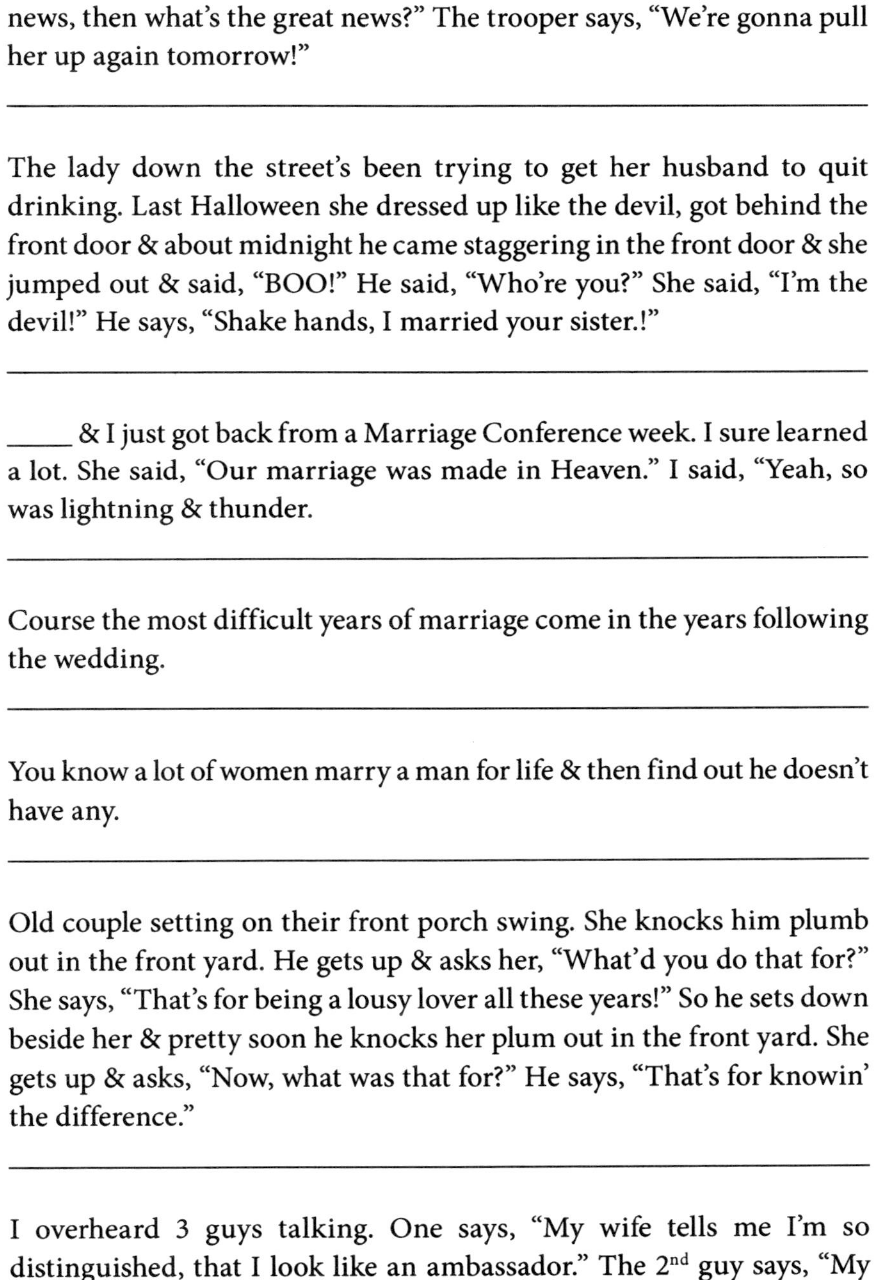

news, then what's the great news?" The trooper says, "We're gonna pull her up again tomorrow!"

The lady down the street's been trying to get her husband to quit drinking. Last Halloween she dressed up like the devil, got behind the front door & about midnight he came staggering in the front door & she jumped out & said, "BOO!" He said, "Who're you?" She said, "I'm the devil!" He says, "Shake hands, I married your sister.!"

_____ & I just got back from a Marriage Conference week. I sure learned a lot. She said, "Our marriage was made in Heaven." I said, "Yeah, so was lightning & thunder.

Course the most difficult years of marriage come in the years following the wedding.

You know a lot of women marry a man for life & then find out he doesn't have any.

Old couple setting on their front porch swing. She knocks him plumb out in the front yard. He gets up & asks her, "What'd you do that for?" She says, "That's for being a lousy lover all these years!" So he sets down beside her & pretty soon he knocks her plum out in the front yard. She gets up & asks, "Now, what was that for?" He says, "That's for knowin' the difference."

I overheard 3 guys talking. One says, "My wife tells me I'm so distinguished, that I look like an ambassador." The 2nd guy says, "My wife tells me I'm so intelligent I'm the best read man she has ever met." & the 3rd gentleman says, "My wife's proud of me too, every time a deliveryman comes to the door, she announces, 'My husband's home, My husband's home!"------------------------

---

I'm going home after the show & run our wedding movies backwards---I wanta remember what it's like to be a free man.

A man is incomplete until he's married, & then he's really finished.

I wish I had as much fun as my wife thinks I do.

() Did you see that girl back there on the back row?
Yeah.
() That's my girlfriend.
No it isn't, I came with that girl.
() Well, I guess we'll just have to divide her, so I'll take the top half. I can talk to my half.
I can take a walk in the woods with my half.
() I can hold hands with my half.
I can sit on a log with my half.
() I can kiss my half.
Well, if you want to be that way about it, you can kiss my half of her too!

I've worked around engineers a lot & this story fits them to a 'T'. Two engineering students were talking. One asked the other; "Where'd you get that great motorcycle?" The other one says, "I was minding my own business when a gorgeous woman rode up on it, jumped off, threw the bike to the ground, tore off her clothes & said, 'Take what you want!' The 1st engineer nodded his approval. He said, "Good choice, the clothes probably wouldn't have fit you anyway."

They had a 'Beautiful Body' contest this week in Tight Wad, Mo. & a telephone booth won.

I interviewed a prisoner down here at the jail. He was in for breaking into a dress shop 3 times. I asked him, "Why did you go back to the same shop 3 times?" He said, "It was my wife's fault, she kept changing her mind!"

A man & his wife were celebrating their 50th wedding anniversary, so the man bought his wife a $250 see-through night gown. Later that night she was getting ready for bed & realized the nightgown was still in the box downstairs. Walking naked through the house, she passed her husband who said, "My word, for $250 they could've at least ironed it!"

Desperate for a child, a couple asked their priest to pray for them. The priest says, "I'm going on sabbatical to Rome, I'll light a candle for you." So, the priest comes back 3 years later, finds the wife pregnant, tending 2 sets of twins. Of course the priest was elated & he says, "Where's your husband, I want to congratulate him!" She said, "He's gone to Rome to blow out that candle!"

Two of my neighbors appeared in court, each woman accusing the other of causing trouble in the neighborhood. The judge says, "Let's get to the evidence!" "I'll hear the oldest woman 1st !" The case was dismissed for lack of testimony.

You know my wife didn't get me anything for my birthday this year! So I confronted her about it & she says, "Well, you didn't use what I bought you last year!" I said, "What'd you give me last year?" She says, "A funeral plot!"

There are 2 times when a man doesn't understand a woman---before marriage & after marriage.

I came home from work & found my wife crying. She says, "The dog ate the pie I made for you!" I said, "Don't worry, I'll buy you another dog!"

Now my wife's getting a double chin. I think it was just too much work for one.

I'm in the doghouse again. We were getting ready for bed the other night & my wife says, "I look in the mirror & see an old lady. My face is all wrinkled & I'm sagging & bagging all over, & look at this flab on my arms!" Folks, I kept my mouth shut for a change. Finally she says, "Hey! Tell me something positive to make me feel better about myself!" So, I said, "Well, your eyesight's still great!"

I used to date a girl with a wooden leg, but she broke it off. She took me to court, but she didn't win. She didn't have a leg to stand on! Her name was Eilene, but I called her Peg.

But I gave him some advise. I told him that men who have pierced ears are better prepared for marriage. They've experienced pain & bought jewelry!

How are a Texas tornado & a Tennessee divorce the same? Somebody's gonna lose a trailer.

We can stay out late tonight, my wife's gone for a 2 week vacation in the Caribbean.

() JAMAICA?
No, it was her idea.

An invisible man marries an invisible woman. The kids were nothing to look at either.

A man meets a genie. The genie tells him he can have whatever he wants provided that his Mother-In-Law gets double. The man thinks for a minute & then says, "Okay, give me a million dollars & beat me half to death."

Two of my neighbors appeared in court this week, each woman accusing the other of causing trouble in the neighborhood. The judge says, "Let's get to the evidence, I'll hear the oldest woman 1st . " The case was dismissed for lack of testimony.

A woman was walking along in front of the building here with a duck under her arm. A drunk met her & says, "Where'd you get that ugly thing?" The woman says, "Sir, that happens to be a duck!" He says, "I know, I was talking to the duck."

Well, I played for another wedding the other day. Yeah, the groom wanted me to give him some advice since I've been married so long. I told him, "Even if the cooing stops with the honeymoon, the billing goes on forever."

Speaking of marriage, my wife's Aunt Aggie is looking for an older gentleman with a strong will---made out to her.

The 1st time _____ visited his girlfriend's home, he waited in the living room while she prepared a snack in the kitchen. Left alone, he noticed a small attractive vase on the mantelpiece. He picked it up & was looking at it when the girl walked back in. He says, "What's this?" She says, "Oh, my Father's ashes are in there." He says, "Oh, I'm sorry!" She says, "Yeah, he's too lazy to go to the kitchen & get an ash tray."

A child asks his father, "How are people born?" Dad says, "Adam & Eve made babies, then there babies became adults & made babies & so on." Then the child went to his Mother, asked her the same question & she told him, "We were monkeys, then we evolved to become like we are now." The child went back to his Father & said, "You lied to me!" His Father said, "No, your Mom was talking about her side of the family."

I went out on the farm to see _____. There he was out in the barn dancing naked around his John Deere. I said, "What in the world are you doing?" He stops dancing & says, "My wife's been ignoring me lately so I talked to my psychiatrist & he said I needed to do something sexy to a tractor."

Joke for an anniversary couple: _____ & ______ were down by the hog lot one day recently & she says, "You know _____ our anniversary's coming up, we oughta butcher a pig." _____ say, "Aw shucks ______, I can't see punishing a hog for something that happened ____ years ago.

I was out walking my dog today & it got away from me & attacked a woman right there in her own front yard. She ran in the house & sent out her husband. Of course I was beside myself & I said; "Sir, how about a settlement, will $50 do?" He said, "Sure, & if you come around next week, I'll give you more!"

You know, my wife didn't get me anything for my birthday this year! So, I confronted her about it & she says, "Well, you didn't use what I got you last year!" I said, "What did you get me last year?" She said, "A funeral plot!"

My Grandson wants to get married so he asked me; "Grandad, how much does it cost to get married?" I said, "I don't know Son, I'm still paying for it."

My wife finally convinced me to sign what's called a 'living will'. It's a document that gives her the right, if I become attached to some mechanical device, to terminate my life. So yesterday, I'm on the exercise bike-----.

I asked my wife, "Where do you want to go for our anniversary?" She says, "Somewhere I have never been!" I told her, "How about the kitchen?"

I don't need your criticism, I've got a wife at home!!

Went on vacation out in California. Early one morning I took a walk along the beach & came upon a bottle with a cork in it. I picked it up, pulled the cork & out came a genie. He says, "For freeing me from the bottle I'll give you any one wish you want, what'll it be?" I had a map in my pocket of the Middle-East, so I unfolded it, showed it to the genie & I said, "I wish to see peace in all these countries!" The genie got a real worried look on his face & I said, "What's wrong?" He says, "Do you realize how many thousands of years these people have been hating & warring with each other?" I said, "Okay, would you like for me to make another wish?" He says, "That would really please me!" I thought for a little bit & I said, "Could you make my wife a wonderful cook?" He says, "Let me see that map again!"

My Grandmother began walking 5 miles a day when she was 82. Now we don't know where in the world she is!

I overheard 2 women talking out here. One says, "For ages I couldn't figure out where my husband was spending his evenings." The other lady says, "Well, you should have hired a private detective!" & the 1st one says, "I didn't have to, I went home early one night & there he was!"

My wife & I hardly ever have a quarrel. We made a rule: If we quarreled, the one who was wrong would walk around the block. My wife hasn't been out of the house since1997!

I call her my 'baseball girl.
() Why do you call her that?
Cause she was throw'd out at home.

I saw an ad in the paper today. It said, "For sale---Complete 25 volume set of Encyclopedia Britannica, latest edition, never used, wife knows everything.

We have a couple here tonight from Tight Wad. They got their luggage mixed up at the airport with another couple from Tight Wad. They both had 'K-Mart' shopping bags.

Mother's Day or Labor Day: I knew a lady from my home town that had 24 children. She never did celebrate Mother's Day. However she did celebrate Labor Day twice a month.

Did you see that pretty girl on the 5th row?
() YEAH

She has nice even teeth. 1, 3, 5, 7 & 9 are missing.

Took my wife out to eat on Mother's Day to the Hyatt Regency Hotel in that Revolving Restaurant. Wouldn't you know it, that revolving mechanism quit working while we were up there & I thought we'd never get done eating, cause we had to get up & move to the next table about every 3 minutes.

There was a man & a very attractive woman sitting next to us & all of a sudden the man starts slowly sliding out of his chair & under the table. Funny thing was, the woman didn't seem to notice as her companion disappeared out of sight. About that time the head waiter came over & said, "Pardon me Madam, but I think your husband is under the table." She said, "No he isn't, my husband just walked through the door."

We finally got rid of our water-bed. I never did like that thing. My wife called it the 'Dead Sea'.

My neighbor came home & told his wife: "I've just been made a vice-president of our company!" She says, "So what, Vice-presidents are a dime-a-dozen, why the supermarket where I shop even has a vice-president in charge of prunes!" Well, he didn't believe her so he called up the supermarket & asked for the Vice-President of Prunes, & the guy asks him, "Packaged or Bulk?"

What do you call an Irishman who knows how to control a wife? A bachelor.

Definition of an Irish husband: He hasn't kissed his wife for 20 years, but he will kill any man who does.

Retirement is nice. This morning my wife said, "Whatcha doin' today?" I said, "Nothin'." She said, "You did that yesterday!" I said, "I wasn't finished."

() I'm gonna give you a driving test ______. If your wife were driving ahead of you & she put her hand out & gestured with her index finger toward the approaching corner, what would it mean?
It would mean the window's open.

It was our anniversary yesterday. We fell in love right before I went to the Navy. I remember writing home to my Mother: Dear Mom, I miss you. I miss Pa. But most of all, I miss the little potty under my bed." A couple weeks later she answered: "Don't worry son, you missed it when you were home too!

Well, I hope I can keep up with you tonight, I was out kinda late last night.
() Did your wife have much to say when you got home?
No, but that didn't keep her from talking for 2 hours!

She was already mad at me though. At supper last night she said, "This is rabbit stew we're having." I said, "I thought so, I just found a hair in mine."

She changes her tune though whenever she needs money. She calls me 'handsome' . She says, "Hand some over!"

You know, there are only 2 ways to handle a woman---& nobody knows either of them.

My neighbor had a terrible accident last week & he was in surgery for

12 hours. They messed up though. They sewed a woman's lips on him & now they can't get him to shut up.

He's the one that didn't have air conditioning until this summer. His wife told him she'd leave him if he didn't get an air conditioner. So he goes to the store & a salesman asked him, "Can I help you?" He said, "Yeah, I want to buy one of them window units." The salesman says, "What size?" He says, "I need one with enough BTU to cool a BUT as big as a TUB."

I just had another fight with the wife. Yeah, when it was over she came to me on her hands & knees. You know what she said? She said, "Come out from under the bed & fight like a man!"

My wife says she knows what Victoria's Secret is. The secret is that nobody older than 30 can fit into their stuff.

I used to do some marriage counseling years ago, but after this I quit. This nice young couple came to me before they got married, only they didn't come in together, they came in individually. The young lady was first, & she said, "I'm real worried about a personal problem I've got now that I'm about to get married." I said, "What's that?" She said, "Well, when I wake up in the morning, I have terribly bad breath." I said, "That's no problem, just keep your mouth closed until you get up & go brush your teeth & use some mouth wash." Then her fiance' came in to see me & he says, "I've got a real problem, my feet stink something terrible when I wake up in the morning." I said, "That's a problem we can overcome, all you have to do is wear socks to bed, get out of bed in the morning, wash your feet or shower & there you are." So they got married & everything went real smooth for about 2 weeks. Then one morning about 4:30am he woke up & found one of his socks was missing. Now folks, he'd been alright if he hadn't panicked, but commenced to thrashing around in the covers lookin' for that sock & he woke her up & she forgot to keep her mouth shut & she says, "What in the world are you a doin'?" & he says, "You done went & swallowed one of my socks!"

My wife came home the other day & found me stalking around with a fly swatter. She asked me, "Killed any yet?" I said, "Yep, 2 males & a female." So she asked me, "How could you tell?" I said, "2 were on a beer can & one was on the telephone."

My wife went to bed before I did last night, so I took her a glass of water & an aspirin. She said, "Why are you bringing me that, I don't have a headache?" I said, "Gotcha!"

One couple in a small town got married to each other 3 times. The town is so small, they keep getting introduced.

() They tell me you married your wife cause her aunt left her a fortune. Well, that ain't so. I'd a married her no matter who'd left it to her.

My Mom & Dad got married to each other twice. Yeah, the 1st time it didn't work out.
() Why'd they get married again?
Oh, he got behind on his alimony payments so she repossessed him.

The lady down the street's been trying to get her husband to quit drinking. Last Halloween she dressed up like the devil, got behind the front door & about midnight he came staggering in the front door & she jumped out & said, "BOO!" He said, "Who're you?" She said, "I'm the devil!" He says, "Shake hands, I married your sister.!"

She's been on a banana & coconut diet. She didn't lose any weight, but she can sure climb a tree like greased lightning!"

She must me half Italian & half Irish. She made potatoes, but she mashed 'em with her feet.

A bald fellow took a seat in a beauty shop. The stylist said, "How can I help you?" The guy says, "I went for a hair transplant, but I couldn't stand the pain. If you can make my hair look like yours without causing me any discomfort, I'll pay you $5000. She said, "No problem, & real quick, she shaved her head.

Women should not have children after 35---35 children are enough.

I love being married. It's so great to find that one special person you want to annoy for the rest of your life.

There's 2 theories to arguing with a woman. Neither one works.

The Mayor of Tightwad has had bad luck with wives. The 1st one left him & the 2nd one won't.

Done your taxes yet? This year the government allows you $1200 for your wife. I'm gonna turn her in before the price goes down.

She gave me her hand, her lips, her heart---I was doing piecework at the time.

Now, she's getting a double-chin. I think it was just too much work for one.

We went to this hotel while we were on our trip & all the rooms were rented except the Bridal Suite. I told the desk clerk, "We've been married ___ years, what're we gonna do with the Bridal Suite?" He says, "Well Sir, I could rent you the Ball Room, but that doesn't mean you have to dance.

You know, bachelors have no idea what married bliss is--& that's true of a lot of married men too!

Did you see that good-lookin girl I was talkin to back there?
() Yeah, she is good lookin'!
She has an upper plate though.
() So, how'd you find that out?
Oh, it just came out in the conversation.

Fifty percent of marriages end up in divorce? Yeah, the rest just fight it out to the bitter end.

There's 2 things you need to know to understand a woman----& nobody knows what either one of them is.

The wife & I went to Branson last week & it was busy. Finally we got a room in this hotel for one night & I came down to pay the bill the next morning. The clerk says, "That'll be $300." I said, "Why so high?" He said, "Well, when you pulled in to the hotel, there was a valet to park your car & carry your bags in." Then I told him, "Sir, we did that ourselves!" He says, "That's your fault, he was there for your." I said, That still seems way too high priced!" He says, "Well, Sir, after you all checked in, there was a fellow who took your bags to the room, unlocked the door, turned the bed down & made you folks comfortable." I said, "Good land man, we did all that ourselves!" He says, "That's your fault, he was there for you." I said, "Well, in that case, you owe me $150!" He said,, "Why would I owe you $150 ?" I said, "After we got settled in, I went down to the 7-11 & got us some soda-pop & chips & while I was gone you were huggin' & kissin' on my wife!" He says, "That's ridiculous, I've never seen, let alone touched your wife!" I said, "That's your fault, she was there for you!"

Saw an ad in the paper today. It said, "For sale-----complete 25 volume set of Encyclopedia Britannica, latest edition, never used. Wife knows everything!"

You know why men don't live as long as women? We don't want to.

I told my wife that it looked like she was drawing her eye-brows too high. She looked surprised.

I've been hearing a lot of complaints about women drivers. I say, If you don't like the way women drive, get off the sidewalk!

My wife & I were setting on the couch the other night & she asked me; "Do you remember when you used to nudge my neck & nibble my ear lobes?" Well, I jumped up & headed out of the room & she says, "Where are you going?" I said, "I'll be right back, I've gotta get my teeth!"

My wife got on me today. She said, "You're always pushing me around & talking behind my back." I said, "What do you expect? You're in a wheel chair!"

A woman was sitting at a bar enjoying an after work cocktail with her girlfriends when a tall, handsome man came in. He was so striking that she couldn't take her eyes off him. So, he noticed her staring at him & he walked directly over to her & whispered in her ear; "I'll do anything, absolutely anything, that you want me to do, no matter how kinky, for $20--on one condition, you have to tell me what you want me to do in just 3 words." She slowly removed a $20 bill from her purse, which she pressed into the guy's hand, along with her address. She looked deeply & passionately into his eyes, barely concealing her anticipation & excitement, & slowly & meaningfully said----"CLEAN MY HOUSE!"

Ran on to a young fellow this week that wants to be on our show. So, I told him I'd need to know some things about him. And he said, "Just so you'll know, I'm single. I don't have anything against marriage. I think marriage is a fine institution. I just ain't ready to be institutionalized."

() WHAT'S _____ SO MAD AT YOU FOR?:
I haven't the slightest idea. We met backstage & we were talking just as friendly as could be, when all of a sudden he flared up & tried to hit me.
() WHAT WERE YOU TALKING ABOUT?
Oh, just ordinary small talk. I remember he said; "I always kiss my wife 3 or 4 times every day."
() AND, WHAT DID YOU SAY?
I said, "I know at least a dozen men who do the same---& then he had a fit!

I was a traveling salesman on the way to Chicago in the winter time & I had a lower bunk in a Pullman car. There was a young lady on an upper bunk & she woke me up about 3:00am in the morning. She says, "Mr., I'm cold, would you get me a blanket?" I said, "Young lady are you married?" She said, "No." I said, "How would you like to pretend you're married?" She says, "Oh, that sounds like fun!" I said, "Good, get up & get your own blanket!"

Here's a love story about Ralph & Edna. Now Ralph & Edna were both patients in a mental hospital. One day while they were walking past the hospital swimming pool, Ralph suddenly jumped into the deep end. He sank to the bottom & stayed there. Edna promptly jumped in, dived to the bottom & pulled him out. When the head nurse became aware of Edna's heroic act she immediately ordered her to be discharged from the hospital, as she now considered her to be mentally stable. So the nurse went to tell Edna. She said, "Edna, I have good news & bad news. The good news is, you're being discharged because you had the sense to save the person you love. The bad news is, Ralph hung himself in the bathroom with his bathrobe belt right after you saved him. I'm sorry, but he's dead." Edna says, "He didn't hang himself, I put him there to dry. How soon can I go home?"

Our anniversary's coming up in a week or so. I guess you might say I married Miss Right. I just didn't know her 1st name was Always

---

Lady down the street hears a knock on the door just as she gets out of the shower. She can't find a towel, so she goes to the door & says, "Who is it?" A man says, "The blind man!" So, she figures, what can it hurt & she opens the door & says, "How can I help you?" He says, "I'm the blind man, where do you want these Venetian Blinds?"

My wife & I've been having short-term memory problems, so we went to this Dr. we read about & the program he put us on really works good.
() I'D LIKE TO SEE THAT DR. TOO, WHAT'S HIS NAME?
Help me with this. I need the name of a flower---it has a long stem---& thorns.
() A ROSE?
Yeah, that's it. Hey Rose, What's the name of that Dr.?"

A man knocks on Heaven's gate wanting to get into Heaven. St. Peter asks him, "Did you die a natural death or a violent death?" The man says, "Well, it's like this. I live on the 13th floor of the Regency Arms Apartments in Greenville, S.C.. I came home off the road as a traveling salesman, I got near our apartment door, I smelled cigar smoke, I opened the door & there was my wife standing near an open window. I looked out the window & saw a man on the 12th floor balcony smoking a cigar. I went into a rage, picked up our refrigerator, threw it out the window, it fell on the guy, killed him, I was arrested, convicted, executed & here I am. St. Peter says, "Whew! Stand over there! Next: " Did you die a natural death or a violent death?" The guy said, "St. Peter, I live on the 12th floor of The Regency Arms Apartments in Greenville, S.C.. It was a hot night, our air conditioner quit, so I stepped out on our balcony to smoke a cigar & the last thing I remember was a refrigerator falling on me!" St. Peter says, "Good Lord, stand over there! Next." Did you die a natural death or a violent death?" "Well, it's like this, I was inside of this refrigerator!"

I was staying in a Motel when the maid knocked on the door. She said, "Can I come in & clean up?" I said, "Sure, I don't care!" So she came in & took a shower.

A couple expecting a baby lived in the middle of Wyoming, 30 miles from town. One afternoon the wife said to her husband, "It's time!" So the guy picked up the phone, called his neighbor & said, "Get over here right away! Help me get some rags, soap & hot water!" The neighbor says, "Well, is she gonna have the baby there?" The future father says, "Naw, we're gonna wash the pickup truck so we can take her to the hospital."

My wife just bought one of those thigh masters they were advertising on TV.
() HAS SHE LOST ANY WEIGHT?
No, but she can crack a walnut with her knees.

A couple celebrating their 50th wedding anniversary had many well-wishers stop by to congratulate them. After all their guests had left, the two settled into their recliners. The man said, "Mother, our marriage is tried & true." She replies, "What's that you say? You know I can't hear without my hearing aid." He says, "I said, our marriage is tried & true." She says, "Oh, that's all right, I'm tired of you too!"

() MY WIFE DOESN'T UNDERSTAND ME, DOES YOURS?
I don't know, I've never even heard her mention your name!"

My wife has the worst memory I ever heard of.
() FORGETS EVERYTHING EH?
No, remembers everything.

Did you see Debbie's boyfriend?
() YEAH, WHERE DID HE MEET HER?
Oh, they met in a revolving door & he's been going around with her ever since.

One of the great mysteries of life is how the idiot that your daughter married can be the father of the smartest grandchildren in the whole world.

One of the most difficult things in life for me is to try to buy something for my wife. Like, the other day I went to a department store & I told the clerk I'd like to buy a pair of stockings for my wife & the clerk said, "Sheer?" I said, "No, she's at home."

When I first met my wife, she was a schoolteacher. I used to write her passionate love letters---& she'd send them back with the grammer & punctuation corrected. I must be the only man in the world who returned from his honeymoon & received a report card. It said, "Larry is neat & friendly & shows a keen interest in fun & games."

My wife used to feed me dehydrated food---right out of the package. One day I went out in the rain & put on 73 pounds.

Did I tell you my wife's training for congress. She's always bringing new bills to the house.

() MY WIFE DOESN'T UNDERSTAND ME, DOES YOURS?
I don't know, I've never heard her even mention your name.

_____ & his wife have been married for 25 years, so while back she asked him if he wanted to renew their vows. He got so excited--he thought they'd expired.

I had bad luck with girls too. One time a girl phoned me & said, "Come on over, there's nobody home." I went over--nobody was home.

Last night I dreamt I was stuck on a deserted island with 3 beautiful women, each beckoning me to come to her.
() WOW! WHICH ONE DID YOU GO TO FIRST?
I couldn't go to any of them, I told you I was stuck.

My wife says, "Men are like parking spaces; All the good ones are taken, the rest are handicapped.

Trains run a lot faster nowadays than they did when I was young. I was a traveling salesman years ago & I got on this slow train. I said, "Conductor, can't you go any faster that this?" He said, "Yeah, but I gotta stay with this train." Pretty soon we stopped on the tracks. I said, "What's wrong conductor?" He says, "There's a cow on the track!" We got going & in about 20 minutes we stopped again. I said, "Now what's wrong conductor?" He said, "Well, we caught up with that cow again." Finally when we got fairly close to where we were going, a young fellow ran up to the conductor & says, "Quick, do something, my wife's about to have a baby!" The conductor says, "Young man what ever possessed you to bring your wife on this train in that condition?" & the young fellow says, "Well, she wasn't in that condition when we got on the train!!!" I tell you folks, trains were slow back then.

I remember another time I was on a business trip by train & I had a lower berth in a Pullman car. I was just about to get to sleep when the young lady in the upper berth said, "Would you get me a blanket? I'm cold." I said, "Are you married?" She said, "No." I said, "How would you like to pretend you're married?" She says, "Oh, I think that would be fun!" So I said, "Okay then, get up & get your own blanket!"

She said, "Before we got married, you told me you were well off." I said, "I was, & I didn't know it!"

Yeah, if they'd have had electric blankets when I was a lad, I'd never got married.

_____ (COUGH, COUGH, COUGH)
My cousin had a cough like yours & he died. Of course he was hidin' under his neighbor's bed at the time.

The manager of a megastore came to check on his new salesman. "How many customers did you serve today?" The new guy says, "One." Manager says, "One, only one? How much was the sale?" Salesman says, "$58,334." Manager asks, "Well, how'd you do that?" Salesman says, "1st I sold the man a fish hook, then I sold him a rod & reel. Then I ask him where he was planning to fish, & he said, "Down the coast." So, I suggested he'd need a boat & he bought that 20 foot runabout. When he said his Volkswagon might not pull it, I took him to the automotive department & sold him a full size SUV." The boss says, "You sold all that to a guy who came in for a fish hook?" The salesman says, "No, he actually came in for a bottle of aspirin for his wife's migraine. I told him, "You're weekend's shot. You should probably go fishing."

When I came home last night, my wife greeted me with a triple strand of natural pearls around her neck.
() CHOKER?
No, but I wanted to.

For Christmas she wanted a mink. I wanted a new car. We compromised. We bought a fur coat, but we keep it in the garage.

She went to the Dr. yesterday & asked him, "Dr. what should I take when I'm run down?" He says, "The license number!"

I guess we don't communicate very well at our house. I said, "Your Mother has been living with us for 5 years now, don't you think it's about time she gets out on her own & makes a life for herself?" My wife says, "My Mother! I thought she was your Mother!"

A woman applies for a job at a citrus grove. The foreman asks her; "Do you have any experience picking lemons?" She says, "Well, I've been divorced 3 times!"

Did I tell you; My neighbor won a trip for 2 to Hawaii.
() DID HE TAKE HIS WIFE?
No, he went twice.

Do you remember your 1st date? I knew my 1st date wasn't gonna go so well right from the start.
() WHAT WAS YOUR 1ST CLUE THAT IT WAS GONNA BE A LOUSY DATE?
Well, when I showed up, she was wearing this 'T' shirt that said, "If you can read this, you're too close!"

We went over to _____'s for supper last night. We sat down to the meal & _____ said, "The best thins I cook are meatloaf & peach cobbler." I said, "Which is this?"

I'm not about to say what kind of cook she is, but she's got her an oven that flushes.

She must be half Italian & half Irish cause she made potatoes, but she mashed them with her feet!

When I was young man I dated a girl with a wooden leg. But I broke it off. She took me to court, but she didn't win. She didn't have a leg to stand on. Her name was Ilene, but I just called her Peg.

I overheard 2 ladies talking before the show. One said, "I wonder if my husband will love me when my hair is grey?" The other lady says, "Why not? He's loved you through 3 shades already."

When I was a young man, I was in love with a twin.
() DID YOU EVER KISS THE WRONG ONE BY MISTAKE?
Are you kidding, her brother had a mustache!

In all the years I've been married, I've never stopped being romantic. If my wife finds out--I'm dead.

Office manager goes to an office party & his secretary gets drunk, so he takes her home. He didn't tell his wife because she's insanely jealous of him. That night he & his wife go out to dinner. He stops at a traffic light & something slides out from under the seat & it's a high-heeled shoe. He throws it out the window while his wife is distracted. They get to the restaurant & his wife is rummaging around under her seat. He says, "What's wrong Dear?" She says, "I can't find my shoe!"

Did you know that _____ was engaged to a nudist? Yeah, but they broke up.
() WHY?
Oh, they decided they were seeing too much of each other.

A 330 pound man went to his minister & says, "I'm so depressed & I can't get any dates. I've tried everything to lose weight to no avail. The preacher says, "Be dressed in a jogging outfit at 8:00am every morning." The next morning his doorbell rings at 8:00am & it's a beautiful woman. She says, "The pastor says to tell you, "If you can catch me, you can have me." So off they went jogging every morning. After several months, he'd lost an appreciable amount of weight & he was getting closer every day to catching her. One day, he almost caught her & he thought, 'tomorrow I'll have her' . The next morning the door bell rang & he opened the door to a 300 pound woman. She says, "The pastor told me, 'If I can catch you, I can have you'"

Did I tell you my Grandson's getting married in July? I've been giving some advice to help make the marriage last:
Whenever you're wrong---admit it. Whenever you're right----shut up.

One day, a man came home & was greeted by his wife dressed in a very sexy nightie. She says, "Tie me up & you can do anything you want." So, he tied her up & went golfing.

With all the new technology regarding fertility recently, a 65 year-old friend of ours was able to give birth. When she was discharged from the hospital & went home, we went to visit. Shirley said, "May we see the new baby?" She said, "Not yet, I'll make some coffee & we can visit a while first. 30 minutes had passed & I asked, "May we see the baby now?" She said, "Not yet." So I said, "Well, when can we see the baby?" She said, "When he cries!" I said, "When he cries, why do I have to wait 'til he cries?" She says, "Cause, I forgot where I put him, Okay?"

I just got off the phone with a friend living in Northern Mn. Near the Canadian border. She said that since early this morning the snow has been nearly waist high & is still falling. The temperature is dropping way below zero & the North wind is increasing to near gale force. Her husband has done nothing but look through the kitchen window & just stare. She says, "If it gets much worse, she may have to let him in."

So this lady was having an affair with a pest-control inspector. One afternoon her husband came home unexpectedly & found the man hiding in the closet. "Who are you?" he husband demanded. "An inspector for 'Bugs-Be-Gone' ", the guy says. "What are you doing in there?" The inspector says, "Looking for moths." "And where are your clothes?" The inspector looked down at himself & said, "Those tricky little devils!"

I bumped into a woman out here on the sidewalk & I said, "Oh, pardon me." She said, "That's quite alright, you know, you look like my 5th husband." I said, "Your 5th husband! How many times have you been married?" She said, "Four."

Henry goes to confession & says, "Bless me Father, for I have sinned. Last night I was with 7 different women." The priest says, "Take 7 lemons, squeeze them into a glass & drink the juice." Henry says, "Father, will that cleanse me of my sins?" The priest says, "No, but it'll wipe that silly grin off your face."

I've got a neighbor that buys all of his wife's clothes, even her underwear. He went into the Jones Store to the Ladies Underwear Department & tells the clerk, "I want to buy a bra for my wife." The clerk asks him, "What size?" He says, "6 & 7/8." She asked him, "Sir, how did you measure that?" He says, "With my hat."

I came upon a wreck on the way here. There was a man pinned under his car, so I made conversation with him while the ambulance & rescue team was comin'. I asked him, "Are you married?" He says, "No, this is the worst fix I've ever been in!"

My son's been out of town on his job & his wife being the romantic sort, sent him a text: "If you are sleeping--send me your dreams. If you are laughing--send me your smile. If you are eating--send me a bite. If you are drinking--send me a sip. If you are crying--send me your tears. I love you." My son, the typical non-romantic, replied; "I'm on the toilet, please advise."

And God promised men that good & obedient wives would be found in all corners of the world. Then he made the Earth round---& laughed & laughed & laughed.

Know what I did before I got married? Anything I wanted to.

John was on his deathbed & gasped pitifully, "Give me one last request, Dear." His wife says, "O course John." He says, "6 months after I die, I want you to marry Bob." She says, "But I thought you hated Bob!" With his last breath John said, "I do!"

I got stopped by a police officer for driving without a tail light while we were on vacation & I guess he could tell I was a little distressed. He said, "Don't take it so hard, it's only a minor offense." I said, "That's not the point, what worries me is, what happened to my trailer & my wife?"

I can think back to the years when I had dark brown hair. I had a little sports car with a stick shift & I picked up my girlfriend up in Carrollton. We got to Waverly & I shifted down at a stop sign & my hand slipped off the gearshift & on to her leg. I said, "Oh, I'm sorry." She said, "That's okay, you can go further if you want to." So I drove on to Marshall.

This new technology is wonderful, but it can sure get you in trouble. There's a young couple that hadn't vacationed together for awhile. He's a traveling salesman & took a business flight to Florida. After he settled in, he decided to 'E-mail' his wife, but he got one digit wrong & the 'E-mail' ended up on the computer screen of a lady whose husband had died 2 days before. The family found her passed out on the floor in front of the computer & when they saw the screen, it said, "Honey, I made it here fine. Look forward to seeing you tomorrow. It sure is hot down here."

() HEY, I HEAR YOU & YOUR WIFE HAVE BEEN FIGHTING AGAIN---LIQUOR I SUPPOSE??
No, she licked me this time.

You know why most women don't play football? It's because 11 of them would never wear the same outfit in public.

We were back in the dressing room before the show & I asked ____. "How long have you been wearing that bra?" He said, "Ever since my wife found it in the glove department."

A man was stranded on a deserted island for years. One day he was relaxing on the beach when a beautiful woman in a wet suit swims up on the beach, unzips one of her pockets, pulls out a Cuban cigar & says, "How long has it been since you've had a good cigar?" He says, "Oh that would be wonderful!" So, she lit it up & gave it to him. Then she asked him, "How long has it been since you've had a candy bar?" He says, "Wow, I'd die for a Baby Ruth candy bar!" She pulled one out of another one of those pockets, gave it to him & he was in hog heaven. Then she said, "How long has it been since you've played around?" He says, "Don't tell me you've got a set of golf clubs in there too?"

Life's all about making the best of a bad situation. For instance years ago my Grandfather took a wagon load of produce to town & made more than he'd expected, so he decided to buy himself a new suit of clothes, hide them under the wagon seat to surprise Grandma. On the way home, he stopped in the middle of this river bridge. He said, "Whoa, Maude, let's put on these new duds & surprise the woman." He threw his old clothes into the river, but when he reached under the wagon seat, his new clothes weren't there. So, he sat there & thought a bit. Then he said, "Giddap Maude, we'll surprise her anyhow!"

A lady down the street went to the police station with her next door neighbor to report her husband was missing. The policeman asked for a description. She said, "He's 35 years old, 6'4", has dark eyes, dark wavy hair, an athletic build, weighs 185#, is soft spoken & is good to the children." The next door neighbor protested; "Your husband is 5'4", chubby, bald, has a big mouth & is mean to your children!" The wife replied, "Well, I don't want him back!"

What do you call a woman who always knows where her husband is? A widow.

Say, do you know your dog bit my Mother-in-law yesterday?
() NO, IS THAT SO? WELL, I SUPPOSE YOU'LL SUE ME FOR DAMAGES?
Not at all. What'll you take for that dog?

My wife hit the ceiling yesterday. She's always been a lousy shot.

She's so fussy, she even irons shoelaces. I get up in the middle of the night to go to the bathroom, I come back & the bed's made.

You know what a bachelor is? It's a guy who never made the same mistake once.

A while back ____'s wife was looking kind of peeked, so he took her to the Dr. The Dr. checked her all over & they were all in the examination room & the Doc was scratching his head for a diagnosis. Finally the Dr. leaned over & kissed ____ on the cheek. In a manner of 30 seconds she was a picture of health she is today. _____ says, "Gee Doc. What's the deal here?" The Dr. says, "Well, _____, your wife needs to be kissed at least twice a week." _____ says, "Well, I guess I could bring her in on Tuesdays & Thursdays."

This cold weather's bothering me. My wife's been pulling the covers off of me in the middle of the night. Yeah, the worst part of that is we sleep in twin beds.

Once upon a time 2 brooms fell in love & decided to get married. Just before the ceremony, the bride broom informed the groom broom that she was expecting a little whisk broom. Well, the groom broom was aghast. He says, "How is this possible? We've never even swept together!"

() IS YOUR WIFE WITH YOU TONIGHT?
Oh yes, it's better to have your wife with you than after you.

____'s single, but he's advertising. He put an ad in the paper titled: "Looking For A Wife". He got 500 replies, all from guys that said he could have theirs.

An old woman was sipping on a glass of wine, while sitting on the patio with her husband. She says, "I love you so much, I don't know how I could ever live without you." Her husband asks, "Is that you, or the wine talking?" She says, "It's me--talking to the wine.

Went to my neighbor's 25th wedding anniversary party this afternoon. The husband seemed very sad, so I tried to console him. He explained, "On our 5th anniversary I wanted to kill my wife but my lawyer told me I'd get 20 years. Just think, today I coulda been a free man!"

My wife lost her glasses the other day. She spent 20 minutes nagging the coat rack.

Now she isn't talking to me & I'm in no mood to interrupt her.

I wouldn't object to my wife having the last word if only she'd get to it.

Hey Boss, we're doing some heavy housecleaning at home next Saturday & my wife needs me to help with the attic & the garage, moving & hauling stuff.

() NOW ____, WE'RE SHORT-HANDED NEXT WEEK SO I CAN'T GIVE YOU THE NIGHT OFF!"
Thanks ______, I knew I could count on you!

Did I tell you what happened at home? The other night my wife came into our bedroom & said, "Take off my blouse." & I did. Then she said, "Take off my skirt." & I did. Then she said, "Take off my pantyhose." & I did. Then she said, "Now, don't let me catch you wearing my clothes again!"

() HOW LONG HAVE YOU BEEN MARRIED ______?
30 odd years.
() WHY DO YOU SAY 30 ODD YEARS?
Just wait 'til you meet my wife!

But she worships me. Yeah, she places burnt offerings before me every evening.

I have a terrible headache & I want something to cure it.
() NOW, YOU DON'T NEED ANY MEDICINE. I HAD A TOOTHACHE YESTERDAY & I WENT HOME & MY LOVING WIFE KISSED ME & SO CONSOLED ME THAT THE PAIN SOON PASSED AWAY. WHY DON'T YOU TRY THE SAME?
I think I will, is your wife at home now?

When I was about 15 I had a crush on 3 neighbor girls. They were beautiful. Out of a scale of 1 to 10, they were about 17 & a halfs.
They didn't know I existed cause I was 15, & they were 16, 17 & 18 years old. Folks, because their folks were maybe a little over protective, they'd never had a date. Finally, they talked their parents into letting them have a date on a Saturday night & the old man goes out on the front porch swing & sets there with his shotgun across his knees. The 1st boy shows

up & says, "My name is Freddie, I'm here to pick up Betty, we're gonna go steady, is she ready?" They leave. Then the 2nd boy shows up & says, "My name is Joe, I'm here to pick up Flo, we're going to the show, is she ready to go?" They left. The 3rd guy shows up & says, "My name is Rex!" & the old man shot him.

Two times a week, my wife & I go to a nice restaurant, have a little beverage, good food & companionship. She goes on Tuesdays, I go on Fridays.

Bought the missus a hamster skin coat last week. Took her to the fair last night, & it took me 3 hours to get her off the Ferris wheel.

A Kansas tornado hit a farmhouse just before dawn one morning. It lifted the roof off, picked up the twin beds on which the farmer & his wife slept, & set them down gently in the next county. Suddenly the wife began to cry. He says, "Don't be scared Mary, we're not hurt." She continued to cry & said, "I'm not scared, I'm happy 'cause this is the 1st time in 14 years we've been out together."

Shirley & I were talking last night; I said, "Every time I chastise you, you never fight back. How do you manage your anger like that?" She says, "I clean the toilet seat." I said, "How does that help?" She says, "I use your toothbrush!"

I'm gonna do a survey tonight. Now you women get your elbows ready, cause you may have to use them. Ready? Those men who're in love with their wives, stand up. Very good. Now, those women who're in love with their husbands, stand up. Okay. Now then, those men who're in love with someone else's wife, keep your seat.

() GEORGE IS MAD AT YOU LARRY!
Why?
() BECAUSE OF WHAT YOU SAID ABOUT HIS GIRLFREND. YOU SAID, "SHE HAD A WART ON HER KNEE!"
Oh, no, I didn't say that!
() WELL, WHAT DID YOU SAY?
I said, "It felt like she had a wart on her knee."

You know, sometimes it doesn't pay to be nice to people. I was at a church meeting the other night when a Mother came in late, sat down beside us & apologized. She said, "I'm sorry I'm late, I've been having a lot of trouble with my sitter." I said, "I know how you feel, I have hemorrhoids myself!"

It's funny how times have changed. On the way here, I saw a girl in the nude & never gave it a 2nd thought---I was too busy with the 1st thought.

Everything's wonderful. My wife & I've finally become totally compatible. Last night we both had a headache!

This cold weather's been bothering me. My wife's been pulling the covers off of me in the middle of the night. The worst part is, we sleep in twin beds!

I'm glad to see Winter coming again. Did you know that married couples have fewer arguments in the Winter?
() WHY'S THAT?
That's cause a lot of husbands wear ear-muffs in the Winter.

Course I did have this one big fight with my wife last week about whether it's alright to spend one night out with the boys.--I don't think she should!

At Sunday School they were teaching how God created everything including human beings. Little Johnny seemed especially interested when they told him how Eve was created out of on of Adam's ribs. Later in the week his Mother noticed him lying down as though he were ill & she said, "What's the matter Johnny?" He says, "I have a pain in my side, I think I'm gonna have a wife!"

A nice, calm & respectable lady went into the pharmacy, walked up to the pharmacist, looked straight into his eyes, & said, "I'd like to buy some cyanide." The pharmacist asked, "Why in the world do you need cyanide?" She says, "I need it to poison my husband." The pharmacist's eyes got as big as saucers & he explained, "Lord have mercy! I can't give you cyanide to kill your husband, that's against the law, I'd lose my license! They'll throw us both in jail! Absolutely not! You cannot have any cyanide!" So, the lady reached into her purse & pulled out a picture of her husband in bed with the pharmacist's wife. The pharmacist looked at the picture & said, "Oh, you didn't tell me you had a prescription!"

So this couple had gone together for several years & they finally got married. After the honeymoon, he was cleaning one of his antique cars for an upcoming show. She was watching him quite a while & she says, "Honey, I've just been thinking, now that we're married, maybe it's timea you quit spending all your time out here in the garage & you probably should consider selling all your cars along with your gun collection. So, he gets a horrified look on his face. She says, "Darling, what's wrong?" He says, "There for a minute you were starting to sound like my ex-wife." She screams, "Ex-wife, you never told me you were married before!" He says, "I wasn't!"

My friend's been married 3 times. He says, "Instead of getting married again, he's gonna find a woman he doesn't like & just give her a house.

When I was in high-school, I had a buddy named Hugh. Now Hugh was a good friend. He came from a very poor family & they ran a saw mill. When Hugh was about 12 years old he was working at the saw mill & got a splinter in his eye. The eye got infected & they had to remove it. Now Hugh had an uncle that was good at whittling & that uncle whittled Hugh an eye. His Mother painted that wooden eye & from 10 feet, it looked real, but kids in school would make fun of him relentlessly. Because of that, he wouldn't date girls & pretty much kept to himself except for me. When we got into our senior year & it got close to Prom time, I started working on Hugh to get him to go to the Prom. Finally, I got him to go, but no way was he gonna get a date. So, there we were setting like wallflowers. The band was playing & it was 11:45pm. I said, Hugh you ought to dance at least one time, the band's gonna quit in a few minutes. He said, "No, she'd probably make fun of my wooden eye." I said, "See that heavy set girl over there? She's just as sensitive about being overweight as you are about your eye, now go over there & ask her to dance." So, he sidled up to her & said, "Care to dance?" She said, "Would I!" He said, "Fatty-fatty-fatty!"

We had a power failure at our house this week. My wife lost her voice.

() _____ I'M SORRY TO HEAR THAT YOUR WIFE'S MIND IS COMPLETELY GONE.
I'm not surprised, she's been giving me a piece of it every day for _____ years!

My niece called the builder of their new house to come over & examine the poor workmanship. She told him, "It's the most poorly-constructed thing I've ever seen, the vibrations are so bad that when a train goes by

4 blocks away it nearly shakes me out of bed! Just lie there & you'll see!" He said, "Now, that's hard to believe, but he accepted her challenge. He had just stretched himself out on the bed when my niece's husband came home. Of course he said, "What are you doing in my wife's bed?" & The poor contractor trembled & said, "Would you believe that I'm waiting for a train?"

My wife bought a new line of expensive cosmetics, guaranteed to make her look years younger. After a lengthy sitting before the mirror applying the 'miracle' products, she asked me, "Darling, honestly, what age would you say I am?" So, I looked her over carefully & I said, "Judging from your skin--20, your hair,--18, & your figure--25." She says, "Oh, you flatterer!" I said, "Hey, wait a minute! I haven't added them up yet!"

My wife ran off with my best friend. I sure do miss him.

Oh well, the only time we went out together was when the gas stove exploded.

I love the Alps. They've given me some of my happiest moments.
() WHY? YOU'VE NEVER EVEN BEEN IN SWITZERLAND!
No, but my wife has.

() WHO ARE YOU STARING AT ?
I beg your pardon, but if it wasn't for the mustache, that lady would look just like my wife!
() BUT THAT LADY DOESN'T HAVE A MUSTACHE!
No, but my wife has.

Do you know why most after-dinner-speakers are men? Because, women can't wait that long!

Say, do you know your dog bit my Mother-in-law yesterday?
() NO, IS THAT SO? WELL, I SUPPOSE YOU'LL SUE ME FOR DAMAGES?
Not at all. What'll you take for that dog?

My neighbor's wife met him at the door wearing a sheer negligee. Unfortunately, she was just coming home.

Why did the Amish couple get a divorce? He was driving her buggy.

_____'s boss said, "You're a liar, you took a day off to bury your Mother-in-law & I met her last night in the supermarket." _____ says, "Oh, I didn't say she was dead. I just said I would like to go to her funeral."

My neighbor's wife told him, "I'm sick of the whole thing. You won't work & all you do is mope around the house & bellyache all day. I'm getting a divorce!" He says, "Oh, you don't really mean that, you're just trying to cheer me up!"

So, the next day he goes to a bar & says, "Give me a double!" The guy next to him asks, "Why are you so upset?" He says, "Cause, I just had words with my wife & she move out." A guy at the end of the bar looked up from his drink & said, "Do you remember exactly what those words were?"

I'm glad my wife & I get along so well. Like the other day she says, "Let's go out tonight & have some fun." I said, "Okay, but if you get home first, leave the porch light on!"

I overheard 2 ladies talking while ago. One of them had recently had triplets & she told the other lady that triplets happened only once in

15,000 times. Her friend says, "My goodness, how did you find time to do your housework?"

While I was out with some other guys the other night, a burglar broke into our house.
() DID HE GET ANYTHING?
I'll say he did, my wife thought it was me coming home!

_____'s boyfriend told her, "If you don't marry me, I'll jump off a 300 foot cliff." & she said, "That sounds like a lot of bluff to me!"

He says, "I always kiss the stamps on your letters cause I know that your lips have touched them. She says, "Oh dear, & to think that I wet them on Fido's nose."

My cousin told a young lady many years ago, "If you refuse me, I shall die." Well, she refuse him, he kept his word & 60 years later he died.

_______went deer hunting & he was out there in the woods & he came upon this beautiful girl & she says, "What are you doin'?" He says, "I'm huntin' game." She says, "Well, I'm game." So, he shot her!

My neighbor's in a heap of trouble. A cop pulled him over & said, "I saw you put your seatbelt on when I pulled you over, I'm gonna give you a ticket for not wearing a seatbelt." My neighbor denied it, he said, "I had it on all the time!" & the cop said, "No, you didn't!" & they argued back & forth 'til my neighbor's wife got sick of it. She said, "Officer, I learned a long time ago, never argue with my husband when he's been drinking!"

A good salesman is a fellow who can convince his wife that she looks fat in a fur coat.

A retiring farmer needed to get rid of his farm animals, so he went to every house in this little town. To the houses where the man is boss, he gave a horse. To the houses where the woman is boss, a chicken was given. He got to the end of the last street & saw a couple out gardening. He asked, "Who's the boss around here?" The man says, "I am." The farmer says, "I have a black horse & a brown horse, which one would you like?" The man thought a minute & said, "The black one." & the man's wife said, "No, no, no, get the brown one!" & the farmer said, "Here's your chicken."

A man walked into a bar looking sad, & the bartender asked him, "What's the matter?" The man says, "My wife & I had a fight, & she told me she wasn't going to speak to me for a month, & the month's up today!"

A young woman saw a funeral procession going by. There was a black hearse, followed by an older woman leading a pit-bull on a leash, & after that was another hearse, & behind that was a line of about 200 women walking single file. The young woman walked up to the older woman & said, "I'm sorry to intrude on your moment of grief, but I can't help asking, whose funeral is it?" The women says, "Well, my husband is in that hearse up there. The pit-bull killed him when it discovered him with his girlfriend, she's in that hearse back there." The young woman asked, "Can I borrow that dog?" The older woman replied, "Get in line!"

() DID YOUR WIFE HAVE MUCH TO SAY WHEN YOU GOT HOME LAST NIGHT?
No, but that didn't keep her from talking for two hours.

A married couple, both 60 years old, were celebrating their 35th anniversary. During their party, a fairy appeared to congratulate them & grant them each one wish. The wife wanted to travel around the world. The fairy waved her wand & poof---the wife had tickets in her hand for a world cruise. Next, the fairy asked the husband what he wanted. He said, "I wish I had a wife 30 years younger than me." So, poof---the husband was 90.

My wife & I can't agree on a vacation, I wanta go to Bermuda & she wants to go with me.

She doesn't treat me the way she should---& I'm thankful.

Oh, it's true, we fight, but we've never gone to bed mad. Course, one year we were up for 3 months.

The formula for a happy marriage is the same as the one for living in California. When you find a fault, don't dwell on it!

I overheard 2 ladies talking while ago. One of 'em had recently had triplets & she told the other lady that triplets happened only once in 15,000 times. Her friend says, "My goodness, how did you ever find time to do your housework?"

As a kid, I had trouble finding myself cause my parents were always telling me to 'Get Lost'. Every family tree has some sap in it.

We had 10 kids in our family. I never slept alone 'til I got married.

() SAY, HOW'S YOUR WIFE _____?
Oh, she's breathtaking. Every time she stops talking, she takes a breath.

Did I tell you my Grandson's getting married in July? I've been giving some advice to help make the marriage last:
1. Whenever you're wrong---admit it. 2. Whenever you're right---shut up.

I overheard 2 ladies talking. One says, "Does your husband lie awake at night?" & the other one says, "Yes, & he lies in his sleep too!

My grandson asked me the other day, "Grandad, did Edison make the 1st talking machine?" I said, "No, son, God made the 1st talking machine, but Edison made the 1st one that could be cut off."

() SAY, WHAT WERE YOU & YOUR WIFE FIGHTING ABOUT THE OTHER NIGHT?
Oh, she was trying to drive a nail in the wall with a hair brush & I said, "You can't drive that nail with that brush."
() IS THAT ALL YOU SAID?
Well, I added, "Why don't you use your head?"

You can tell a lot about a woman's mood just by her hands. If they're holding a gun, she's probably very angry.

A woman's prayer: Dear Lord, I pray for wisdom, to understand a man, love to forgive him, & patience for his moods. Because Lord, if I pray for strength, I'll just beat him to death.

A man walked into a super market & bought a loaf of bread, a pint of milk, & a frozen dinner for one. The woman at the checkout said,

"You're single aren't you?" The man says, "Yeah, how did you guess?" She said, "Because, you're ugly.

I cleaned the attic with the wife last week. Now I can't get the cobwebs out of her hair.

A husband & wife are talking; She asks, "What would you do if I died? Would you get married again?
He says, "Definitely not!
"Why not, don't you like being married?
"Of course I do!"
"Then why wouldn't you remarry?"
"Okay, okay, I'd get married again"
"Would you live in our house?"
"Sure, it's a great house!"
"Would you sleep with her in our bed?"
"Where else would we sleep?"
"Would you let her drive my car?"
"Probably, it's almost new."
"Would you take her golfing with you?"
"Yes, those are always good times."
"Would she use my clubs?"
"No, she's left handed."

I'm gonna see if I can get my wife on the show here.
() WELL, WHAT CAN SHE DO?
Oh, for one thing, she does bird imitations---she watches me like a hawk!

You know bachelors have no idea what married bliss is---& that's true of a lot of married men too.

Our next door neighbors are getting a divorce because of illness. They're sick of each other.

Right now my wife isn't talking to me---& I'm in no mood to interrupt her.

My wife is really against smoking. Yesterday she spent 3 hours trying to convince a fellow to stop smoking. She said, "Just look at the tips of your fingers, they're yellow!" He said, "I know, I'm Chinese!"

() I HEARD YOUR WIFE CAME TO YOU ON HER HANDS & KNEES YESTERDAY.
Yeah, she did. She dared me to come out from under the bed & fight like a man.

My wife & I have a joint checking account.
() ISN'T THAT HARD TO KEEP STRAIGHT?
No, I put in the money & she takes it out.

Did you ever play 'Spin-The-Bottle' when you were a kid? I used to play. A girl would spin the bottle, & if the bottle pointed to you when it stopped, the girl would either kiss you or give you a quarter. By the time I was 14, I owned my own home.

When my oldest son was about 3 we were having a violent thunderstorm & Shirley was tucking him into bed & she was about to turn off the light when he asked with a tremor in his voice, "Mommy, will you sleep with me tonight?" She says, "I can't Marty, I have to sleep in Daddy's room." & Marty says, "The big sissy."

Yeah, Marty's always been a trouble-maker. One day his teacher caught him making faces at some other kids on the playground. So she went over to him & said, "Marty when I was a child, I was told that if I made ugly faces, it could freeze & would stay like that." Marty said, "Well Mrs. Smith, you can't say you weren't warned."

There's no better time for me to give marital advice than around Valentines Day. So here goes: There are 2 times when a man doesn't understand a woman---before marriage & after marriage.

So this couple died & went to Heaven. They were strolling around & the wife says: "Look how beautiful it is, with all the trees, flowers & grass & the air's so fresh & clean." & He says, "Yeah, & we'd a been here 10 years sooner if you hadn't fed us that oat bran."

A woman has the last word in any argument. Anything a man says after that is the beginning of a new argument.

() IS IT TRUE THAT MARRIED MEN LIVE LONGER THAN SINGLE MEN?
Naw, it only seems longer.

() WELL, DO YOU BELIEVE IN LOVE AT FIRST SIGHT?
I think it saves a lot of time.

She asked me today; "Do you love me still?" I said, "I might if you'd stay still long enough!"

() DIDN'T YOU TELL ME YOU"VE BEEN MARRIED ALL THESE YEARS & YOUR MOTHER-IN-LAW'S ONLY BEEN TO VISIT YOU ONCE?

Yeah, she came the day after we were married & never left.

Debbie rushed into the supermarket to pick up a few items. She headed for the express check-out & the clerk was talking on the phone with his back to her. She says, "Excuse me, I'm in a hurry, could you please check me out?" The clerk turned, stared at her for a second, looked her up & down, smiled & said, "Not bad."

Ad in the paper: Wedding dress for sale. Worn once by mistake. Call Stephanie.

Dennis, there's a lady in the audience that's 111!
() LET ME SEE THAT NOTE LARRY. "IT SAYS THERE'S A LADY IN THE AUDIENCE THAT'S ILL!"

A hunter & his friend were sitting in a tall deer stand early one cold December morning. Suddenly a huge buck walked out over the corn they'd spread. This buck was magnificent, a once in a lifetime animal. The hunter's hand shook in anticipation. He carefully aimed the scope on his 300 Winchester Magnum at the buck, but as he was about to squeeze the trigger, his friend alerted him to a funeral procession passing slowly down Highway 7. The hunter pulled away from the gunstock, set the rifle down, took off his hat, bowed his head & then closed his eyes in prayer. His friend was stunned, "Wow, that is the most thoughtful & touching thing I have ever seen you do. You let that trophy deer go to pay respects to a passing funeral procession. The hunter shrugged & said, "Yeah, well, we were married for 37 years.

I had a very funny childhood. My Mother used to tell me so much about the 'birds & the bees' that it took me years & years to get interested in girls.

Getting married is an important decision for guys, It's the last one they're ever gonna make!

In being married, the hardest thing to get used to is being bought gifts with your own money.

My wife is going to a self-help group for compulsive talkers. It's called "On & On Anon".

I overheard 2 ladies talking. One says, "It is I who made my husband a millionaire." The other says, "What was he before?" She says, a multimillionaire!"

Marriage is grand---& divorce is about 10 grand.

My wife & I were sitting at a table at my last high-school reunion, & I kept staring at a drunken lady swigging her drink as she sat alone at a nearby table. Shirley asked, "Do you know her?" I said, "Yes, she's my old girlfriend. I understand she took up drinking right after we split up those many years ago, & I hear she hasn't been sober since." Shirley says, "My Lord, who would think a person could go on celebrating that long?" And that's when the fight started.

My neighbor took his wife to a fancy restaurant. The waiter for some reason took his order 1st & my neighbor says, "I'll have the strip steak, medium rare please." The waiter says, "Aren't you worried about the mad cow?" He says, "Nah, she can order for herself!" & that's when the fight started.

For more than an hour a scrawny little guy sat at a bar staring into his glass. Suddenly a burly truck driver sat down next to him, grabbed the guy's drink & gulped it down. The poor little guy just burst out crying & the truck driver said, "Oh, come on pal, I was just joking. Here, I'll buy you another." The little guy says, "No, that's not it. This has been the worst day of my life. I was late for work & got fired. When I left the office I found out my car had been stolen, so I walked 6 miles home. Then I found my wife with another man, so I grabbed my wallet & came here, & just when I'm about to end it all (sob), You show up & drink my poison!"

And now we take you to the Garden Of Eden, where a fig leaf is slowly wafting down from a tree. Eve looks up & says, "Look Adam, look, the Invisible Man!"

You know, I've been telling jokes on stage for many years, & I've found that PMS jokes aren't funny; PERIOD!

The theory used to be: You marry an older man because they're more mature. The new theory is that men don't mature, so you might as well marry a young one.

A mother takes her 3 sons to enroll them in school. The teacher asks, "What are your sons names?" The lady says, "This boys name is Leroy, this other boy's name is Leroy & Leroy here is my 3rd son's name." The teacher asks, "Isn't it confusing having all 3 boys named the same. The lady says, "Oh, no, you see when it's time for lunch, I just holler out the door, "Leroy, it's time for lunch, or Leroy it's time for dinner, & they all come a runnin" The teacher says, "Okay, but what do you do when you want a specific boy?"
The lady says, "Oh, well then I just holler out their last name."

Yeah, the 1st time I met ______ he was going with one of the tank sisters. You know---Sherman & Septic.

If love is blind, why is lingerie so popular?

Two ladies died & went to Heaven. One asked the other, "How did you die?" She said, "I froze to death." The 1st one says, "Boy, that sounds horrible!" The 2nd one says, "Oh, no, I just got cold & sleepy & that was it. How did you die?" She says, "Well, I knew my husband was cheating on me, so I came home in the middle of the day & I looked all over for his girlfriend. I looked in the attic, in the closets, in the basement, under the beds, & I got so frustrated that I had a heart attack & died." & the other one said, "Well, if you'd a looked in the freezer, we'd both be alive!"

An old couple were setting on the front porch. She knocks him out in the yard. He says, "What'd you do that for?" She says, "That's for being a lousy lover all these years!" He sets back down & pretty soon he knocks her out in the yard. She says, "What'd you do that for?" He says, "That's for knowin' the difference!"

() YOUR SISTER SEEMS TO BE A SENSIBLE WOMAN. WHERE CAN I GET HOLD OF HER?
I don't know---she's awful ticklish.

I've been studying a book on efficiency & I did a case study on my wife's routine for cooking breakfast. Now, after a few days of observation, I determined what was slowing her down & I made her some suggestions. You know, ways to speed up the process.
() DID IT WORK?
It sure did. Instead of taking her 20 minutes to cook my breakfast, it takes me only 7.

My neighbor came home from work the other day & his wife was crying. He said, "What's wrong?" She says, "The pharmacist just insulted me!" So, he jumped in his car & drove down to the pharmacy & confronted the guy. The pharmacist says; "Listen to my side! First, my alarm didn't go off & I overslept. Of course I was in a rush & I went out & I locked both my house & car keys inside the house & I had to break a window to get them. Then I got a flat tire. When I finally got behind the counter, there was a long line & the phone was ringing. After bending over to pick up a roll of nickels, I cracked my head on a drawer & fell backward, shattering the perfume case. Meanwhile the phone was still ringing. I picked up & Your wife asked me how to use a rectal thermometer. I swear, all I did was tell her!"

My wife's on a 3 week diet.
() OH YEAH? HOW MUCH HAS SHE LOST SO FAR?
Two weeks.

I take my wife everywhere---but she keeps finding her way back.

God promised men that good & obedient wives would be found in all corners of the world. Then he made the Earth round---& laughed & laughed & laughed.

Some people ask the secret of our long marriage. We take time to go to a restaurant 2 times a week. A little candlelight, dinner, soft music, & a slow walk home. She goes on Tuesdays; I go on Fridays.

When it comes to telling her age she's shy though. Yeah, about 10 years shy.

I remember, Mom & Dad were so proud of me when I graduated from High School---so were my wife & kids.

A farmer's wife nagged him all the time, morning, noon & night, nag-nag-nag. One day he was out in the field & his wife brought him his lunch. So, he led his mule under a shade tree, & sat down to eat his lunch. And there she started in on him---nag-nag-nag. "Your rows aren't straight; you're plowing too slow, blah-blah-blah." Out of nowhere that mule hee-hawed & kicked that woman in the head & knocked her dead on the spot. A couple days later after the funeral, the preacher noticed that lots of neighbors came up to say words of comfort to the farmer. But the preacher noticed that every time a woman talked to him, he farmer would nod his head & every single time a man said something to him, he shook his head. So, the preacher's curiosity got the best of him & he asked the farmer: "Why do you nod when the women talk to you & shake your head when the men talk to you?" The farmer says, "Well, the women always have something nice to say, like don't she look pretty, or ain't that a nice dress they've got her laid out in. But the men, they all want to know if the mule is for sale."

I'm recovering from a bad fall. My Mother-IN-Law stayed with us in October & November.

She talks so much that the phone company gave her her own area code.

My wife's mad at me again. The other night we were going to a banquet & I'm waiting on her & finally she says, "I'm ready now!" So I said, "I'm not." She says, "I thought you said you were ready while ago!" I said, "I was, but now you'll have to wait for me. I've got to shave again."

The other day she called desperate for help. She said, "The car is stalled & I'm at the corner of 'Walk & Don't Walk'."

I tell you folks, that woman uses her credit cards so often that she's using money that hasn't even been printed yet.

She hinted about our next anniversary that she would like something on her wrist that would last forever, so I'm making arrangements to have her tattooed.

Remember, behind every great man is a woman rolling her eyes.

Took my wife to that revolving restaurant on top of the Hyatt Regency Hotel to celebrate our anniversary last Tuesday. It didn't turn out so well. The revolving mechanism quit working & so every 2 minutes we had to get up & move to the next table.

How many divorced men does it take to change a light bulb? Who cares? They never get the house anyway.

Did I tell you my wife had plastic surgery? I cut up her credit cards.

I met my wife at a dance. It was so embarrassing, I thought she was at home with the kids.

() I UNDERSTAND THAT YOU & YOUR WIFE HAD SOME WORDS.
I had some, but I didn't get a chance to use them!

I told my wife that a husband is like a fine wine—he gets better with age. The next thing I know, I'm locked in the cellar.

I'm kinda worried. I got a letter from a feller who says if I don't stay away from his wife, he'll shoot me!
() WELL, ALL YOU HAVE TO DO IS STAY AWAY!
Yeah, but he didn't sign his name.

Drove by your house last night. You know, you ought to close your shades, cause I saw you and your wife a hugging and kissing something fierce.
() THE JOKES ON YOU, I WASN'T EVEN HOME LAST NIGHT!

I was over to Sam's house & I was amazed at how well he treats his wife. He's always telling her how pretty she is, compliments her cooking & he's always hugging & kissing her. I said, "Gee, Sam, you really make a big fuss over your wife." He says, "Yeah, I started to appreciate her more about 6 months ago & it has revived our marriage & we couldn't be happier!" So, that really inspired me, so I hurried home hugged my wife & told her how much I love her & I told her I wanted to hear all about her day. But then, she burst into tears. I said, "Honey, what's wrong?" She said, "This has been the worst day. This morning I sprained my ankle doing aerobics, then the washing machine broke, now, to top it off, you come home drunk!"

We had a power failure at our house this week. My wife lost her voice.

Did you see that girl in the 9th row? She has nice even teeth. 1, 3, 5, & 7 are missing.

I told him I didn't need his criticism, I've got a wife at home.

Did I tell you she puts popcorn in her pancakes so they'll turn over by themselves?

() DID YOU HEAR ABOUT THE GUY IN PLEASANT HILL THAT WAS CHARGED WITH POLYGAMY.
What do you mean?
() WELL, HE'S GOT THREE WIVES!
Three! Why, that's not polygamy, that's trigonometry!

Do you know why it's wrong to have more than one wife? It states it right there in the Bible: "No man can serve two masters."

I would have been 2 years older, but my Father stuttered real bad.

I remember my Mother always put so much starch in everything that it was ridiculous. One time my brother fell out of bed & broke his pajamas.

() WOW! YOU MUST HAVE HAD A STRANGE CHILDHOOD LARRY.
Oh, I guess. I'm descended from a long line that my Mother fell for.

A minister congratulated a gentleman at a men's meeting on his 50th wedding anniversary. The minister asked the man to take a few minutes & share some insight into how he managed to stay married to the same woman for 50 years. The man stood up & said, "Well, I've always respected her & listened to what she had to say, but mostly I took her traveling on special occasions." So, the minister asked him, "Trips to where?" He says, "Well, for our 25th anniversary, I took her to Italy." The minister says, "Sir, you are a terrific example to all husbands. Please tell the audience what you are planning for your wife on your 50th anniversary?" He says, "I'm gonna go back & get her."

Shirley & I were down by the hog lot last week & she says, "We ought to butcher one of them hogs bein's our anniversary's comin' up purty soon." I said, "I can't see no sense in takin;' out on a hog something that happened 59 years ago.

Did you see that good lookin' girl I was talkin' to back there?
() YEAH, SHE WAS GOOD LOOKIN'.
She has an upper plate though.
() SO, HOW'D YOU FIND THAT OUT?

Oh, it just came out in the conversation.

I hate it when you offer someone a sincere compliment on their mustache & suddenly she's not your friend anymore.

This morning I woke up to the unmistakable scent of 'Pigs In A Blanket'. That's the price you pay for letting the relatives stay over.

June is the marriage month. I'm experienced. The other day I said; "Let's go out & have some fun tonight. She said, "Okay, but if you get home before I do, leave the hallway light on."

If you have wedding plans in the future, here's some questions & answers that might help you:

1. Is it alright to bring a date to the wedding? Not if you're the groom.
2. How many showers is the bride supposed to have? At least one within a week of the wedding.
3. What music is recommended for the wedding ceremony? Anything except 'Release Me & Let Me Love Again'.

I went to my class reunion & there's my old buddy George. He told me he'd been married 3 times. I said, "Tell me about it." He said, "The 1st one died of eating poisoned mushrooms." "What about the 2nd one?" "She died of eating poisoned mushrooms too." "And the 3rd one?" "Well, she died of a fractured skull." "Really?" "Yeah, she wouldn't eat the poisoned mushrooms."

Two cannibals were sitting by a fire & one says, "Gee, I hate my Mother-In-Law." & the other says, "So, try the potatoes!"

I'm sorry I'm late. It takes my wife forever to change a flat.

My wife's on a diet now, & I'll bet she weighs herself 20 times a day. Do you know how she weighs?
() NO, HOW?
Naked! The other day she embarrassed me to death. She took off her clothes & stepped up on the scales, right in front of me.
() WHAT'S SO EMBARRASSING ABOUT THAT?
Well, we were right in the middle of Wal-Mart

I knew a girl so skinny she could change clothes in a shotgun barrel.

A honeymoon couple picked up a man's suitcase by mistake & took it to their room. The man went up to their room, & just before knocking, overheard the couple talking inside. The groom said, "Whose little nose is that?" She says, "It's yours Honey." He says, "Whose little mouth is that?" She says, "It's yours Honey." Then the groom says, "Whose little eyes are these?" She says, "They're yours Honey." About that time the man hollered through the door & said, "When you get to that little suitcase, that's mine!"

I was taking a walk yesterday & for some reason I ended up walking through the cemetery. Here was this guy about 50 years old kneeling down by a grave that certainly wasn't recent cause it had grass all over it & looked nice. So there he was with tears streaming down his face & he was saying; "Why did you die, oh why did you die?" I said, "Was it your Mother?" "Oh, why did you die?" "Was it your Father?" "Oh, why did you die?" "Well, who was it then?" He said, "I was my wife's 1st husband, why did you die, oh, why did you die?"

A newly married sailor was stationed on a remote island in the Pacific for a year. A few weeks after he got there he sent a letter to his new wife. "My love, we're gonna be apart for a very long time. I'm already starting to miss you & there's really not much to do here in the evenings. Besides that, we're constantly surrounded by young attractive native girls. Do you think if I had a hobby of some kind, I wouldn't be tempted?" So, his wife sent him a harmonica saying, "Why don't you learn to play this?' Eventually his tour was up & as he rushed into the house, he said, "Darling, I can't wait to hold you!" She kissed him & said, "First, let me hear you play that harmonica!"

I was watching a film with some creepy organ music on the TV & suddenly I yelled, "NO, no, don't enter that church you stupid idiot!" My wife asked me, "What are you watching?" I said, "Our wedding video."

My wife asked me to buy organic vegetables from the market. I went & looked around & couldn't find any. So, I grabbed one of the employees & said, "These vegetables are for my wife, have they been sprayed with any poisonous chemicals?" The produce guy looked at me & said, "No Sir, you'll have to do that yourself."

My wife & I were driving home after a party last night & she asked me, "Honey, has anyone ever told you how handsome, sexy & irresistible to women you are?" I said, "No, Darling, not lately.:" She said, "Then what gave you that idea at the party tonight."

_____ is so conscientious that he goes down to the county courthouse once a month to see if his marriage license has expired.

_____'s getting married next week. You know there's nothing like a wedding to bring two married people together.

For 20 years my wife & I were happy---then we met.

The neighbor lady caught a peeping Tom last night, & she'd have killed him if we hadn't stopped her!
() HE MUST HAVE MADE HER VERY ANGRY PEEKING AT HER HUH?
No, that's not what made her the maddest.
() IT'S NOT?
No, she got the maddest when he reached in & closed the curtains!

I got on one of those scales that tell you your fortune & weight & dropped in a quarter. It spit out this little white card. I read it to Shirley, It said, "You're energetic, bright, resourceful & a great lover!" Shirley says, "Ha, I bet it has your weight wrong too!"

I don't know what to get my wife for our anniversary this year. Last year I bought her a mink---she keeps the cage so clean.

It was so cold that my wife forgot about her headache.

I've got a girl in a grass skirt tattooed on my arm. Do you know what happens when I make my muscle go up & down? I get tired.

A census taker in a rural area of Mississippi went up to a farmhouse & knocked. A woman came to the door & he asked her how many children she had & their ages. She said, "Let's see now, there's the twins, Sally & Billy, they're 32. And the twins, Seth & Beth, they're 26. And the twins, Penny & Jenny, they're 24." The census taker says, "Hold on! Did you get twins every time?" She says, "Heck no, there were hundreds of times we didn't get nothin!"

Elijah came home late the other night, took off his shoes, climbed the stairs, opened the bedroom door & closed it without being detected.

Just as he was about to get into bed Jesse raised up half asleep & said, "Is that you Fido?" For once in his life Elijah had real presence of mind---he licked her hand.

A fellow driving down I70 at 70 MPH notices a State Patrolman in his rear-view mirror so he speeds up to 93 MPH & of course the patrolman pulls him over. The officer asks, "What were you thinking of sir, driving so fast?" He says, "Gee, officer, my wife ran off with a State Patrolman last week, & I thought that might be you trying to bring her back!"

My son Mike's been out of town on his job & his wife, being the romantic sort, sent him a text: "If you are sleeping, send me your dreams. If you are laughing, send me your smile. If you are eating send me a bite. If you are drinking, send me a sip. If your crying, send me your tears. I love you." Mike, the typical non-romantic, replied; "I'm on the toilet. Please advise."

My neighbor's husband died & I went to the visitation. I told his widow, "I'm sorry my dear, tell me, what were his last words?" She says, "His last words were, "You don't scare me with that shot-gun Martha. You couldn't hit the side of a barn!"

That good- looking girl on the back row is annoying me?
() BUT, SHE'S NOT EVEN LOOKING AT YOU!
I know it, that's what's annoying me!

Do you know what you get when you have 32 women from Arkansas in a room? A full set of teeth.

I've got a girl I'd like to bring on the show next Saturday night.
() DOES SHE DRESS LIKE A LADY?

I don't know, I never saw her dress.

() DO YOU LIKE THOSE LONG DRESSES WOMEN ARE WEARING THESE DAYS?
It doesn't bother me, I've got a good memory.

Kevin tell you what happened to him? He was in a fancy restaurant & there is a gorgeous redhead sitting at the next table. Of course,he's noticed her, gut he didn't have the nerve to talk to her. Suddenly she sneezes, & her glass eye comes flying out & Kevin reflexively reaches out & grabs it right in mid-air & hands it back. The girl pops her eye back in place & says, "Oh my, I am so sorry, I'm sure that must have embarrassed you, so let me pay for your dinner to make it up to you." They enjoy a wonderful dinner together & afterwards they go to the theatre followed by drinks. They talk, they laugh, they share their deepest dreams & after paying for everything, she asks him if he would come to her place for a nightcap & stay for breakfast. The next morning, she cooks a gourmet breakfast with all the trimmings. Now folks, Kevin is amazed & totally impressed. He told her, "You know, you are the perfect woman. Are you this nice to every guy you meet? She says, "No, you just happened to catch my eye."

A naked woman jumps into a taxi & gives the cabbie an address. The cabbie just looks at her, making no attempt to drive. She says, "What are you staring at, haven't you seen a naked woman before?" He says, "I'm not staring!" She says, "Well, if you're not staring, what are you doing?" He says, I'm just wondering where you're keeping the money to pay me."

Kevin took his girlfriend to Alaskan furs before Christmas. He told her to pick out the coat she wanted. She picked out the most expensive sable coat on the place. $37,000.00 was the price, so Kevin wrote out a check. The salesman said, "Okay, we'll hold on to the coat until your check clears Sir." So the following Monday, Kevin goes back into Alaskan Furs & that salesman jumps on him. He says, "Have you lost your mind writing a check like that? You don't have $500 in that account!" Kevin says, "Now don't get all shook up, I just came in to thank you for the best weekend I EVER HAD!"

I was sleeping in yesterday morning & about 8:00 O'clock the phone rang & woke us up & I listened for a while & said, "Well, how would I know, it's 2000 miles from here!" I slammed the receiver down & the wife says, "Who was that?" I said, "I don't know, some guy wanted to know if the coast was clear."

How ya doin' _____?
Well, I'm locked in a major custody battle. My wife doesn't want me, & my Mother won't take me back.

One lazy Sunday morning as the wife & I were sitting around the breakfast table, I said, "When I die, I want you to sell all my stuff immediately." She asked, "Now, why would you want me to do something like that?" I said, "Well, I figure you'd eventually remarry, & I don't want some other jerk using my stuff." She looked at me intently & said, "What makes you think I'd marry another jerk?"

MISCELLANEOUS HUMOR?

What's a crick? That's the sound of a Japanese camera.

That was a small joke otherwise known as a mini-ha-ha.

As a child, I was very young.

I was born on a farm & I guess it shows. To this day, in the wintertime, I still put on my coat to go to the bathroom.

() I'm looking for a place to live. __ How much are they asking for your apartment rent now?
About twice a day.

Years ago, I became a renowned artist & painted portraits. This lady came to me one time & wanted me to paint her in the nude. I said, "Oh no, I couldn't do that Mam!" She says, "I'll give you $10,000 if you'll paint me in the nude!" I thought about it & I said, "Okay, but I at least want to wear my socks, cause I need someplace to keep my brushes."

---

3 guys are talking about what constitutes 'fame'. The 1st guy defines it as being invited to the Whitehouse for a chat with the President. The 2nd guy says, "Nah, real fame would be if the red phone rang when you are there & the President wouldn't take the call."

The 3rd guy says, "You're both wrong. Fame is when you're in the Oval Office & the red phone rings, the President answers it, listens for a second, then says, "It's for you!"

After a sad song: Boy! If that don't make you 'tear-up' you might need to jerk a nose hair out.

A lot of people wonder why I'm the way I am, but I had a very funny childhood. One day my Father took me aside & left me there.

Did you notice that I don't worry about anything anymore?
() Yeah, you used to worry about everything, what happened to you______?"
I hired a professional worrier for $1000 a week, & I haven't had a single worry since.
() A thousand a week!! How're you gonna pay him?"
That's his worry.

Well, I had another neighbor to die this week. It was sad. For the last several years he thought he was a rooster. The day after he died, everybody in the whole neighborhood overslept.

I joined the Army cause I was 18 & bored with the tenth grade.

When I was a kid I had a friend who worked at a radio station. Whenever he walked under a bridge, you couldn't hear what he said.

Why do KU graduates put their diplomas on the dashboards of their cars? So they can park in handicapped spaces.

_____ went on vacation in Colorado, got up early in the morning and came upon an old gold mine with a vertical shaft. He dropped a rock in it to see how deep it was. No sound. He dropped the biggest rock he could carry into that mine---no sound. Then he found an old railroad tie, drug it over to the hole & dropped it in. About that time, a goat ran by him & jumped into the hole. A young man came up & asked, "Have you seen a goat around here? " _____ says, "Yes, one just jumped into this mine shaft, where'd you have him?" The young fella says, "I tied it to a railroad tie!"

Wanta have some fun? The next time you go on a roller coaster, take a handful of nuts & bolts with you & just as the car starts forward, hand them to the people in front of you & tell them you found these under their seats.

Well, I did some work in the Outlying Community of_____ this week. The people out there can out lie anybody.

This town was so small that the barbershop quartet only had 2 members.

I was so sorry to hear about the recent passing of Robert Kearns, the man who invented the intermittent windshield wiper. At his funeral, there wasn't a dry eye in the house. Then there was, then there wasn't.

A young couple hit's a golf ball through a window of a nearby house. So, they rushed up to the house & there stands a handsome fellow in a turban. The husband says, "We're so sorry! We'll pay for the damage." The guy says, "Not at all, I'm a genie & I was trapped for 1000 years 'til your ball broke the bottle that was my prison. Allow me to grant whatever you wish!" So, the woman says, "Could you make us millionaires?" The genie says, "Done! You'll have $100,000 put into your account every month for the rest of your life." The husband says, "How can we ever thank you?" The genie says, "Well, I've forgotten what it's like to hold a woman. Could I give your wife a single perfect kiss?" So, the couple decided they could live with this & after the embrace the genie asks the woman her age. She says, "I'm 29." & the genie says, "I see, & you still believe in genies?"

I nearly got mobbed yesterday. I went to an antique show & said, "What's new?"

I was wearing a leather vest & a lady came up to me & pointed at my vest. She said, "You know a cow was murdered for that vest?" I said, "I didn't know there were any witnesses. Now I'll have to kill you too."

There are a lot of lessons to be learned in life: Like, never under any circumstances take a sleeping pill & a laxative on the same night.

A friend of my wife's confused her valium with her birth-control pills. She had 14 kids, but she doesn't really care.

Did you hear about the lady that got her saccharin mixed up with her birth control pills? She had the sweetest little baby.

Have you seen that 'Ancestry' site on the internet? I sent them some information on my family tree. They sent me back a pack of seeds, & suggested that I just start over.

Every 3rd person in the world is ugly. So, if you look to your right & that person is nice looking & you look to your left & that person is nice looking, you know where that leaves you.

There's a mute who wants to buy a toothbrush. By imitating the action of brushing one's teeth, he successfully expresses himself to the shopkeeper & the purchase is done. Now, if there is a blind man who wishes to buy a pair of sunglasses, how should he express himself?" He opens his mouth & says, "I would like to buy a pair of sunglasses."

Hard work never killed anybody, but why take a chance?

If all the cars in the U.S.A. were placed end-to-end, it would probably be Labor Day Weekend.

Labor Day Weekend is a celebration of the economic achievements of American workers. I hope those 3 people have a great day.

One seventh of your life is spent on Monday. However, the only person to get his work done by Friday was Robinson Crusoe.

I quit my job at the helium gas factory. I refuse to be spoken to in that tone.

Why do mermaids wear seashells? Cause, B shells are too small & D shells are too big.

Last week we were out in Arizona. I was drivin' along out there & spotted a cowboy by the side of the road with his ear to the ground. So, I stopped & asked him, "what's going on?" He said, "Two horses, one gray, one chestnut, pulling a wagon carrying 2 men. One man was wearing a red shirt, the other a black shirt. They're heading East." I said, "Wow, you can tell all that just by listening to the ground?" He said, "No, they just ran over me!"

I'm sure glad you folks are here tonight. Like the warden said to an incoming prisoner; "The world will be a better place because you're here."

Every 3rd person in the world is ugly, so if you look to your right & that person is nice looking & you look to your left & that person is nice looking---you know where that leaves you.

Life is one contradiction after another.
() No it's not!

I was gonna write an article on women's bathing suits, but I couldn't find enough material.

The guy who invented Velcro died---which is sad, cause his family was very attached to him.

(harassment) Did I bother you when you went up before the parole board?

My Mom & Dad were 1st cousins, that's the reason why I look alike.

I once sued someone for saying I was clumsy, but I dropped the charges.

I'm not what you'd call coordinated. When you see me walk down the street, you'd swear it was my 1st time on skis.

I hung up on an obscene phone call last night. I couldn't think of anything else to say.

What's gray, has 4 legs & a trunk? A mouse on vacation.

We received a letter delivered to us by mistake the other day. Before I noticed it wasn't to us, I opened it & some guy had written to this company complaining about the product he'd evidently bought mail-order. It said; "Dear Sir, I used 6 bottles of your corn syrup & my feet are no better."

It's wonderful to be in show business. When I got out of High School I wanted to join the circus as a 'Human Cannonball' but they wouldn't hire me, I was the wrong caliber.

So, I asked the manager, "Isn't there some other job opening you might have?" He says, "Well, we have an opening for an assistant lion tamer." I said, "What does that consist of?" He said, "Come with me & I'll show you." He took me over to the lion training cage & here's a huge lion on a pedestal in the middle of the cage. In walks a beautiful girl with a whip in her hand. She cracks the whip & that lion jumps down off that pedestal & goes over & licks her boots. The manager says, "Do you think you could do that?" I said, "I sure can, you just get that lion out of there!"

Listen ____ I'm awfully sorry, I can't pay you this month.
() That's what you said last month!
Well, you see, I keep my word.

() What time is it?
I don't have a watch anymore. I bought one that was waterproof, dustproof & shockproof.
() Well, where is it?
It caught fire.

The last thing I want to do is hurt you, but it's still on the list.

At what age do you think it's appropriate to tell a highway it's adopted?

It was so cold the other night my teeth chattered all night. I finally had to get up & take 'em out of the glass.

(No laughter?) Is this an audience or a jury?

(sour crowd?) I'd like to see you all again, but not as a group.

The wife & I were out in California for a couple of months last summer. We were at San (J) Jose & went swimming every day.
() Don't you mean San (H) Jose? Out in California all the 'Jays' are pronounced as 'H'es. By the way, when were you there?
In Hune & Huly.

A man with a serious stuttering problem looked for a job as a Bible salesman. Being interviewed, his speech problem caused concern . So the interviewer said, "We don't see how you could be very affective at selling Bibles with your speech problem . The man says, "If you'll g-g-g-give m-m-me a try for t-t-two weeks, if I c-c-can't do a good job, you don't have to p-p-pay m-m-me." He came back in after 2 weeks & he'd sold twice as many as their best salesman.. They said, "Okay, how did you do this?" He said, "Come out with me & I'll s-s-show you. They went up to a house & knocked on the door. A lady answered the door & he says, "M-m-maam, I'm selling Bibles. You can either b-b-buy one or I can c-c-come inside & r-r-read it to you."

The best thing about getting older is that you gain sincerity. Once you learn to fake that, there's nothing you can't do.

Did you hear about the Pepsi executive who got fired? He tested positive for Coke.

Years ago Jon, Don & myself were traveling up from Arkansas on old 2-lane roads about 2:00 in the morning when our van broke down. We were in the middle of nowhere but we saw a farmhouse light in the distance & we walked up to the house & knocked on the door. The farmer answered the door & asked if he could help us. I said, "Our vehicle broke down, could we use your phone to call a tow truck?" He says, "Ain't got no phone." I said, "I see you've got a pickup truck, could you take us to town to get help?" He said, "No, cause that old pickup's lights don't work, but you can stay all night & I can take you for help tomorrow." We said, "Well, thanks, that's mighty kind of you sir." He said, there's just one thing, I've got a leven year old boy that doesn't have no ears & he's real sensitive about it, so don't look at him." We said, "That's fine, we'll be okay." Next morning they invited us to breakfast & the boy caught Don looking at him & the boy says, "Mr. you lookin' at me?" Don says, "I was just admiring your full head of hair, take care of it or you'll go bald like me!" Pretty soon he saw Jon looking at him & he says, "You starin' at me?" Jon says, "No, I was just admiring your pearly white teeth, you take good care of them or you'll have to have false teeth like me!" Yeah, you guessed it, he caught me looking at him & he says, "Mr., you're lookin' at me ain't you?" I said, "Yes, I guess I was. I was just admiring your beautiful blue eyes, you take good care of them, cause you can't wear glasses like I do!"

Epitaph: "Here lies Johnny Yeast. Pardon him for not rising.

You know this outsourcing business is getting out of hand! I was feeling depressed the other day, so I called the 'Suicide Help Line'. I was put through to a call center in Pakistan. I explained that I as feeling suicidal. They were very excited at this news & wanted to know if I could drive a truck or fly an airplane.

Did I ever tell you I was caesarean born? You can't really tell, although whenever I leave a house, I go out through the window.

I stopped at a drugstore last night & asked the pharmacist if he had anything for the hiccups. He said, "I've got just the thing, wait right here, I'll be right back. So, I was looking around & he snuck up behind me & hit me over the head with a wet mop. I said, "What did you do that for?" He says. "Well, you don't have the hiccups anymore do ya?" I said, "No, but my wife does out in the car!"

I went to my class reunion last week. I didn't recognize anyone. Finally I saw a lady I thought looked familiar & I went over to her & said, "Excuse me, but you look like Helen Green." She says, "Well, you don't look too good in blue either mister!"

Most accidents occur in the home or on the highway; the surest way to be safe is to leave home & sell your car.

You don't think times have changed? Now the Swiss Army Knife has an ear-piercing tool on it.

I didn't get much sleep last night. I plugged the electric blanket into the toaster by mistake & I kept poppin' out of bed all night!

Flew to New York on business & I hailed a cab from the airport. We were going down the street there in the middle of the night on the way to the hotel & I wanted to ask the driver a question. So, I tapped him on the shoulder. Folks, he went berserk. He ran up on the sidewalk & almost crashed into a store window. The cabby says, "Don't ever do that again!" I said, "I'm sorry, I didn't think a little tap on the shoulder would scare you." The cabby says, "I'm sorry too, but you see, this is my 1st day driving a cab, for the last 25 years I've been driving a hearse.'

Once upon a time there were 3 old maids who made some porridge. It was too hot to eat, so they took a tramp/walk in the woods while it was cooling. They came back & the oldest one said, "Somebody's been eatin' my porridge!" & the middle one says, "Somebody's been eatin' my porridge too!" & the youngest one says, "Somebody's been eatin' my porridge & it's all gone! Then the oldest one went into the living room & said, "Somebody's been sittin' in my chair!" & the middle one says, "Somebody's been sittin' in my chair too!" & the youngest one says, "Somebody's been sittin' in my chair & it's broken all down!" Then the oldest one goes up to her bedroom & says, "Somebody's been sleepin' in my bed!" & the middle one says, "somebody's been sleepin' in my bed too!" & the youngest one looks in her bedroom & says, "Goodnight Girls!"

A guy walks into a bank, points a gun at the teller & says, "Give me all your money or you're geography!" She says, "Don't you mean 'history' ?" He says, "Hey lady, don't be changing the subject!"

Well, here we are again. Just goes to show you, no matter where you go--there you are.

Hot weather. You know, this is my favorite time of the year. I remember when I was a kid, I'd ask my mom if I could go swimming & she'd say, "Wait'll you eat something!"

Did I ever tell you how I learned to swim? My Dad took me down to the lake & threw me in about 10 feet & I thrashed & thrashed until in about 10 minutes, I got into the bank. He said, "Naw, that ain;t good enough." So the next day he took me to the lake & threw me plumb out into the middle of it. Well, I thrashed & thrashed for 45 minutes, but I finally got out on the bank. I'll tell you the hardest part though & that was getting out of that burlap bag!"

We were so poor that my folks couldn't afford kids, so the neighbors had me.

We couldn't afford Ex-Lax, so Mom'd set me in the outhouse & tell me ghost stories.

And we never had curtains in the outhouse. Dad said Mom would want 'em in the house too!

But now look at us, we al live in the suburbs trying to keep up with the Joneses. The hottest thing in the suburbs now is an aftershave lotion that smells like chlorine. It makes the guys at the office think you have a pool.

Did you hear about the guy who fell into the machine at the upholstery shop? He's completely recovered now.

This business man was self conscious because he had no ears. So when he hired a manager, he asked each candidate, "Notice anything unusual about me?' The 1st one replied, "You have no ears." He was shown the door. The 2nd one's response was the same so they tossed him out too. But the 3rd guy had a different answer. "You're wearing contact lenses!" The businessman was flabbergasted, he said, "How did you know?" The 3rd guy says, "Cause people who don't have ears have to wear contacts."

We were so poor when I was a kid that people used to break into our house & leave things.

I didn't have anything to wear 'til I was 7 years old & my Dad bought me a hat so I could look out the window.

A man meets a genie. The genie tells him he can have whatever he wants provided that his Mother-In-Law gets double. The man thinks for a moment & then says, "Okay, give me a million dollars & beat me half to death!"

Just got a bill in the mail that said: "FINAL NOTICE." So that's a relief.

A man walks into a bar & sits down. The bartender asks him if he wants a drink. Old man says, "Tried liquor once, didn't like it." "Care for a pretzel?" "Nope, tried a pretzel once, didn't like it." "Wanta watch the baseball game?" "Tried watching baseball once, didn't like it. Don't mind me, I'm waiting for my son." The bartender says, "Let me guess. Your only child?"

How many of you folks are against audience precipitation? When I hold up my hand everybody say 'WONABAKA'.
Ready? When I was in the Navy, we visited this island where a primitive tribe lived. I get to thinking at my young naïve age about how much they might be missing from the modern world, so I got up on a stump & addressed them. I said, "I come from a land where there is great peace!" In unison, the natives said, (hold up hand) 'WONABAKA!" "Each man is treated equally!" (hold up hand) "WONABAKA!" "I have come here to show you our ways so you can become truly happy!" (hold up hand) "WONABAKA!"
About that time some of the tribe's cattle appeared out there on the

pasture & I said, "May I go over & touch them?" The head chief said, "Yes friend, but don't step in the WONABAKA!"

Only in America; can a pizza get to your house faster than an ambulance.

A widow was lonely & decided to maybe get a pet. She went to a pet store & when she walked in she saw a real ugly frog, but it winked at her. She looked at the dogs, cats, birds, & the fish but they all seemed to be too noisy or messy, so she decided to leave, but on the way out she saw that frog again. The frog said, "Take me home with you, I can make you happy!" So, she bought the frog & as she was driving down the road, she heard the frog say, "If you'll kiss me, something truly amazing will happen!" She pulled over, took the frog out of his box, closed her eyes & kissed that frog & zap that frog turned into a handsome prince! Then she started feeling a metamorphosis coming on & do you know what she turned into? A Holiday Inn.

What do Eskimos get from setting on the ice too long? Answer: Polaroids.

() HOW WAS YOUR TRIP, DID YOU HAVE A GOOD TIME?
Well, yes & no.
()WHAT DO YOU MEAN?
To start with, the bus was late.
() OH, THAT'S BAD
No, that was good.
() WHY'S THAT?
Cause I got a taxi.
() OH, THAT'S GOOD!
No, that was bad.
() WELL, WHY?
Cause, the transmission went out on the taxi & it would only go in reverse.

() OH, THAT'S BAD!
No, that was good.
() WHY?
Well, see'ns how we could only go backwards, by the time we got to the hotel, he owed me $37.95.

Rap is to music what Etch-a-sketch is to art.

The human mind is a wonderful thing. It starts working the moment you are born & never stops until you stand up to speak in public.

Remember, time is what keeps everything from happening at once.

My Father always said, "If you keep your feet firmly on the ground, you'll have trouble putting on your pants.

My Father was a very smart & frugal man. He invented the 'LIMBO'. He was trying to get into a pay toilet without paying.

A man went to a restaurant, intending to order some brains for supper. The menu read: Fiddle player brains--$2.00 an ounce; Guitar player brains--$3.00 an ounce; Drum player brains--$4.00 an ounce; Piano player brains--$100 an ounce. The man asked the waiter, "Why are Piano player brains so expensive?" The waiter says, "Do you know how many Piano players it takes to get one ounce of brains?"

I went to the bank & went over my savings. I found out I have all the money that I'll ever need, if I die tomorrow.

We came across a creek on the way here that was out of it's banks so we had to wait in this little town called Burnt Mattress,. Arkansas. That's a little bit South of Hot Springs. I struck up a conversation with one of the local fellers & I asked him, "How much rain have you had lately?" He says, "Well, it rained twice this week. Once, for 3 days & then again for 4." Well, I got to watchin' all that water go by with limbs, old tires, sofa cushions & such & I noticed a straw hat goin' up stream & down stream & up stream & down stream, so I asked this local character, I said, "Hey, what's the deal with that hat?" He said, "What hat?" I said, "That hat that keeps goin up stream & down stream etc. " He said, "Oh, that must be old man Johnson, he said he was goin to mow his yard today come hell or high water!"

I'm sure glad you folks are here tonight. Like the warden said to an incoming prisoner; "The world will be a better place because you're here."

So a guy goes to a psychiatrist & says, "I think I'm an umbrella." The Dr. says, "A cure is possible if you'll open up." & the patient says, "Why, is it raining?"

It's that time of the year again. Just about the time a man is cured of swearing---he gets his real-estate tax bill.

A guy hails a cab in New York City & they're goin' down the street when the passenger taps the cabby on the shoulder. Well, the cab driver goes berserk, runs up on the sidewalk & almost crashes into a store window. The cabby says, "Mister, don't ever do that again!" The passenger says, "I'm sorry, I didn't think a little tap on the shoulder would scare you." The cabby says, "I'm sorry too, but you see, this is my 1st day driving a cab. For the last 25 years I've been driving a hearse."

My neighbor knocked on my door at 2:30 am this morning. Can you believe that? Lucky I was still up playing my bagpipes.

Ever wonder about those people who spend $2.00 a piece on those little bottles of Evian Water? Try spelling Evian backwards: NAÏVE.

If 4 out of 5 people suffer from diarrhea, does that mean that 1 enjoys it?

What hair color do they put on the driver's licenses of bald men?

We don't bother our neighbors in the suburbs. Like there's a couple next door. They just sit around hugging & kissing & cooing all day long. Two of the nicest guys I've ever met.

You know, for a long time I had the feeling that someone was following me.
() BUT YOU DON'T FEEL THAT WAY ANYMORE?
Oh, I still feel that way--but I found out what it was. It was just my underwear creeping up on me.

Class reunion: A lady came up to me & said; "Hey, do you remember me?" I said, "No, who are you?" She said, "I'm Georgette, I used to be your best buddy George in high school." I said, "Wow, that's amazing, do you miss anything you had when you were George?" She said, "Yeah, I sure wish I could remember how to parallel park."

There was a fire when I was a kid in my home town. It was in the only 2-story building we had in town. The fire department tried to put it out but they couldn't, so some other fire districts came in to help with the same results. Finally this little red fire truck from a rural fire district with all volunteer firemen came into town, didn't even slow down hardly. In fact, they drove that fire truck straight into the middle of that building, jumped out, fought like madmen & put it out. Well, the town folks were so grateful that the mayor took up a collection of donations. The mayor handed the money to that Fire Chief with thanks from all & asked him what they were gonna do with the money. The Chief said, "Well, I'll tell you one thing, the 1st thing we're gonna do is get the brakes fixed on that fire truck!"

A cowboy appeared before St. Peter at the Pearly Gates. St. Peter asked him, "Have you ever done anything of particular merit?" The cowboy says, "I can think of one thing. On a trip to the Black Hills of South Dakota, I came upon a gang of bikers who were threatening a woman. I directed them to leave her alone, but they wouldn't listen. So, I approached the largest & moat tattooed & I smacked him in the face, kicked his bike over, ripped out his nose ring, & threw it on the ground. I yelled, "Now back off or I'll kick the stuffins out of all of you!' St. Peter was impressed, & he asked the cowboy, "When did this all happen?" The cowboy says, "A couple of minutes ago!"

Trains today run a lot faster than when I was a young man. I was on this slow train in the old days & I said, "Conductor, can't you go any faster than this?" He says, "Yes, but I gotta stay with this train!" Pretty soon we totally stopped on the tracks. I said, "Conductor, what's wrong?" He said, "There's a cow on the tracks." We got to going again & in about 20 minutes we stopped again. I said, "Conductor, now what's wrong?" He said, "Well, we caught up with that cow again." When we got fairly close to our destination a young man ran up to the conductor & said, "Conductor! Conductor! Do something, my wife's about to have a baby!" The conductor says, "Young man, what were you thinking when you brought your wife on the train in that condition?" He says, "Well sir, she wasn't in that condition when I brought her on the train!" I tell you folks, trains were slow in those days.

When I got out of high school my buddy Pete says, "Hey, I just bought me an old Ford convertible & I'm gonna tour the United States, do you wanta go with me?" I had $55 saved up so I said, "Sure, let's go!" But before we left the word got around the neighborhood about our trip & there was a lady who's son had left home a year ago who called me & asked if we'd look for him. I said, "Do you have any ideas about where he might be & what is his name?" She said, "His name is John Dunn & he mentioned that he wanted to go to New York City." I said, "We'll sure look for him Mrs. Dunn." Well, Pete & I traveled around the country & finally got to New York City. We were driving down Wall Street when I saw a sign that read: 'Dunn & Bradstreet', I said, "Pull over Pete, I bet that's him!" Pete double parked while I went in & there was a lady behind a desk there. I said, "Is there a John here?" She said, "Last door down the hall on the right." I headed down the hall & a young fella came out of that door & I said, "Are you Dunn?" He says, "Yeah. " & I said, "Well, call home."

A blind man goes into a Department store, gets in the crossroads of an aisle & starts swinging his dog around in a circle. The manager comes over & asks him; "May I help you?" The blind man says, "No, I'm just looking around."

Did you hear about the German scientists who dug down 50 yards deep & discovered small pieces of copper in core samples taken at several sites in the country? They announced that 25,000 years ago ancient Germans had a nationwide telephone network.

Naturally, the British didn't want to be outdone, so they dug down 100 yards deep & found small pieces of glass. After some study, they announced that 35,000 years ago ancient Englishmen had a nationwide fiber optic network. Well, as you can imagine, the French scientists were outraged. They dug down 200, 250, then 300 yards deep, but found nothing but dirt & rock. Finally, they announced proudly; 55,000 years ago, the ancient French used cellular phones.

When I was a kid, we had a quicksand box in our back yard. I was an only child--eventually.

Recently the IRS was baffled by a letter from a man who explained that he hadn't been able to sleep since 1973 when he cheated on his income tax. Enclosed in the letter were five $100 bills. He closed the letter by saying that if he didn't sleep better now, he'd send in the rest.

I finally got my tax sent in, but before I did I called the IRS Tax Question Answering Service, & it said, "You have reached the IRS tax question answering service. To blow off steam--press1. To beg & plead--press 2-----------

---

This year the government allows you $1200 for your wife. I'm gonna turn her in before the price goes down!

A man with an alligator walked into a bar & asked the bartender; "Do you serve IRS agents here?" The bartender says, "Sure do!" & the man says, "Good, give me a beer & my gator'll have an IRS agent."

_____ named his farm 'Margarine Acres' .
() WHY'D HE NAME IT THAT?
Cause, it's just a cheap spread.

I ran into a smart-aleck today. I was buying myself a new pair of shoes. You know, some wing-tips for dress. So, I was trying some on & I said, "They're a little too tight." And this salesman says, "Try pulling the tongue out." & I said, "Nath, theyth sthill feelth a bith tighth."

Three passengers strike up a conversation in the airport in Bozeman,

Montana. One is an American Indian passing through from Lame Deer. Another is a cowboy on his way to Billings & the third is a fundamentalist Arab student, newly arrived at Montana State University from the middle East. Their discussion drifts to their diverse cultures. Soon, the two westerners learn that the Arab is a devout, radical Muslim and the conversation lulls. Finally, the Indian clears his throat & softly speaks, "At one time my people were many, but sadly, now we are few." The Muslim raises an eyebrow & leans forward & says, "Once my people were few, and now we are many. Why do you suppose that is?" The cowboy says, "That's because we ain't played cowboys and Muslims yet, but I do believe it's a comin'."

I had a friend once who had a love of limburger cheese. He had to have it three meals a day. When he became middle-aged he made his wife promise to put a big jar of limburger cheese in his coffin when he died. So, when he died, she did just that and when the pallbearers were carrying the coffin out, they had to go down some stairs with it and when they did, that jar of limburger cheese fell over & spilled in the coffin. Folks, they dropped that coffin & started walking off when the funeral director said, "Hey, what're you guys doing?" They said, "Well, if he can do that, he can get up & walk!"

Two green beans are crossing the freeway when one of them is hit by an 18 wheeler. His friend scrapes him up & rushes him to the hospital. After hours of surgery, the Dr. says, "I have good news & bad news." The healthy bean says, "Okay, give me the good news first." The Dr. says, "He's going to live!" So, what's the bad news?" "The bad news is, he'll be a vegetable he rest of his life!"

Jobs are sometimes hard to find. When I was a young man I worked at a lot of different jobs. I used to work in a blanket factory, but it folded. Then it was the orange juice factory. I got fired there, cause I couldn't concentrate. Then I worked at a fire-plug factory, but I quit. Folks, you couldn't park within a mile of that place. After that I got a job at a Pork-&-Bean factory, but I got fired there. See, I was puttin' the beans in the "Pork & Bean" cans upside down & people were getting the hiccups.

Things have sure changed over the years. I remember my 1st job. I was selling vacuum cleaners. Of course they gave me the worst territory to work. One day I was out in the 'boonies' & I went to this old farmhouse. The lady let me come in & I was in her kitchen going into my sales pitch & I pulled a sack of dirt out of my briefcase, threw it on the floor & I said, "If this vacuum cleaner won't clean that up, I'll eat that dirt!" She says, "Well, you better get to eatin' cause we ain't got no electricity."

_____ went to buy a new car while back. He picked out a Cadillac he liked & the salesman priced it at $33,334. _____ says, "Well, how much will you knock off if I pay cash?" The salesman says, "Twelve & a half percent." So _____ goes to a café across the street & tries to figure the cost on a napkin, but he couldn't do it. So he calls the waitress over to refill his coffee & he asks her, "How much would you take off for twelve & a half per cent of $333,334?" She says, "Everything but my earrings!"

So, two peanuts walk into a bar & one was a-salted.

Well, I lost my job this week.
() WHAT HAPPENED, WHY AREN'T YOU WORKING?
Oh, the boss & I had a fight & he won't take back what he said.
() WHAT DID HE SAY?
He said, "You're fired!!"

I've got a quiz for you. What do you call frozen water?
() ICED WATER.
What do you call frozen ink?
() ICED INK.

You're telling me!

I just got back from spending a few days in Branson. I went fishing with Shoji Tabuchi. Boy, I'll never do that again.
() WHY?
Cause, he kept eating all the bait!

Yeah, we've known each other a long time. There's nothing I wouldn't do for him & there's nothing he wouldn't do for me. So, we just go around doing nothing for each other.

A new supermarket opened in our area. It has an automatic water mister to keep the produce fresh. Just before it goes on, you hear the sound of distant thunder & the smell of fresh rain. When you pass the milk cases, you hear cows mooing & you experience the scent of fresh mown hay. In the meat department there is the aroma of charcoal grilled steaks with onions. When you approach the egg case, you hear hens cluck & cackle, & the air is filled with the pleasing aroma of bacon & eggs frying. The bread department features the tantalizing smell of fresh baked bread & cookies. We don't buy toilet paper there anymore.

Leading a buffalo on a rope, a man walks into a café, sits his shotgun on the counter & orders coffee. After drinking one gulp, he blasts the buffalo with the gun & leaves. He returns the next morning with gun & another buffalo in tow. "Coffee please." The waiter says, "We're still cleaning up after the mess you left yesterday. What was that all about anyway?" The man smiled real big & says, "I'm training for upper-management. I come in, drink coffee, shoot the bull, leave a mess for others to clean up & disappear for the rest of the day."

This morning I was sitting on a park bench next to a homeless man. I asked him how he ended up this way. He said, "Up until last week, I still had it all! A cook cooked my meals, my room was cleaned, my clothes were washed, pressed, I had a roof over my head, I had TV, internet, I went to the gym, the pool, the library, I could still go to school." So I asked him, "What happened? Drugs? Alcohol? Divorce?" He said, "Oh no, nothing like that, I just got out of prison."

Course, a lot of men are homeless. Some are just home less than others.

Saw my friend Frank again the other day. He had on some $500 Gucci shoes & a suit that was a dazzler & he was getting out of a BMW. I said, "Frank, I remember just a year ago you were down & out, broke & ready to end your life & I told you to go home, get your bible, set it on the table, close your eyes, open your bible, put your finger on the page, open your eyes & be guided by what it says." Frank says, "Well, that's exactly what I did! I said, "What did it say?" He said, "Chapter eleven."

What do you get if you take the interior from a Ford, the exterior from a Toyota, & the transmission from a Chevy?
Three years behind bars & two years probation.

Took my cousin to the airport before the holidays & I asked the clerk; "Why is there mistletoe hanging over the baggage counter?" He said, "So you can kiss your luggage goodbye."

I wonder what happens if you get scared half to death twice?

What do you call the clone of a police officer? A copy.

What do you call a frozen police officer? A copsicle!

(MC) COUGH-COUGH-COUGH, TAKE OVER FOR ME ____.
Okay--cough-cough-cough.

Listen ______, I'll give you $100 to do my worrying for me.
() THAT'S GREAT, WHERE'S THE HUNDRED?
That's your 1st worry.

It's bad to suppress laughter--if you do, it'll go down & spread your hips

---

How many men does it take to change a roll of toilet paper? Nobody knows, it's never been done.

I come from a Dutch background. In fact, I recently found out that one of my great-great-great-ancestors invented the wooden shoe. But he died trying to put out a campfire.

Did you ever stop to think & forget to start again?

I guess I have too much time on my hands. I like to go into Wal-Mart; show people my driver's license & demand to know "whether they've seen this man!"

Remember, if the world didn't suck, we'd all fall off.

According to a recent survey by the Academy of Incomplete Research, 9 out of 10--------.

---

51 years ago, Herman James, a North Carolina mountain man, was

drafted by the Army. On his 1st day in basic training, the Army issued him a comb. That afternoon the Army sheared off all his hair. On his 2nd day, the Army issued Herman a toothbrush. That afternoon the Army dentist yanked 7 of his teeth. On the 3rd day, the Army issued him a jock strap. The Army's been looking for Herman for 51 years.

A Polish immigrant went to the DMV to apply for a driver's license. 1st, of course he had to take an eye exam test. The Optician showed him a card with the letters 'CZWIXNOSTACZ'. So the optician ask him; "Can you read this?" & the Polish guy says, "Read it, I know the guy!"

I went out of town this week & I'd been driving all night so I pulled into this city park of a little town & went to sleep in the front seat. Pretty soon a jogger knocks on my window, I roll it down & he says, "What time is it?" I said, "8:15." After that, I made a sign, put it in the windshield reading: 'I don't have the time!" & I went back to sleep. In a few minutes another jogger knocked on the window. I rolled it down & he said, "It's 8:30."

The other day I got my tie caught in a FAX machine---before I knew it, I was in San Francisco.

Sometimes I feel as useless as an ashtray on a motorcycle.

You know what one of my favorite things to do? I go in a Wal-Mart to the Men's Clothing Section, take something in a dressing room to try on & a book to read. Pretty soon a salesperson will come over & say; "Is everything alright in there sir?" & I say, "Hey, do you know you're out of toilet paper in here?"

Prejudging our fellow man: A Jew & an Oriental were sitting on a park bench. All of a sudden the Jew knocks the Oriental off the bench.

The Oriental asks, "What'd you do that for?" The Jew says, "That was because of Pearl Harbor!" The Oriental says, "Well, that was caused by the Japanese, I'm Chinese!" The Jew says, "Japanese, Chinese, it's all the same to me!" The Chinaman sets back down & pretty soon he knocks the Jew off the bench. The Jew asks, "What'd you do that for?" The Chinaman says, "That was because of the Titanic!" The Jew says, "The Titanic was caused by an ice berg!" The Chinaman says, "Iceberg-Goldberg, it's all the same to me!"

Did I tell you about my trip to Europe? Of course I went to my barber to get a haircut before I left & I told him about my plans & I almost decided not to go after talking to him. He asks me how I was going to travel. I said, "We'll fly, of course." He says, "You won't like that. The ride is rough, they lose your luggage, they never arrive on time." Then he asked where we were staying. I said, "We have reservations at the Hilton in Rome." He says, "You won't like that, the beds are hard & the foods weird." "What are you wanting to do in Rome?" I said, "We want to see things like the Sistene Chapel & maybe try to see the Pope." He said, "Man, you won't be able to understand anybody & besides there's always 10,000 people trying to see the Pope." Well, we went & when we got back, I went to get another haircut & the barber gave me the 3rd degree. I told him the flight was great, they didn't lose our luggage, the hotel was great, the food was awesome & we could speak to English-speaking people everywhere we went. He says, "Well, you didn't get to see the Pope did you?" I said, "We sure did, we didn't have to wait more than 5 minutes." "What did he say?" I said, "Well, I knelt down by his feet to receive his blessing. He pulled me up by my shoulders & whispered in my ear." The barber asked, "What did he say?" The Pope said, "For Pete's sake man, where'd you get that terrible haircut?"

The YO-YO was 1st introduced on this day in 1929. Of course this was a huge improvement over its predecessor the YO.

An officer stopped me. He said, "Let me see your license." I said, "I wish you people would make up your mind. Yesterday you took my license, today you want to see it again."

So, he took me down to the city jail, but they couldn't keep me because somebody had stole all the bathroom facilities. But they couldn't catch cause they didn't have anything to go on.

I don't think I'll travel by air anymore. The last time I flew the flight attendant approached a gentleman who was protesting rather loudly. The gentleman said, "I want to complain about this airline, every time I fly, I get the same seat. I can't see the in-flight movie, & there are no window blinds, so I can't sleep." & the flight attendant said, "Aw, captain, just shut up & land the plane."

This is a story how intelligence prevails over brawn. A timid little man was seated in the window seat of an airplane next to a scowling brute of a guy. The little man was terrified of flying, & as soon as the plane took off, he felt sick. But his seatmate was fast asleep & he couldn't figure out how to get past him to the bathroom. And then it was too late; he got sick all over the big guy. As he frantically wiped up the mess; careful not to wake the giant, the brute's eyes flew open. The timid man smiled & said in a shaky voice, "Feeling better now?"

Went out West to an Indian reservation & I got acquainted with an old chief there. I asked him, "What's your name?" He said, "Chief Hockawristwatch, I'm a Pawnee." I said, "Well, that's a rather unusual name, what's your wife's name?" He said, "Wife's name is 'Three Horses'." I said, "That's certainly a funny name for a woman!" He said, "Indian name---mean nag-nag-nag."

Did you ever notice how irons have a setting for 'Permanent Press', I don't get it.

Boy, I've been busy. I'm conducting a seminar on 'Multiple Personality Disorders' & it's taking me forever to fill out the name tags.

Our neighbors across the street caught a burglar in their bedroom the other night. The burglar said, "Now that you've seen me, I'm gonna have to shoot you." So, he pointed the gun at the woman & said, "I like to know the names of my victims. What's your name?'
She said, "Elizabeth." The burglar says, "I can't go through with this, my Mother was named Elizabeth." So, he pointed the gun at the husband & asks, "What's your name?" My neighbor says, "My name is Joe, but all my friends call me Elizabeth!"

Remember: A bird in the hand is worthless when you want to blow your nose.

How many ears did Davy Crockett have? Three. His left ear, his right ear & the wild front ear.

The origin of profiling: The day it all started was March 6, 1836. On that fateful day Davy Crockett woke up & rose from his bunk on the main floor of the Alamo & walked up to the observation post along the West wall of the fort. William B. Travis & Jim Bowie were already there, looking out over the top of the wall. These 3 great men gazed at the hordes of Mexicans moving towards the Alamo. With a puzzled look on his face, Crockett turned to Bowie & said, "Jim, are we by any chance having any landscaping done today?"

Remember folks, if you think nobody cares, try missing a couple of payments.

Good advice from a cowboy: Don't squat with your spurs on.

In closing, I'd like to announce that '____ ____' has just signed a recording contract with Columbia Records. It's a pretty good contract. We send them $20 a month & they send us 24 Cds a year.

I've given up on social media for now & I'm trying to make friends outside Facebook while applying the same principles. Every day, I walk down the street & tell passersby what I've eaten, how I feel, what I did the night before& what I will do tomorrow. Then I give them pictures of my family, my dog, & me gardening. I also listen to their conversations & tell them I love them. And it works. I already have 3 people following me--2 police officers & a psychiatrist.

There's something to be said for older methods of communications---like the mail. Here's an example: Dear Charlie, we've been neighbors for 6 tumultuous years. When you borrowed my snowblower, you returned it in pieces. When I was sick, you blasted hard rock music. And when your dog decorated my lawn, you laughed. I could go on, but I'm not one to hold grudges. So I'm writing this letter to tell you that your house is on fire. Cordially, Harry.

How come Sherlock Holmes never paid any income tax? Brilliant deductions.

Some things you never want to hear at the tattoo parlor: "Eagle? I thought you said beagle! Or, "Anything else you want to say, you've got all kinds of room back here."

An Englishman, a Frenchman & a New Yorker are captured by cannibals. The cannibal chief says, "We're going to kill you, eat you & use your skins to make a canoe. But, you get to choose how you die." The Englishman pulls out a revolver, yells,"God save the Queen" & shoots himself in the head. The Frenchman grabs a bottle of cyanide, shouts, "Vive La France", drinks the poison & dies. Now it's the New Yorker's turn. He pulls out an ordinary table fork & as he stabs himself all over his body he shouts, "The heck with your dat-gum canoe!"

I've been busier than a one-eyed man at a topless bar.

When I left the ranch, I was a 3-letter man.
() WHY, DID THEY HAVE A FOOTBALL TEAM?
No, I sat on a branding iron.

() SAY LARRY, CAN YOU TELL ME, HOW DO YOU GET RID OF FLEAS?
That's easy. Taka a bath in sand & rub down in alcohol. The fleas get drunk & kill each other throwing rocks.

-Did you hear about the ship bound for San Francisco with a cargo of yo-yo,s that got caught in a violent storm? It sank 42 times.

A miracle happened in downtown K.C. A guy fell off a 10 story building & landed on the sidewalk without a scratch. A big crowd gathered around him & a cop came over to the guy & asked him, "What happened?" The guy says, "I don't know, I just got here!"

Did anybody drop a roll of bills with a rubber band around them?
() YEAH, I DID
Well, I just found the rubber band.

() YOU KNOW LARRY, I PASSED YOUR HOUSE LAST NIGHT.
Thanks.

() YOU KNOW LARRY, ANTICS LIKE THAT COULD GET YOU KILLED!
Oh, I don't worry about that. I've already picked my pallbearers for my funeral. Yeah, I've got 6 bankers. I figure they've carried me so long now, that they might as well finish the job.

You know, I feel like I'd like to punch the boss in the jaw again.
() GEE LARRY, DID YOU SAY 'AGAIN'?
Yeah, I felt like doing it last week too.

What do you call a guy who never has gas in public? A private tutor.

You know I've seen some amazing things in life, but the most amazing is the thermos bottle.
() WHAT'S SO AMAZING ABOUT A THERMOS BOTTLE?"
It keeps hot things hot & cold things cold.
() SO?
How does it know? I've got one back stage.
() WHAT'VE YOU GOT IN IT?
Two cups of coffee & a popsickle.

Prom season is here again. Reminds me of my buddy Hugh. Hugh was a good friend when I was growing up. He came from a poor family & they had a sawmill. When Hugh was about 13, he was working at the sawmill & he got a splinter in his eye. It got infected & had to be removed. So, his uncle was good at whittliing & he made Hugh a wooden eye. Hugh's Mom painted that eye to make it look pretty real but he was teased unmercelessly in school. His classmates would call him 'Woodeye'. So Hugh kept to himself & wouldn't have anything to do with girls. Come the time nearing the Prom on his senior year in high school, I started trying to get him to go to the Prom. Finally he relented & said he'd go, but he wouldn't dance or anything. About 11:45pm, I told Hugh, "Hugh the band's gonna quit playing soon, why don't you go over there & ask that heavy-set girl to dance before it's too late." He says, "No, she'd probably make fun of my wooden eye." I said, "Now Hugh, she's just as sensitive about being overweight as you are about your wooden eye, so go over & ask her to dance!" So Hugh sidles over to that girl & says, "Care to dance?" She says, "Wood I!" & he says "Fatty-fatty-fatty."

A scientist invented a salve that could bring inanimate objects to life & he decided to try it out on the statue of a great general. Sure enough, the statue gave a quiver & a moment later the General climbed down from his pedestal. The scientist asked him, "I've given you back your life! Tell me General, what's the 1st thing you're going to do?" The General replies, "I'll tell you exactly what I'm gonna do! I'm gonna kill about a million pigeons!"

() YOU KNOW, I'VE BEEN MEANING TO ASK YOU LARRY, IT MUST BE KIND OF DIFFICULT TO EAT SOUP WITH THAT MUSTACHE?
Yeah, it's quite a strain.

I feel like reciting something. Would you like prose or poetry?
() WHAT'S THE DIFFERENCE?
I'll show you: "There once was a young man named Rutt who went into the sea up to his ankles." That's prose. Now if the water'd been 2 feet deeper.
() THAT'S QUITE ALRIGHT, YOU DON'T HAVE TO EXPLAIN!

_______ & I've known each other for a long time. There's nothing I wouldn't do for him & there's nothing he wouldn't do for me. We just go around doing nothing for each other.

Word of wisdom: A bird in the hand is worthless when you want to blow your nose.

Well, it rained twice this week, once for 3 days & again for 4.

I hardly ever complain about the rain though cause I can remember some awful drought years. For instance, in 1954 the corn crop was so bad that we cooked some for dinner & my Father ate 14 acres of corn at one meal!

Yeah, we fed an old hen sawdust instead of oatmeal----she laid 12 eggs & sat on them & when they hatched, 11 of the chickens had wooden legs & the 12th one was a woodpecker.

I had a funny dream last night & I actually chewed the insides out of my pillow.
() WELL, DO YOU FEEL SICK TODAY?
Naw, just a little 'down' in the mouth.

I feel like reciting something . Would you like prose or poetry?
() WHAT'S THE DIFFERENCE?
I'll show you: There once was a young man named Rutt who went into the sea up to his ankles. That's prose. Now if the water'd been 2 feet deeper---
() (Push him away from the microphone.)

I don't care if the basement wall is cracking, please stop telling everyone you come from a broken home!

Russia is planning to build a base on the moon where astronauts will live permanently. When asked if they really wanted to spend the rest of

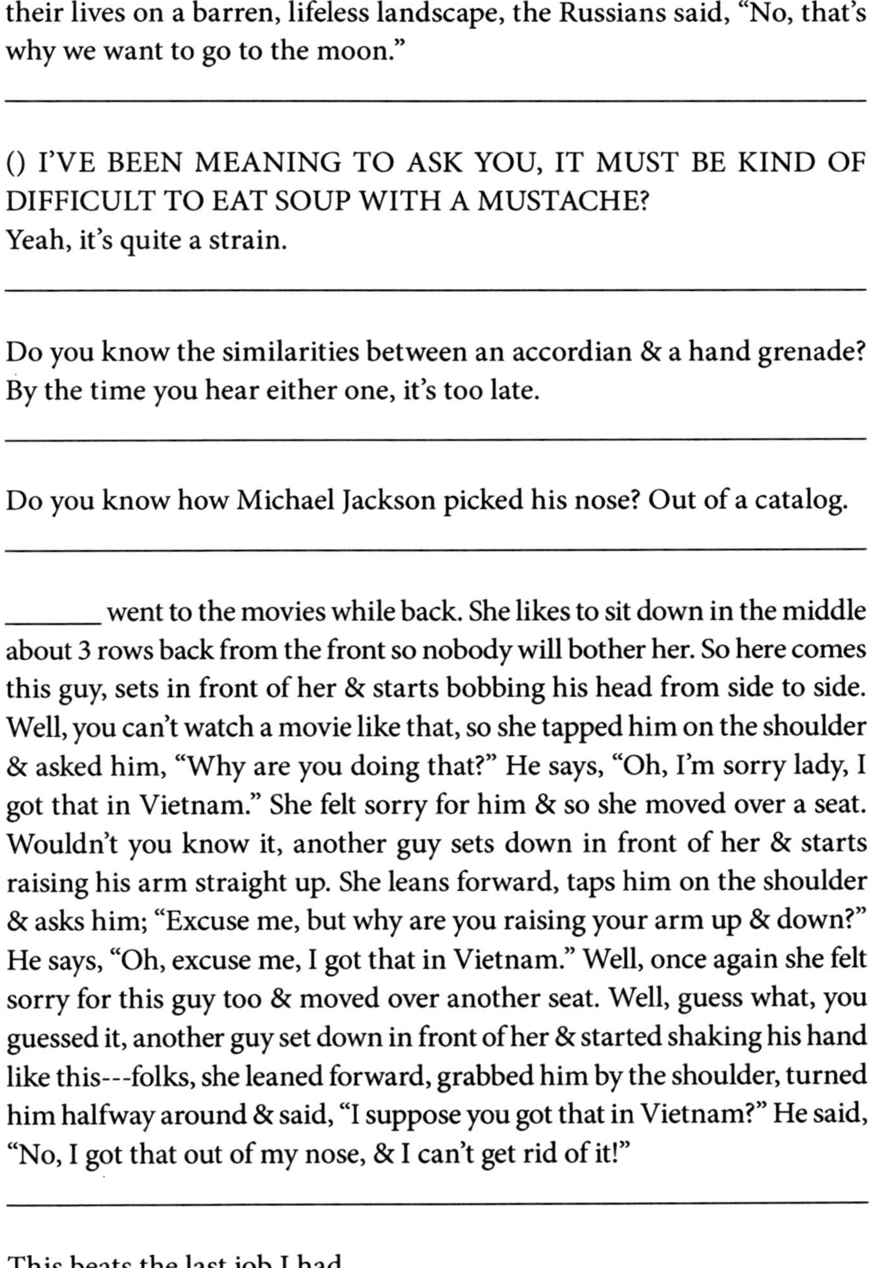

their lives on a barren, lifeless landscape, the Russians said, “No, that’s why we want to go to the moon.”

() I’VE BEEN MEANING TO ASK YOU, IT MUST BE KIND OF DIFFICULT TO EAT SOUP WITH A MUSTACHE?
Yeah, it’s quite a strain.

Do you know the similarities between an accordian & a hand grenade? By the time you hear either one, it’s too late.

Do you know how Michael Jackson picked his nose? Out of a catalog.

_______ went to the movies while back. She likes to sit down in the middle about 3 rows back from the front so nobody will bother her. So here comes this guy, sets in front of her & starts bobbing his head from side to side. Well, you can’t watch a movie like that, so she tapped him on the shoulder & asked him, “Why are you doing that?” He says, “Oh, I’m sorry lady, I got that in Vietnam.” She felt sorry for him & so she moved over a seat. Wouldn’t you know it, another guy sets down in front of her & starts raising his arm straight up. She leans forward, taps him on the shoulder & asks him; “Excuse me, but why are you raising your arm up & down?” He says, “Oh, excuse me, I got that in Vietnam.” Well, once again she felt sorry for this guy too & moved over another seat. Well, guess what, you guessed it, another guy set down in front of her & started shaking his hand like this---folks, she leaned forward, grabbed him by the shoulder, turned him halfway around & said, “I suppose you got that in Vietnam?” He said, “No, I got that out of my nose, & I can’t get rid of it!”

This beats the last job I had.
() WHAT WERE YOU DOING?
I was workin’ in a bloomer factory, pullin’ down about $300 a week.

At one time, when I was younger I was quite an artist. I became very popular at painting peoples portraits. One day a lady came to me & said, "I want you to paint me in the nude." I said, "Oh no, that wouldn't be right. I couldn't do that!" She said, "Well, I'll give you $10,000 if you'll paint me in the nude." I said, "Well, okay, but I'll at least have to wear my socks, because I need someplace to keep my brushes!"

Know what thr mayonaise said to the refrigerator? Close the door, I'm dressing.

Let's talk about one of the world's most disgusting inventions---The Answering Machine. People are getting so used to these answering machines---I called & got a real person last week, & neither one of us spoke. We were both waiting for the beep.

Everybody's got these answering machines. My folks bought one, & thay don't even have a phone!

I guess we gotta get used to it. Everything is going to be automated in the future. Even Emergency 911: Thank you for calling 911. If you're being murdered--press 1. I you're suffering from a split personality--press 2,3 & 4. If you're battling Satan--press 666. If you're being assaulted--press ###. If you're already dead--Stay on the line, & an operator will be with you shortly.

The YO-YO was 1st introduced on this day in 1929. Of course this was a huge improvement over its predecessor the YO.

People are always asking me; "Larry, why do you always have a smile on your face?" & I just tell them, "Cause, it looks silly on other parts of my body."

Did anybody drop a roll of bills with a rubber band around them?
() YEAH, I DID!
Well, I found the rubber band.

I was walking past a mental institution last week & there was a high wooded fence. It was a nice day & I could hear the patients playing some kind of game. They were hollering 13, 13, 13 & I couldn't see over the fence, but I found a knothole & I bent over & peeked into that knothole & some guy poked me in the eye with a stick. Then they started shouting 14, 14, 14.

Never say anything bad about a man until you've walked a mile in his shoes. By then he's a mile away, you've got his shoes & you can say whatever you want to.

How much do pirates pay for corn? A buccaneer.

It was so cold: The politicians had their hands in their own pockets.

It was so cold: We had to chop up the piano for firewood---but we only got 2 chords.

A family went on vacation to the ocean. The son wandered back down the beach to his dad dragging the top half of a bikini bathing suit along the edge of the beach. His dad said, "Son, show Daddy exactly where you found that."

Did you tell Jake down at the barber shop that I'm a thieving, lying shyster?
() NO, I DON'T KNOW HOW HE FOUND OUT.

I've been out of town all week & I stayed at some 'dilly' motels. One of them you had to be real careful---when you turned on the 'hot' water faucet, cold water came out, & when you turned on the 'cold' water faucet, 'hot' water came out. But it didn't make any difference.
() WHY NOT?
Because, there was no hot water.
() WHAT WAS THE NAME OF THAT MOTEL?
I don't know, I'll have to look through my towels.

How to keep salesmen away: A sign was posted on the front door of an Arkansas home that read: We shoot every 3rd salesman, & the 2nd one just left.

We had a one-row corn picker when I was a kid, which reminds me of a young fellow who went to the Marine Recruiter's office & said, "I want to be a Marine!" The recruiter said, "Well, young fella, what makes you think you've got the grit to be a marine?" The boy says, "I'll tell you what sergeant, I was in the cornfield pickin' corn & the schucks & stalks got hung up in that contraption & instead of shutting it down, I tried to clear it out, but I got caught & it tore my arm off. So, I shut it down & got my arm out of there, went to the house, there was nobody home, so I sewed that arm on myself!" The recruiter was about to faint after listening to all this, He says, "Son, that's what I call true grit, you can be a Marine!" The boy sticks his thumbs out (one up, one down).

Shirley & I have several great grandchildren & we've learned a lot from them. For instance:
A king size water-bed holds enough water to fill a 2000 square foot house 4 inches deep
Or, when you hear the toilet flush & the words uh oh, it's already too late.
Also, No matter how much Jell-O you put in a swimming pool, you still can't walk on water.

Did you hear about the skeleton they found in Sani-Flush, Ark. Last week? Yeah, it was the winner of the 1965 Centenial Hide & Seek Contest.

A salesman walks into a bar & asks, "You know where Bubba lives?" The bartender says, "Sure, but you got to be careful. Don't honk your horn when you pull up in front of Bubba's house." The salesman asks, "Why not?" & the barkeep says, "Well, you see about 3 months ago, Bubba's wife ran off with a banjo player named _____ & every time Bubba hears somebody honk, he's afraid the banjo player's bringing her back."

I was at this banquet & my false teeth were hurting me, so the guy sitting next to me reaches into his pocket & pulls out some dentures & says, "Try these." So, I do, but they're too tight. He gives me another set & says, "Try these!" I try them & they're fine. I wear them for the rest of the banquet, then I gave them back. I said, "Thanks, lucky for me I was sitting next to a dentist." He says, "No, I'm an undertaker."

Did you know that half of all people are below average?

() I HEAR YOUR GRANDSON'S GOING TO COLLEGE.
Yeah, that's right.
() SO, WHAT DO YOU THINK HE'LL BE WHEN HE GRADUATES?
Oh, probably about 35 or 40.

Say, I'm gonna buy a plot for my brother.
() DID HE PASS AWAY?
Oh no, he's writing a story.

I like to write poems you know. Here's one:
Roses are red, Violet's are white---
() VIOLET'S ARE BLUE LARRY.

No, Violet's are white, I saw 'em on the clothesline this morning.

What has 4 legs, is big, green, fuzzy & could kill you if it fell out of a tree? A pool table.

A man goes for a skydiving event. He jumps out of the plane, pulls the rip cord---nothing happens, he pulls the emergency cord----nothing happens. When he gets about 100 feet from the ground he sees a fellow flying up. He asks, "Know anything about parachutes?" The other guy says, "No, do you know anything about gas stoves?"

Did you notice that Cuba doesn't have a rowing team in the Olympics? That's because every Cuban who can row already lives in Florida.

What company originated the phrase: 'Good To The Last Drop' ? The Otis Elevator Company.

Why is a person who plays a piano called a pianist, but a person who drives a race car not called a racist?

Why do women wear evening gowns to nightclubs? Shouldn't they be wearing night gowns?

I went into a book store & I asked the woman behind the counter where the 'self-help' section was, She said, "If I told you, that would defeat the purpose!"

You know, there's a lot of 'self-help' cds out there. I bought one called, "How to handle disappointment", I got it home & the case was empty.

Speaking of self-help, do you know what the word 'buffet' means? It's a French word that means; Get up & get it yourself.

Say! The coffee business is getting ridiculous. There's a new coffee company that delivers overnight. It's called 'Federal Expresso'.

Did you ever stop to think & forget to start again?

I have too much time on my hands. I like to go into Wal-Mart; show people my driver's license & demand to know whether they've seen this man!

() WELL LARRY, HOW'S YOUR NEW JOB?
I quit.
() WHY?
For several reasons. The unfriendlyness, sloppy workmanship, terrible language---my boss just wouldn't put up with it!

I have an uncle that's conceited. He's 7 feet tall & plays the flute.
() WHAT MAKES YOU THING HE'S CONCEITED, JUST BECAUSE HE'S 7 FEET TALL & PLAYS THE FLUTE?
Well, that's high-falutin' ain't it?

Life on the farm was always interesting. I remember one time Ma was in the kitchen & she hollered out, "Pa, you need to go out & fix the outhouse." Pa says, "There ain't nothing wrong with the outhouse!" She says, "Yes there is, now get out there & fix it!" So, Pa mosies out to the outhouse, looks around & yells back, "Ma, there ain't nothing wrong with the outhouse!" Ma says, "Stick your head in the hole!" Pa yells back, "I ain't stickin' my head in that hole!" Ma says, "Ya have to stick your head in that hole to see what to fix!" So, Pa sticks his head in the hole, looks around & yells back, "Thar ain't nothing wrong with this outhouse!" Ma hollers back, "Now, take your head out of the hole!" Pa proceeds to pull his head out of the hole, then starts yelling; "Ma, help, my beard is stuck in the cracks in the toilet seat!" Ma says, "Hurts don't it?"

I just arrived from Canada. I came by dogsled. We had a woman driver. She hollered 'mush'!, I hollered 'mush' & while we were mushing, somebody stole my sled!

On New Years Eve, I go crazy. Last year just at the stroke of midnight, I grabbed the person next to me & kept kissing until 'Auld Lang Syne' was finished. I'll never forget that night. I don't think Henry will either!

I'm very proud to be a friend of his--& it's not easy to be a man's only friend.

I slept like a log last night---I woke up in the fireplace.

I just got out of the hospital last week. I don't like hospitals. As soon as the hospital made me put on one of those little gowns, I knew the end was in sight.

I got hit in the head with a can of soda today. I was lucky it was a soft drink.

A man & his wife moved back home to Kentucky from Indiana. The husband had a wooden leg & to get insurance on it back in Indiana it cost them $1700 a year. When they arrived in Kentucky, they went to an insurance agency to see how much it would cost to
Insure his wooden leg. The agent looked it up on the computer & said,

"It'll be $39.00." The husband was shocked & asked why it was so cheap here in Kentucky. The insurance agent turned his computer screen to the couple & said, "Well, here it is on the screen, it says; Any wooded structure with a sprinkler system above it is $39.00. You just have to know how to describe it!"

My Father taught me to be frugal. In fact, my Father originated the Limbo Dance. He was trying to get into a pay toilet without paying.

You think I'm looney, I had one aunt who thought she was the Goodyear Blimp. Sure, it sounds crazy to you, but she got to see a lot of football games for free!

One night on stage I was singing Zipdeedoodah Zipadeeday, my Oh my what a ---& a woman on the front row started singing, Zipadeedoodah-zipadeedoodah. I looked down & I'd forgotten to zip up my doo-dah.

O'brien crossed a four-leaf-clover with poison ivy.
() WHAT DID HE GET?
A rash of good luck

I come from a big family. I slept in the same bed with 5 brothers. We had a bed-wetter. It took us 3 years to find out who it was. I always came home late so I could sleep on top. Then my oldest brother got married & we slept 7 to the bed.

Yeah, 5 brothers. That's how I learned to dance---waiting in line to get into the bathroom.

Change is inevitable except from a vending machine.

He's proof that every family tree has some sap in it.

My Mother got up at 5:00 o'clock in the morning no matter what time it was.

A man walked into the barber shop. He asks, "How much for a haircut?" The barber says, "$12.00." "How much for a shave?" "$10.00." The man says, "All right, shave my head."

() NOW LARRY, LET'S SEE HOW SHARP YOU ARE TONIGHT. GIVE ME A SENTENCE WITH THE WORD 'DIADEM' IN IT. Okay, people who drive onto railroad crossings without looking 'DIADEM' sight quicker than those who stop, look & listen.

A man stopped in at Jim's barber shop this week. He took off his toupee & said, "I want a shampoo & haircut & I'll be back in half an hour."

My Mother would try to rock me to sleep as a child, but I kept dodging the rocks.

One time we went to a Middle Eastern Restaurant where I knew they served camel meat. I asked the waiter for a glass of water, & they didn't bring it for 10 days. I ordered a camel burger & the waiter asked, "One hump or two?"

We were settiin' there & my wife said, "Get your elbows off the table!" I did, & my face fell in the soup.

Every morning I make coffee in my pajamas, someday I'll try a pot.

Don says he only has 3 gray hairs on his head. But hey, 3 out of 4.

Dennis is having a celebration. He told us all to meet at Denny's & say it's our birthday. (he's tight)

There's a new invention--it's self-cleaning restrooms for gas stations. The maker says it won't take anyone's job, because noone has ever cleaned them.

Ladies & gentlemen, as a public service, the show you are about to see will not be seen by our Armed Forces over seas.

I called Ty the other day & you wouldn't believe how he answered the phone. "Incontinence hot line, can you hold please?"

Recently a poll of people in New York City showed that 80% of them wouldn't live anywhere else in the world. Besides, it was reported, it would violate the terms of their parole.

I see you just set your hair. What time does it go off?

I have a friend that specializes in Mohawk Hairstyles. He doesn't do it for a living though. He just cuts hair on the side.

I got in a long line at the Super Market the other day. It took me so long to get up to the cashier, my fruit was no longer in season, my coupons had expired & I got a discount for day-old-bread.

I saw a man out here at the ticket booth tonight & his right arm seemed to be frozen in this position with his hand glued to his hip. (demonstrate) I said, "Sir, I know it isn't polite to ask, however, I"ve never seen a deformity like yours. What happened to your arm?" The man looked down at his arm & said, "Oh, no, I've dropped my pumpkin!"

With all this refreshing patriotism that abounds nowadays, it's great. If I was a young man I'd probably go right down & enlist again. I remember when I was 18 & I went to the recruiter, there was a young man about my age in front of me saying; "But, you've got to take me, I've told my boss what I think of him, I proposed to 3 girls & I sold my car!"

I'm afraid I lost us a customer tonight Dennis. There was a lady setting in the middle, about the 3rd row from the back & she got there about 7:00 O'clock. I'd never seen her before, so I thought I'd make her welcome & get acquainted, so I sat down beside her & introduced myself. She says, "What time does this show start anyhow, I've been settin' here so long, my rear's gone to sleep!" I said, "I know, I heard it snoring awhile ago."

My little 9 year-old great grandaughter has decided what she wants to be when she grows up. She says, "I wanta be a 'garbage collector." I said, "That's a strange ambition Cozy, why do you want to be a 'garbage collector'?" She says, "Cause, 'garbage collectors' only work on Tuesdays!"

Did you ever go to the ballet? The costumes are what get me--I mean they're so tight, if you have a tattoo, you have to wear it outside your leotards!

I guess my problem is, I don't understand ballet. I don't understand calculus either, but I've never paid $50 to go watch calculus.

I was so bored this week, I was about to run around the house naked but then I drank a bottle of Windex & it kept me from streaking.

An Arkansasyer walks down the road wearing one shoe. He meets a man from Missouri who says, "How did you lose your shoe?" The Arky says, "Didn't lose a shoe, I found one."

Had a bit of confusion at the grocery this morning. When I was ready to pay for my groceries, the cashier said, "Strip down facing me!" At first I made a mental note to write my congressman & complain about Homeland Security running amok, bu I did just as she instructed. When the hysterical shrieking & alarms finally subsided, I found out she was referring to how to insert my debit card. I've been asked to shop elsewhere in the future, but I told them they need to make their instructions a little clearer.

() LARRY, DO YOU HAVE A BURIAL PLAN?
Don't need one, I'm gonna be buried in the Wal-Mart parking lot.
() NOW, WHY WOULD YOU WANT TO BE BURIED THERE?
Cause, I figure if I'm buried there, at least my wife will visit me 2 or 3 times a week.

A Mexican bandit made a specialty of crossing the Rio Grande off & on, robbing banks in Texas. A reward was offered & a Texas Ranger decided to track him down. Finally, after months of searching, he traced the bandit to his favorite cantina, snuck up behind him, put his six-shooter to the bandit's head & said, "You're under arrest. Tell me where you hid the loot or I'll shoot you!" But the bandit couldn't speak or understand English, & the Ranger couldn't speak or understand Spanish. The Ranger asked the bartender to translate his message. The terrified bandit blurted out, in Spanish that the loot was buried under the oak tree in back of the cantina. The Ranger asks the bartender, "What did he say?" The bartender says, "He say, 'He no afraid to die'."

The latest survey shows that 3 out of 4 people make up 75% of the population.

A traveling salesman stops for gas in Billings, Montana & asks how far it is to Bozeman. A fellow says, "180 miles, but don't try to go cause there's gonna be a blizzard. The salesman says, "Oh that doesn't stop a traveling salesman, & he drives on & the snow gets deeper & deeper. Finally his car won't go. He sees a light from a farmhouse miles away. He gets out & walks until he's exhausted. So he's crawling on his hands & knees & he finally reaches the back porch on the farmhouse. He scratches on the screen door. The farmer comes to the door & asks, "What can I do for you?" The salesman says, "I'm a traveling salesman & I'd like to stay in your house for the night please." The farmer says, "Okay, but I'll tell you right now, I don't have a daughter!" The salesman says, "How far is it to the next farmhouse?"

I got so bored last Saturday night that I drove downtown, found a great parking spot. Then I just sat in my car & counted how many people ask me if I was leaving.

Be kind to your friends--without them, you'd be a total stranger.

I used to be a grave digger but I quit. I got tired of the 'hole' business.

For my last birthday I got a humidifier & a de-humidifier. I put them in the same room & let 'em fight it out.

Now, I'll do something & you guess what I'm doing.
() ALL RIGHT
What am I doing?
() NOTHING.
Yes, I am.
() WHAT ARE YOU DOING?
I'm going upstairs.
() BUT YOU'RE NOT MOVING!
I know, I'm on an elevator.

() I THINK YOUR ELEVATOR DOESN'T GO ALL THE WAY TO THE TOP FLOOR LARRY.

This is a good job. I used to work at the Unemployment Office. I hated it because when they fired me, I had to show up for work anyway.

I'm reading a book about ANTI-GRAVITY. I just can't put it down.

Had a nightmare last night. I dreamt I ate a whole box of shredded wheat. I woke up & half my mattress was gone.

Had a nightmare last night. I dreamt I ate a 5 # marshmallow. I woke up & my pillow was gone.

Well then, how do you feel? Oh, I'm a little down in the mouth.

Look at that man with one eye. (COVER ONE EYE)

I had an aunt & uncle who lived in Oklahoma & they leased their land for oil exploration for years. So these geologists decided there was oil under their property & they came in there & drilled down 5000 feet without striking oil, so they decided to cap the hole off & leave. My uncle said, "Hold on there, how about settin' my outhouse over that hole, shucks, I won't have to dig another hole for the rest of my life." They said, "Sure, we'd be glad to." The next day my uncle was down in the corn field cultivating & one of the oil riggers came down there & stopped him. He said, "What's wrong?" The guy says, "Well, your wife's been in that outhouse for over an hour, something's wrong!" So, my uncle gets down off the tractor & walks up to the outhouse, opens the door, & there she sets all blue in the face. He starts back to the field & the rigger says, "Hey, ain't there something wrong with her? My uncle says, "Naw, she always holds her breath 'til she hears it hit bottom.

I was just thinking. What a good thing Adam had. When he said something, he knew nobody'd said it before.

Adam was created 1st ---to give him a chance to say something.

I just got back on a flight from Hot Springs. That's a little bit below Burnt Mattress. That flight was so rough that the flight attendants poured the food directly into the 'sick-sacks'.

Do you know that every time I breath, a man dies?
() WELL, WHY DON'T YOU TRY USING A LITTLE MOUTH WASH NOW & THEN?

If a man is standing in the middle of the forest speaking & there's no woman around to hear him---is he still wrong?

Why do they put Braille on the drive-through bank machines?

Would a fly without wings be called a 'walk'?

______'s a police reporter---Once a week he reports to the police.

Why do KU graduates put their diplomas on the dashboards of their cars? So they can park in handicapped spaces.

My Father had a good sense of humor. One day he was out along the edge of the cornfield next to the road with his ear to the ground. A tourist spots him & stops to ask questions. Dad looked up & said, "Shhhhhhh!" Then he went on listening with even greater intensity. Well, curiosity got the best of the tourist, so he dropped to his knees & listened for a full 3 minutes. Finally he says to Dad; "I don't hear anything!" Dad says, "I know, it's been that way all day long!"

How do you get a KU graduate off your front porch? Pay him for the pizza.

I sent this 'ancestry' site some information on my family tree. They sent back a pack of seed, & suggested that I just start over!

Phil spent $5000 to search his family tree & found out he was the sap.

A silly young man from the Clyde,
In a funeral procession was spied,
When asked, "Who is dead?"
He giggled & said,
"I don't know, I just came along for the ride."

Advice: Never hire an electrician with no eyebrows.

Everything is relative. Like to a bald man---dandruff is a thrill.

They even sell imitation dandruff for people who wear wigs.

My wife has dyed her hair so often, she's got technicolored dandruff.

Did I tell you? I got this great new hearing aid the other day & boy is it fabulous!
() ARE YOU WEARING IT NOW?
I sure am. It cost me $3000, but it's worth it.
() WHAT KIND IS IT?
It's about 8:15.

When I got out of high school in 1957, my buddy Pete asked me if I would like to go on a tour of the United States with him. He'd bought a used 1954 Ford convertible, I had $55 saved up, so I said, "Sure, let's go." Now, before we left, a neighbor lady, Mrs. Dunn had heard rumors of our trip & she called me. She said, "You probably don't know my son John as he graduated 3 years ago, but I want you to look for him & if you find him, have him call home." I said, Well, Mrs. Dunn, this is a big country, do you have any idea where he might be?" She said, "I heard he was in New York City & that's all I know." I said, "Okay, we'll sure look for him." So, we went all over the country & ended up in down-town New York City. We were driving down Wall Street & I saw a sign that said, 'Dunn & Bradstreet' . I said, "Pull over Pete, I bet that's him!" I went inside & up to a lady at a desk & I said, "Is there a John in here?" She says, "Yes, 3rd door down the hall on the right." I walked down the hall & here come a young feller out of that door, I said, "Are you Dunn?" He says, "Yes." I said, "Call home."

On the way here tonight, I was stopped by an officer for speeding. I begged the officer to give me a warning. So, he fired 3 shots over my head.

Ty went to buy a new Cadillac. He found a model & color he liked & he asked the salesman the price. The salesman said, "$33,333.00." Ty says, "How much would you knock off if I paid cash?" The salesman says, ";Twelve and a half percent." Ty says, "I'll think about it." He then goes across the street to a café for a cup of coffee & tries to figure this on a napkin. He's having trouble, so he calls the waitress over for a coffee refill & asks her, "How much would you take off for twelve & a half percent of $33,333.00?" She says, "Everything but my earrings!"

Tonight folks we have a galaxy of international stars performing for us: From Indonesia, Mr. Frank Sumatra; from South America, the gorgeous Bolivia Newton-John; from Bermuda, the acrobatic midgets, the popular Burmuda Shorts, & the Olympic Czechoslovakian Trampoline Team, the sensational 'Bouncing Czechs'.

I saw a strange sign in a jewelry shop window this week. It said, "Ears pierced while you wait."

My home town is so small that the Masons & the Knights of Columbus knew each other's secrets, so they formed a coalition, & they called themselves the Masonites.

My family was poor. We had eleven kids in our family & had to wear each other's clothes. It wasn't funny either. I had 10 sisters.

Introduction: Here's a man who's been like a brother to me. In fact, just yesterday he beat me up & took my bicycle.

But _______ has always been a trendsetter. He was the 1st one in the office to wear brown & white shoes. Then he lost the brown one.

_______ 's been compared to the Vice President of the United States. No one can figure out what either one does.

If a deaf person swears, does his Mother wash his hands with soap?

Did you hear that Fairchild Electronics & Honeywell are merging? Yeah, it'll become 'Fairwell Honeychild'.

Grey Poupon & Docker Pants are expected to become: 'Poupon Pants'.

It's been cold this week. It was so cold the other night that my teeth chattered all night. And we don't even sleep together.

Did you ever buy a cured ham & wonder what it had?

I find it ironic that the colors red, white & blue stand for freedom, until they're flashing behind you.

I got pulled over last week. I was gonna give him a nasty look, but he already had one.

The officer was a really nice guy. He told me about an interesting case he had last week. He called in to the sergeant & told him; "I have a woman out here who just shot her husband for stepping on the floor she's just mopped!" The sergeant asked him, "Have you arrested her?" He said, "No, not yet, the floor's still wet."

On another case, during a bank robbery, the robber's mask fell off. He puts it back on, turns to a man & says, "Did you see my face?" The customer says, “Yes, I did!” & the robber shoots him. Then he turns to a woman & says, “How about you?” She says, “No, but my husband did!”

Show me a man with both feet firmly on the ground, & I’ll show you a man who can’t get his pants off.

Pedro was trying to get into the United States legally through immigration. The officer said, “Pedro, you have passed all the tests, except there is one more test. Unless you pass it you cannot enter the United States.” Pedro says, “I’m ready.” The officer says, “Make a sentence using the words: YELLOW, PINK & GREEN.” Pedro thought for a few minutes & said, “Mister officer, I am ready.” The officer said, “Go ahead.” Pedro says, “The telephone goes green-green-green, I pink it up & say, yellow, this is Pedro.” Pedro now lives in a neighborhood near you.

How many of you are here for the first time or you’ve been here before?

I feel like you’re watching TV & you’re about to change channels.

My great aunt Matilda died this week at the age of 107, but they saved the baby.

Some days you’re the dog & some days you’re the hydrant.

If you spin an Oriental man in a circle 3 times, does he become disoriented

---

Here’s an idea for a new business. I don’t know why the U.S. Government didn’t think of this. A friend of mine just started his own business in

Afghanistan. He's making land mines that look like prayer mats. He's doing well. He says prophets are going through the roof.

Somebody get a plumber, there's a drip in here.

I've been saving for a rainy day & I'm happy to report that in 2 more months I'll have enough to buy that umbrella I've always wanted

---

On this day in 1869 the waffle iron was invented for people who had wrinkled waffles.

On our way back from Chicago, we stopped to sleep a few hours at an old Navy buddy's apartment. It was real late & my buddy's a drinker, so he wanted to show me around the apartment & there was this big brass gong. So, I asked him, "What's that brass gong for?' He said, "That's not a gong, it's a talking clock!" I said, "A talking clock, how's that work?" He said, "Watch." He picked up a hammer, gave the gong an ear shattering pound & stepped back. Someone on the other side of the wall screamed: "Hey, you jerk, it's 3 in the morning!!!"

We're gonna have to fatten up _____ he's lost so much weight. I mean, he's so skinny that he can't keep his seat down at the movies.

And he's the kind of guy who likes to walk up to overweight people in the supermarket & say, "Haven't you had enough already?"

A bum came by our house today & my wife answered the door. He says, "Have you a piece of cake Lady, to give a poor man who hasn't had a bite to eat for 2 days?" She says, "Cake? Isn't bread good enough for you?" He says, "Ordinarily, yes ma'am, but this is my birthday."

If someone with multiple personalities threatens to kill himself, is it considered a hostage situation?

If a parsley farmer is sued, can they garnish his wages?

If a turtle doesn't have a shell, is he homeless or naked?

It's easy to grin when your ship comes in & you've got the stock market beat, But the lad worth while is the lad who can smile, when his shorts are tied up in his seat.

The economy is so bad---that I got a pre-declined credit card in the mail.

And Motel 6 won't leave the light on anymore.

With all the sadness & trauma going on in the world at the moment, it is worth reflecting on the death of a very important person, which almost went unnoticed last week. Larry LaPrise, the man who wrote 'The Hokey Pokey', died peacefully at age 93. The most traumatic part for his family was getting him into the coffin. They put his left leg in & then the trouble started.

THE POLECAT

Once upon a morning dreary, as I staggered weak and weary
Making my way homeward bleary from the festive night before.
I was feeling less than steady for the punch had been quite heady,
And I hoped my bed was ready waiting just inside my door;
That's of course providing I could recognize my own front door
I wanted sleep and nothing more.

I saw a furry little creature and I hurried up to reach her,
Though I beheld a double feature with my eyes so red and sore.
Just a lost and lonely kitty with her fur so soft and pretty
And my heart was filled with pity knowing not what lay in store.
If I could have only known the evil fate that lay in store
I'd have wished to live no more

Much too late I saw my error and I cried out then in terror
For I found myself the bearer of an aromatic gore.\
This was neither half nor whole cat, but a lousy stinking polecat,
And I wished there was a hole that I could hide in ever more.
I was deep in desperate trouble, up the creek without an oar—
And the skunk had declared war.

Suddenly my eyes were burning and my stomach started turning
And my nose hairs all were churning; I felt rotten to the core.
Oh, I tasted it and felt it for the skunk had not withheld it
And I bet you could have smelled it all the way to Ecuador;
Strong enough to make a buzzard lose his lunch upon the floor—
And the skunk poured out some more.

As the polecat sat there gloating, I was filled with fear and loathing.
I would have to burn my clothing and go bathing far offshore
I was perfumed so completely, I was reeking indiscretely.
Would I ever smell as sweetly as I always had before?
Would my friends still come to see me or invite me to their door?
Said the polecat, "NEVERMORE!"

Boy! That song gave me chills & made my skin crawl. Does your skin ever crawl like that?
() YES!
Well, how'd your armpits smell when they went by your nose?

If you get cheated by the Better Business Bureau, who do you complain to?

Did you hear about the claustrophobic astronaut? He just needed a little space.

Two guys moved to Mexico to open a bungee-jumping business. They built a tower & on the 1st day they put on a demonstration to get the local people interested. One of the guys attached the cord to his ankles & dived off the tower. He soared toward the crowd & then sprang back up. But when he got near the top, his buddy noticed that his clothes were torn & the next time he popped up, he had a few scrapes. The 3rd time he looked bruised. Finally he came to a stop & staggered up the ladder. So, his partner says, "What happened buddy?" & the guy says, "I don't know, what's a piñata?"

Did you hear about the ship bound for San Francisco with a cargo of YO-YO's. It got caught in a violent Pacific storm. It sunk 42 times.

On the show tonight will be those fine Filipino contortionists, 'The Manila Folders' & from Dover Delaware, the remarkable 'Dover Twins', Ben Dover & Eileen Dover, who will demonstrate their unusual hobby of twisting animals into the shapes of balloons.

I'll say this. You have a very good nose as noses run.

I need to refer Dennis to a self-help group for compulsive talkers. It's called 'On & on anon'.

Listen Dennis, I'm awful sorry, I can't pay you this month.
() THAT'S WHAT YOU SAID LAST MONTH!
You see, I keep my word.

They say an entertainer will be less nervous if he pictures his audience naked----so, just give me a few seconds, okay?

A recent study shows that 75% of the body's heat escapes through the head. I guess that means you could ski naked if you had a good hat.

We were gonna have a sick comedian on the show tonight, but he called in well.

Humorous epitaphs:
"If you can read this, you're too close, get off my grave idiot."
Another: Grave of a hypochondriac: "See, I told you I was sick!"

A man is writing in his diary: I'm an ideal man---I don't smoke, drink or go to nightclubs. I 've always been faithful to my wife & don't flirt with strange women. I sleep at 8 o'clock & wake up early. I exercise daily & work regular hours. But all this will change as soon as I get out of prison.

Any internet addicts out there? You might be an internet addict if---you refer to going to the bathroom as downloading.

Two guys were riding on an airplane, when one says, "I think I'm gonna throw up!" The other guy says, "Just grab that air sick bag in front of you!" & the 1st guy says, "I would, but I'm afraid she'll slap me silly!"

How many telemarketers does it take to change a light bulb? Only one, but she has to do it while you're eating dinner.

I want to see a show of hands; How many of you folks are opposed to audience participation?

When I was young, I lived in the country.
() WHEN YOU WERE YOUNG, EVERYBODY LIVED IN THE COUNTRY!

When I got out of The Navy, I wanted to start a business out on the farm, so I went to the bank & talked to the loan officer. His name was Dexter Cobb. He said, "What can I do for you young man?" I said, "I'd like to borrow some money to start a business on the farm." He said, "Ha-ha, do you know what we do with hicks like you in the city?" I said, "No, but I know what we do with cobs in the country!"

We were a poor family. Schucks, I didn't have anything to wear 'til I was 7 years old & my Dad bought me a hat so I could look out the window.

& People used to break into our house & leave things.

We were so poor that we couldn't afford to buy laxative, so they used to set me in the outhouse & tell me ghost stories.

() HAVE YOU GOT ANY BROTHERS OR SISTERS?
No, my parents were orphans.

But, as my Dad used to say---------------My Dad wasn't much of a talker.

I've learned some of the facts of life though:

1. If at 1st you don't succeed, skydiving is not for you.

2. Always take time to smell the roses---& sooner or later, you'll inhale a bee.
3. It's always darkest before dawn. So if you're gonna steal the neighbor's newspaper, that's the time to do it.
4. If you're pulled over by a policeman, never say; "I'm surprised you stopped me, Dunkin Donuts has a 3 for one special."

Last night I lay in bed looking up at the stars in the sky & I thought to myself, "Where the heck is the ceiling?"

My brother has a new hairdo. He parts it from ear to ear. He combs the front part forward & the back part backward. I asked him how he liked his new hairdo. He said, "I like it pretty good, but I get tired of people whispering in my nose."

What do you call twin policemen? Copies.

I bought one of those tapes to teach you Spanish in your sleep. During the night, the tape skipped. Now I can only stutter in Spanish.

My neighbor was on vacation last week in Miami & decided to walk the beach & gather some shells. Mostly he found .38 specials & .357 magnums.

A window salesman called ______'s house today. He said, "Hello Mr. ______ I'm calling because our company replaced all the windows in your house with our triple-glazed weather-tight windows over a year ago & you still haven't sent us a single payment!"

_____ said, "But you said they'd pay for themselves in 12 months!"

We were poor folks. I was 10 years old before I found out my name wasn't 'Get Wood'.

Before we go on with the show, I have something to say to all the fans who've written me---I can only say in all sincerity---"The same to you!"

Larry, I passed your house last night. Thanks

Do you remember that grandfather clock of mine that just goes tick-tick-tick, instead of tick-tock, tick-tock? Well, I took it to clock repair shop the other day & this old shopkeeper had a real heavy German accent. He asked me, "Vat sims to be zee problem?" So, I told him that instead of going tick-tock, tick-tock, it goes tick-tick, tick-tick. So, the old boy rummages behind the counter, pulls out a flashlight & walks over to the clock. He shines the beam directly on the face of the clock & he says in menacing tones, "Ve haf vays of making you tock."

How much money do pirates pay to have their ears pierced: a buck-an-ear.

How did the pirate stop smoking? He used the patch.

The world's getting too complex for me. I go to the grocery store & go through the check-out: They ask me, "Paper or plastic?" I just say, "It doesn't matter to me, I'm bi-sacktual!"

Criminals are getting more brazen these days. Thieves broke into the Lee's Summit Jail & took all the toilet fixtures. So far, the police have nothing to go on.

I made a killing on the stock market this week. I shot my broker.

My neighbor's constantly working on their washing machine & his language is often colorful. One day their daughter returned home from a movie & they asked if she'd learned anything from it. She said, "Only a lot of 4-letter words, that until now I always thought were parts of our washing machine."

A teacher asked her middle school class to tell a story with a moral. Kathy went 1st; "Once we were driving a basket of hen eggs to market & we hit a big bump in the road. The eggs broke. The moral is 'don't put all your eggs in one basket'."

Joyce was next, "Once we had a dozen chicken eggs, but when they hatched, we got only ten chicks. The moral is, "Don't count your chickens before they hatch."

Then it was Johnny's turn. "When my Aunt Gertrude was in desert storm, her plane was hit. She bailed out over enemy territory with only a bottle of whiskey & a machine gun. She drank the liquor on the way down so it wouldn't break, & landed in the middle of 100 enemy soldiers. She killed 70 with the machine gun, & when she ran out of bullets, she killed the rest with her bare hands."

The teacher asked, "What is the moral of that terrible story?" Johnny says, "Stay away from my Aunt Gertrude when she's been drinking."

How good are you at algebra? How much is 5q plus 5q?
() TEN Q.
You're welcome.

The difference between a yard sale & trash pickup is how close to the road the stuff is placed.

() LARRY, WHAT'S YOUR WORK EXPERIENCE?
Oh, from time-to-time I was a door-to door salesman, selling wall-to-wall carpeting on a day-to-day basis with a fifty-fifty commission in Walla-Walla.
() AND HOW WAS BUSINESS?
Oh, so-so.

Cliff & I were drivin' down the road & saw stranger walkin' along with a burlap bag over his shoulders. So, we pulled over & gave him a ride. He got in the back seat with his bag & I asked him what was in the bag. He said, "None of your darn business!" I didn't think too much about it, but it bothered Cliff, so pretty soon he asked him what was in the bag & he told Cliff the same thing, "None of yo0ur darn business!" Now, that was all the malarkey I could stand, so I told the guy, "You either tell us what's in the bag, or you can get out & walk!" He says, "Okay, let me out." We let him out, but he left his bag in the back seat.
() WHAT WAS IN IT?
None of your darn business!

Bob was sitting on the plane, waiting to fly to Detroit, when a guy took the seat beside him. The guy was an emotional wreck, pale, hands shaking, obviously in fear. I said, "What's the matter, flying bother you?" He said, "No, I've been transferred to Detroit. I've heard things are terrible there. They've got lots of shootings, gangs, race riots, drugs poor public schools & the highest crime rate in the nation." Bob says, "I've lived in Detroit all my life. It's not as bad as the media says. Find a nice home, go to work, mind your own business & enroll your kids I a nice private school. It's as safe a place as you want to make it." The guy relaxed & stopped shaking, & said, "Oh, thank you, I've been worried to death, but if you live there & say it's okay, I'll take your word for it. By the way what do you do for a living?" Bob says, "I'm a tail gunner on a Budweiser truck."

Our old friend, Gary Bagley got a job as a Sheriff's deputy down in Douglas County. One of his 1st jobs was to patrol a nudist colony & he called in to report to the dispatcher. "Deputy Bagley reporting." The dispatcher asked; "How are things out there Gary?" Gary says, "No problems, except this badge is killing me!"

Did you hear about the lady that got her birth control pills mixed up with her saccharin tablets? She had the sweetest little baby.

MOTHER JOKES

My Mother always told me that lima beans would put hair on my chest. I don't know how she got my sister to eat 'em.

I really don't think my Mother loved me. She used to pack my school lunch in a roadmap.

When I was real little she used to rock me. She used rocks about this size.

One time I played hooky from school & my teacher sent my Mother a 'thank-you note'.

I was thinking today, you know it's been over 40 years since I joined the Navy. Yeah, I was fresh off the farm & I remember writing home to my Mother: "Dear Mom, I miss you, I miss Pa, but most of all, I miss the little potty under my bed. A couple of weeks later she answered: "Don't worry Son, You missed it when you were home too."

My Mother taught me about 'time travel'. She'd say, "If you don't straighten up, I'm going to knock you into the middle of next week.

Three sons left home, went out on their own & prospered. Getting back together, they discussed the gifts they were able to give their elderly Mother.

The 1st : "I built a big house for Mother."
The 2nd : "I sent her a Mercedes with a driver."
The 3rd : Smiled & said, "I've got you both beat. You remember how Mom enjoyed reading the Bible? & you know she can't see very well. I sent her a remarkable parrot that recites the entire Bible. It took elders in the church 12 years to teach him. He's one of a kind. Mama just has to name the chapter & verse & the parrot recites it."

Soon after that their Mother sent out her letters of thanks: "Melton, the house you built is so huge. I live in only one room, but I have to clean the whole house." "Ralph, I am too old to travel. I stay home most of the time, so I rarely use the Mercedes. And the driver is so rude!" "Dearest Donald, you have the good sense to know what your Mother likes. The chicken was delicious."

The things my Mother taught me:
Religion--"You better pray that'll come out of the carpet!"
Time Travel---"If you don't straighten up, I'm going to knock you into the middle of next week!"
Logic---"If you fall out of that swing & break your neck, you're not going to the store with me!"
Contortionism---"Will you look at that dirt on the back of your neck!"
Humor---"When that lawn mower cuts off your toes, don't come running to me!"

MUSICIAN JOKES

Two explorers, camped in the heart of the African jungle, were discussing their expedition. One said, "I came here because the urge to travel is in my blood, city life bored me, the smell of exhaust fumes made me sick, I wanted to see the sun rise over new horizons & hear the flutter of birds that never had been seen by man. I wanted to leave my footprints on sand unmarked before I came. In short, I wanted to see nature in the raw. What about you?" The other guy says, "Oh, I came because my son is taking saxophone lessons!"

A patrolman stopped me for running a red light. I said, "Have mercy on me, I'm a poor musician." He said, "I know, I've heard you."

He says, "Do you have any ID?" I said, "About what?"

How is playing the bagpipes like throwing a javelin blindfolded? You don't have to be good to get everyone's attention.

The Lone Jack Symphony Orchestra had to cancel its performance of Beethoven's 5th . The fellow who played 1st ukulele quit.

And now presenting our 1st musical score of the evening: Brahms 6, Beethoven 2, at the top of the 5th.

What's the difference between a pizza & a drummer? A pizza can feed a family of four.

What's the difference between an Uzzi & an accordion? The Uzzi stops after 20 rounds.

I went to see a friend who's been in a mental institution for a while this week. As I came up on the big front porch of the place, here were these bunch of guys setting on the steps & each one of them had an apple in one hand & a pencil in the other & they were tapping on their apples with the pencil, keeping time & they were singing 'Ave Maria' all in harmony.. I tell you folks, it was the most beautiful singing I had ever heard. I told one of the guys, I said, "That was beautiful, what do you call your group?" He said, "Well, isn't it obvious? We're the Moron Tap-An-Apple Choir."

I went home feeling really good about myself last Saturday night. Some lady told me I had a mellow voice. So, I went home & looked up 'mellow' in the dictionary. It said, "Overripe & almost rotten".

I tried to write a song about drinking, but I couldn't get past the 1st two bars

---

What do you call a guitar player who breaks up with his girlfriend? Homeless.

Two people were walking down the street. One was a musician. The other didn't have any money either.

Do you know the similarities between an accordion & a hand grenade? By the time you hear either one, it's too late.

Three souls appeared before St. Peter at the Pearly Gates. St Peter asked the 1st one, "What was your last annual salary?" The soul replied, "$200,000; I was a trial lawyer." St. Peter asked the 2nd one the same question, The soul answered $95,000; I was a realtor." St. Peter then asked the 3rd soul the same question. The answer was $8000.00. St. Peter says, "Cool, what instrument did you play?"

The doorbell rang at (piano player's) house the other day & _____ discovered a workman, complete with tool chest on the front porch. _____ says, "Can I help you?" The guy says, "I'm the piano tuner." _____ says, I didn't send for a piano tunerl" The man says, "I know, but your neighbors did."

I sure like Dennis' singing. Why I'd rather see Dennis sing than eat. Of course you can understand that if you've ever seen Dennis eat.

Wow, 35 years with the Big Creek Country Show. Before this show came to town in 1982, the only exciting thing to do on the weekends was to see who rented the room at the Tucker Hotel.

Phil composes music in bed. It's called 'sheet' music.

Why are violins smaller that violas? They're the same size, but violinists have bigger heads.

A policeman came up to me on the street & asked, "Excuse me, Sir, Do you have a license to play that violin on the street?" I said, "No sir." & the cop says, "In that case, I'm going to have to ask you to accompany me." & I said, "Of course officer, what would you like to sing?"

What's the difference between a 5-string banjo & a Harley-Davidson Motorcycle? You can tune a Harley-Davidson Motorcycle.

A beautiful girl was sitting on the banks of a brook when a frog hopped up & said, "Lady, lady, I'm really a great guitar player. Kiss me & we'll live happily ever after!" So, the girl put the frog in her pocket & started walking to her car & the frog called out again, "Hey Lady, I'm really a great guitar player, kiss me & we'll live happily ever after!" So, she got to her car & started driving home & the frog was getting mad at being ignored. He said, "Hey, why don't you kiss me? I told you I was a great guitar player!" She says, "I would, but you're worth a lot more as a talking frog!"

A guy goes on vacation on a tropical island, & the 1st thing he hears is drums. He goes to the beach & hears drums; he eats lunch, he hears drums; he tries to sleep, he can't---drums. Finally he storms over to the manager. "I've had it! Can't you stop these drums?" The manager says, "No! It's very bad if the drums stop." The tourist says, "Why?" The manager says, "Cause, when the drums stop, the bass solo begins."

What do you say to a banjo player in a 3-piece suit? Will the defendant please rise?

What's the 1st thing a musician says at work? Would you like fries with that?

Two people were walking down the street. One was a musician. The other one didn't have any money either.

St. Peter is checking ID's at the Pearly Gates. First comes a Texan. St. Peter asks him, "Tell me, what have you done in life?" The Texan says, "Well, I struck oil, so I became rich & I divided all my money among my family in my will." St. Peter says, "Come on in!" The 2nd guy says, "I struck it big in the stock market, & I donated 5 million dollars to 'Save The Children'." The 3rd guy had been listening & he says timidly with a downcast look, "Well, I only made $5000 in my entire lifetime." St. Peter says, "Heavens! What instrument did you play?"

Before the show a fellow out here asked me if I knew the 'Road To Mandalay'. I said, "Yeah, do you want me to play it?" He said, "No, take it!"

Why did "Beethoven get rid of his chickens? All they said was, "Bach, Bach Bach."

All the musicians you see here on stage studied 7 years at the suppository of music.

Did you hear my last recital?
() I HOPE SO!
What do you call a guy that plays 2 saxophones at once? Bisaxual!

Here's a song I helped make popular by never singing it before.

General George Custer is getting ready for the Battle Of The Little Big Horn & he hears drums over the hill. He turns to his captain & says, "That doesn't sound too good!" A voice hollers back over the hill: "This isn't our regular drummer!"

OLD/RETIREMENT JOKES

Retirement is nice. This morning my wife said, “Whatcha doin’ today?” I said, “Nothin.” She says, “You did that yesterday!” I said, “I wasn’t finished.”

An older widow was rather lonely & decided she needed a pet to keep her company. So, she goes to a pet shop. When she walked in the shop, she noticed an ugly frog in a cage & it winked at her. She looked at the dogs & cats, the birds & fish, but something drew her back to that ugly frog. She went to his cage & she heard him whispered, “I’m lonely too. Buy me & take me home with you. You won’t ever be sorry.” So, she bought the frog, put him in the front seat beside her, started down the road & the frog whispered to her, “Kiss me & something truly amazing will happen!” She figures, what have I got to lose & she kisses the frog. Immediately the frog turned into a handsome prince. Then the prince returned the old lady’s kiss. Suddenly the old lady felt a metamorphosis coming on. You know what the old lady turned into? A Holiday Inn.

When ______ was younger, all he wanted was a nice BMW. Now, he doesn’t care about the W.

Gotta go, I’ve got some mechanical work to do. I’ve gotta put a rear end in a recliner.

There’s always a lot to be thankful for if you take time to look for it. For example, I was looking in the mirror this evening & thinking how nice it is that wrinkles don't hurt.

Yeah, old age. 1st you forget names, then you forget faces. Then you forget to pull up your zipper.

My memories not as sharp as it used to be. Also, my memories not as sharp as it used to be.

I went to a funeral today & I asked the lady; "How old was your husband?" She says, "98", 2 years older than me. I said, "So you're 96?" She says, "Yeah, hardly worth going home is it?"

Everything's starting to click for me. My knees, my elbows, my neck.

I knew I was going bald when I realized it was taking longer & longer to wash my face.

To help the economy, the government will announce this month that the Immigration Department will start deporting seniors, instead of illegals, in order to lower Social Security & Medicare costs. Older people are easier to catch & most of them won't remember how to get back home. I got upset when I thought of you----then it dawned on me--oh well--I'll see you on the bus.

() SAY___ HAVE YOU EVER THOUGHT OF COLORING YOUR HAIR? Naw, I figure, what's the use in putting a new top on a convertible when the engine's wore out.

You know, I used to eat a lot better when Ronald Reagan was President.
() AH--SO YOU THINK TIMES WERE BETTER BACK THEN?
No, I had my own teeth!"

Just came across this exercise suggested for older people, to build muscle strength in the arms & shoulders. It seems so easy, so I thought I'd pass it on to you folks my age & older. Begin by standing on a comfortable surface, where you have plenty of room at each side. With a 5# potato sack in each hand, extend your arms straight out from your sides & hold them there as long as you can. Try to reach a full minute, then relax. Each day you'll find you can hold this position for just a bit longer. After 2 weeks, move up to 10# potato sacks. Then 50# potato sacks & then eventually try to get to where you can lift a 100# potato sack in each hand & hold your arms straight for more that a full minute. (I'm at this level). Now folks, after you feel confident at that level, put a potato in each of the sacks.

I feel like my body has gotten totally out of shape, so I got my Doctor's permission to join a fitness club & start exercising. I decided to take an Aerobics Class for Seniors. I bent, twisted, gyrated, jumped up & down, & perspired for an hour. But, by the time I got my Leotards on, the class was over!

You know why retirees are so slow to clean out the basement, attic or garage? They know as soon as they do, one of their adult kids will want to store stuff there or move back in.

Talked to my cousin---his dad lives next door to him. I said, "How's your dad doing?" He says, "Dad says, the Lord helps him in everything he does." I said, "Give me an example cous." He says. "Well, for one thing when he gets up in the middle of the night to go to the bathroom---the Lord turns the light on for him." I said, "Oh, no! He's using the refrigerator again!"

I feel like my body's gotten totally out of shape, so I got my Doctor's permission to join a fitness club & start exercising. I decided to take an aerobics class for seniors. I bent, twisted, gyrated, jumped up & down, & perspired for an hour. But by the time I got my leotards on, the class was over!

Two ladies at John Knox got bored at the 'day room' yesterday, so they cornered this old guy & told him; "Take off your clothes & we'll tell you how old you are." He says, "That's ridiculous, you can't tell how old you are just because you're naked!" They said, "Well, you take your clothes off & we'll prove it to you!" So, he did. He said, "Okay, how old am I?" They said, "You're 84 years old." He said, "That's amazing, how did you know?" They said, "Cause, you told us yesterday."

Two ladies at John Knox got bored at the 'day room' & decided to streak across the room. Two old boys were playing checkers & one says to the other, "What were they wearing?" The other one says, "I don't know, but it sure needed ironing."

A tough old cowboy once counseled his grandson that if he wanted to live a long life, the secret was to sprinkle a little gunpowder on his oatmeal every morning. The grandson did this religiously & he lived to the age of 93. When he died, he left 14 children, 28 grandchildren, 35 great grandchildren & a 15 foot hole in the wall of the crematorium.

Be nice to your kids. They're the ones who will be choosing your nursing home.

I was walking down the street & saw 2 guys trying to steal an old lady's purse. She was putting up quite a fight & I didn't know if I should get involved or not. Finally, I decided to help, & it didn't take the 3 of us very long to get it away from her.

My memory has gotten so bad it has actually caused me to lose my job. I'm still employed. I just can't remember where.

An old man was in the hospital recovering from a serious operation. It was his birthday & he'd received no cards or presents from his family. The next day 3 of his teenage sons came to visit, all empty handed. The old man says, "Well, I see you all forgot it was poor old Dad's birthday." The sons were embarrassed & said they'd all been busy & just forgot. The old boy says, "That's okay, I guess I can forgive you. Forgetfulness runs in our family. I even forgot to marry your Mother." The boy said, "Good Heavens, why that means we're----!" The old man says, "That's right, & darn cheap ones at that!"

Went out to John Knox Care Center & did some entertaining for the old folks the other day. I must have played & sang for this one bedridden fellow for 15 minutes & he never said a word. So, I packed up to move on & as I was leaving, I said, "I hope you get better! & he said, "I hope you do too!"

This is what seniors go through. The other day I went over to CVS Pharmacy. I went straight back to the Pharmacist's counter & took out my little brown bottle along with a teaspoon & laid them on the counter. The pharmacist came over with a smile & asked if he could help me. I said, "Yes! Could you please taste this for me? I guess cause I'm old he went along with me & he picked up a spoon & put a tiny bit of the liquid on his tongue & swilled it around. Then he got the most terrible look on his face & spit it out on the floor & began coughing. When he finally was finished, I looked him right in the eye & said, "Now, does that taste sweet to you?" He was mad folks & he said, "Heck no!" I said, "Oh thank God! That's a real relief! My Dr. told me to get a pharmacist to test my urine for sugar! Well, I can never go back to that CVS, but I don't care, cause they aren't very friendly there anyway."

A man is feeling poorly, so he goes to his Dr. After numerous tests the doc says, "I'm sorry, but you have an incurable condition & there is nothing more that I can do for you." The man pleads with the Dr. to suggest anything he might do to improve his condition, & the Dr. then suggests that he go to a SPA & take a daily mud bath. So the guy asks, "Is there any hope for a cure?" The doc says, "No, but it'll help you get used to the dirt."

An old fellow called the newspaper office & demanded to know where the Sunday edition was. They told him; "Sir, today is Saturday, the Sunday paper is not delivered until tomorrow, on Sunday." (long pause) Finally the old coot says; "Well, that explains why no one was at church either."

An 82 year old man went to the Dr. to get a physical. A few days later, the Dr. saw the old boy walking down the street with a gorgeous blonde on his arm. The Dr. called him up & said, "Wow, you're really doing great aren't you?" He says, "I'm just doin' what you said Doc; "Get a hot mama & be cheerful!" The Dr. says, "I didn't say that, I said, 'You've got a heart murmur, be careful'."

Two old boys out at John Knox Village discussing life. One turns to the other & says, "Slim, I'm 83 years old now & I'm just full of aches & pains. I know you're about my age, how do you feel?" Slim says, "I feel like a newborn baby." "Really?" "Yep, no hair, no teeth & I think I just wet my pants.

The neighbors down the street are gonna have another baby. Yeah, he's getting up in years too. Of course the best time for men to have babies around the house is when they're 80 years old. That's when they have to get up from 3 to 10 times a night anyway.

I called my Mother the other day & the conversation went something like this:
How are your eyes Mama? Do you still see spots in front of them? Put your glasses on Mama. How is it now? Oh, you see the spots much clearer.

Today I was thinking about the perks of being over 70.

1. Kidnappers are not very interested in you.
2. In a hostage situation you're likely to be released 1st .
3. No one expects you to run--anywhere.
4. Your secrets are safe with your friends cause they can't remember them either.

Folks, here's my inconclusive travel plans for 2019:

I've been many places, but I've never been in CAHOOTS. Apparently you can't go home. You have to be in CAHOOTS with someone.

I have however been IN SANE. They don't have an airport, you have to be driven there. I've made several trips there, thaks to my friends, family & Dennis.

I would like to go to CONCLUSIONS, but you have to jump, & I'm not much on physical activity anymore.

One of my favorite places to go is in SUSPENSE. It really gets the adrenalin flowing & pumps up the old heartF! At my age, I need all tht stimuli I can get.

I may have been in CONTINENT, & I don't remember what country I was in. It's an age thing.

I've got a nice pond on the back side of my place & I've got it fixed up nice with picnic tables, horseshoe courts & I fixed the pond for swimming.

One evening about dark, I decided to go down there & as I got nearer, I could hear voices shouting & laughing. As I got closer, I could see it was a bunch of young women skinny-dipping in my pond. As soon as they saw me, they went to the deep end & one of them shouted, "We're not coming out 'til you leave!" I said, "I didn't come down here to watch you ladies swim or make you get out of the pond, I only came to feed the alligators." Old age & treachery will triumph over youth & skill every time.

Went entertaining down at the retirement center this week. They had a little excitement going on. Two ladies were bored so they streaked through the 'day room'. Two old boys were playing checkers & one of them says, "What was that?" & the other one says, "I don't know, but whatever they were wearing sure needed ironing!"

An elderly woman, a member of our church died last month. She never married & she requested 'NO MALE PALLBEARERS'. The instructions she wrote for her memorial stated; "They wouldn't take me out when I was alive, I don't them to take me out when I'm dead."

In celebration of Valentine's Day, Shirley & I invited a couple from down the street for dinner. We were impressed by the way the lady preceded every request to her husband with endearing terms such as: HONEY, MY LOVE, DARLING, SWEETHEART, PUMPKIN, etc. Now folks, this couple had been married almost 70 years & clearly, they were still very much in love. So, while the husband & I were in the living room discussing politics, Shirley told the lady, "I think it's wonderful that after all these years, you still call your husband all those loving pet names!" The lady hung her head. She said, "I have to tell you the truth, his name slipped my mind about 10 years ago, & I'm scared to death to ask the cranky old coot what his name is!"

A very old man lay dying in his bed. He suddenly smelled the aroma of his favorite chocolate chip cookies wafting up the stairs. He gathered his remaining strength & lifted himself from the bed. Leaning against the wall, he slowly made his way out of the bedroom & forced his way down the stairs, groping the railing with both hands. At the kitchen door, were it not for death's agony, he'd a thought he was already in Heaven. There spread out on newspapers on the kitchen table were literally hundreds of his favorite chocolate chip cookies. Mustering one great final effort, he threw himself toward the table. His shaking hand made its way to a cookie at the edge of the table, when he was suddenly smacked with a spatula by his wife. She said, "Stay out of those, they're for the funeral.

Three old men were setting on a park bench, all of them hard-of-hearing. The 1st one says, "Windy ain't it?" The 2nd one says, "No, it's Thursday!" & the 3rd one says, "Me too, let's go get a drink."

Working people frequently ask retired folks like myself what we do to make our days interesting. I just give them this example: The other day I went downtown to a delicatessen for the Wall Street Journal so I could track my investments. I was only there for about 5 minutes. When I came out, there was a cop writing out a parking ticket. I said to him, "Come on man, don't you have anything better to do than write a retired person a ticket? Why aren't you out chasing crooks or child molesters---that's out of your league obviously!" He ignored me & continued writing the ticket. I called him a Nazi. He glared at me & wrote another ticket for having worn tires. So I called him 'Barney Fife'. He finished the 2nd ticket & put it on the windshield with the 1st. Then he wrote a 3rd ticket. This went on for about 20 minutes. The more I abused him, the more tickets he wrote. Personally, I didn't care---I came downtown on the bus.

Do you realize that in about 40 years, we'll have thousands of old ladies running around with tattoos? And RAP music will be the golden oldies.

Two old guys are pushing their carts around Wal-Mart when they collide. The 1st old guy says, "Sorry about that, I'm looking for my wife." The 2nd fellow says, "That's okay, it's a coincidence, I'm looking for my wife too! I can't find her & I'm getting a little desperate." The 1st old coot says, "Maybe I can help you find her, what does she look like?" The 2nd ole boy says, "She's 27 years old, tall, red hair, blue eyes, long legs, & she's wearing short-shorts. What does your wife look like?" & the 1st guy says, "Doesn't matter, let's look for yours."

Old age. 1st you forget names, then faces, then you forget to pull up your zipper. It's worse when you forget to pull it down.

_______ & _______ ______ are here tonight & it's good to have both my friends in one place. They've been having memory problems lately, so they developed the habit of writing things down. So, the other day she says to _____, "Would you mind getting me some ice cream?" He says, "No problem." & he heads for the kitchen. She says, "You better write it down or you'll forget." He says, "No I won't, it's ice cream, how hard can it be to remember that?" So, a few minutes later he walks back into the room carrying a tray with eggs, coffee, cereal & orange juice. She says, "See, I told you to write it down, now look, you've forgotten the toast!"

An elderly couple, were living in Miami with a son in New York & a daughter in Los Angeles. The old man calls the son & says, "Your Mother & I are getting a divorce, I've had all I can take." The son says, "Oh please Dad, not a divorce, after all these years." Dad says, "It's no use son, I can't take it anymore." The son hangs up & calls his sister in L.A., & tells her all about it & she says, "Don't worry, I'll take care of this!" She calls her Dad & says, "What's this I hear about a divorce?" He says, "That's right, I can't take it any longer." She says, "Don't do anything until my brother & I get there. Promise?" Dad says, "Well, okay." After they hang up the old man says to his wife, "Well, that takes care of Christmas, now what'll we do for Easter?"

Well, I just had a thorough physical examination & the Dr. said, "You're fit as a fiddle, you'll live to be 75." I said, "But I am 75!" He said, "See, what'd I tell you?"

My elderly neighbor lady called 911 on her cell phone the other day to report that her car had been broken into. I mean she was hysterical. She told the dispatcher; "They've stolen the stereo, the steering wheel, the brake pedal & even the accelerator!" The dispatcher said, "Stay calm. An officer is on the way." So, a few minutes later the officer radios in. He says, "Disregard, she got in the back seat by mistake."

I had a busy week. I still consider myself a go-getter, of course now, I have to make 2 trips.

I'm not really old yet. 'Old' is when you remember when the 'Dead Sea' was only sick.

I've been doin' some more marriage counseling lately. Your marriage is in trouble if your wife says, "You're only interested in one thing." & you can't remember what it is.

A funeral home called one of its clients & said, "I realize we all grieve in our own way Ma'am, but the crematorium staff did not appreciate the fireworks you put in your late husband's pockets!"

It was entertainment night at the Senior Citizens Center. After the community sing-along led by Phil on the piano, it was time for the star of the show---Claude The Hypnotist! Claude explained that he was going to put the whole audience into a trance. He says, "Yes, each & every one of you & all at the same time! The chatter dropped to silence as Claude carefully withdrew, from his pocket, a beautiful watch &

chain. He says, "I want you to keep your eyes on this watch." He began to swing the watch gently back & forth while chanting, "The Watch-The Watch". 150 pairs of eyes followed the movements of the gently swaying watch. They were all hypnotized. Then, suddenly, the chain broke! The beautiful watch fell to the stage & burst apart. Claude says, "crap"! It took them 3 days to clean up the Senior Citizen Center.

I was a rotten kid. I used to hide my Grandfather's bedpan in the freezer.

Old is when someone compliments you on your alligator shoes & you're barefooted.

My brother, who's 75 is married to a lovely woman who is 89. She's very rich. It's what you might call a football romance. He's waiting for her to kick off.

() LARRY, ARE YOU ON SOCIAL SECURITY?
What's social security?
() THAT'S WHAT KEEPS YOU GOING IN YOUR OLD AGE.
Hmmmm, I thought it was prunes.

It's good to be here tonight. I was busy this evening, blow-drying my eyebrows, before I came over here & I thought to myself; "When I die, I want to go peaceably, like my Grandfather, in his sleep, not like the rest of the passengers in his car.

An old man was walking down the street crying. I asked him, "What's wrong?" He said, "My Daddy whipped me!" I said, "How old are you?" He says, "76". Well, how old's your Dad? He says, "93." Okay, why'd your Daddy whip you? He says, "Cause I made fun of Grandpa." How old's your Grandpa? He says, "109." Well, how were you making fun of your

Grandpa? He says, "Cause, he's getting married." What's he want to get married for? "Oh, he doesn't want to!"

My Grandfather lived to be 103 years old. The truth is nobody knows what's good for you. Every morning he would eat an entire raw onion & smoke a cigar. You know what his dying words were? Nobody knows, they couldn't get near the guy!

POLITICAL/POLITICIAN JOKES

One of our politicians went hiking in the Irish countryside. He came upon a shepherd with a large flock of sheep. He says, "If I can guess how many in the flock, may I have one?" The shepherd says, "Okay, go ahead." Politician says, "287." Shepherd says, "You're exactly right, go ahead & pick you out one!" So the politician slung one over his shoulders to carry it home. The shepherd says, "If I can guess your occupation, may I have that animal back?" Politician says, "It's a deal!" Shepherd says, "You're a politician!" Politician says, "That's amazing! How did you know that?" Shepherd says, "Put that dog down & we'll discuss it."

A bus full of politicians was speeding down the road when it swerved into a field & crashed into a tree. The farmer who owned the field went over to investigate. Then he dug a hole with his backhoe & buried the politicians. A few days later the sheriff drove by & saw the overturned bus. He knocked on the farmer's door & asked where all the politicians had gone. The farmer said, "I buried them." The sheriff asked, "You mean they were all dead?" The farmer says, "Well, some of them said they weren't, but you know how politicians lie!"

Definition of the word 'POLITICS': The word is in 2 syllables, 'POLI' which means 'MANY' & 'TICS' which is blood suckers. There you have it: 'Many blood suckers'.

It seems we have some local heroes. A famous politician was rescued from drowning by 3 young lads here in ______ . Of course the politician was very grateful & he told the boys, I'll give you anything you want!"

The 1st boy said, "I'll take a bicycle!" The 2nd boy said, "I'll take a motorbike Sir!" The 3rd boy says, "If it's all the same to you Sir, I'd like a military funeral." The politician says, "Son, why would you want a military funeral?" The boy says, "Cause when my Pa finds out whose life I saved, he's gonna kill me!"

Politicians are like babies diapers. They both should be changed often, & for the same reasons.

A Cardinal & a U.S. Senator arrived in Heaven at the same time. The Cardinal was given a small room & the Senator got the key to a huge penthouse. The Cardinal asked, "Why do I get a tiny room & he gets such special treatment?" St. Peter says, "We have many Cardinals up here, but he's the 1st Senator we've ever seen!"

Three surgeons were bragging about their skills: 1st one said, "I had a man come in who had his hand cut off in an accident. I put him back together & he is now a concert violinist!" The 2nd one says, " I had a man come in after a terrible car wreck who'd had his legs severed. He is now a marathon runner!" The 3rd surgeon said, "I've got you both beat, I came upon a terrible accident where there was nothing left but the back end of a horse & a pair of eyeglasses. That man is now in the United States Senate!"

Have you heard the latest White House joke?
() Wait, before you begin, I should tell you that I work for the White House.
Oh, don't worry, I'll tell it real slow.

An ATF officer stopped at ______'s farm. He told _____, I need to inspect your farm for illegally grown drugs." _____ says, "Okay, but do not go in that field over there!" The ATF officer verbally explodes saying, "Mister, I have the authority of the Federal Government with me!" & he pulled out his badge & says, "See this badge? This badge means I'm allowed to go wherever I wish--on any land. No questions asked or answers given. Have I made myself clear? Do you understand?" _____ nodded politely, apologized & went about his chores. Pretty soon ______ hears loud screams & sees the ATF officer running for his life chased by ______'s prize bull. With every step the bull is gaining ground & it looks like the officer'll get horned before he reaches safety. ______ dropped his tools, runs to the fence & yells at the top of his lungs---"YOUR BADGE! SHOW HIM YOUR BADGE!!!"

I was driving home this week worrying about all the stuff going on in Washington & how so many lives are falling apart. I saw a sign that said; "Need help? Call Jesus 1-800-005-3787." Out of curiosity, I did. A Mexican showed up with a lawnmower.

Did you ever notice: When you put the 2 words 'the' and 'IRS' together it spells 'THEIRS'.

A man with an alligator walked into a bar & asked the bartender, "Do you serve IRS agents here?" The bartender says, "Sure do!" And the man says, "Good, give me a beer & my gator'll have an IRS agent."

Now they have a tax on funerals---I'll die before I pay that!

Did I tell you my wife's training for congress? She's always bringing new bills to the house.

A New Yorker goes into a bar in Billings, Mt. had a few to drink, stood up & shouted, "All democrats are horses rears!" The crowd jumped on him & beat him up. A week later he returned, had some drinks, stood up & shouted, "All republicans are horses rears!" The crowd beat him into silly putty again. So, he asks the bartender, "Who are these people anyway?" The bartender says, "You don't understand, this is horse country!"

Have you heard the latest joke about the White House?
() LISTEN, I HAPPEN TO WORK IN THE WHITE HOUSE!
That's all right, I'll tell it real slow.

It was already late in the fall & the Indians on a remote reservation in South Dakota asked their new Chief if the coming winter was going to be cold or mild. Since he was a Chief in a modern society, he had never been taught the old weather secrets. When he looked at the sky he couldn't tell what the winter was going to be like. So, to be on the safe side, he told his tribe that the winter was going to be cold & that the villagers should collect firewood to be prepared. To be on the safe side he called the National Weather Service & asked, "Is the coming winter gonna be cold? The meteorologist said, "It looks like this winter is going to be quite cold." So the Chief went back to his people & told them to collect even more firewood in order to be prepared. A week later he called the National Weather Service again. He asks, "Does it look like it's gonna be a very cold winter?" They said, "Yes, it's going to be a very cold winter." The Chief went back to his people for the 3rd time & ordered them to collect every scrap of fire wood they could find. Two weeks later the Chief called the National Weather Service again & asked, " Are you absolutely sure that the winter is going to be very cold?" They said, "Absolutely, it's looking more & more like it's going to be one of the coldest winters we've ever seen!" The Chief asked, "How can you be sure?" The Weatherman says, "Cause, the Indians are collecting firewood like crazy!!!

Always remember this whenever you get advice from a Government Official

---

I think I'll vote for 'Larry The Cable Guy' for president. He says, "Everyone concentrates on the problems we're having in the United States lately: 1. Illegal immigration. 2. Hurricane recovery. & 3. Alligators attacking people in Florida.---not me---I concentrate on solutions for the problems--it's a win-win situation. For instance, Dig a moat the length of the Mexican border. Send the dirt to New Orleans to raise the levees. Put the Florida alligators in the moat along the Mexican border.

Any other problems you'd like to solve today? Think about this: 1. Cows. 2. The Constitution.

COWS: I find it amazing that during the mad cow epidemic our government could track a single cow born in Canada almost 3 years ago, right to the stall where she was born. But they were unable to locate 11 million illegal aliens wandering around our country. Maybe we should give each one a cow.

The Constitution: They keep talking about drafting a constitution for Iraq---why don't we just give them ours? It was written by a lot of really smart guys, it has worked for over 200 years & we're not using it anymore.

Did you know that when the white man discovered this country the Indians were running it. There was no taxes. There was no debt. The women did all the work---------and the white man thought he could improve on a system like that?

Did you hear about the nudist who won a seat in Washington? He was named 'Streaker of the House'.

My great granddaughter asked me, "Granddad, do all fairy tails begin with the words; 'Once Upon A Time', ?" I said, "No, a whole lot of them begin with the words, 'If Elected, I Promise'."

What's the difference between a church bell & a politician? A church bell peals from the steeple. A politician steals from the people.

You've got to give the President a lot of credit for foresight. Last year he told us to tighten our belts, which was a good thing. Cause, what's happening now is enough to scare the pants off you!

The reason America is running low on oil is that most of it is in Alaska & most of the dipsticks are in Washington.

I'm not going to say the mayor's election was rigged, but the winner got votes from 3 out of every 2 people.

George W. Bush Jr., in an airport lobby, noticed a man in a long flowing white robe with a long flowing white beard & long flowing white hair. The man had a staff in one hand & some stone tablets under the other arm. George sidled up beside him & inquired, "Aren't you Moses?" The man ignored George & stared at the ceiling. Again George asked him, "Aren't you Moses?" The man continued to stare at the ceiling. Finally George got right in his face & tugged on his beard & asked, "Aren't you Moses?" The man said, "Yes I am." So George asked him why he was so uppity & Moses replied, "The last time I spoke to a bush I had to spend 40 years wandering in the desert.

I got a letter from the President in reply to one I had sent. He told me that when the time comes, he wants me to serve in an advisory capacity. Well, those weren't his exact words. It was more like, "When I want your advice, I'll ask for it."

RELIGIOUS JOKES

A customs inspector in New York stopped a little ole lady & asked her what she had in her suitcase. She said, "Holy Water." He opened up her suitcase, took out a bottle, uncorked it, sniffed it & said, "But this is Irish Whiskey!" She said, "Saints be praised, it's a miracle!"

I was taking a walk in the park & saw my old friend George setting on a park bench looking down & forlorn. His clothes were in bad shape & he hadn't shaved in a week. I said, "George, what happened, you used to be wealthy & healthy?" He says, "Oh, Larry, I've lost it all & I think I'm gonna commit suicide!" I said, "Oh, don't do that. Before you do anything else, go home, get out your bible, put it on the table, close your eyes, open the bible, put your finger on the page, open your eyes & what ever it says where your finger is pointing; do that!" About a year later I saw George again. He got out of a brand new Mercedes with a beautiful lady. He had a $500 suit on, folks he was looking good. I said, "Hi George, looks like you're doing well." He says, "I just did what you told me Larry, I went home, got my bible out, closed my eyes, opened the book & put my finger on the page." I said, "What did it say George? " He said, "Chapter 11."

Every day a woman stood on her porch & shouted, "Praise the Lord!" & every day atheist next door yelled back, "There is no Lord!" One day she prayed, "Lord, I'm hungry, please send me groceries." The next morning she found a big bag of foods on the stairs. "Praise the Lord" she shouted. Her neighbor jumped out from behind a bush & says, "I told you there was no Lord, I bought those groceries!" The woman said, "Praise the Lord, he not only sent me groceries, but he made the Devil pay for 'em!"

Hypothetical situation: You're going down a road with a steep bank on the left & a steep grade on the right with a church straight ahead down the road with the doors wide open. There's a bear behind you. Where you gonna go, up the left bank, down the right bank or straight ahead into the church?"
() WHY, STRAIGHT INTO THE CHURCH!)
You mean you'd go into a church with a bear (bare) behind?

Took my Great granddaughter to church with me last Sunday. She's 5 years old & says just what she's thinking. The preacher was really getting into the spirit & one of the things he said was, "Dear Lord, without you we are but dust!" My great granddaughter asked me, "Grandad, what's 'butt dust'?"

He's a 'man-of-the-cloth'. He's in charge of towel drying down at the car wash.

In Italy, a man went to a priest & confessed. He said, "Forgive me Father, during WWII, I hid a refugee in my attic. Well, the priest said, "That's not a sin." "Yeah, but I made him pay rent!" The priest says, "That wasn't very nice, but still, you put yourself at risk." The guy says, "Oh thank you Father, but I have one more question, do you think I ought to tell him the war's over?"

I answered the door to 2 Jehovah's Witnesses the other day. I said, "Oh please do come in." I took them into the living room & told them to make themselves comfortable. Then I left my son's house & went home.

I was reading Bible stories to one of my great grandsons. I read, "The man named Lot was warned to take his wife & flee out of the city, but his wife looked back & was turned to salt." My great grandson asked me, "What happened to the flea?"

\We had to fire another preacher. He had some good ideas & built up the church. He was always trying something new & that's what eventually got him in trouble. Here's the story: He got up to the pulpit one Sunday morning & said, "I'll say a word & whatever hymn that reminds you of, congregation--sing it. So he said, "Grace!" We all sang 'Amazing Grace'. Then he said, "Love!" & we all sang 'Love Lifted Me'. Then for some reason or the other he said the word, "Sex!" You coulda heard a pin drop. Finally, a little ole lady on the back row started singing, 'Precious Memories'.

A dead mule lay in front of our church for 2 days, so finally our Pastor called the Department of Health. Some smart-aleck answered the phone & the Pastor told him about the dead mule & the guy said, "Well, don't you people take care of the dead?" & the Pastor said, "Of course, but first we get in touch with their relatives.

Three men die in a car crash & when they get to heaven St. Peter asks them; "What would you like for people to say about you back on Earth? The 1st one says, "I'd like for people to say, "He was a great Doctor!" The 2nd one says, "I wish people would say, 'He was a great Father'." The 3rd one says, "I'd like for people to say, 'Look, he's moving, he's alive!'."

_____'s pastor was telling the banker about _____ . He said, _____ has a marvelous voice, he can hold a note for almost two minutes!" The banker says, "That's nothing, I've held one of his notes for 2 years!"

A guy goes to his priest & says, "I think my wife's trying to poison me." The priest say, "Do you want me to talk to her?" He says, "Yes, I'd sure appreciate it." The next day he stopped by to talk to the priest again. The priest said, "Well, I talked to your wife for about three hours today." "What'd you come up with Father?" "Well, if I were you, I'd take the poison!"

I saw a church sign that needs changing. It said, 'SERMON FOR NEXT SUNDAY---WHAT HELL IS LIKE' & just below that in smaller letters it says: 'Come & Hear Our Choir Sing'.

Two church members were going door-to-door & knocked on my neighbor's door. She was not happy to see them & told themin no uncertain terms that she did not want to hear their message & slammed the door in their faces. To her surprise, however, the door did not close & in fact bounced back open. She tried again & really put her back into it & slammed the door again with all her might, but got the same result. The door bounced back open. Convinced these rude young people were sticking their foot in the door, she reared back to give it a slam that would teach them a lesson, when one of them says, "Ma'am, before you do that again, you need to move your cat."

An old dollar bill & an even older 20 dollar bill arrive at a Federal Reserve Bank to be retired. The 20 dollar bill says, "I've had a pretty good life, I've been to Vegas, the finest restaurants in New York & even on a Caribbean cruise." The dollar bill says, "Wow, you did have an exciting life!" The 20 bill asks, "Where have you been?" The dollar bill says, "Oh, I've been to the Methodist Church, the Baptist Church & spent some time with the Lutherans." & the 20 bill interrupts, "Wait, what's a church?"

Two Jehovah's Witnesses knocked on my door, so I invited them in & had them sit down on the sofa. I said, What do you want to talk about?" They said, "We don't know, we've never got this far before

---

I've been in our church choir now for 19 years? Yeah, our Music Director refers to us as: 'The Prison Ensemble"
() Why does he call you that?
"Because we're always behind a few bars & trying to find the key."

Desperate for a child, a couple asked their priest to pray for them. The priest says, "I'm going on sabbatical to Rome, I'll light a candle for you." So the priest comes back 3 years later, finds the wife pregnant, tending 2 sets of twins. Of course the priest was elated & he says, "Where's your husband, I want to congratulate him?" She says, "He's gone to Rome to blow out that candle!"

Three little boys were bragging about their dads. The 1st little boy says, "My Dad writes on a pad, calls it a poem & they pay him $100 for it." The 2nd boy says, "My Dad writes on a pad, calls it a song & gets $200 for it." 3rd boy says, "I've got you all beat, my Dad scratches on a pad, calls it a sermon & it takes 8 people to pick up all the money!"

I don't know why some people change churches; what difference does it make which one you stay home from?

I met a priest on the street & I asked him, "How come you wear your collar backwards?" He said, "Because I'm a Father." I said, "Well, I have 2 sons myself!" He said, "No, no, you don't understand. You see, I have thousands of children!" I said, "Well then, you should wear your trousers backward!"

Do you know the difference between Baptists & Catholics? Catholics will speak to each other in a liquor store.

You know, just about the time a man is cured of swearing--he gets his real estate tax bill.

Years ago I had an uncle who ran a general store & he was quite a Bible scholar. Every time he sold an item he would quote a scripture. For instance, if a child bought some candy he might say, "Suffer the little children to come onto me, of such is the Kingdom Heaven." One day in November a Texan stopped in & asked my uncle if he could help him. The Texan said, "I've got my prize quarter horse out there in the trailer behind my Cadillac & I need a nice warm blanket for him." So, my uncle goes back in the storeroom & gets a black blanket for him & says, "That'll be 5 dollars." The Texan says, "Oh, that's not good enough for my horse, get me a better one." Now folks my uncle had all different colors of those blankets, but they were all the same quality, so he went back & got a green one & said, "This one is 25 dollars." The Texan says, "That's still not good enough for my prize horse!" So, my uncle went back & got a purple blanket & said, "This is the very best one, it's 50 dollars." The stranger said, "Okay, that one will do." By that time a pretty good crowd was gathered around the cash register to see what scripture my uncle was gonna quote, cause they knew all them blanket's was the same & he didn't disappoint them. He said, "He was a stranger, and I took him in."

Three churches in a little town were having trouble with the squirrel population so the individual congregations had a meeting to decide what to do about it. The Presbyterians decided just to put up with it. The Methodists decided to trap & relocate the squirrels & the Baptists decided to make the squirrels part of the congregation, that way they wouldn't have to put up with them except for Christmas & Easter.

Our preacher was going around to some of our member's homes to get them to come to church on Easter Sunday. You know, the folks he hadn't seen for a while. So he knocks on one door & no answer. He knocks again & no answer. Now the front door was open with the screen door closed, so he took out one of his business cards & wrote Rev. 3:20 on it & slipped it in past the screen door. Sunday morning there was his card in the collection plate with Rev 3:20 written on it, only below it the scripture Gen. 3:10 was written. Well, after thinking about it for a while he decided he'd make sure just what Rev. 3:20 says. "BEHOLD I STAND AT THE DOOR & KNOCK etc.." & then he looked up Gen. 3:10 & it said, "I HEARD THY VOICE IN THE GARDEN, & WAS AFRAID, BECAUSE I WAS NAKED; & I HID MYSELF."

We're having trouble with our Pastor again. He got up there yesterday morning & announced to the congregation: "I have good news & bad news. The good news is we have enough money to pay for our new building program. The bad news is, it's still in your pockets!"

My Great-granddaughter came home from Sunday School last Sunday & asked me, "Grandad, were you & Grandma on Noah's Ark?"
I said, "Of course not!" She said, "Well, why weren't you drowned then?"

A Baptist family here in Pleasant Hill had a death in the family while their minister was out of town. So they called the local Methodist minister to conduct the funeral service. So the minister called his bishop & asked him; "Can I bury a Baptist?" & the Bishop said, "Sure, bury all the Baptists you can!"

A Baptist Missionary was visiting a cannibal tribe & he asked the chief, "Do people know anything about religion?" The chief says, "Well, I got a taste of it when the last missionary was here."

We're having fund raising problems at our church. One Sunday morning our Pastor was preoccupied about how he was going to ask the congregation to come up with more money for repairs to the church building. On top of that he was annoyed to find out that the regular organist was sick & a substitute had been brought in at the last minute. So now the substitute wanted to know what to play. So he told her; "Here's a copy of the service, but you'll have to think of something to play after I make the announcement about the finances." During the service the minister paused & said, "Brothers & sisters, we are in great difficulty; the roof repairs cost twice as much as we expected & we need

$4000 more. Any of you who can pledge $100 or more, please stand up." At that moment, the substitute organist played 'The Star Spangled Banner'." And that is how the substitute organist became the regular organist.

A fellow runs into the Catholic Church in a panic. He says; "Father! Father!, an old man on crutches walked up to the Holy Water a minute ago, he splashed some on his right leg & then threw away his right crutch! Then he splashed some more on his other leg & threw away his left crutch!" The priest says, "My boy, you've just witnessed a miracle! What happened then?" "Well Father, he fell on his rear, he's a cripple you know!"

Did you hear about that guy who was asked to be a Jehovah's Witness? He refused because he hadn't seen the accident.

There are 3 religions truths:

A: Jews do not recognize Jesus as the Messiah.

B: Protestants do not recognize the Pope as the leader of the Christian Faith.

C: Baptists do not recognize each other in the liquor store or Hooters.

A Jew & an Oriental are sitting on a park bench. All of a sudden, the Jew knocks the Oriental plumb out in the grass. The Oriental says, "What was that for?" The Jew says, "That was for Pearl Harbor!" The Oriental says, "Well, that was the Japanese, I'm Chinese!" The Jew says, "Japanese, Chinese, it's all the same to me!" Pretty soon the Chinaman knocks the Jew out in the grass. The Jew asks, "What was that for?" The Chinaman says, "That was for the Titanic!" The Jew says, "The Titanic! The Titanic was caused by an iceberg!" The Chinaman says, "Iceberg, Goldberg, it's all the same to me!"

I took my old aunt to church this morning & she surely did embarrass me. She snored so loud it woke me up! The preacher said, "You'd better wake you're aunty up!" I said, "You wake her up yourself, you put her to sleep!"

Saw a church sign on the way over here. "If you're tire of sin, come on in." Written below in lipstick it said; "If you're not, call 555-2626.

I went to the Dr. about my snoring problem. I told him, "As soon as I fall asleep, I start snoring, what can I do to cure myself? " So, he asked me, "Does it bother your wife?" I said, "Oh, it not only bothers her, it disturbs the whole congregation!"

I was downtown Kansas City the other day when a guy got hit by a bus. So, he's lying there hurtin' & he gasps, "Somebody get me a priest!" So, I went over to him & I said, "I'm not a priest, I'm not even Catholic, but for 50 years I've lived behind the Catholic Church in Lee's Summit & every night I overhear their services. Maybe I can be of some comfort." So, I knelt down beside him & in a solemn voice I said, "B-14, I-19, N-38, G-54, O-72"

Back in the early 70's I worked part time at a full service gas station & there were long lines. This minister I knew had waited a long time. Finally I motioned him in to a pump & I said, "Reverend, I'm sorry about the delay. It seems as if everyone waits until the last minute to get ready for a long trip." He chuckled & said, "I know what you mean, it's the same way in my business!"

I've been to the Dr. about my snoring problem. I told him, "As soon as I fall asleep, I start snoring, what can I do to cure myself?" He asked me, "Does it bother your wife?" I said, "It not only bothers her, it disturbs the whole congregation!"

() OKAY ____ IF YOU'RE SO SMART, GIVE ME A QUOTATION FROM THE BIBLE.
A quotation from the bible eh? Okay, here it is; "Judas went out and hanged himself."
() AND ANOTHER ONE?
"Go thou and do likewise."

A man suffered a serious heart attack & had open heart surgery. When he woke up from the surgery he found himself in the care of nuns at a Catholic hospital. As he was recovering, a nun asked him questions as to how he would pay for his treatment. She says, "Do you have health insurance?" "No health insurance." "Do you have any money in the bank?" "No bank account." "Do you have a relative that would help you?" "I only have a spinster sister who is a nun." The nun says, "Nuns are not spinsters! Nuns are married to God!" He says, "Well then, send the bill to my Brother-in-law!"

My neighbor got arrested for having more than one wife.
() NOW _____, CAN YOU TELL ME OF A SINGLE PASSAGE OF SCRIPTURE WHERIN POLYGAMY IS FORBIDDEN?
I sure can, the Bible says, "No man can serve two masters."

My Pastor caught me on the street yesterday. He said, "I know perfectly well you didn't come to church last Sunday so you could play 9 holes of golf." I said, "That's a lie, & I've got the fish to prove it!"

So I was walking through the mall & I saw there was a 'Muslim Book Store'. I was wondering what exactly was in a Muslim book store, so I went in. As I was wandering around, taking a look, the clerk stopped & asked me if he could help me, so I asked, "Do you have a copy of Donald Trump's book on his U. S. Immigration Policy regarding Muslim's &

illegal Mexicans?" The clerk said, "Out, get out & stay out!" I said, "Yes, that's the one. Do you have it in paperback?"

Our Pastor got him a new set of false teeth. The 1st Sunday after he got his new teeth, he talked for only 8 minutes. The next Sunday he talked for only 10 minutes. Last Sunday he talked for 2 hours & 47 minutes & the deacons had to drag him away from the pulpit to get him to stop. They asked him for an explanation & he said, "The 1st Sunday my gums were so sore, I could only talk for 8 minutes. The 2nd Sunday he made it to 10 minutes. But the 3rd Sunday, I put my wife's teeth in by mistake & I couldn't shut up!"

An old fellow called the newspaper office & demanded to know where the Sunday edition was. They told him; "Sir, today is Saturday. The Sunday paper is not delivered until tomorrow, on Sunday." (long pause) Finally the old coot says, "Well, that explains why no one was at church either."

We had to fire another preacher. He tried something new. He said, "I'll say a word & whatever hymn that word reminds you of--sing it." So, he said, "Grace." & the congregation sang "Amazing Grace." Then he said, "Love." & they sang "Love Lifted Me". Then for some reason he said the word "Sex." & you coulda heard a pin drop. Finally a little ole lady on the back row started singing, "Precious Memories."

Bubba goes to see his pastor. The pastor asked him, "What's wrong Bubba?" Bubba says, "I need you to pray for my hearing." The pastor put his hands on Bubba's ears & prayed. When he was done, he asked, "So how's your hearing?" Bubba says, "I don't know, it ain't 'til next Tuesday."

A Baptist preacher & his wife decided they need a dog. Worried about the congregation, they knew the dog must also be a Baptist. They visited an expensive kennel & explained their needs to the manager. He said,

"I believe I have just what you're looking for." He brought the dog & said, "Fetch the bible!" The dog went to the bookshelf, looks around, finds the Bible & brings it. The manager says, "Find Psalms 23!" The dog leafs through the Bible, finds the correct passage & puts his paw on it. The couple was very impressed & they bought the dog. That evening a group of the church members came to visit. The preacher shows off the dog having him locate several Bible verses. They were amazed. Finally one man asked, "Can he do normal dog tricks too?" The preacher says, "Well, let's see." He pointed a finger at the dog & commanded "Heel"! The dog immediately jumped up on a chair, placed a paw on the preacher's forehead & began to howl. The preacher turned to his wife & said, "Good grief! We bought a Pentecostal dog!"

One day George was at the track playing the ponies & all but losing his shirt & he noticed a priest who stepped out on the track & blessed the forehead of one of the horses lining up for the 4th race. Lo & behold, that horse-a very long shot-won the race. So, George kept an eye on that priest & sure enough as the 5th race horses came into the starting gate he made a blessing on the forehead of one of the horses. So, George made a beeline for a betting window & even though it was another long-shot, the horse the priest had blessed, won the race. The same thing happened on the 6th race. George bet big & won big. This kept going on & George was pulling in some serious money. Then came the last race. George made a quick dash to the ATM, withdrew all his savings & waited the priest's blessing on a horse. Sure enough, the priest stepped onto the track & blessed the forehead of an old nag that was the longest shot of the day. George new he had a winner & bet every cent he owned on the old nag. Then he watched dumbfounded as the old nag came in last. So, he got hold of that priest & asked him, "Father, what happened?" Son, that's the problem with you protestants, you can't tell the difference between a simple blessing & the last rites."

A young minister was asked by a funeral director to hold a grave-site service for a homeless man with no family or friends. The funeral was to be held at a cemetery way back in the country, & this man would be the 1st to be laid to rest there. The young preacher wasn't familiar with the area & he got lost & he arrived an hour late. He finds the burial crew there with a backhoe & they were eating lunch, but the hearse was nowhere in sight. He apologized to the workers for being late & stepped to the side of the open grave, where he saw the vault lid already in place. He started his burial service & the workers gathered around, still eating their lunch & I'm telling you, he poured out his heart & soul. When he really got into it the workers began to say "amen, praise the Lord, & glory"! Folks, he preached & preached like he'd never preached before, from Genesis all the way through Revelations. At the end of his closing prayer, he was walking to his car & he overheard one of the workers saying to another, "I ain't never seen anything like that before & I've been putting in septic tanks for 20 years!"

We got another minister & he's stirring things up already. He was addressing the congregation: "There's a certain man among us today who is flirting with another man's wife. Unless he puts ten dollars in the collection plate, his name will be read from the pulpit." When the collection plate came in, there were 19 ten dollar bills & a 5 dollar bill with this note attached saying, "Another 5 dollars payday."

I had an unusual dream last night. I dreamt I had died, went to Heaven & they immediately gave me an important job. The angel told me to go back to Earth & make a survey of the people committing 'hanky-panky'. So, I went back & got started but I could see it was going to take me forever, so I went back to the angel & asked, "Could I make a survey of those people who are not committing 'hanky-panky' instead?" The angel said okay & I was done in 2 weeks. I turned in the survey & the angel said, "I want you to write a letter & sent it to all those good folks who are not committing 'hanky-panky' thanking them & you know what else it said?"
() NO, WHAT'D IT SAY?"
Oh, you didn't get one either!

Announcement: The Pastor would appreciate it if the ladies of the congregation would lend him their electric girdles for the pancake breakfast tomorrow.

Church sign: The sermon this morning---'Jesus Walks On Water' The sermon for tonight---'Searching For Jesus'.

_____ went to one of those tent revivals last summer. He saw some folks getting in line on the platform for healings, so he got in line & when it was his turn the preacher asked him, "What do you want me to pray about for you?" _____ says, "I want you to pray for my hearing." So the preacher puts his fingers in _____ 's ear, prays over him, removes his hands, stands back & asks, "_____, how's your hearing now?" _____ says, "I don't know, Reverend, it ain't 'til next Wednesday."

My great granddaughter was saying her prayers the other night in a real low voice. So, I said, "I can't hear you Sweetheart." She said very seriously, "Wasn't talking to you." Another humbling experience.

The pastor announced in his sermon last Sunday that there are 726 kinds of sin. Now he's being besieged with requests for the list, mostly from folks who think they're missing something!

Our pastor noticed a group of boys standing around a small stray dog. He asked them, "What are you boys up to?" One of the boys says, "We're telling lies. The one who tells the biggest lie, gets the dog." The pastor says, "Why, when I was your age, I never even thought of telling a lie!" Well, the boys stared at each other & finally one of them shrugged & said, "I guess he wins the dog."

A psychiatrist talked to his patient on the couch. The Dr. asked, "Do you talk in your sleep?" The patient says, "No, I talk in other people's sleep." The Dr. says, "I don't understand, how can that be?" The patient says, "I'm a preacher!"

A man who stuttered applied for a job at a Bible factory. He said to the interviewer; "I_I_If you hire me, Y_Y_You won't have to P_P_Pay me if I_I_I don't sell as many B-B-Bibles as your b-b-best salesman. So they hired him & he came back in after a week & he'd sold twice as many as their best salesman. They asked him how he did it, so he said, "C-C-Come with me & I'll show you." They went out into a neighborhood, went up to a door & knocked on it & a lady answered the door. She says, "May I help you?" He says, " M-M-Maam, I-I-I'm selling Bibles, you can B-B-Buy one or I can come inside & R-R-Read it to you."

We had quite a time at church last Sunday. Instead of preaching for a ½ hour he preached for 2 hours, so I asked him why, & he said, "I apologize, I got a hold of my wife's false teeth by mistake!"

My grandson was with me when we went out of the church & shook the pastor's hand & my grandson says, "Pastor, when I grow up, I'm gonna give you some money." The pastor said, "Well, thank you son, but why would you do that?" He says, "Because, my grandad says you're the poorest preacher we've ever had."

My grandson was in Sunday School last Sunday & the teacher asked him where God's home was. Of course she figured he's say 'Heaven', but he said, "In the bathroom at my house." She asked him, Why do you say that?" & he says, "Cause, every morning my Daddy says, 'My Lord, are you still in there?'"

I had another dream this week. I dreamed I died & went to Heaven & St. Peter was showing me around & the place was full of these huge warehouses, & the warehouses were full of clocks & the clocks were all running different speeds. So, I asked him what the deal was & he said, "Well, Larry each person dead or alive is represented by one of these clocks & the speed of the clock shows how sinful the person is or has been." I said, "Wow, where's _____'s clock?" He said, "Now over here's Abraham's clock." Folks, you'd have to watch it a week to see it move a minute. I said, "That's really something, but where's _____'s clock?" He said, "Check this one out, its Moses' clock." I said, "Okay, but where's _____'s clock?" He said, "Oh it's in the office. The air-conditioning's out, so we're using it for a fan."

I went to a fortune teller & I said, "Tell me, are there golf courses in Heaven?" She said, "I have good news & bad newss." I said, "What's the good news?" She says, "The good news is--that the golf courses in Heaven are beautiful beyond anything you could imagine!" I said, "That's wonderful, what's the bad news?" She said, "You'll be teeing off at 8:30 in the morning."

I've got a riddle for you: What do you get when you cross a Jehovah's Witness with an Atheist? Someone who knocks on your door for no apparent reason.

You know they have a Dial-A-Prayer for atheists now. You can call up & it rings & rings & rings, but nobody answers.

() ARE YOU GONNA PAY ME WHAT YOU OWE ME?
Yes, I'll pay. Here's a dollar down.
() WHAT ABOUT THE REST OF IT?
I'll give you a dollar every day I work.
() THAT'S FINE. WHAT DO YOU DO?
I decorate Christmas trees.

A young priest enters a monastery where you take a vow of silence. The rule is, you can say 2 words every 10 years. So he was there for 10 years & went into the holy father's presence & said, "FOOD COLD." Another 10 years go by & he goes in & says, "BED HARD". Ten more years go by, making 30 years he's been there, & he goes in to the holy father & says, "I QUIT!" The holy father says, "I'm not surprised, you've been complaining ever since you've been here!"

St. Peter is waiting at the Pearly Gates when 2 guys wearing hoodies arrive. St. Peter says, "Wait here, I'll be right back." St. Peter goes over to God's chambers & tells him who is waiting to come in. God says to St. Peter; "How many times do I have to tell you, you can't be judgmental here. This is Heaven. All are loved. All are brothers. Go back & let them in!" St. Peter goes back to the Gates, looks around, goes back to God's chambers & says, "Well, they're gone!" God says, The guys wearing the hoodies?" & St. Peter says, "No, the Pearly Gates!"

Last Sunday, my 7 year old great grandson went to church with me & he got to staring up at a large plaque. It was covered with names & small American flags mounted on either side of it. Attison asked me, "Grandad, what is that?" I said, Well Son, it's a memorial to all the young men & women who died in the service." & Attison says, "Which service, the 8:30 or the 11:00am?"

You know what my greatest fear is? I fear that one day I'll meet God, he'll sneeze, & I won't know what to say.

A deaf old lady had a tendency to shout when she went to confession, so the priest told her she should write down what she had to say in advance. At her next confession she knelt & handed a piece of paper to the priest. He looked at it & said, "What is this, it looks like a grocery list!" She says, "Mother of God, I must've left my sins at the Piggly-Wiggly!"

Cliff was on an ocean cruise while back & they hit a reef & the ship was sinking. The captain yelled; "Does anybody know how to pray? Cliff says, "I do!" The captain says, "Good, you start praying. The rest of us will put on the life vests, we're one short."

I was listening to Christian radio & heard a lady call in, She said, "Pastor, I was born blind, & I've been blind all my life. I don't mind so much being blind, but I have some well-meaning friends who tell me that if I had more faith I could be healed. So the radio pastor asked her, "Do you carry one of those white canes?" She says, "Yes, I do." He says, "Then the next time someone tells you that, hit him or her on the head with your cane & say, "If you had more faith that wouldn't hurt!"

My elderly neighbor lady came home from church the other night & caught a burglar ransacking the place & she yelled; "STOP! ACTS 2:38! REPENT & BE BAPTIZED IN THE NAME OF JESUS CHRIST FOR THE REMISSION OF YOUR SINS SO YOU MAY BE FORGIVEN!" The burglar stopped in his tracks & the lady calmly called the police & explained what she had done. So, the police come & one of them is handcuffing the burglar & he asks the burglar, "Why did you just stand there? All the old lady did was yell a scripture to you." & the burglar says, "Scripture?! She said she had an axe & two 38s!"

I was substitute teaching a Sunday School class last Sunday of mostly 7 & 8 year olds. I described how Lot's wife looked back & turned into a pillar of salt. One little boy spoke up, "My Mommy looked back & turned into a telephone pole!"

_____ has been retired for several years & he's got plumb tired of shaving himself every morning & he decided he'd had enough. He decided he'd go to the barber shop & let the barber shave him every day. Now, the barber shop was owned by the pastor of the Baptist Church. The barber's wife, Grace was working that day, so she performed the task. Grace shaved him & sprayed him with lilac water & said, "That'll be $20." _____ thought that was a little steep but he paid her & went on. The next morning he looked in the mirror & his face was as smooth as it was the day before, so he decided he didn't have to shave every day. Two weeks later he still didn't need a shave so he went back to the barber shop & the told the barber's wife, "You must have done a great job, it's been 2 weeks & my whiskers still haven't started growing back." With a straight face she says, "Well, you were shaved by Grace. Once shaved, always shaved."

This may be a surprise to those of you not familiar with Las Vegas, but there are more Catholic Churches there than casinos. Not surprisingly some worshipers at Sunday services will give casino chips rather than cash when the basket is passed. Since they get chips from many different casinos, the churches have devised a method to collect the offerings. The churches a priest with all their collected chips to a Franciscan Monastery for sorting & then the chips are taken to the casinos of origin & cashed in. This is done by the chipmonk.

I was raised in Sani Flush, Arkansas which was 12 miles from Toilet, the county seat. We had two churches there in town, Methodist & Baptist & that's all I knew of. Dad sent me up to the general store to get some chicken feed & while I was in there a stranger asked me where Tilly Jones lived. I told him, "Two miles South of town on that dirt road, you can see her name on her mailbox right there on the right side of the road, but how come you got your shirt on backwards?" He says, "Young man, I'm a Catholic priest, & this is the way we dress." I said, "Well, then, how come you wear those beads?" He said, "These are called a rosary, we use these in our worship." Then I asked him, "How come you got that cast on your arm?" He said, "I was setting on the commode this morning, tying my shoes, when I fell off & broke it." Folks, he left & I ain't seen him again to this day, but my cousin Clem had to know what we were talking about, so he comes over & asks me, "Larry, who was that?" I said, "That was a Catholic Priest Clem, don't you know nothin'." Clem says, "What's the deal with his shirt, he had it on backwards?" I said, "That's the way they're supposed to dress if they're Catholic Priests." He says, "Why does he wear those beads?" I said, "Now, Clem, that's called a rosary, they use them in their worship." Clem asks, "How come he had a cast on his arm?" I told Clem, "He told me he was settin' on the commode this morning tying his shoes & he fell off & broke it." Clem says, "Larry, what's a commode?" I said, "I don't know, I ain't Catholic."

This lady visited our church for the 1st time last Sunday. The sermon seemed to go on forever & many in the congregation actually fell asleep, including me. After the service, to be social, she walked up to me, extended her hand in greeting, & said, "Hello, I'm Gladys Dunn." I said, "You're not the only one, Ma'am. I'm glad it's done too!"

An Irishman is stumbling through the woods, totally drunk, when he comes upon a preacher baptizing people in the river. He proceeds into the water & he bumps into the preacher. The preacher turns around & is almost overcome by the smell of alcohol & he asks the drunk, "Are you ready to find Jesus?" The drunk shouts, "Yes I am!" So, the preacher grabs him & dunks him in the water. He pulls him back & asks, "brother, have you found Jesus?" The drunk says, "No, I haven't found Jesus." The Preacher dunks him again for a little longer & asks again, "Have you found Jesus?" "No, I haven't found Jesus!" He's dunked again for about 30 seconds & he's kicking his arms & legs & the preacher pulls him up. The preacher says, "For the love of God, have you found Jesus?" The drunk staggers upright, wipes his eyes, coughs up a bit of water & says, "Are you sure this is where he fell in?"

My grandson's teacher asked the students to bring something to school that has to do with their religion, so of course Devan brought a crucifix, his Jewish friend brought a star of David & another buddy who was a Southern Baptist brought a tuna casserole.

A priest, a minister, & a rabbi want to see who's best at his job. So, each one goes into the woods, finds a bear & attempts to convert it. Later, they all get together. The priest begins; "When I found the bear, I read to him from the catechism & sprinkled him with holy water. Next week is his 1st communion." The minister says, "I found a bear by the stream, & preached God's Holy Word. The bear was so mesmerized that he let me baptize him." They both looked down at the rabbi, who is lying on a gurney in a body cast. He says, "Looking back, maybe I shouldn't have started with the circumcision."

An elderly priest speaking to the younger priest. "You had a good idea to replace the 1st four pews with plush bucket theater seats. Worked like a charm. The front of the church always fills first now. & you told me adding a little more beat to the music would bring young people back to church, so I supported you when you brought in that Rock & Roll gospel choir. Now our services are consistently packed to the balcony. But, I'm afraid you've gone too far with the Drive-Thru-Confessional." The young priest says, "But Father, my confessions & the donations have nearly doubled since I began that!" & the old priest says, "Yes, and I appreciate that, but the flashing sign saying 'Toot-Tell Or Go To Hell' cannot stay on the church roof!"

Once upon a time many years ago, there was a monastery where all the monks did was copy thed Holy Writ. Brother Andrew was responsible for training new scribes in the art of copying by hand, word-for-word the Holy Writ. One day an eager new scribe asked if anyone had ever made a mistake. Brother Andrew said, "Oh, no, these words have always been correctly copied from generation to generation." So, the new monk asked, "How do you know?" Brother Andrew says, "I'll prove it to you, I'll show you the original manuscript!" So, off to the monastery's library the old monk shuffled. Many hours pass, so the young monk decided he'd better check on the old man. So, he goes to the library & there's Brother Andrew sitting alone in a candle-lit corner, tears running down his wrinkled cheeks. The young monk asks, "What's the matter Holy

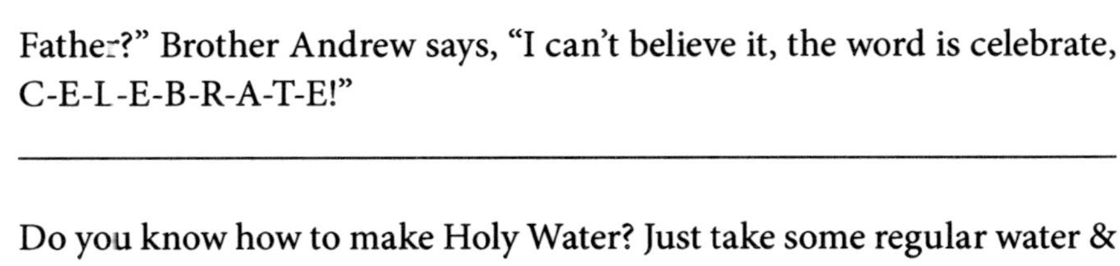

Father?" Brother Andrew says, "I can't believe it, the word is celebrate, C-E-L-E-B-R-A-T-E!"

Do you know how to make Holy Water? Just take some regular water & boil the hell out of it.

Cliff, as a Pastor has started up an emotional support group for middle aged men experiencing hair loss. Apparently they close every meeting with the benediction, 'Go, & thin no more!'

Last night I dreamt I died & went to Heaven & as I approached the pearly gates there was a long table with an enormous book on it. To the side of the table was a ladder that stretched out of sight up into the sky farther than the eye could see. St. Peter met me & asked my name. Then he looked in that big book until he found it. He says, "Ah yes, Mr. Ellis, won't you come this way. You have one small thing to do before we can admit you to Heaven. Here is a piece of chalk. I will count out from this book the number of sins you've committed, & for each sin you must place a chalk mark on a successive rung on the ladder. When you've done that for all your sins, we'll let you in." I thought, this ought to be a snap. So, St. Peter began counting & I made my chalk marks as I climbed, 1, 2, 593, 2,967, 7,953. By now I was so high I could barely see St. Peter & I hollered down, "How many more?" He says, "Only 3 more." So, I reached my hand up to grab the next rung. All of a sudden I felt an excruciating pain in my left hand. I looked up & saw a big foot pinning my hand to the rung. I looked higher & saw that it was _____ coming down for more chalk.

One day I looked out the window & noticed Attison playing with our cat. He had the cat sitting quietly, & he was preaching to it. I went back to fiddling & a while later I heard some loud meowing & hissing. So, I looked out the window & he had the cat in a tub of water. I said, "Attison stop that! That cat is afraid of water!" He looked up at me & said, "Well, he should have thought about that before he joined my church."

Three men die in a car crash & when they get to heaven St. Peter asks them; "What would you like for people to say about you back on earth?" The 1st one said, "I'd like for people to say, 'He was a great doctor!'" The 2nd one says, "I'd wish people would say, 'He was a great father.'" The 3rd one says, "Look, he's moving, he's alive!!!!"

RESTAURANT-EATING-FOOD JOKES

Sometimes I don't have the spirit of giving. For instance I was downtown Kansas City & a bum came up to me & said, "Mr., will you give me a buck for a sandwich?" I said, "Let me see the sandwich!"

He said, "But Mr., I haven't had a bite in 3 days!" So I bit him.

Took my wife out to dinner last night & I ordered the whole meal in 'French'. Boy was the waiter surprised. It was a Chinese restaurant.

I had a dish called 'Poulet-A-La-Chevrolet'. Which is a chicken what was run over by a pickup truck.

Shirley & I went out for a meal at a Chinese restaurant & we ordered the "Chicken Surprise' . The waiter brought the meal, served in a lidded cast iron pot. Just as Shirley started to serve herself, the lid of the pot raises slightly & she briefly sees 2 beady eyes looking around before the lid slams down. She says, "Good grief, did you see that?" I said, "No!" So she says, "Well, you look in the pot!" So, I reach for the lid & again it rises & I see 2 little beady eyes looking around before it slams down. So I called the waiter over & read him the riot act. He said, "Please, Sir, what did you order?" I said, 'Chicken Surprise'." He says, "So solly, I bring you 'Peking Duck'."

My wife decided after all these years, she'd go out & get a job. So, she got a job as a waitress at 'Joe's Truck Stop Café . Well, on her 1st day she got an order from a truck driver for, "2 flat tires & 2 headlights." So, she went back to the chef & told him she didn't understand the order & the chef said, "Oh, he's pullin' your leg, that's 2 pancakes & 2 fried eggs." So, Shirley thought for a bit & said, "In that case, give me a large bowl of beans first." She took that bowl of beans out to that truck driver & he said, "Hey, I didn't order these beans!" & Shirley says, "Well, when you get your car parts, you'll have the gas to make 'em go!"

My neighbor's moved his restaurant to a better locale, so last week he had a grand opening & people sent cards & flowers & everything was great. So, he was reading one of the cards that came with some flowers & it said, "Rest In Peace." He called the florist & asked, "What does this card mean?" & the florist says, "I don't know, but there's a card on some flowers at a funeral somewhere saying, 'Good Luck In Your New Location'."

We're in a restaurant & the waiter brings me this chicken & I say, "What's wrong with this chicken? It's all bruised." He says, "It was in a fight." So I said, "Well, take it back & bring me the winner."

I was on the road this week & on Wednesday morning I stopped at a Waffle House & the waitress says, "So, what'll it be mister?" I said, "I'll tell you what. I want my eggs hard & burned around the edges, I want my bacon burnt to a crisp, & I want my toast blackened & hard. I want my coffee bitter, & when you bring me my food, I want you to yell at me. She says, "What, are you, crazy?" I said, "No, I'm homesick."

I just got back from Africa. On the way back I got stopped by a customs agent & he asked me if I had anything to declare. I said, "No I don't." He said. "Are you sure?" I said, "Of course I'm sure!" He says, "Well, what about that elephant standing behind you with bread in his ears?" I said, "Sir, what I put in my sandwiches is my own business!"

I'm having a hard time getting into the spirit of giving this year. For instance, I had a bum come up to me on the street. He says,"Mr, will you give me a buck for a sandwich?" I said, "Let me see the sandwich!"

He said, "But Mr., I haven't had a bite in 3 days!" So, I bit him.

Another bum walked up to me today & said; "Could you spare $140 for a cup of coffee?" I said, "Sir, coffee is only 75 cents!" He said, "I know, but I couldn't go into a restaurant dressed like this!"

My wife is a very adventurous cook. She hollered out from the kitchen; "How does this sound? 'Bonito, surimi & anchovies in a decadent, silky broth?" I hollered back, "Is that what we're having tonight?" She says, "No, I'm reading this from a packet of cat food!"

We were so poor that Mom would insist that we all sit at the table, & she'd read recipes to us. My kid brother was deaf, so he starved to death.

I went to a new restaurant last night & our waiter handed me my filet mignon with his thumb firmly pressed against it. I said, "What are you doing pawing my steak?" He says, "What? You want it to fall on the floor again?"

Practice safe eating---always use condiments.

I was on a business trip & I saw a sign in the window of a small town café. It said, "$500 reward to anybody who orders something we can't furnish." So I went in, sat down & said, "Bring me an elephant ear sandwich." This waitress' face fell & she hurried back to the kitchen & told the chef; "Better get ready to fork over $500, there's a guy out front who wants an elephant ear sandwich." The chef roared, "What! You mean to tell me we're out of elephant ears?" She says, "No, but we're out of those great big buns!"

SONG TITLES

"The Peach I Picked In Georgia, Didn't Cling To Me Too Long"

"When They Operated On Father, They Opened Mother's Male"

"Get Out Of The Wheat Field Grandma, You're Going Against The Grain"

"Walk Me Down To The Corn Field Baby, And I'll Kiss You Between The Ears"

"Walk Me Down To The Rock Pile Baby, And I'll Be A Little Bolder There"

"I Quit Kissin' The Girl At The Bank, Since I Found Out She's A Teller"

"I Call My Sugar Candy, Cause She's Built Like A Peanut Cluster"

"She Had An Hourglass Figure, Only Time Stood Still In The Wrong Places"

"She Wouldn't Kiss Me In My Canoe, So I Paddled Her Back"

"If I'd A Met You Sooner, I'd A Been Rid Of You Long Before Now"

"It's Not That He's Bald, It's Just That His Part Won't Quit"

"How Can I Miss You When You Won't Go Away"

"I Baked My Sweetie A Pie, But He Left With A Tart"

"I Don't Want That Floozy In My Jacuzzi"

"There Ain't Been No Trash In My Trailer Since I Throwed You Out"

"Don't Tear Your Hair Out Over A Woman, It'll Be Harder To Meet The Next One If You're Bald"

"He Used To Be Called 'Tall-In-The-Saddle' 'Til His Blisters Broke"

"Help Keep Your City Clean, Eat A Pigeon"

"I'm Dancing With Tears In My Eyes, Cause The Girl In My Arms Is My Brother"

"He Must Be A Good Gardener, He And His Plants Are Both Potted"

"She Was Only A Moonshiner's Daughter, But I Love Her Still"

"Hang Down Your Head Tom Dooley, Cause You Got Your Tie Caught In Your Fly"

"She Chews Tobacco, But She Won't Choose Me"

"You're The Reason Our Kids Are So Ugly"

"It's Better To Have Loved A Short Girl, Than Never To Have Loved A Tall"

"I Call Her My Melancholy Baby, Cause She's Got A Shape Like A Melon And A Face Like A Collie"

"I Walked Her Down To The Meadow And She Listened To My Bull."

"Don't Kiss A Girl Under The Mistletoe, It's More Fun Under The Nose"

"I've Been Flushed From The Bathroom Of Your Heart"

"The Shades Of Night Were Falling Fast, But I Got A Pretty Good Look Anyhow"

"I'd Rather Have A Bottle In Front Of Me Than A Frontal Lobotomy"

"If I Can't Be Number One In Your Life, Then Number Two On You"

"I Still Miss You Baby, But My Aim's Getting Better"

"I'm So Miserable Without You, It's Like Having You Here"

"Here's A Song That The Jolly Green Giant Had A Big Hit On: 'There Will Be Peas In The Valley'"

"A Girl Who's Built Like A House Has A Reason To Get Plastered"

"Mama Get A Hammer, There's A Fly On Papa's Head"

"I Keep Forgettin' I Forgot About You"

"I Wouldn't Take Her To A Dog Fight, I'm Afraid She Might Win"

"What Makes Wyatt Earp"

"Let's Sing The Income Tax Song, "Everything I Have Is Yours"

"His Face Was Flushed, But His Broad Shoulders Saved Him"

"If I'd A Met You Sooner, I'd Been Rid Of You Long Before Now"

SPORTS JOKES

A Detroit Tigers scout flies to Baghdad to watch a young lad play baseball & is very impressed & invites him to come over to the States. So, the Tigers are in a close game with the Indians & the Manager gives the young Iraqi reliever the nod & on he goes. Folks, this kid is a sensation, he strikes out everyone he faces for the rest of the game & wins it for the Tigers! The fans are delighted, the players & coaches are delighted, & the media loves the new star. When the kid comes off the field he phones his Mom to tell her about his 1st day in the majors. "Hello Mum, guess what! I played for 3 innings today, the bases were loaded but I struck out everyone I faced, & we won. Everybody loves me, the fans, the media, they all love me!" His Mom says, "Wonderful, let me tell you about my day. Your Father got shot in the street & got robbed. Your sister & I were ambushed & beaten & your brother has joined a gang of looters, & all the while you were having such a great time." He says, "What can I say Mum, but I'm so sorry." She says, "Sorry?!!!, Sorry?!!! It's your fault we moved to Detroit in the 1st place!"

He who drives well on the fairway does not always fare well on the driveway.

I was at a Royals game while back & was seated by this lady with an empty seat beside her. I asked her about it & she explained that it was her husband's, but he died. I said, "Oh, I'm sorry, isn't there someone else in the family who could use the ticket?" She said, "No, they're all at the funeral!" Now that's a baseball fan for sure.

In my position as a homicide detective, I've been investigating the murder of Juan Gonzalaz. It looks like he was killed with a 'golf' gun.
() A GOLF GUN? WHAT IN THE WORLD IS A GOLF GUN?
I don't know. But it sure made a hole in Juan.

_______ went out golfing yesterday & 2 little boys were watching him like a hawk. Finally _____ said, "You boys will never learn to play golf by watching me. They said, "Oh, we're not interested in golf mister, we're goin' fishing as soon as you dig up enough worms!"

Baseball is the 1st sport mentioned in the Bible. It starts right out there in Genesis: "In The Big Inning."

() ISN'T IT SINFUL THE WAY ______ PLAYS GOLF EVERY SUNDAY MORNING?
Yeah, the kind of golf ______ plays is sinful every day.

Seven wheelchair athletes have been banned from the Paralympics after they tested positive for WD40.

A 1st grade teacher can't believe her student isn't hopped up about the Super Bowl. She says, "It's a huge event, why aren't you excited?" The student says, "Because, I'm not a football fan. My parents love basketball, so I do too." The teacher says, "Well, that's a lousy reason. What if your parents were morons? What would you be then?" The student says, "Then I'd be a football fan."

Can you believe it? Here it is football season again. When I played football, I was known as 'crazy legs' until I was 12 years old. That's when I learned to put my pants on with the zipper in front.

I went out for football in my freshman year in high school. I played 'tight end', which meant I sat on the end of the bench & held on tight. One day I was at practice & the quarterback threw a long pass, hit me in the nose & broke my finger.

It's the men's Olympic figure skating. Out comes the Russian competitor. He skates around to some classical music in kind of a dull costume, performs some excellent leaps but without any great artistic feel for the music.

Judges scores: Britain--5.8, Russia--5.9, U.S.A.--5.5, Ireland--6.0,
Next comes the American in a sparkling stars & stripes costume, skating to some Rock & Roll music. He gets the crowd clapping, but it is not as technically as good as the Russian, but artistically, it is a more satisfying performance.

Judges scores: Britain--5.8, Russia--5.5, U.S.A.--5.9, Ireland--6.0.
Finally, out comes the Irish competitor wearing a tatty old sports coat, with his skate laces tied over his trousers. He reaches the ice, trips immediately & bangs his nose which starts bleeding. He tries to get up, staggers a few paces, then slips again. He spends the entire 'routine' getting up & falling over again.

Judges scores: Britain--0.00, Russia--0.0, U.S.A.--0.00, Ireland--6.0.
The other judges turn to the Irish judge & demand in unison, "How in the world can you give that mess a 6.0?" The Irish judge says, ":Well, you gotta remember, it's darn slippery out there!"

Hey, I heard your nephew won a swimming match last week.
() OH, YES, HE'S BEEN SWIMMING FOR 20 YEARS.
Well, I bet he's tired by now.

June--the main month for marriage. Advise: Marry not a tennis player, for 'LOVE' means nothing to them.

If at 1st you don't succeed skydiving is not for you.

_____ went to college. He was the string changer on the YO-YO squad.

Did you know that bullfighting is the number one sport in Latin America?
() THAT'S REVOLTING!
No, that's the number two sport.

Our track team had a cross-eyed discus thrower. He wasn't that great, but he kept the crowds loose.

() Larry, what do you run the mile in?
Shorts & a T-shirt.

There's a big ole boy fishin' down in Truman Lake wile back & he came up on a boat that had capsized with several guys in it. He would grab them one by one, by the hair of the head & drag them into his boat. All of a sudden, a bald-headed man came bobbin' out of the water. The man hit him on top of the head with a boat paddle & said, "You go down & come up head first next time!"

Why is Cinderella bad at sports? Cause she has a pumpkin for a coach, & she runs away from the ball.

I guess you didn't know I'm an expert skydiver. One time I was getting ready for a jump when I spotted another man outfitted to dive wearing dark glasses, carrying a white cane & holding a seeing dye dog by a leash. I really admired this blind man for his courage, so I asked him; "How do you know when the ground's getting close?" He said, "Easy, the leash goes slack."

Baseball season is starting up again, so I have a riddle for you: Two old maids set huddled together watching a baseball game. Nearby is an empty whisky bottle. What inning is it? It's the end of the 5th & the bags are loaded.

I sure hope it stays cold a little longer cause I ain't been ice fishin' in years. I remember the last time I went. I go down to the lake & here's this maybe 11 year-old boy. He's got a hole cut in the ice. He's got maybe 5 or6 nice bass he's already caught, so I cut me a hole about 10 or 12 feet from him & I go fishin'. An hour goes by & I ain't caught a thing & he's caught 6 more! So I go over to him & ask him; "What's your secret to catchin' all them fish?" He says, "MM-Mm,: I said, "What'd you say?" He says, (spit) "Keep your worms warm."

() _____ WHY DON'T YOU PLAY GOLF WITH _____ ANYMORE?
Well, would you play golf with a man who moves the ball & puts down the wrong score while you're not looking?
() I CERTAINLY WOULD NOT!
Well, neither will _____.

TALL TALES/ JOKES

I've been ocean fishing & I caught a 500# fish.
() I'VE BEEN OCEAN FISHING TOO & I THOUGHT I CAUGHT A FISH, BUT IT TURNED OUT TO BE A LANTERN FROM THE TITANIC & IT WAS STILL LIT!
Listen, I'll take 200# off that fish I caught if you blow out that lantern!

THANKSGIVING JOKES

What kind of music did the Pilgrims like? Plymouth Rock.

If the Pilgrims were alive today, what would they be most famous for? Their age.

() THANKSGIVING'S COMING UP IN A COUPLE OF WEEKS, LET'S FIND OUT WHAT YOU KNOW ABOUT HISTORY.
Okay.
() WHO WERE THE PURITANS?
Huh?
() WHO WERE THE PURITANS? WHO WERE THE PEOPLE WHO WERE PUNISHED IN STOCKS?
Oh, that's easy. The small investors.

() CAN YOU TELL ME WHAT THE FORMER RULER OF RUSSIA WAS CALLED?
The Tzar.
() CORRECT, & WHAT WAS HIS WIFE CALLED?
The Tzarina
() RIGHT. WHAT WERE THE TZAR'S CHILDREN CALLED?
Tzardines!

_____ are you a Russian spy?
() NO, I'M A MINCE PIE.
You've got a lot of crust.

You know I think when you're born into a big family it makes you appreciate things even more. For instance, when I was born, I was so surprised, I couldn't talk for a year & a half.

It was 'Black Friday' the morning after Thanksgiving, & the crowd was huge & getting antsy. A small man pushed his way to the front of the line, only to be shoved back. On his 2nd try he was picked up & thrown to the end of the line. On his 3rd attempt, he was knocked to the ground, kicked & again, dumped in the back. He says, "That does it, if they hit me one more time, I won't open the store!"

TRAVELING-MOTELS-SHOWS, ETC.

Jon, Don & myself were traveling up from Arkansas on the back roads from a Bluegrass Festival. It was about two o'clock in the morning & our van broke down. We saw a light from a farm house up the road, so we walked up there & knocked on the door. The farmer answered the door, we told him about our misfortune & asked him if we could use his phone. He said, "We don't have a phone." Could you take us to town so we could get help? "No, the lights don't work on my old pickup, but you fellows look alright, so why don't you just stay all night, we'll have breakfast & I'll take you to town. There's just one thing. I've got a boy that has no ears. Please don't stare at him, he's real sensitive about people looking at him." Next morning we were at the breakfast table & the boy caught Don staring at him. The boy says, "Mister, you lookin' at me?" Don says, "Aw, I was just admiring your full head of hair--you take good care of it or you'll be bald like me." Pretty soon he caught Jon looking at him. He says, "Hey, are you staring at me?"

Jon says, "I was just admiring your pearly white teeth--you take good care of them or you'll have to wear false teeth like me." Yes, it happened, he saw me looking at him. He says, "You starin' at me?" I said, "No, I was just admiring your pretty blue eyes--you take good care of them, cause you can't wear glasses like me!"

Yeah, I've done my share of traveling. How do you know when you're staying in a Mississippi hotel? When you call the front desk & say, "I've gotta leak in my sink!" And the person at the front desk says, "Go ahead!"

One night I had a blonde knockin' on my door 'til 3 in the morning. Finally, I got up & let her out.

I have a lot of good memories playing these shows since I was a young man. I remember one time I was singin' "Zipadeedoodah, Zipadeeday, my oh my what a beautiful day." This lady on the front row kept singing, "Zipadeedoodah, Zipadeedoodah." I looked down & I'd forgot to zip up my dooda.

My landlord told me; "I'm gonna have to raise your rent." I said, "I wish you would cause I sure can't raise it!" So, he kicked us out.

So, we moved into this chintzy hotel. I had to carry my own bags up to the room. I wouldn't have minded if I was a bigger tipper.

Phil gets on an Amtrak train. Tells the steward, "I get nauseous when I travel on trains, so I'm gonna take a heavy sleeping pill, but please do whatever you can to make sure I get off when it stops in St. Louis, I really don't want to miss my aunt's funeral. The steward says, "Sure thing, we'll make sure you get off!" 'Seven hours later the train stopped in Chicago & Phil jumped out of his seat in a panic, "What the heck, I asked you to wake me up in St. Louis!" A guy setting behind Phil tells his wife, "Oh boy! He looks mad!" She whispered back, "Not half as mad as that other guy they carried off back in St. Louis!"

CPSIA information can be obtained
at www.ICGtesting.com
Printed in the USA
FFOW05n2227130817

9 781640 696501